# Two Ways to Sunday

By:

Tom Starita

Copyright © 2012 by Tom Starita

ISBN 978-0-7414-8048-4   Paperback
ISBN 978-0-7414-8049-1   eBook
Library of Congress Control Number: 2012918324

Printed in the United States of America

Published November 2012

INFINITY PUBLISHING
1094 New DeHaven Street, Suite 100
West Conshohocken, PA 19428-2713
Toll-free (877) BUY BOOK
Local Phone (610) 941-9999
Fax (610) 941-9959
Info@buybooksontheweb.com
www.buybooksontheweb.com

*Dedicated to Kristina.*
*The first of many*

# ACKNOWLEDGEMENTS

It's not often in life when you get a chance to publicly thank the individuals that had a direct impact on you. When I started writing this book five years ago I promised myself that if it ever saw the light of day I would take the time to thank everyone who had a hand in shaping me.

First, I want to thank my wife, Kristina aka "Lady." Without you there is no book. Without you, I'm probably still living in an attic somewhere getting by on "Hungry Man" dinners and wrinkled shirts. There were a couple of times I wanted to give up and you refused to let me. I cannot thank you enough both publicly and privately for having a ridiculous amount of faith and confidence in me. I love you.

Next comes the family...

My parents, Bill and Kathy. On the night of November 30, 2007 I showed you four pages of what would eventually turn into this accomplishment. You loved the idea that night and you have loved every single revised edition ever since. Thank you for continuing to read even when you knew how the story would end. Most of all, thank you for all the support, belief and love that you have given me.

Lisa, Terry and Allison. You were one of the few who saw this early on and I thank you for the ideas, suggestions and encouragement. And thanks to Terry for giving me a couple of lines that I permanently borrowed. You guys are now officially in charge of getting the word out in the Carolinas!

Greg, Melissa, Brooke, Matt, Paige and Ryan. Early on, when I wasn't sure what I had your opinions greatly mattered and gave me confidence to continue. I knew if you guys liked it I actually had something. Thanks for always being there for me.

Aunt Ann and Uncle Bob. If I say thanks for everything I think that also covers the countless tablecloths, carpets and glass shelves I have ever stained, ruined or destroyed.

Nana, Pop-Pop, Uncle Richie, Auntie Ro, Uncle Johnny, Uncle Joe, Grandma, Pop, Uncle Jimmy, Aunt Claudia, Jimmy, Karoline, Kirsten, Gunnar, Melissa, Manny, Aunt Janet, Uncle Walter, Brian, Denise, Kassandra, Erica, Jason, Avery, Uncle Dennis, Aunt Carol, Michael and Derek. I'd say you guys had a big hand in creating who I am today. Now I would say that's a good thing but I might be biased. I'll let you decide.

Terry, Bob, Nick and Melissa. Thanks for accepting me the moment I walked through your door and thank you for not throwing me out when I proposed to Lady seemingly three minutes later. I love you guys.

Thanks to the best landlords ever, Aunt Angie and Uncle Dom. As well as Johnny, Cyara, Anthony, Nicole, Michael, Fabiana, Abuela, TiTi TeTe, TiTi Cuchi, Uncle Eddie Aunt Donna, Katie, Sean, Evey, Kelly, Ariana, Jim, Carolyn, Baby O'Gara, Uncle Phil, Aunt Lisa, Andrew, Elizabeth, Uncle Teddy, Amanda Rand, Gladys, Frank, Lisa, Danny and Uncle Reuben. You're all nuts, every…single…one of you. Thanks!

Nick Tacopino, JoJo Iacono, Mike Sblendorio, Rich Sblendorio, Mike Saccenti, Jon Saccenti and Tony LoConte. My crew, my guys, my wedding party. Nothing more needs to be said because then it will get creepy and weird. See you next Sunday for football.

Amanda Grossman, Dana Cristino, Tamara Iacono, Rachel Saccenti and Stephanie Saccenti. Thank you for being awesome. And thanks for putting up with my nonsense.

Now the professionals…

Way back when, my first real job was at Major Leagues in the Staten Island Mall. Thanks to Roger and Bonnie for the opportunity and the four years of insanity that transpired.

From St. Peter's High School for Girls thank you Monsignor Dorney, Florence Bricker, Steve Fayer, Joe Yannantuono, Leslie Bozza and Lucy Ewing. Without the four of you my teaching career would have crashed and burned within the first week. Thanks for all your help and advice.

From Paramus Catholic High School thanks to Jim Vail, Joe Agostino, Bill Brieden, Tiffany Connelly, Felicia Cowie, Jean Cousins, Mike Dorrian, Tiina Fischgrund, Luke Frangione, Beth Grusenski, Larry Hughes, Marlena Johnston, Andrew Kent, Mary Pat Leon, Camille Lewandowski, Jim Loranger, Danielle Moore, Jim

Mulligan, Tim Murphy, Justin Pedrick, Ann Marie Quattrocchi, Lynn Raimo, Stella Scarano, Amy and Mike Shea and Ed Wilk. You all made coming to work that much better.

If I didn't give Father Larry his own blurb I would hear about it for the rest of my life. Thank you for marrying Lady and me and for being a great friend. I always know if I want honesty all I have to do is pick up the phone.

Now it is impossible to name every single student I taught at St. Peter's High School for Girls and Paramus Catholic High School. It would take way too long and some of you have difficult last names to spell. Therefore I'm just going to thank all of you for the laughs, stories, memories, overall classroom insanity, basketball games, soccer games, every softball team, class trips and the epic amount of free food you guys either bought or made me.

From the Associated Press I cannot thank Jack Stokes and Santos Chaparro enough for their help and advice they gave a guy who was clearly over his head. I learned a tremendous amount in my short time there. Thank you.

From Aflac thanks to Rey Rostami, Mike Paine, Andrew Higgins, Mike Trainor and Marty Conroy. In the sales world, for someone to give their time and patience to someone just starting out is unheard of yet that's what each and every one of you did for me. Thank you.

She's not a work person but she deserves her own paragraph. I cannot give enough credit, thanks and love to Kara LoConte, who spent hours turning my random words and fragment sentences into something coherent and grammatically correct. Without your editing I don't have a book.

Finally, thanks to Nicole Beniamini, Brooke Townsend and Jessica Nastasi. The three of you helped me either through reading, suggesting or inspiring. Thank you.

I think that covers everyone I ever met in my entire life. If I left you out I'll make a note of it and give you a two paragraph spread in the next book!

# CHAPTER 1

## September 17, 2052

The faded white door closed with a thud and Chris could feel some embarrassment rise up in his cheeks. His right hand had betrayed him again. He turned around and used his cane to feel for the kneeler hidden in the dark. As if he wasn't making enough noise already, a pair of seventy six-year-old knees announced his landing with a series of pops and cracks. An audible breath escaped while he used the cane to guide him down. Despite his age, Chris could make out the shadowy figure on the other side of the screen; Monsignor Bob Davis had been Monsignor at St. Clare's for as long as Chris had been a parishioner, although he preferred to be called Father Bob. The few times he found himself in conversation with the man had been pleasant. A random memory came to mind at the same time the confessional window slid open and at once Chris began to speak.

"Bless me Father for I have sinned. It has been a couple of years since my last confession."

"Go on."

"I suppose you could say I make the same mistakes most men make. I fight with my wife. I can be short with my children at times."

"Yes."

"I curse. Some say I have a problem with my temper."

"And you say?"

"I'd say they're right," he said with a laugh. "As I've grown older I'm able to control it better, but there are still times where it comes roaring out of me." While he spoke he flexed his right hand a couple of times.

"Anything else?"

Chris thought for a second before answering, "Hmmm. I don't always go to church."

"About how often do you go?"

"I'd say about twice a month." He could feel the pressure building on his shoulders and he tried to rotate the right one as casually as he could.

"Any specific reason why?"

"To be honest no there's not. My wife is a regular; she goes with at least one of my children and a grandchild or two."

"And you?"

"Like I said I do go, just not as often."

He could see the silhouette of Father Bob lean forward, "Can I ask you a question?"

Chris was caught off guard by the casualness of the question and stammered, "Yeah sure."

"What kind of relationship do you have with God?"

Chris tossed the question about in his mind and said, "I think I have a good one. I try to pray every night before I go to sleep."

"What prayers do you say?"

"Normally some sort of combination of the Our Father and Hail Mary."

"Do you ever have a conversation?"

"More so when I was younger. As the years passed I guess only when I needed something." Chris heard a touch of shame in his voice.

"What do you need now?"

"Father?"

"Sounds like there is more on your mind than fights with your wife or your temper."

His breath slowly escaped between his teeth and he felt the weight of each word as he said them. "Yeah, I'd say so. Is it obvious?"

"When you've been a priest as long as I have it is."

Chris could feel a wave of emotion rise up from his throat and he did his best to choke everything back. "Father I'm about to turn seventy-six-years-old and there is an excellent chance I won't see seventy-seven."

"Why?"

He attempted to speak, but the only sound to come forth was a small cough. He gathered himself and continued. "I'm sick. Nothing official, not yet anyway."

"You're sure?"

"I'm as sure as you were about me a minute ago. There are pains where there shouldn't be and what used to be routine is now a struggle."

"Which is why you're here." He could hear genuine sympathy in Father Bob's voice.

"Father, in my heart of hearts I'm confident I did the right thing all my life. There were times I screwed up, although nothing major. I just want to make sure everything is order before things get out of control."

"Sounds like you've already made your peace."

"If you told me at eighteen to write what would be the perfect life I don't think I would have come close to the life given to me. To complain now after everything would be like spitting in His face."

"Good to hear. Although you know it is perfectly natural if negative feelings do arise."

"I know. I'm going to do my best to stay positive, if not for myself than for my wife and family." A pause lingered in the air before the priest spoke again.

"God knows both your heart and your intentions. I absolve you from all your sins. Go out and say three Our Fathers and a couple of Hail Mary's. And remember no matter what there is a God and He loves you very much."

"Thank you, Father. I appreciate it."

Father Bob smiled and replied, "All credit goes to God. I'm just the guy in-between. In the meantime, I'll be praying for you."

"Thanks again. Oh and Father, I might as well tell you this one in advance. When I get home tonight I'm most likely going to get drunk. Even though I am at peace a casual drink or two couldn't hurt."

"Better make it three Hail Mary's then. Go in peace, my son. In the name of the Father and the Son and the Holy Spirit Amen."

# CHAPTER 2

## October 6, 2052

## Celebrated novelist, Christopher Marcum, diagnosed with bone cancer

*October 4, 2052*
*Web posted at: 11:21 a.m. EDT (1621 GMT)*

**NEW YORK — Christopher Marcum, author of "Weight of the World," "The Knot" and "The Other Side" revealed Thursday that he has been diagnosed with grade three chondrosarcoma, a form of bone cancer. The award winning novelist will be meeting with doctors from John Hopkins to discuss his next course of action.**

Mr. Marcum declined to meet with bloggers. Instead there was a simple message on his Facepage informing the public of his state of mind.

"On behalf of Jen and the rest of my family, I would like to thank each and every one of you for your love, concern, and support. This isn't the story I would have written for myself but apparently the Great Author in the sky had other ideas. Fortunately I believe there are still hundreds of pages left in my book."

Starlight Publishing president **Allison Wullford** addressed the world on the company page:

"This morning, Christopher Marcum informed the world of the looming battle that lies ahead. All of us at Starlight Publishing have watched over the years as Christopher has led us on various adventures with ordinary men and women who have accomplished the extraordinary. We have no doubt he will rise to the challenge and expect many more of his novels to be published under the Starlight banner for years to come."

*(Story continues below)*

\*\*\*\*\*\*\*\*\*\*\*\*\*\*\*\*\*\*\*\*\*\*\*\*\*\*\*\*\*\*\*\*\*\*\*\*\*\*\*\*\*\*\*\*\*\*\*\*\*\*\*\*\*\*\*\*\*\*

Christopher Marcum arose from a deep slumber unsure of his surroundings. His pale blue eyes fluttered as he attempted to focus on whatever it was he was looking at. The room was filled with light, temporarily hindering his attempt at recognition. After a couple of beats Chris understood he was looking up at a white ceiling. Still unable to determine where he was his eyes began to circle the room.

Turning his head to the right brought an old cherry nightstand into focus. He could see the iTV remote sitting within reach, an old fashioned brown leather wallet overstuffed with cards of various kinds, an old tuna can painted random colors and filled with coins, and the holo-clock that read: 8:29am - Fri - 10/6/52, in a soft green hue. As he attempted to look past the table, the holo-clock began to flutter. Chris's eyes squinted again, but the shapes beyond remained in their muddled state. After a couple of seconds he closed his eyes and swiveled his head back up towards the ceiling. As if he was easing into a cold pool, Chris took a deep breath and opened his eyes. The ceiling was still white. He started to turn his head to the left before pausing momentarily.

Somewhere off in the distance a shrill whistle signaled the arrival of something unknown. The sound grew increasingly louder and louder in his ears until he realized it wasn't a whistle—it was a sharp pain, like knives stabbing his arms. Chris attempted to sit upright before a gust of what felt like fire swirled up and down his body. With a shout, he announced his return to the waking world. What felt like an hour passed before his wife came charging into the bedroom, carrying a glass of water and a couple of pills. "I have your meds, it'll be over in a second," she said in a soothing tone.

Chris let out an incoherent grunt and opened his mouth. Jen dropped the pills down his throat in one breath and the water in the next. He was so anxious to alleviate the pain that most of the water wound up on his plain white t-shirt.

"Chris I know it hurts, but please go easy! Do you need more water?"

Instead of answering, Chris collapsed back into his king size bed. A cool wave cascaded over his body and the fires began to subside. He sighed, "No. I'm okay, I'm okay. Thanks hun."

Jen ran her hand through his thinning white hair.

"You nearly gave me a heart attack with that scream!"

"Honey all I know is that when I woke up, I forgot all about these." He looked down at the useless arms at his side. "I had no idea where I was, but at this point I would gladly trade pain for confusion."

"I know. I wish there was something more I could do for you." Despite dealing with these episodes daily, Jen could not grow accustomed to seeing and hearing her husband in agony.

"You just put out another fire babe; considering what I was feeling two minutes ago, you've done more than enough."

"Do you want to shower or eat first?"

"I think I want to shower first. Mind helping me out?" Chris leaned forward and waited for his wife to wrap her thin arms around his increasingly frail body.

"If I can carry you through fifty years of marriage, I can easily carry you fifty feet to the tub."

Chris had been suffering from pain in his shoulders and fingers for months, which he attributed to a lifetime of typing. Believing it was nothing more serious than a cough, he chose to not say anything to Jen, or anyone else. Chris had reached his breaking point two weeks ago when he was in his office working on the first draft of his latest book. He was jolted with a sensation so intense he swore someone dropped an axe into his left shoulder. Jen heard the blood-curdling cry and charged in from the living room. A visit to his private doctor was mandatory; after some basic tests he suggested a follow up at John Hopkins. Pokes, prods, and various body scans followed and Chris felt more like a pincushion than a person. The results came back within hours and they were only positive in one respect—grade three chondrosarcoma, which Chris quickly learned was a serious form of bone cancer. The first tumor they found was in his right shoulder, and the cancer had spread up and down both of his arms. The physician said that despite various advances in battling cancer, in his case the necessary surgeries would be like plugging a leaking dam with gum. Dourly, his doctor concluded the forecast was terminal and Chris was given somewhere between two and six months. To a seventy-six year old man who had a family history of vitality, six months was an impossibility. He planned on living at the very least until ninety, not until March.

Since the diagnosis, Chris spent his time holed up inside the house. He was still allowed inside the car as long as he left the actual driving up to the auto pilot. Chris, however, was too vain to allow others to see him in his weakened condition. Writing was now out of the question as well, which was like asking him not to breathe.

Long ago, Christopher Marcum shattered his own expectations as an aspiring author. The original dream was to see his first novel, *The Weight of the World,* on a shelf at his local bookstore. Money, fame and awards were the furthest thing from his mind. Instead the twenty-eight-year-old Marcum sought affirmation. Publication gave his life meaning, no matter what else he did or did not accomplish. He knew critics would find fault with his work, as their title would imply, but he hoped the average man and woman would enjoy the story and want seconds.

Instead what he received was both critical acclaim and national attention when his novel shot to the top of numerous best sellers lists and was optioned by Sony Productions. Suddenly his days were no longer spent standing in front of teenagers while teaching about World War II, but in dealing with his agent and publicist. While it wasn't his intention to get involved in the movie business, Chris' stories were a natural fit for the big screen. In the blink of an eye he was in his early thirties, somewhat a celebrity, and having his door knocked down by a public clamoring for more. Over the years and throughout numerous interviews Christopher has always made sure to credit his success to two people— his wife, Jennifer and his muse who he jokingly referred to as Gus.

"Before there were awards and praise, there was only Jen's smile," he said in a recent interview given to the *New York Post home page*. "I owe everything I have due to this wonderful woman of mine. To this day she is the only person allowed to read along while I work because I trust her judgment. In fact, my *lesser* works are merely examples of what happens when I think I know more than she does."

# CHAPTER 3

## August 29, 2003

As early as he could remember, adults told Chris he was going to be a writer. Friends, family members, his teachers, they all saw the potential. The only question was what would he write? Chris had a best friend growing up named Sammy whose only dream was to be a firefighter. Their private joke was Sammy would live an exciting life filled with burning buildings and saving orphans and Chris would put all his stories down on paper. Together they would make a kajillion dollars and live the high life together. Unfortunately, Sammy's time on the job was brief as he died on 9/11.

At the time of Sammy's death, Chris was working on several short stories with the hope of finding a common thread between them. The way he figured, find that common thread and presto, he would have his first novel. Whether it was because he couldn't find the thread (his conscious belief), or because Sammy's death was so devastating he didn't want to write anymore (his subconscious belief) his dream of becoming a famous novelist appeared to be just that, a dream.

In Jen's eyes, Chris seemed to accept this defeat too willingly. She knew her at the time future husband as well as anyone could know anybody. As happy as he was in his personal life, Chris had only one goal professionally and that was to get published. She couldn't believe he would give up so easily. Of course she didn't want to nag so at first she kept silent. Her next excuse was their wedding was coming up, June 22$^{nd}$, 2002 and she didn't want to add any additional pressure to his plate. The seasons continued to change and by the winter of 2002 the keyboard inside the spare bedroom remained quiet outside of the random AOL session. Enough time had passed and Jen felt it was her duty as his wife and best friend to try and shake him from his doldrums. So Jen started to gently prod. Then poke. A casual question at dinner whether or not he was watching television with her or knocking out one thousand words. An innocent request to tell her a story before they fell asleep. Every time she did this Chris would try to deflect just as nonchalantly as Jen had asked. For eight months they played this little game until one night, just before another school year was set to begin, Jen decided to stop dancing.

Chris was at his desk in the spare room, typing up the first two weeks of lesson plans. He had taught Global History to freshmen and sophomores his first three years at Tottenville High School and knew the material inside and out. Not only that, he was already growing a little bored of the same subject five times a day, five times a week for three years. That was why he immediately agreed to switch classes and teach U.S. History. Sure he now had to prep like it was his first year but he enjoyed the process. Chris had just finished the outline for his first Friday when Jen opened the door and said,

"Anything good?"

"Huh," he blurted out, more of a statement than a question.

"I was wondering if you were writing anything good?"

"Nope, just the exciting world of lesson plans."

"Huh." Chris stopped typing and swiveled his flimsy desk chair to face his wife standing in the doorway.

"What's huh?"

"No big deal." Jen tried to keep her voice light and even. She didn't want to come across as judging, judging meant fighting. This was to be as airy as possible. "It's just that I haven't seen you typing away at your desk in a long time. Thought maybe you had an idea."

"Nope, not for a long time. I'm starting to think that ship has sailed." Chris started to swivel back to the computer screen when Jen said,

"I don't think it's the ship, I think it's you." She could tell by the way his back straightened that she got his attention.

"I'm not following."

"Two years Chris. It's been two years since you even tried to write something. The guy I first met would go into withdrawals if he went two days without getting something down on paper, even if it was a napkin."

"I just haven't had anything to say," he sort of mumbled.

"I don't think it's that. I think you have plenty to say. I think you're afraid." Jen started to take a step into the room and was cut off by Chris.

"Please don't try and psychoanalyze me. You're not a doctor and I'm not laying on a couch." They were teetering on the edge right now she thought to herself. If she didn't regain control of the conversation fast this would get ugly and God knows when she would be able to bring this up again.

"I'm not psychoanalyzing you, I'm stating the obvious."

"Fine, you know what? I'm basically finished with these plans anyway. I'll indulge you. What am I afraid of?" Chris ran both of his hands threw his hair and made a mocking show of facing her completely. He completed the performance by putting his hands underneath his chin like a child. Jen followed his lead and sat down on the guest bed two feet away.

"When's the last time you spoke of Sammy?"

"Hold on. Time out," he said while pantomiming the signal. "We're not talking about this."

"See? Look at you? I bring up your best friend's name and I can already see the sweat forming on your forehead. You've already run your hands through your hair once and you're about to do it again." Chris looked slightly up and saw his wife was right; his hands were itching to pour through his hair again.

"Jen please not tonight. It's late. Another night, hell tomorrow afternoon we'll talk about this I promise."

"I know you're being sincere right now but honestly, you won't. Tomorrow there will be another excuse and before we know it two years will turn into four."

"What's wrong with that? Why is it so important to you that we talk about this?"

"Because we haven't. For two years you have kept everything you felt about Sammy inside bottled up. While you haven't changed in the way you act towards me you have changed."

"If I haven't changed the way I am with you then what's the problem?" He asked with the slightest hint of exasperation.

"We just got married Chris and you already have a thin wall up. Sure there's a door on that wall and you let me come in but what happens in ten years when that door gets boarded up and grows thicker…"

"Hold on, you lost me." Jen couldn't help herself and let out a laugh. Even during serious conversations her husband had a way of making her laugh.

"Okay you're right sorry. I'm not going to make this about us, although a part of me is concerned. What this is about is you. Your writer's block is due to you bottling up your emotions. How can you expect to write and let ideas and emotions flow out of you if you don't deal with the worst day of your life?" Chris took a deep breath, part annoyance and part frustration that Jen was right.

"What do you want to know Jen? Do I miss Sammy of course I do! He was my best friend and would have been the best man at our wedding. He's dead, I'm alive the end." Once again Chris attempted to swivel around away from her gaze and Jen was having none of it. She stood up from the bed, walked over and placed her hands on his shoulders. With a slight bend, she looked into his eyes and said,

"Not the end. Far from the end. I'm not looking for tears and I'm not saying you should go to a therapist although I wouldn't be against the idea either. How about just trying to write something about him? Something stupid you guys did in high school, or a story involving him that you could make up. Something, anything just as long as you're writing about him." Chris kept her gaze for a couple of seconds before he looked down and quietly said,

"I don't want to." Jen sat herself on the floor and looked up at her husband. He was getting upset. Not angry, not overly emotional but there were cracks in his veneer. She took his right hand and began to gently massage the back of it.

"Why not?" His answers were taking longer to come by. A couple of beats passed before he replied,

"I don't want to exploit him."

"Exploit him?" Now Chris perked back to life. He climbed up on the chair so that he was in a catcher's position. Jen remained sitting down and listened.

"I don't want to write about 9/11. It feels dirty, like I'm benefitting from the pain and misery of others."

"Then don't write about 9/11. Write a story with a character based on Sammy. Write something that would honor his memory. Set it in 1985 or 2025. Didn't you tell me when we first started to date that Sammy would live it and you would write it all down?"

"I wouldn't know the first thing about firefighting or the men who wear the uniform."

"But you do know about a man who wore the uniform. You know the type of person he was. Use that. You don't even have to show me what exactly you write. Just do something. Trust me, you'll be better off."

"Of course I'd show you, I show you everything." Now it was his turn to take her hands and hold them tight.

"So then write this story for me. When you're finished I'll read it and you can shred it for all I care. Except I know you won't because I know it will be good."

"And if it's not good?"

"Then at least I'll know and more importantly you'll know that you tried. And I promise to never bring this up ever again."

"Alright. Okay. One short story. One thousand words tops. When it's done I'm done."

"Whatever you say," and she stood up and kissed him.

One thousand words turned into ten thousand words. Ten thousand words turned into thirty chapters and suddenly not only did Chris have an idea, he had his novel. Every night Chris would spend an hour in the spare room chopping down his metaphorical tree until he hit a bump in the road.

With ten pages to go Chris had finally hit his first roadblock, he couldn't figure out the ending. To be more accurate, he couldn't write the ending. From the moment he started this little project eight months earlier Chris knew how the story would end. In his mind it was obvious. The novel would trace the journey of a young man who wanted to become a firefighter and his father who wanted him to do anything but that job. Terry O'Malley, the main character, would ignore his father's wishes and become a firefighter. Not just a firefighter, a damn good one. Eventually the story would climax inside an abandoned building in the Bronx, with Terry saving his father who was trapped inside. They would walk out of the burning building together and off into the sunset. It was the Disney ending, the happy ending that he thought the readers would want. The only problem was after close to one hundred ten thousand words, it wasn't the right ending. It felt cheap. It felt fake. Most of all, it was a lie. Whenever Chris thought about this he would laugh. How could it be a lie when he was the one writing the story? Yet he knew, if he wrote the happy ending he was lying to himself and his audience. There was only one way the story could end, Terry had to die saving his father.

The realization hit Chris so hard he couldn't continue. There was no way he could write Terry's death. Jen wanted a story about Sammy and she got one. And now, after all of this, all the hard work and nights plugging away he couldn't see his best friend die again. Finally, he decided it was time to put the story away. Jen understood and was proud of him for dealing with everything. She insisted that one day he would be ready again and the story would be there waiting for him.

Six months later Jen was right.

One night Chris had awoken from a terrible nightmare that he couldn't remember. All he knew was he was freaked out and would not be falling asleep again for the near future. He got up in order to not disturb his still sleeping wife and made his way to the kitchen, passing the spare room. One glass of ice tea later he was on his way back to bed when the urge to sit down at his desk overcame him. A greater urge to open up an old Microsoft WORD document also became an itch that needed scratching and suddenly there he was, staring at the screen with his abandoned still untitled novel staring back at him. The blinking cursor almost seemed to curse him and call him a deadbeat dad. Enough was enough, he couldn't let this story waste away in book purgatory. This would be upsetting and he was probably going to get emotional but he didn't care. He had to finish the book.

Jen woke up the next morning and noticed Chris wasn't there. She slowly ambled out of the bedroom and was startled to see her husband sitting at his desk and apparently crying. Actually, crying wasn't the word, more like openly sobbing. In all the years she knew him the only time she saw her husband cry like that was at the cemetery for Sammy. Chris had stayed strong throughout, taking charge at the wake, delivering a heart felt eulogy at the church and Jen attributed his strength to still being in shock. It wasn't until it was time to drop a rose on Sammy's casket that Chris lost it. Since then his emotions had been all walled up. Now the dam had finally burst. She came running in and with a shout called his name. Chris swiveled the chair around and simply said,

"He's dead."

Before Jen could ask another question he leaned into her stomach and continued to cry. As Jen stroked her husband's hair she looked over at the printer, where two hundred and thirty seven pages sat, freshly printed. A couple of minutes passed before Chris was able to collect himself.

"Thank you."

"For what?"

"You know exactly what. I needed to do this for so many reasons. And now, because of you I have a real legitimate book on my hands. Most of all, it feels like the weight of the world has been lifted off of my shoulders."

"Did you figure out a title?"

"Not yet."

"Well I think you just did."

# CHAPTER 4

## October 6, 2052

Not only had Jen saved his novel, Chris believed she had saved his life. Without that book, he would have been doomed to a much less desirable existence.

Fourteen books (the majority of which were well received by the public, although according to the critics there were a couple of clunkers) and five movies later, Christopher Marcum evolved from someone writing for his wife to someone who was read all over the world. There were some critics who derided the stories as "absurdity meets predictability," but Chris insisted that he wrote "for the guy on the train and not for the professor in Maine." The line had eventually made for a great sound byte.

Chris was adept in handling the media, seeing it as part of the job. Truth be told, Chris adored the attention. He loved to entertain and had an innate sense of how to hold a room. Whether it was an autograph request at the supermarket or an interview on the iTV, Chris never said no. The only time he shirked from the spotlight was if he was out with his family. While Chris had chosen to be a public figure, his family had not. As far as dealing with the press, Chris learned early on that he enjoyed being out front rather than behind closed doors. Besides, his fans wanted access and in giving numerous print and video interviews, he could control his image and in some odd way retain some semblance of privacy. It was Jen's idea to set up his own Facepage where Chris could react and respond to the fans who submitted questions. This would end up being the same page he used to announce his "medical condition."

Upon discussing this with his wife and three adult children—James, Brittany and Peter—he decided to be cute with his words and not let the public know the full extent of his situation. Not wanting to endure reading his obituary while still alive, the family decided it would be best to project an image of optimism to the media. The world had Chris for almost fifty years without complaint from his family; it was now time for the Marcums to be selfish.

Jen was resolute in keeping her husband's spirits up, even though it was growing increasingly more difficult. Simple activities such as taking a shower, dressing and even eating were now dependent on his wife. Despite the loss of his independence, Chris was quick to adapt and somewhat accept his new lifestyle. The only issue he could not come to terms with was losing the ability to type. The loss was too painful to even think about, thus Chris asked his wife to keep the door closed to "The Hatch." If he couldn't use it he didn't want to see it.

"The Hatch" was what his kids called the room where Chris wrote his books. His youngest son Peter had come up with the nickname after his dad gently coerced him into watching "LOST." Peter saw the similarities between John Locke and his dad, both had an obsession with pressing buttons in dark rooms. Of course Chris loved the name and it stuck ever since. Located off the downstairs kitchen and down a long hallway in the back corner of the house, the room was perfectly situated away from everything and everyone. Upon entering the room, the wall directly ahead and to the left were made up entirely of bookcases. The wall to the right had a solitary window, which either had the curtains drawn or opened depending on whether or not Chris was working at the given moment. When he was in the midst of writing, Chris preferred to be cut off from the outside world, thus the drawn curtains. It was hard to write when you could look outside and see your kids playing in the in-ground pool. The room had proven to be a womb for his subconscious, helping give birth to the characters and situations of his stories.

Underneath the window sat his desk. A simple flat twentieth century wooden desk, stained a light brown with three drawers to his right filled with pens, papers, old manuscripts, magazines and other assorted junk he dumped in there through the years. If Chris wanted or needed a distraction, opening up one of those drawers would do the trick. There had been a long drawer running directly above his legs, but Chris had it taken out years ago. Without realizing it, he would get the jimmy legs if he was in a great flow, and his knees would bang against the drawer. The extra space gave his lanky six-foot frame plenty of room to maneuver. The only items on the desk itself besides the iTV, keyboard and speakers for his mood music were two framed pictures. One was of himself with his wife and kids at the beach in Belmar, New Jersey. The other was taken three years ago when the New York Mets won the World Series. It was of him with his youngest grandson John. Chris was pouring a bottle of water on his grandson's head and if he closed his eyes he could still hear the shriek of delight emanating from his grandson's lips. Any time writing became an object of frustration he could calm down by staring at those pictures and remembering when. Writer's block was easier to overcome when he had the smiling faces of those he loved staring back at him.

In the middle of the room, sitting on the hardwood floor, was an old faded blue couch with an even older New York Mets fleece blanket to curl up in. When Chris wanted to watch an antiquated New York Mets Blu-Ray using his "ancient" computer he would turn the couch towards the screen and enjoy. If Jen or the kids heard a ballgame on they knew it was safe to go in the room. Directly above the couch was the only source of artificial light in the room—a single bulb in the ceiling. Chris did his best writing in the dark, as it mimicked a physical form of tunnel vision. However, when he needed to read something the single beam of light provided a small circle of illumination.

The rest of the house was your basic four-bedroom colonial. "The Hatch" and the master bedroom were located on the first floor; his children's old bedrooms (now for his grandchildren) were upstairs. The Marcums had lived in their Staten Island residence for almost forty-five years and never had any inclination to move. They were all the way out in Tottenville, Atoz Court to be precise, and could see New Jersey from their kitchen window. They loved both their privacy and the fact that their neighbors treated them like everyone else.

Chris sat in his motorized chair and was chewing the last morsel of eggs Jen fed him when she once again tried to bring up a strained conversation.

"Chris, I was wondering. Your latest story had a really good flow and if you wanted to…"

"Jen, listen to me. I'm not dictating the story to you. My hands have to be in control."

Jen took a deep breath and tried to remain patient with her frustrated husband. "I understand what you're saying, I just think you're saying that because…"

Chris cut her off before she could go any further.

"Believe me if I could get this out of my head I would. When I close my eyes all I see is the story and it's driving me nuts, but I can't! In my mind dictation is the same as surrendering."

"I wouldn't be…"

"It's impossible. Case closed."

His face turned a slight shade of red and Jen knew they were another volley or two away from raised voices and an argument. Chris hated the conversation; Jen knew this just like she knew writing gave him a sense of purpose. Without that purpose who knew how long he would fight, if at all. At the same time, after a marriage filled with smiles and laughter, she didn't want to spend their remaining time locked in battle. She conceded this round and changed the subject.

"Do you want to go outside and get some fresh air? It looks like it's going to be a beautiful day."

Chris was still somewhat defensive and responded in suit, "I think I'd rather just go back to our room and play on the iTV." Apple had finally figured out how to combine the television, computer and phone years ago. Chris felt like it was straight out of "The Jetsons."

Jen put on a smile, wiped her husband's face and pushed him back towards their bedroom. After helping him get back into bed she said,

"I'll leave you be for a bit. Let me know if you need anything."

Chris had regained his composure and wanted to reach out and grab his wife before she left his side. Unable to, Chris simply said, "Thanks Jen. I'll try not to bother you."

Sensing a change in his demeanor, Jen didn't have to put on a smile, one naturally appeared. Without skipping a beat she said, "I love you," turned on the iTV and closed the door.

A couple of hours later, the door opened and Jen reappeared.

"Chris?"

"Yeah babe."

"Joe Brady messaged me to see how you're doing. Feel like talking?"

"Yeah, just put the privacy button on so he can't see me."

Jen walked over to the iTV on the wall facing the bed, and changed the setting from entertainment to phone. She flipped her way through a couple of publicity shots Chris used when he didn't want to be seen. Since it was Joe she decided to open up the family shots and chose a picture of Chris taken at his seventieth birthday party. Peter had smeared icing on his father's face and Brittany was lucky enough to take a picture before Chris cleaned it off and went after his son. The grandkids especially loved that picture.

Joe Brady was a well-known novelist who dealt mainly in horror stories. Ten years Chris' junior, Joe and Chris had been friends for many years now and often critiqued each other's works. Just as Jen closed the door behind her, Chris heard the distinctive baritone voice that could only belong to one man.

"Chris! How you doing buddy?"

"Hey, Joey. Hanging in there. How about you?" Chris said in his best nonchalant voice.

"Did I catch you at a bad time? Although I have to admit, seeing that picture is much better than staring at your face!" A hint of concern was found in Joe's voice, although he tried to keep a cheery presence up on the screen.

"Hey Jen, our ugly friend Joe is trying to be funny again! You would think after all these years he would have given up," and the men exchanged a mutual laugh.

Joe was sitting in his own version of "The Hatch." The room was filled with souvenirs he had accumulated from his years of travel and didn't have a window. The only source of light was the screen itself, illuminating his roundish, pale face and giving off a ghostly image. Chris referred to this look as "living the gimmick" and often joked that he was the palest ghost Chris ever saw. Joe believed in writing in darkness and letting his mind run wild, which was effective he supposed if you're writing horror.

"I don't want to bring down the mood but I saw the statement on your page."

Chris took a deep breath and was going to make a dumb joke before deciding otherwise.

"Yeah the family decided I should say something before the rumors started."

"Well they're still flying around; I'll do my best to shoot them down."

"Thanks, Joe." Chris found himself getting strangely emotional and swallowed hard before continuing. Fortunately Joe didn't hear the change in his voice, or if he had, didn't acknowledge it.

"Don't worry about it. If you or Jen need anything, don't hesitate to ask."

"Thanks." Another pause lingered in the air.

"So how are things on your end?"

Joe leaned back on his chair and put his hands behind his head. Chris thought he gained some weight since the last time they saw each other.

"Same old. I'm getting ready to promote the next book. Were you able to read it?"

"Yeah, actually Jen has been reading it to me at night."

"And?"

"It reminded me of "*Empty Faces*." Took awhile to kick in, but once it did it was worth the wait."

Joe laughed. "Are you saying I'm wordy?"

"All I'm saying is ever since Jen started reading to me I haven't had any problems falling asleep." They chuckled.

"Listen, Chris, I don't want to keep you. Just wanted to see how you were doing."

"I appreciate it Joe. We'll talk soon."

"Yes we will. Bye for now."

"Bye."

Chris stared at the blank screen for a couple of seconds before Jen walked back into the room. "You know I don't listen in on your conversations…"

"Here comes the but."

Jen laughed. "No buts, just an observation. You are amazing Christopher Marcum. You truly missed your calling as an actor."

"Maybe in my next life," he said with a satisfied look on his face.

"Very funny." Jen sat down on the bed and brushed a white hair off Chris' face.

"What? I'm not going to complain to Joe. He might steal my pain and use it in his next book!"

"Did I say actor, I meant comedian," she said sarcastically. "Do you need anything?"

"Nah, I think I'm going to close my eyes for a little bit."

"Well if you do, call me. I'll be folding laundry inside."

"Okay."

Jen stood up, ran her hand down the left side of his face and kissed him.

"Love you."

"I know you do and I love you too."

# CHAPTER 5

## January 4, 2053

The past two months had taken their toll on Chris. At first the pain was like the tide, coming and going in waves. As the calendar flipped over into 2053, the pain had become an ocean and Chris was without a life preserver. His physician had kept the medication coming, allowing him to spend half his time where he had made his living--his own fantasyland. The Marcum family was now making statements on behalf of their father on his Facepage. He had receded into the background, his name having permanently replaced his face in the eyes of the public. Privately, his children had begun discussing what happens next. They were all in agreement that the conversation would be kept from their mother. Let her concern herself with today; they would handle tomorrow.

Chris always had a baby face, which he credited to his half Italian half English heritage, but now his face looked like time had finally caught up to him. He looked haggard and perpetually tired. Not long ago the only wrinkles on his face were from laughing. Now his cheeks looked like a road map with lines zig zagging across. What had been his proudest feature; his clear blue eyes were now hidden due to his proclivity to squint. Long ago his hair was a dark chestnut brown with hints of gray sprinkled throughout. Seemingly overnight the hints of gray had been replaced by white and swept through the landscape, to match his beard.

The entire family, including his brother Eric and sister-in-law Danielle, celebrated Christmas and New Year's together. What was once a raucous affair was now somewhat muted. For a family used to such a high-energy husband, father, and grandfather, this shift in personality was almost heartbreaking to watch. The head of the table no longer led the conversation and his silence was felt. Brittany quietly commented to her younger brother Peter how her father looked like he aged fifty years since the diagnosis. Worse, his sickness was taking a toll on Jen, who at seventy-four was having a difficult time keeping up with his needs.

Due to his lack of dexterity, Jen had taken over grooming, making sure his beard and hair were well maintained. During those lucid moments Chris would comment that it made no difference anymore. The slight case of vanity he carried throughout his life had been exchanged for a crate of apathy. His children attempted to broach the idea of a nurse helping out but were swiftly rebuked by their mother. There was no need for someone else to do the job; she would take care of her husband. She always had and always would.

A couple of nights after Christmas, Jen tiptoed into the bedroom, being extra careful not to wake her slumbering husband. She took off her faded gray robe and hooked it up on the bathroom door to the left of the bed. She slowly pulled back the blankets and sat down when her husband stirred.

"That you?"

"Yes, love."

"Jen?" His voice was no longer larger than life. He was reduced to a rasp.

"Yes it's me. Go back to sleep."

"I want to talk."

Now under the covers, Jen rolled on to her side and propped her head up with her hand. She knew this was an opportunity that might not present itself in the morning. They had not shared a real conversation for two days.

"What's on your mind, love?" she cooed.

"All I ever do is sleep. I miss out on everything because either the pain is intolerable or because I can't keep my eyes open." He attempted to kick his right leg out from under the blankets in disgust and instead only managed to cause a ripple.

"Do you want to cut back on the pain meds? I can call the doctor tomorrow if you want."

"No, don't do that. I'm not that strong anymore."

"Are you comfortable? I could…" Before she could finish the sentence Chris cut her off and went straight to the matter at hand.

"Am I old?"

"What do you mean?" In spite of her best intentions she chuckled at the question. Out of all the things to be on her husband's mind she did not expect to hear this one.

"Is seventy-six an old number?"

Jen wanted to blow off his question in favor of something more important. What stopped her was the realization that anything said by her husband at this point was important. "It used to be, but not really. Not anymore."

"How long are we married?" Chris' voice remained calm and even keeled. It was as if he had already written the conversation out in his mind and was now reading the from the script.

"You know the answer to that."

"I know, but I want you to tell me."

"Fifty wonderful years," she said and added a kiss to punctuate the remark.

"And how long do you know me?"

Jen saw there was a point to the line of questions and patiently played along.

"Fifty-four glorious years."

"And did you ever wonder what would have happened if you didn't get in my car?"

"You've never given me a reason to wonder."

# CHAPTER 6

## May 7, 1999

Chris was referring to the day they met. They were at the local bar called Leo's, Chris was with his friends while Jen was there on a blind date. For a Friday night the place was empty, which, by Leo's standards meant half filled. Chris watched his two friends Sammy and Richie finish a game of darts and he offered to buy the next round to resounding cheers. He took their order, made his way over to the bar and rested both elbows onto the counter. Things were moving a little slow due to the new bartender named Valerie and Chris patiently waited while she looked through the fridge below for a Beck's. The jukebox was playing "Time" by Pink Floyd and Chris nodded his head with the song. He passed the time by fiddling with the wrinkled ten dollar bill in his hand and looking absent mindedly at himself in the mirror behind the bar. He hadn't shaved in a couple of days and liked the way it looked. Finally, Valerie came over for his order and Chris rattled off what they wanted. The only drink left to mention was his Budweiser when something or rather someone caught his attention in the mirror.

Her face was tan and absolutely flawless, causing her deep blue eyes to pop on the glass. The blonde hair was pulled tightly back in a no frills ponytail. Chris couldn't get over her eyes, and when they seemed to meet his in the reflection his stomach flipped. If this was a movie, time would have stopped and Chris would have enjoyed the moment for as long as he wanted. Instead, she continued her walk directly behind him, around the bar and over to one of the tables on his left. The plan was a simple one, drop the drinks off and move immediately over to her table. Except there was a slight problem, and he was flashing a set of perfect teeth. With a smile out of a Sears catalogue the guy stood up from the table and slid her chair in. "Lucky guy," he muttered while the bartender stood in front of him and for the second time yelled out, "seven dollars." Startled, Chris noticed the two beers he ordered. Without a second thought Chris handed over the ten, forgetting to order his own beer in the process and walked back to his friends.

Twenty minutes later, Chris joined his friends outside in the back alley for a casual smoke. Even though he didn't indulge, the alley was a place where you could hold conversations with various strangers without the concern of an overly loud jukebox. His friends were just about finished with their cigarettes and were talking something work related although Chris stood there quietly. He had let his mind wander and had begun counting the number of damaged tiles on the side of the bar. He was up to seventeen when he noticed the same girl from before standing in the back of the alley on the pay phone. Her face had turned slightly towards his and seemed a little agitated. Naturally, Chris moved a couple steps closer to get a better handle on the conversation. It was at that moment when he overheard her exclaiming how badly the date was going. Sensing an opportunity, Chris decided to go for it. The moment the phone hit the handle he approached her with his best conversation starter.

"Hey, can I borrow a cigarette?" said in his most nonchalant voice.

He was afraid his voice cracked and hoped she hadn't noticed.

Jen turned around and looked at him quizzically. "Do you plan on giving it back when you're done?"

"Sure. Maybe you'd like to keep it as a souvenir." He waited for a laugh and instead received a slight smirk as well as a possible eye roll.

"I don't know about that. I'd let you keep it if I had one. Sorry." She started to walk back to the bar before Chris blurted out,

"Honestly you look like you need one yourself."

This time he received a small sigh, perhaps laced with a hint of frustration and watched as she stepped back and leaned against the brick wall with her hands behind her back.

"Actually, I'm on a date right now and to be honest it's not going well."

Chris took a step closer and whispered, "ugly or boring?" Jen gave a surprised laugh and said,

"To be honest neither. He's an okay guy, great smile. There just isn't a spark. Everything about tonight seems forced."

Chris sensed an opportunity forming. "Does he know you're outside?"

"No, I said I was going to the bathroom and instead slipped outside to make a phone call."

"So why not go back inside and tell the guy something came up and you have to leave?" Chris said with a sly grin.

"That's why I called my friend Stephanie, except she can't come to rescue me."

"I could rescue you." The words came out fast and Jen let out a laugh,

"I don't even know you!"

"Not to sound overly confident but I'm assuming the past minute of our brief conversation tops whatever you've been getting for the past twenty."

"I'm pretty sure that statement would apply to anyone out here," she said in jest.

"Okay true true but you're talking to me and that's the important thing."

He wasn't sure if she was squirming because she wanted out of the conversation or because he was starting to make sense to her.

"Give me one good reason why I should leave one blind date for another."

"Time out; you're on a blind date? And you didn't take your own car?"

"Two things," she said while making the hand gesture. "One, he offered like a gentleman to pick me up and two I don't have a car of my own. What other choice did I have?"

Without missing a beat, Chris responded. "I hear the bus is lovely this time of night."

They both laughed and Chris caught Sammy gesturing from the corner of his eye. He made a motion to say they were going back inside and Chris nodded to go on without him.

"All right. Hypothetically let's say I agree to hang out with you instead--then what?"

"Same thing you would have done if your friend picked you up. You go back inside and tell your blind date you are so sorry, but your brother just beeped you and you have to leave."

"And when he offers to drive me home?"

"Say your brother is on his way."

"Yeah, and what do I do when Henry walks me outside and there's no car waiting for me?"

"Ah-ha. That's when I'll pull up, you hop in my car and we'll go grab a bite to eat." She smiled and seemed to weigh out his proposition.

"Did you just think of all this off the top of the head or is this the usual Friday for you?"

"I can be diabolical when I have to be" he said with a devilish grin.

"Remind me again why I'm getting in the car with a complete stranger?"

"Complete strangers? We're practically best friends."

"Best friends, huh? I don't even know your name," she said with a smirk. He was starting to love that smirk.

"Chris Marcum," and he gave an exaggerated bow.

"Jen Polanski," she curtseyed in reply.

"See, we are now officially best friends." Jen wrinkled her nose in reply.

"Hey, all I'm saying is you have two options. Either you go back inside, hang out with Mr. Personality, and count the minutes till the end of the night or get in the car with me and laugh all night."

Jen thought about it, smiled and said, "I can't believe I'm doing this."

"To be honest I can't believe it worked. I'll meet you outside in five."

Jen walked back inside the bar with Chris right behind her. He immediately made a beeline towards his friends.

"Sam listen no time to talk I need your car keys fast."

"Woah Marcum slow down. What's going on?"

"No time to explain. Give me your keys and I'll owe you my life."

"What about us?" Richie said.

"Please guys trust me she's worth it."

"If it's the same girl you were talking to outside I'd steal a car if I had to," Richie said with a grin.

"That's my second option, what do you say Sam?"

Sam looked at Richie and shrugged. "Whatever, I'll call Jaime and see if she wants to come down with some friends. Just promise me you'll call me tomorrow and explain what happened."

"You got it."

Chris grabbed the keys from his best friend's hand and ran out the door. From the corner of his eye he could see the disappointment in Henry's face while Jen told her story. "Thank God Sam parked across the street and not down the block" he thought to himself. A minute later he pulled the Camry in front just as Jen reached the sidewalk with Henry trailing behind her.

"So I'll give you a call?"

"Umm sure. Sorry for the rush but there's my brother." She gave Henry a kiss on the cheek and opened the car door. Chris could feel his heart thumping as he watched her sit down. He thought of giving Henry a wave but didn't want to be a dick about things. Instead, he pulled out while Jen dropped her head back on the headrest.

"Am I a bad person for doing this?" she wondered out loud.

"Maybe if you guys were dating then yeah but people leave blind dates early all the time."

"And get in the car with a complete stranger" she said with some exaggeration in her voice.

"Okay, then yeah, you are a bad person" and they both laughed.

He stopped at the light on the corner of Hylan Boulevard and the melodious tones of "Elderly Woman Behind the Counter in a Small Town" came on the radio. To his shock she started to sing along. Jen saw his surprised look, laughed and said, "That's just the tip of the iceberg." If he wasn't already giddy for the girl, he was now. They never went for that bite to eat, instead finding it much more enjoyable to drive up and down Hylan singing along with the radio and making each other laugh. By the time Chris pulled up in front of her house the word, "swooning" could be applied to the both of them.

"I must say this has been the worst and best blind date of my entire life." Jen said with her now ever present smile shining brightly.

"To think I left my house tonight with the intention of making it an early one."

"And without shaving."

"Yeah imagine if I got myself all pretty? You wouldn't stand a chance."

"Thank God I don't care about looks...clearly." They both laughed for the umpteenth time that night.

"What time is it?" Jen inquired.

"12:41 and that would be the AM."

"That was just horrible" followed by an insincere over laugh.

"They all can't be winners. Although I'm fairly confident I was definitely more hit than a miss tonight."

"Eh, if you say so."

Without the slightest thought, Chris suddenly leaned in and kissed her. Jen smirked and said,

"Cheesy jokes and lousy kissing. You really know how to make a girl feel special." Chris let out a booming laugh that startled her.

"I suppose if there is another date I'll have to get used to that."

"That's just the tip of the iceberg; just wait till I really laugh."

"Fantastic" Jen said sarcastically.

"What are you doing tomorrow?" Chris said with a big cheeseburger smile on his face.

"Tomorrow? Wow we move fast!" she said with that smile.

"It wouldn't be fair to make you wait the regular three days."

"Really? Okay then. Call me and you'll find out."

"I don't have a pen."

"Then you better memorize 555-4341."

By this point Chris could tell anyone the locations of the four beauty marks on her face, memorizing her phone number would be a breeze.

"I'll try my best."

"I'm sure you'll do more than that. Good night, Chris."

"Good night, Jen."

Before she opened the car door, she leaned over and kissed him again.

"All right getting better."

"I'll have to practice."

"Only with me" she said as she gracefully left the car. He was too smitten to respond back and just watched her as she walked up her front steps. When she opened the front door she turned, gave a wave and went inside. Chris drove away with the world's biggest cheeseburger grin permanently attached to his face.

# CHAPTER 7

## January 4, 2053

Thinking Chris might have fallen asleep, Jen sat up on the bed and leaned in closer to her husband. Instead of seeing his face plummeting into a deep sleep, she saw his eyes wide open. Chris had paused and was carefully weighing the next question in his mind.

"Did I make you happy?" It was the way he asked the question that caused a small lump to rise from her throat.

"Of course, Christopher. You always make me happy." Jen noticed how he had said it and forcefully remained in the present tense.

"Forget about the books. Was I a good husband to you?"

Jen eased back down next to him and once again turned to face him. Placing her right hand on his she said, "I think the qualities that make you a great writer are the same qualities that make you a great husband. It's all about the details and you never forget that." Chris' eyes glistened and his raspy voice cracked.

"Jen I'm afraid to die."

Jen leaned forward and looked deep into her husband's eyes. They were glassy and she was on the verge of tears. Being careful to mind his right arm she drew close to him so that he was lying on her left shoulder and began scratching his head. In the past whenever Chris grew agitated or stressed she would run her fingers through his hair.

"Chris, I want you to hear this because it's the truth and you need to hear it. I know you're depressed and feeling helpless. I also know you're scared and you're nervous and the truth of the matter is so am I. Christopher, I love you. It kills me to see you in pain and know that there is nothing I can do for you. I would give anything to switch places with you right now. You are my love and you are my life. I love you."

Silence sat between them for a brief moment before Chris resumed. "Jen, can you do me a favor?"

"Of course."

"When the time comes will you be right by my side holding my hand? I think I'll be able to handle it better knowing you're with me."

Throughout the course of their marriage, Chris and Jen had always been blunt with each other. He credited their longevity to how open they were with each other. There was no guessing for the most part and that made the relationship work. Up until this point the both of them had avoided acknowledging Chris' mortality.

Jen had been trying her best the entire conversation to control her tears; however, it was now impossible. She had seen Chris vulnerable at times, but this was raw. Her husband was scared and needed his wife. The tears began falling like raindrops on his pillow as she spoke.

"I promise you, God forbid that time ever comes, I will be right beside you."

"I don't know what I would do without you. I would be lost without you." He barely managed to spit out the last couple of words before succumbing to emotion. They laid there, allowing their dams to burst and let the grief pour forth. It had been a long time coming. In between sobs she said,

"And I can't imagine life without you."

"I thought I knew this before, but I didn't. I understand now. Nothing in this world means more to me than you." Jen was used to Chris getting the last word in so she leaned in and kissed her husband. Their faces were wet but that was inconsequential. A couple of minutes later they fell asleep, with Jen's right arm draped over her husband.

Less than a week later Chris developed a cough and began running a fever. Jen knew this was serious and called his doctor at John Hopkins. He told her it was time to admit her husband into Staten Island University Hospital. An ambulance was sent over and Jen went downstairs to unlock the front door.

Barely conscious, Chris understood what was going on. He would be leaving their home for the final time. A wave of panic came over him as he closed his eyes and tried to imagine what their bedroom looked like. They bought this house with the money they made when his second book, "*One of These Nights*," went into paperback. About forty-four years ago they bought their dream house and they never looked back. What color were the drapes in the bedroom? What about the basement carpet? Closing his eyes, Chris struggled to remember if his coins were all in the decorative can Brittany made for him in kindergarten or if they spilled onto his nightstand. Then another wave hit him when he couldn't remember what "The Hatch" looked like. He was leaving his home and apparently his memories as well.

Taking a deep breath, Chris counted to ten and pictured his wife laughing. Then, he asked himself what color was the chair he sat in to write? Black. On what shelf did C.S. Lewis' book, "*The Screwtape Letters*," reside? The wall to the left of the door, middle section, top shelf, fourth book from the left. Where was his favorite mug? The pantry to the left of the sink, second shelf on the right. Taking another deep breath, Chris managed a meager smile.

Closing his eyes, Chris began to think of milestone moments that occurred there in the house. Showing James and Brittany their new brother Peter, shutting off all the lights and playing with his children while their mom went out to the movies with her girlfriends, Brittany's pre-prom party, the night Jen woke him up and they discovered Peter trying to sneak out with the car. Watching Mets games as a family in the living room, especially celebrating the championships. What about the weekends when Jen's parents took the kids, giving them the house all to themselves. Family dinners, Christmas, birthdays; a lifetime of memories, all contained inside a two-story white colonial.

Chris felt himself succumbing to fatigue and struggled to remain awake. He didn't want to fall asleep now and wake up in a cold hospital. It was no use, the harder he tried to fight, the more fatigue set in. By the time Jen led the EMTs to their bedroom, he was already asleep.

# CHAPTER 8

## January 11, 2053

James and his son John were sitting in the fourth floor waiting room down the hall. Visiting hours were over in five minutes and James had left early to give his parents some privacy. Peter and Brittany had already said their goodbyes and taken the elevator down to the first floor. Chris' eldest son and youngest grandson sat silently together, the only sound coming from James' fingers gently tapping his son's shoulder. John was being a good little boy, content to stare out the open window. The world outside was dark except for the random street lights off in the distance. James felt his son stir and thought he was drifting off to sleep. The past week had been exhausting and the idea of passing out on his king size bed sounded appealing. He felt his own eyes grow heavy and as his head began to droop he heard John say something.

"I'm sorry, Johnny. Daddy closed his eyes for a second. What did you say?"

"You weren't listening?"

"Of course I was listening. Like Pop-Pop says I'm hanging on your every word."

"You didn't say that in the funny voice."

"Sorry. Daddy's just tired. What's up?"

John looked up at his father with his brown doe eyes and said, "I don't want Pop-Pop to die."

James pulled him even closer and let out a deep sigh. "Neither do I, John."

"So then why does it have to happen?"

James didn't want to look at his son. The emotions of having his father in the other room combined with his son discovering death for the first time would be best dealt with by staring straight ahead. He thought for a second and said honestly, "I don't know. That's just the way it is."

John waited a moment before another thought came to him. His big brown eyes grew wide and he asked, "Do you know when you're going to die?"

"Not till I'm really old like Pop-Pop and then you'll be talking to your little boy like we are now."

"Can I go in and see him?"

"Well, he's talking with grandma right now. You'll see him tomorrow."

"Can I see him after they're done talking?"

"Grandma is putting Pop-Pop to sleep. He has to get plenty of sleep so he'll get better."

"Well, I just want to see him for like a minute."

"I'll tell you what; we'll get here earlier tomorrow so you can have extra time with him."

"Daddy I just want to go in for like a second and just tell him something very important."

"What?"

"Don't die." A large lump formed in the back of his throat and James could feel his eyes getting glassy. Okay, for his son's sake he would let John go in and see his Pop-Pop. However, if James was honest he wanted to see his dad just as much, if not more.

"Okay, Johnny, once grandma is finished you can go in for a minute. But then you have to let Pop-Pop get his rest."

James' iPhone rang and he scrambled through his jacket pockets to grab it. He held his right index finger up to his son to make sure he knew to wait for daddy before saying hello to his sister on the screen.

"I thought you left, Dannie."

"Yeah I did. You interested in coming back to my place for a late dinner?"

Before James could answer a nurse walked by and reminded him, "Sir this is a phone-free zone. If you want to talk you're going to have to do it outside."

James gave an awkward smile and acknowledged the nurse's presence. "Listen, Dan, I have to go. I'll drop off John first and if I have the energy I'll pop over."

"Sir…"

"Sorry, sorry. Gotta go, bye."

Notwithstanding that one particular nurse, the staff on call at Staten Island University Hospital was top of the line. The administration at the hospital had respected the Marcum's wishes and placed Chris in a secluded room up on the fourth floor, away from any curious fans or paparazzi. The room was big enough to hold four patients with a fantastic view of the water and of Brooklyn beyond. The hospital also provided a three sectional leather couch, which Jen used as her bed.

Over the past four days, Chris' body had begun to rapidly deteriorate. His weight had already dropped substantially and what was a thirty-six inch waist was now down to a barely twenty-eight. Conversations were minimal, at best, due to the high levels of pain medication coursing through his frail body. The doctors told Jen and his children to prepare for the inevitable as it was just a matter of time now. At this point, all they could do was make sure he was comfortable and not in pain. The day he was checked into the hospital James recorded a message on Chris' Facepage. To end any sort of speculation, his words were brief and to the point.

"Today my father, Christopher Marcum, was checked into the hospital due to his battle with bone cancer. I am here to inform you that things aren't well and I would like to ask anyone watching to keep my father in their prayers tonight. Please respect our privacy during these trying times. Thank you." Jen was proud of how her son handled himself in addressing the issue and thanked him several times for it.

Despite his outward appearance, inside Chris was alert and doing what felt natural, writing a narrative in his head. Whether it was a coping mechanism or just ingrained after a lifetime of doing so, in capturing the moment he was outside himself. The worries and stress were now just two more characters in the story. He allowed his unconscious tell the story for him.

*I'm tired, yet I'm afraid to go to sleep. What if I don't wake up? What if I do wake up? Do I really want to deal with another day of unbearable pain? Worse, not being able to talk to my family? I had the whole crew here today, including the seven grandchildren and all I could do was make sure I didn't scare them with my moans. It's not fair to Jen, it's not fair to the kids and most important of all, it's not fair to me. So why am I sticking around? Why is this good Catholic*

36

*suddenly afraid to cross the street? I guess it's a hell of a lot easier to be brave and face death when you're thirty. And then there's the worst and scariest question of all, what if there isn't anything after this? What if this is all there is? Did I do enough? I pray God is more than just another character in a story.*

A tired Jen slowly made her way over to James and John in the waiting room. If Chris had aged fifty years in three months then his wife had aged twenty-five. James had just about come to terms with the thought of losing his father. The thought of losing his mother was a whole different story.

"You ready to go, Jimmy?"

"One second, Mom. I told John he could go back in one more time and say goodbye." Jen bent over slightly and looked into her grandson's eyes.

"Even if it doesn't look like it, he can hear every single word."

"Okay, grandma."

James and John walked down the hall to Chris' room. A nurse mentioned that visiting hours were over and he said they were just saying goodbye. When they reached the room, James stood at the door and watched his son walk in. He was small for seven, still waiting for that first growth spurt. Wiping his long brown mop-top hair from his eyes, he gingerly creeped into the room and to the side of the bed. Standing on the tips of his toes, he leaned forward and whispered into his grandfather's ear.

"Pop-Pop, I know you're sleeping, so I'll whisper really quiet. Daddy promised he would take me to a Mets game this year and I want you to be there too. I love you Pop–Pop, so you have to get better."

Try as he might, Chris couldn't utter a syllable. He tried to blink to show John he was listening, but that wasn't even an option. He thought to himself again.

*I'm going to try Johnny, I really am. I just don't think I have another four months in me.*

Six hours later, Chris was wide awake and staring up at the ceiling. He had been writing a short story in his mind about an old man who was about to die and had hit upon a great line, "the toughest part of dying is everyone else." Of course this story would eventually be filed where all those great ideas between awake and sleep go. Even if he somehow pulled through there was no way he was remembering it, and it's not like he could go grab a pen and scribble on his bed sheets.

Barely managing to register above a whisper he exclaimed, "If that's the toughest, the second toughest part is waking up in the middle of the night alone." As he counted the holes on each ceiling tile, Chris felt a rustle come from the direction of the bathroom and the unmistakable feeling of being watched.

"You can always talk to me." Chris stopped counting and looked around the room desperately searching for the source of the voice he heard. Believing that he imagined the noise, he closed his eyes and tried to fall asleep.

"Christopher Marcum," the words were as clear as a bell and caused goose bumps to run up and down his fragile body.

"I know I'm sick," Chris mumbled. "This has to be an affect of whatever drugs the nurses are giving me."

"I am not a hallucination, nor the byproduct of any drug. Nor is my appearance the result of an undigested bit of beef." Chris began to tremble. He had accepted the demise of his body on the condition that his mind stayed sharp. The side deals one makes with God when one has no choice. With this new addition to the story, he firmly believed his mind was breaking down as well. The thought sent panic up and down his body.

"I can't go crazy now. Please God, take me before that happens," he managed to get out in a rough, raspy voice.

"You aren't going crazy, Christopher. I am right over here. Would you prefer to actually see me or continue to just hear my voice?" Christopher nodded and thought,

"This has to be the morphine talking,"

Suddenly, a faint gray outline appeared to be growing out from the corner of the room. In a matter of seconds it became a tangible form, if you could call light a form. He could see a being somehow within the aura. Whatever it was, it was beautiful. Chris couldn't tell if it was a man or woman or how old or young it was. Yet he couldn't take his eyes off the figure. Before he could even annunciate a syllable of questionable thought, the light provided an answer.

"Christopher. I am a type of angel sent to those who are about to cross over. Don't worry, you aren't going to die right now, however the moment is rapidly approaching. I'm here to make sure your final hours are comfortable. Do you need anything?" To himself, Chris was shocked and his mind was drowning in thoughts. This is why he considered it somewhat of a personal triumph when he managed to get out a faint "no."

"I understand this is a shock to the system," the voice went on. You obviously have plenty of questions to ask. We'll get to them. For now let's talk about you. Are you satisfied with the way your life turned out?"

"Yes," Chris stammered. The angel softened its tone and leaned in closer.

"Christopher, listen to me. Take a deep breath. I am here and you are not dreaming. We can have a conversation, but not if you are afraid to talk. Is there any particular reason why you're happy with the way your life turned out?" Chris took that deep breath and smiled. He still couldn't believe this was happening, but he wasn't going to fight it.

"Well, yeah several reasons actually."

"Okay good, that is a good start. Give me one."

"I married my best friend; I have three great kids and seven wonderful grandkids."

"Do you have any regrets?"

"Who doesn't have regrets? Sure I have some, but all in all I'm really happy." At that Chris propped himself up using his hands and was surprised when he didn't feel an ounce of pain.

"Ahh yes. You have discovered the absence of pain. For the purposes of this conversation I think you would function better if the thought of pain wasn't over your head like the Sword of Damocles."

"Thank you," he said while twirling his hands like a pinwheel.

"What about other areas of your life? Did things work out the way you wanted them to?"

"Never in my wildest dreams could I have imagined the life I lived. All I ever wanted was to be published and somehow I became a celebrity. Outside of my family, doing what I love for a living was the greatest gift God could have ever given me."

"Funny you should mention Him. You feel this way even though He took the ability away from you?"

"Sure, I still have plenty of stories to write, at the same time how can I complain when I've had the career I've had?"

"Interesting. Christopher, may I ask you a question?"

"The fact that I somehow regained use of my arms and hands means you can do whatever you'd like" he said while rotating his arms and flexing his fingers.

"Do you believe in God because He's been so good to you?"

Chris heard the words but didn't know what to say. "What do you mean?" Out of all the possible questions, Chris didn't see that one coming. It both concerned and scared him a bit to hear his faith questioned by a corporeal being.

"Well let's say things didn't go the way you wanted. Would you still have the level of faith you possess at this very moment, outside of actually seeing and talking to a being such as myself?"

"I'd like to say I would. I was religious long before Jen came into my life and before I was published. I don't see how the gifts I received would impact my level of belief."

"Christopher Christopher Christopher. I have talked with many types of people at this moment in their life and they all give me the same answer you just did. For the purposes of this conversation I'm going to let you in on a little secret. What you think and what you do can be two different things."

"I'm assuming you know everything about me. What is it that makes you question me like this? Have I done something wrong?"

"No, and that's the point. The perfect life with the perfect wife...the perfect career...everything coming out in your favor. Don't you think a life like that would give someone more reason to believe than someone who wasn't as blessed as you were?"

"A seventy six-year-old man who is about to die has no reason to say otherwise." The being paused and then took a step forward, if you could describe light moving in that respect. There was a tone in its voice as it said,

"Enough dancing around the issue, I'm going to be blunt. I don't believe you truly mean it. I think you believe because God has given you so much. If you lived a less privileged life, I'm confident your tune would be different right now." Chris' face wrinkled in puzzlement.

"I'm confused; I thought you were here to help me." The being paused again and softened its voice.

"Yes. Yes of course I am Chris. That's the point. Do you want to die with doubt in your heart? What if you could know for sure?"

"You mean we could find out just how strong my faith is?"

"Correct."

"How would you do that?"

"Let's just say I have the ability to rewind the clock and let you live your entire life over again. You wouldn't have the knowledge you have right now and you wouldn't be given the gifts you were given. You would live an entire lifetime again and we would be right back here when it is over."

"You're telling me that I could live my entire life all over again all in a couple of seconds?"

The offer was seemingly too good to be true. An opportunity to leave the body that betrayed him and receive another opportunity at life had Chris' heart beating fast. The point was driven home when he ran his fingers through his hair. He hadn't done that in months.

"Seventy-six years would pass and we would be right back here before you knew it. Once you came back we would know for sure how strong your faith is. You don't want to face the Lord God Himself with any hesitation in your heart?" Chris began to talk excitedly. A pleasant thought had come to mind.

"Would I get to meet and marry Jen all over again? Would I get to experience the thrill of having James, Brittany and Peter?"

"I can't guarantee that. You will live your life and the chips will fall as they may. Does your faith rest on your wife and children?"

"No, but I couldn't imagine a life without them."

"God gave us all free will and I'm sure you'll make the correct choices when the time comes around. You will live a less successful life. Your wife and kids may be the same, but your job may not. Who knows what will happen? The only thing I can guarantee is your life will be a much harder one."

"And I won't remember anything from this life right now?"

"Have you ever experienced déjà-vu? You might hear a song or a name and you'll remember something, you just won't know what."

"And what if my faith isn't as strong as I think it is?"

"You know yourself better than I do. Can you see yourself ever refusing God's love?"

Chris rolled the question over in his mind. He had experienced some tough moments in the past, but never wavered in his faith. Now in his final hours, here was an opportunity to show just how much faith he had. How could he say no?

"Okay, let's do it. When do I leave?"

"Before you go I have to say this, for what you would call legal reasons. If, at the end of this other life you don't believe in God at all, things will get a little complicated."

"Meaning what?"

"Christopher, do you ever see yourself out and out denying your faith?"

"No."

"Then do not worry yourself with inconsequential details. Just think of everything you'll get to experience again. All the people you've missed and those loved ones who died. You're getting an opportunity most would kill for." A smile came over Chris' face.

"I haven't seen my parents in over twenty years."

"And now you will. Enjoy your second chance and I'll see you soon enough."

# CHAPTER 9

## March 26, 2010

The faded white door slammed with an inadvertent thud, due to the frustration he felt, which had only grown worse as the day grew long. Of course frustration and anger weren't new to Chris; they had been his traveling buddies for a long time now. Chris dropped to his knees and let out a long sigh. The priest on the other side paused, as if he was bracing himself for a battle. He slid open the confessional screen and waited. Chris closed his eyes and began.

"Bless me Father for I have sinned. It has been seven months since my last confession."

The priest was startled at how calm his voice was and said in a surprised tone, "Tell me your sins, my son."

"Well, Father, I tend to curse a lot. I have a short fuse and occasionally I fly off the handle."

"How often?"

"More than I should. I guess I have some anger issues."

"Any specific reason why?"

Chris smiled. There were millions of reasons why and only one which truly mattered. "I suppose it comes from my family life, or lack thereof. I'm divorced and we don't exactly get along."

"Any children?"

"My son, James. He turns eight in a couple of days."

"How's your relationship?"

"Honestly, I don't know. I think we have a good one. The problem is my ex. She has no problem using James to prove a point."

"How so?"

"Whenever we get into fights, suddenly fa…plans fall through." He had almost cursed during confession and the shame rose up in his cheeks.

"What do you mean?"

"I was supposed to see James this weekend. I was going to take him out for his birthday; cake, presents the whole nine yards. Then came Wednesday when the ex and I got into a fight over something stupid."

"Okay."

"So now, coincidentally, I get a text from the ex an hour ago saying his best friend Bobby is having a party on Saturday and James doesn't want to miss it. That means he misses out on me tonight and I miss out on his eighth birthday. Of course according to mommy that's okay because I'll understand." Chris said in a mocking tone.

"You just found this out?"

"I worked a long day at work, made the hour commute home to Staten Island, hopped in my car to Brooklyn and got the text on the Verrazano Bridge."

"I'm sorry to hear that."

"Honestly the only reason why I'm here is because I needed an outlet for my anger. I saw your church and hoped there was someone here to listen."

"I'm happy I could help."

"So anyway, when I do see him it's tough because I'm not his friend; I'm his dad you know? And 'no' isn't a popular word in her house, making me the bad guy whenever I do say it."

"It sounds like you need a lawyer more than a priest."

"I just need a break, Father." He said with a touch of desperation.

"Is there anything else you'd like to confess?"

"Umm. I lie. And I suppose I could treat people in general better."

"Well, my son, I absolve you from all your sins. Go out and say two Our Fathers and a couple of Hail Mary's. Most importantly, try to keep in mind that no matter what, a son needs his father."

"Thank you, Father. Oh and Father, I might as well tell you this one in advance. I'm going to the bar tonight and I'm going to get really drunk."

"My son I hear the pain in your voice and I can tell you that the solution is not to drink the pain away. In fact the only thing you'll be doing is making a bad situation worse."

"I know Father I know. I'll try not to."

"Do you really want the last thing you say in this confessional to be a lie?"

More shame flooded over him and Chris said, "You're right Father, I'm going to drink, I won't deny that. I'll just try and not get too drunk."

"I'm sure you know about the programs provided for people in need. When you get to the point where you realize you're in need come and see me, Father Jim."

"Thank you Father. I appreciate that."

"Dear God, look over this man in his time of need and help him remember Your love is always there for him. In the name of the Father and the Son and the Holy Spirit Amen."

The last dying gasp of winter blew through Brooklyn when Chris stepped outside. He buttoned up his heavy coat, tucked his hands into the pockets and quickly made his way to the parking lot. The sun was on the verge of setting when he walked into Our Lady of Angels Church and now the parking lot was illuminated by an artificial glow. He climbed into the used Mazda he owned for eleven years and cranked up the heat. While he waited for the car to warm up he rubbed his hands together and flipped on the radio. The first sound to come through his speakers was a DJ spouting off the cliché, "Thank God It's Friday!" In reality, Chris couldn't care less. The only thing special about Friday was that it was the end of another long work week. The parking lot was empty, except for a plastic bag riding the wind. "There was a movie about a lonely kid filming a plastic bag," he said out loud to the empty water bottles littered throughout his car. Putting the car in drive, Chris pulled out of the parking lot and headed to his home away from home.

When he was younger, Chris found the best way to work out whatever was bothering him was either by writing about it or driving. Sometimes words alone couldn't make sense of things and driving would, at the very least, compose him. The car was his escape hatch, as he called it, and he would jump in and cruise up and down Hylan Boulevard. During those stressful times there had to be rock music blaring from the stereo, his version of comfort food. However, with life being what it was, no amount of driving or music could help alleviate the stress he felt, even if a thirty minute commute to Staten Island was in the cards.

He sure as shit didn't see this future when he was ten-years-old. A thirty-three-year-old divorcee, working a job he hated, and spending a Friday night at the confessional and then the bar. Chris merged onto the Belt Parkway and casually looked in his rear view mirror. For a second he didn't recognize the man staring back at him. Apparently the weight he felt on the inside had expressed itself on the outside. The dark chestnut brown hair he had grown up with had been invaded by an army of gray coming up the sides, with spies mixed in at the top. His normally neatly trimmed goatee had merged with a five o'clock shadow and his blue eyes looked like someone installed a dimmer on them. Chris reached over and grabbed the black Mets hat resting on the backseat, pulling it down to the point where it almost covered his eyes. There was only one solution for the anxiety, which occupied all his thoughts: Budweiser--at least three or maybe eight.

At one time, Chris believed the use of alcohol to cope with life was a crutch for the weak. Then he got divorced and alcohol became more of a comfy rocking chair. As he crossed the Verrazano Bridge, the peaceful image of the lights clashed violently with his present thoughts. Namely, how in the hell did he get to this point? Eleven years ago he thought for sure he made the right choice. Sure, she had her flaws, although who didn't? No, he made the right choice and together they had a beautiful son. So why was he hanging out with strangers in a bar, instead of with his family in the living room?

Traffic was surprisingly light for a Friday night and Chris made the drive as if he was on auto-pilot. The EZ-Pass toll blended in with the expressway which blended in with his exit. Without a second thought Chris made his way down Richmond Avenue, reached his destination and parked the car. His legs did the thinking while his mind continued to fret, random memories playing on the big screen. The trance like walk ended when he walked up the green metallic steps and gripped the door knob.

Chris wandered into Leo's bar, although a Leo hadn't owned it for a number of years. The place had fallen on hard times in recent years and the inside reflected it. There were the worn bar stools with some of the seats torn, a couple of tables scattered about, pretzels, dart board, a pool table with a worn fabric and a color that was almost green. The multiple televisions were always tuned to some sporting event for the degenerates who couldn't resist betting their last dime on the tip they heard from a guy at work. When someone once asked

Chris to sum the place up in three words or less he simply said, "Paradise it's not."

But home it was. This was where Chris came to take refuge from the day. A day of pushing buttons in front of a computer screen. A day spent wearing a tie and being told by a guy five years his junior his work should be better. Chris always thought if he opened up a bar he would name it "Sanctuary," A place to protect you from life's troubles. Yup, paradise this wasn't, nevertheless it was still his little slice of heaven.

Chris sat down at his usual stool, the one lined perfectly with the far left corner of the bar. The owner was named Gus and he worked behind the bar. Chris had been a regular for so many years now that Gus had a Bud waiting for him the moment he walked in. When it came to Chris' beverage of choice, a simple Budweiser would do. He reasoned that hard liquor was for alcoholics and drinks with names were for girls. Budweiser simply said to anyone interested that you're thirsty.

Gus was in his mid-forties, with a shaved head due to losing a battle with premature baldness years ago. He was the type of man who was taller around the belly than in the legs. Many a person had commented that he "looked like a Gus," whatever that meant.

"Usual, Chris?"

"Yeah, thanks Gus."

"Rough day?"

"You know it."

"I'll leave you be. Just wave when you want a refill."

"Thanks."

With his Bud in hand, Chris removed himself temporarily from his barstool to flip through the choices of the jukebox. This was one of those new computerized jukeboxes. If you didn't see your song listed as an option you could download your choice for an extra ninety-nine cents. Fortunately for Chris, every jukebox in the world carried the Dark Side of the Moon album by Pink Floyd so finding "*Time*" wasn't an issue. Fifty cents later he strolled back to his stool, content to wait for his song to play. The jukebox wasn't popular tonight and Chris' song came on a couple of minutes later.

Chris was quietly singing along when he heard, "You say something, buddy?" Some guy had sat down next to Chris and apparently thought Chris was making conversation.

"Nope, just singing into my bottle. Hey Gus, slide another down here."

"How about this, your car keys for a free round?" Gus said knowing Chris' mindset.

Chris didn't take long to answer, "It's a deal."

The man sitting next to him was impressed. "Wow, the way you get service around here you're either some kind of big shot or the luckiest guy I know."

Chris paused with the bottle inches from his lips. "If there's a third choice, go with that, otherwise I'd appreciate some privacy."

"Hey no offense, pal," said the stranger as he moved one bar stool over.

Another night and Chris probably would have laughed and bought him a drink. Lucky? Chris Marcum? In his world, luck was pollen and he was allergic. Chris couldn't get the word out of his head. When was the last time he thought he was getting a break? The pity party was in full swing and Chris was the guest of honor. And so it went for the rest of the night. Buds sliding down the bar, Chris barely singing and the memories pouring fourth from his own personal tap.

# CHAPTER 10

## July 16, 1995

At eighteen-years-old, Christopher Marcum screamed one word—average. He stood a touch over six feet, making him the tallest one in the family and his face showed slight evidence of a battle with hormones fought fairly recently. His brown hair was only a legend due to a proclivity for a certain lucky blue Structure hat. He wasn't the best looking guy in the world, yet he had a certain look, which would only improve as the calendar flipped. Although right now, to see him in the mall wouldn't merit a second look.

He didn't project confidence or trepidation. Chris was simply there. In high school he had a modicum amount of friends, although he seemingly got along well with everyone. Athletic to a certain point, talkative to a degree, if you had to compare him to any animal it would probably be a chameleon. He simply blended in.

Chris would never say he was lucky, except in one respect: he never lost anyone close to him. Sure, Chris had gone to wakes before. His long time neighbor, Mr. Dorney, had died when Chris was seven years old and there had been a couple of times when he went to the wakes of his parent's friends. His dog, Jerry, died a couple of years ago too. That was tough. Yet when it came to those he loved, Chris was extraordinary lucky.

This was why the summer after his freshmen year at St. John's was such a shock. The sight of his maternal grandfather hooked up to wires and tubes was jarring. Here, in the sterilized room at Staten Island University Hospital, Chris met death for the first time and he was not happy to make its acquaintance. His Pop-Pop was dying of cancer and was on high levels of morphine to mask the pain. The random speck of gray hair was disheveled on his scalp and without dentures his mouth had a peculiar curve to it. Chris was extremely close to his Pop-Pop and made sure to remain near to take advantage of any lucid moment grandpa had in between drips.

His parents and grandma were outside talking to the doctors while his younger brother Eric was downstairs getting something from the cafeteria. Aunt Jean and Uncle Sal would be arriving within the half hour. He had a couple seconds of alone time and Chris wasn't going to waste it.

"Pop-Pop, I know you're in a lot of pain right now. I'm right next to you." Chris looked down at his grandpa's right hand. At one time his hands were his livelihood. His Pop-Pop had been a construction worker for forty-seven years and he could shatter bones with a simple handshake. Now those same hands lay still, old and withered, just like the body it was attached to. Chris hoped that, like in movies, he would see his grandfather's hand stir while he talked to him. Chris looked for any movement, any sign that would acknowledge being heard. When you're eighteen, you're allowed to have that kind of hope. Unfortunately, this wasn't the movies and his hand did not stir.

"Pop… I just want you to know that I love you so much." Chris paused to gather himself.

"Mom said it's a matter of time now. She said you're in a lot of pain and we would be selfish to want you to stay. But I am selfish. I want you to stay. I'm sorry but I do. I want more time with you." Chris looked down again at the hand. He thought he detected movement in the pinkie before realizing it was his eager mind playing tricks. "Pop, can you do me just one favor? Can you open your eyes just one more time? I'm not saying it has to be right now, just look at me one more time. That's all I'm asking."

The only response he received was the steady beeping of the machines which kept his Pop alive. Chris sat there quietly for another ten minutes, waiting for a non-existent miracle.

A couple of nights later his Pop-Pop finally passed. The doctor had prepared the family, letting them now he probably wouldn't last through the night. For the next five hours the Cavalcari family remained at his bedside, at times praying, consoling and remembering. Despite the anguish and hardship, a small miracle was given to Chris' family. An hour before he passed his eyes opened up for less than twenty seconds, long enough for him to say to his wife and his children, "I'm not afraid." To the people there, they would never forget seeing the sudden recognition of peace and the comfort those three words brought to each of them. There was only one person who didn't get to experience the moment--Chris. He was outside on a pay phone talking with his girlfriend Denise. Ten minutes later, he returned and heard what had happened. He never forgave himself for not being there.

His grandfather was laid out at Scalia Funeral Home and the two days seemed to go on forever. He greeted people he either vaguely remembered or had no idea who they were. If his dad was around he would whisper an introduction such as, "that's Pop-Pop's old neighbor Shea" and Chris would kiss her hello. What made the experience somewhat bearable was the constant presence of his friends, specifically Sammy. They had been friends since the fourth grade and lived within biking distance from each other. Sammy was the taller and stronger of the two and dreamed of becoming a firefighter. In fact, their ultimate dream was for Sammy to become a firefighter and for Chris to write down all the stories he would have. The book would make a kajillion dollars and they would be set.

At the end of the first night of the wake, Chris found himself alone in the back of the room with his grandma. They were sitting on the couch, staring ahead at the open casket. Most of the crowd had already said their goodbyes and his mom was telling anyone interested to come back to the house for a cup of coffee. The two of them sat there listening to the conversation yet not really comprehending anything being said. Chris felt something gnawing at him and needed to unburden himself. A couple of minutes passed while Chris thought of the right words to say. Upon realizing there weren't any right words, he blurted out,

"Grandma, can I ask you something?"

His grandma was thinking of something else and absent-mindedly answered, "Sure, lovey."

"Do you think Pop-Pop was disappointed I wasn't there?"

It took a couple of seconds before the words he said sunk in. She started to say something, paused and then turned to face him.

"What do you mean?"

"Well a couple of days before he died I asked him to just open his eyes and look at us one more time. And when he did I wasn't there to see him." Chris could feel a wave of emotion crashing over him and the tears were falling on his white shirt like rain drops. His grandma was crying as well and pulled him in tight for a hug. She whispered haltingly in his ear.

"Oh, lovey, Pop-Pop could never be disappointed in you."

Chris tried to say something and his voice cracked. Bracing himself he tried again, "Still, I asked him to open his eyes and when he finally did I wasn't there to see him."

His grandma had tears streaming down her cheeks. "Then I guess I have you to thank for letting me hear my husband one last time. Thank you."

At this point he was talking in between sobs. "I should have been there though. I should have been there."

"You listen to me. Your Pop-Pop loved you very much and he knew just how much you loved him. Nothing will change that. One moment does not erase 18 years of love. You remember that."

No more words were needed. Chris hugged his grandma and they walked out of the room together.

The days after the burial, Chris found himself praying a lot. He was raised a religious Catholic, mostly due to the efforts of his mom and grandma. His father wasn't a churchgoer, but he did pray. God was everywhere growing up, to the point where Chris debated becoming a priest. Of course that idea went out the window when he discovered girls, still the faith stayed the same.

The focus of these prayers was asking God why. Not why did Pop-Pop have to die. He understood that's the way life is. His guilt lay in the fact that he was not there when his prayer was answered. He was aware that it wasn't God's place to come down and smack the phone from his face but still, did he have to call Denise at that moment? It just didn't seem fair, and when you're eighteen, fairness and justice are two big issues.

A couple of nights later, Chris walked into the den where his father was watching television. His dad was a shade under forty-five years old and starting to look middle aged. The stomach was turning into a gut, his hairline was receding more and more and the black beard was looking whiter every day. Sitting there on the black leather couch, with his glasses and white t-shirt, his dad looked old. Chris wanted to talk, but at the same time felt embarrassed asking what he perceived to be "little kid questions." He decided to scrap the idea and turn around when his father noticed him from the corner of his eye.

"Hey kiddo what's up?"

Chris fumbled for an answer. "Nothing really. Anything good on?"

His dad remained nonchalant, staring straight ahead at the television. "Just flipping around. How you feeling?"

"I'm fine. I mean I'm not fine, but I'm dealing."

"Sounds just like me."

"Really?"

For the first time his dad pivoted away from the screen and looked at his son. "Yup, just trying to maintain right now and be there for your mom."

"Dad, can I ask you a question?"

"Of course. Come sit down." Chris sat down on the couch and turned towards his dad.

"It's kind of dumb, but it's on my mind."

"Okay."

"Do you think life is fair? His father laughed and looked at him.

"Where did you get that idea from? Who ever said life would be fair?"

"I know it's a ridiculous thought, I don't know."

"Well it's not ridiculous, at the same time I hope you're old enough to accept that everyone eventually dies."

"That's not it. I mean I'm upset that he's dead and everything but I understand. I guess I'm wondering if life's fair or just a series of shitty events?"

His father leaned back, took a breath and answered. "Chris, that's something you just have to accept. Shitty things are going to happen to you. There are going to be times where you'll be wondering why. It's funny; I had almost the exact same conversation with your mother after your Great Uncle Tommy died. We were lying in bed one night and I was telling your mother how much I hated dropping the rose on his casket. The more I talked the angrier I grew. Before I knew it I was much angrier than you and instead of railing against the roses I was railing against God. I kept asking her where was God now when I really needed Him? I prayed and I prayed and I heard nothing coming from the other side! You know what your mother told me?"

"What?"

"She said some people perceive the silence as God ignoring them. Others feel like God is acting like anyone would when someone you love is upset. Because there are no words to heal, instead of talking, you simply stay with them and listen. And that's what He was doing, listening to us. I guess you'll have to figure out how you see things." Chris took a couple of seconds to think and then turned to his father.

"Well what do you think?"

His father's eyes returned to the television. "Depends on the day."

"What do you mean?"

"Well there are days when I think I'm being ignored, like when my Uncle Tommy died. Then there are other times when I think He is there and He is listening."

"Well what are you right now?"

"Proud to have an adult conversation with my healthy eighteen-year-old son," he said with a smile. His dad placed his hand on Chris' knee and patted it a couple of times.

"Dad, seriously, what are you right now?"

"What I am is irregardless of this conversation. The question is what are you," and his dad pointed at him emphatically.

"For the first time I think I'm being ignored."

"Well you just lost someone really close. That's a perfectly normal feeling to have. It'll go away eventually."

"What if it doesn't?"

"Chris, if there is one thing your dad has learned, it's that eventually everything goes back to normal. Sometimes it takes longer and other times it occurs pretty fast. Regardless, in the end things go back to the way they were. This is a normal bump. Don't sweat it."

"Thanks, Dad." He stood up and walked out of the room.

"Hey, Chris?"

"Yeah?"

"Don't hold this shit inside. You'll feel much better getting it out."

Later that night Chris was having a difficult time falling asleep so he pulled out his journal. His father's words were rattling about his head and he knew the only way to make sense of them was by writing it out. Chris understood what he was trying to convey, but it seemed strange that one day things would go back to normal. How do you just move on after someone you love dies? He grew more troubled. If he were having a hard time dealing with this how would he deal with more intimate events? What if his parents died? Or what if his future wife died when they were still young? Are those considered bumps as well? Would he be able to get back to normal? The more Chris wrote the more questions arose from his subconscious and he knew there would be no answers forthcoming. All he could do was hope if the time ever came where the bump seemed insurmountable he would have the mental fortitude to live day to day.

# CHAPTER 11

## April 14, 1997

The year 1997 was a significant one for Chris Marcum. The first reason why happened on October 18th when he turned twenty-one-years old. The second was not as important in the grand scheme of things yet very important to Chris, the arrival of a halfway decent beard. For as long as he could remember, his dad had a neatly maintained beard. In his mind, he wouldn't be an adult until he could grow facial hair like his father.

The third reason why had to do with college. By the time his birthday rolled around, Chris would be in his senior year at Saint John's University. He had done most of his course work at the Staten Island campus, occasionally mixing in a class out at the "real" campus in Queens. By junior year, Chris had come to the conclusion he should have gone away, or at the very least dormed out in Queens. It wasn't because of the quality of the University rather due to the finite amount of people available to him. Staten Island felt like a small town where everyone knew everyone else, or their cousin. He had been around the same people for twenty years and desired a change. At the same time, Chris understood it would be foolish to transfer this late into his college career, especially since St. John's was known for their education program. If Chris was going to become a teacher, he might as well stay at a place known for its success inside the classroom.

Even though Chris thought of the future, the real world still seemed far, far away. He had another year of undergraduate work on top of finishing his graduate degree. There was time. Time to relax, time to have fun with his friends, time to date, or attempt to date anyone who caught his eye. In his world, there were only two things Chris took seriously: his love for the Mets and his love for rock music. Both were outlets, different ways to escape whatever looming pressures or concerns were running around his manic mind.

After four relatively quiet years in high school, Chris found himself in college. Somewhere around freshmen year he decided he didn't want to be the guy laughing in the crowd, he wanted to be the guy making the crowd laugh. He began talking more, both in class and out and found people liked his sarcasm. The more laughs he received, the more his confidence grew. Suddenly, the prospect of going over and talking to a random girl wasn't such an intimidating idea. The "nothing to lose" mentality was paying off, bringing several girlfriends into his life as well as the usual heartbreak/cheating/day to day relationship angst found on any quality television show or movie.

By the end of his junior year, Chris didn't see anyone in his worldview willing or interesting enough to chase after. He had quit looking, which wound up being the solution to his problem.

It was a couple of minutes after 11 o'clock on a beautiful Monday morning and Chris' sociology class had just let out. If he hustled he had just enough time to run home, grab a bite to eat before racing off and going to work at Walden Books in the Staten Island Mall. He pulled out of the St. John's parking lot in his blue 1995 Saturn and flipped on FM106.3, only to hear commercials. In Chris' mind, the biggest sin wasn't pride, envy or greed, it was hearing commercials while you were driving. Who wanted to drive down the expressway with 1-800 MATTRES commercials screaming in your ears? Cars were invented to have their windows down while you went a little over the speed limit and a good guitar lick reverberated out of blown out speakers. Chris smacked the play button on his CD player, only to see "NO DISC" pop up on the screen. He opened up the CD player on his dashboard and was going to reach into his glove compartment for a disc before thinking better of it. The situation would be corrected at the next red light.

His car came around the turn on Grymes Hill and he could see the next two lights up ahead were green. The street walking light wasn't flashing yet so they posed no threat of changing anytime soon. Chris knew if he pulled over to pop a CD in it also meant losing valuable eating time before work. Facing an impossible conundrum, Chris made the wrong choice. He deftly maneuvered toward his glove compartment, popped it open and reached for the debut album from Third Eye Blind inches from his right hand. It was leaning off to the right side, so it required even more of a stretch and a quick glance from the road. They say it only takes a second…

## Bam!

Chris failed to remember the third light that came quickly around the next turn. A light that was infamous for not being timed with its two brothers up ahead. Fortunate for Chris, he had his seat belt on, something he was not in the regular habit of doing. This was his first real accident, and knowing he was completely at fault didn't help the situation. He took a quick look in his rear view mirror and surmised there was not a scratch on his face. More importantly, he hoped he could say the same for whoever was coming out of the Ford truck he hit. Chris prayed there wouldn't be a pissed off body builder with an attitude problem. When he looked back later on, he sometimes wished God hadn't answered that prayer.

Chris unbuckled his seat belt and opened his door. Nervously, he took off his hat, ran his hand through his hair and put it back on. He saw the driver side door of the truck open up and Chris tried to think of something appropriate to say. He settled on, "are you okay?" Turned out he didn't have to ask.

From the moment she stepped out of the truck the girl was a lunatic. She screamed and yelled over her truck, her hair, her coffee, her lost time—all said while gesturing wildly with manicured lilac nails. She was at least four inches shorter than he was, with curly black hair, a small face with a button nose, and chocolate brown eyes. Between her explosive temper and her looks Chris guessed she was Italian. Finally she stopped yelling and from the looks of things appeared to have asked Chris, who was still somewhat in shock, a question.

"Hello! Are you blind and deaf? I said, what's the matter with you?"

Chris was embarrassed and mumbled, "Are you talking to me?"

"Please tell me an amateur comedian didn't destroy my truck. Please God, anything but someone who is trying to be funny right now!" She had somewhat of a Staten Island accent when calm, but in a situation like this it was thicker than Manhattan clam chowder.

Chris managed to gather himself and spoke up with a tad more confidence. "I'm not trying to be funny, I'm actually really sorry and not exactly sure what to do right now."

"Here's a tip for you. Next time you're driving and there is a car ahead of you stopped at a red light, don't crash into them!" Her hands were off in a thousand different directions and she punctuated her remarks by slamming her right fist into her open left hand.

Chris turned beet red and glanced over at the truck. The bumper was falling off, and the rest of the back was mangled. The only positive he could think of was at least it wasn't on fire. While he surveyed the damage, the girl paced back and forth.

"There is no way I can drive this! Now I have to call the cops, a tow truck, my grandma to come pick me up, and my job telling them I obviously can't come in today."

In spite of the situation, his curiosity got the best of him. "Can I ask where you work?"

If her eyes could shoot bullets Chris would be riddled with them for asking such a question. Despite the obvious annoyance she answered his question through gritted teeth. "Over at the mall. Abercrombie and Fitch."

"Oh, I work in the mall too, at Walden Books." For some reason Chris thought having common ground might ease the tension of the situation.

"Wow maybe we're soul mates and this accident was meant to be! Did I even ask where you worked? Does anything about me right now scream I care? All I want to do is call the police and get this thing over with." If this was a race, her anger would have edged out her sarcasm, but it would have been a photo finish.

Throughout the abusive conversation, one thought kept creeping up in the back of Chris' twenty-year-old mind—she's hot! Somehow insults are better tolerated when they're coming out of a pretty face. He knew this could only get worse so Chris decided to try and extend an olive branch.

"Listen, I know this is my fault and I'm sorry. So I'm going to walk over to that pay phone over there and report this to the cops. Then we'll exchange insurances and hopefully be out of here soon enough."

This seemed to calm her down a little bit, thus Chris walked over to the phone and reported the accident. A couple of minutes later he hung up and walked back over to the scene. Traffic was building up on the Hill as people stopped to rubberneck. He could never understand why people slow down to see a simple fender bender, although with the Island being what it was, chances were you might know someone involved. When he was a couple of feet away he saw the back of her peeking out of the passenger side. Her head popped in and out of view and it was clear she was somewhat frantic.

"You, okay?"

"Shit Shit Shit! I can't find my insurance card!"

An incredulous smile came over his face. His first instinct was sarcasm before he thought better of it. Instead Chris tried to maintain an even tone and said, "Wait are you telling me you don't have insurance?"

"No, I am not saying that! Did you hear those words come out of my mouth? I'm saying I can't find it!" She said with the same edge in her voice he had come to know and love.

A sigh of relief came over him. "Well if you have insurance the cops can just look that up on their computer. No need to get upset."

The girl paused and stepped out of the truck." Really?" For the first time her voice dropped to a somewhat normal tone.

"Yeah."

There was a pause and the girl leaned against her driver's side door. Her attention was somewhere else and it seemed as if things were finally calming down. While she stared off into the distance, he blatantly checked her out. Was there a slight window of opportunity? Chris took a deep breath and figured he had nothing to lose.

"They said the cops will be here soon so I figure we have at least ten minutes to kill. Is it okay if I ask your name?"

She paused as if Chris had asked her how much she weighed. He braced for more sarcasm or perhaps a shout or two but instead he heard her say in a subdued voice,

"Valerie."

"I'm Chris."

"Oh so this is a regular thing for you? Do you wreck cars to meet girls?" Chris was surprised at her comment and laughed. She might have calmed down a degree or ten yet she still had a mouth on her. He sensed the window opening wider and decided to take a chance.

"Actually I met my first wife that way!"

For a second she gave him a look of complete disgust and Chris figured he blew it. But then her face crinkled up and she giggled. Not a hearty laugh, but the dam had cracked. Over the course of the next twenty-five minutes (thank God the police are never on time) Chris and Valerie had a friendly conversation with smiles and more jokes. He had never dated a girl as sarcastic as he was and this made the attraction deeper. As their cars went up on the individual tow trucks the conversation felt so natural that it wasn't preposterous for Chris to ask, "Any chance we could do this again?"

"If you mean another car accident absolutely not." She tapped him on his left shoulder to reinforce her point. Chris playfully rubbed the spot and replied,

"I'm pretty sure I meant maybe grab a coffee and talk some more."

"As long as you know that you'd be picking me up and driving me around."

He pretended to think it over for a couple of seconds. "I think I could handle that."

"You couldn't handle driving today by yourself, what makes you think you could handle driving with a beautiful girl next to you?"

"Aren't we funny? Is this what I have to look forward to?"

"If you're lucky," she said with a playful smile.

"I'm sure if there are any problems you'll voice them well in advance."

"You know, I'm really a shy girl," said with the utmost sincerity.

"And I'm fat," he replied with obvious sarcasm.

Valerie started to reply when she heard a car horn and saw her grandma across the street. "Grandmas always have the worst timing," Chris thought to himself. Valerie waved back and put up one finger. She reached into her purse, took out a pen and turned his left hand upside down. She scribbled furiously, smiled, kissed his cheek and walked away. Chris was floored and silently watched Valerie climb into the car. The car pulled away and one thought kept repeating itself in his mind, "this was the best car accident ever." His dad would be arriving any second and whether it was to pass the time, or just because he had to keep staring at it to believe it, Chris admired the pen marks written on his left hand.

*Valerie Carreon*
*555-9634*

# CHAPTER 12

## Labor Day - October 1997

Valerie was an amazing girl. Demanding? Somewhat, but what twenty-year old wasn't? Sure she made him shave off the beard but so what? Who wanted a hairy face during the summer? People said they complimented each other perfectly. She was hyper and he was laid back. She was intense and Chris was cool. Looking back, the minutes after the accident summed up their future relationship—Chris wasn't paying attention and Valerie couldn't believe he was so absent minded. Outside of those minor details, things were great. Fortunate for Chris, his parents were generous and helped him pay for the damage to the truck. However, Valerie wasn't so lucky. While her truck wasn't totaled, there was considerable undercarriage damage. In the time her car was incapacitated, it was decided (she had decided) that Chris could make it up to her by driving her wherever she needed to go (which was everywhere).

One night, about a month or so into the relationship, Chris drove Valerie home from work. He had gotten out of Walden Books an hour before she did and killed some time in Major Leagues, the sports memorabilia store. Actually he killed more time than he should have looking at the autographs in the back and as a result met Valerie outside of Abercrombie five minutes late. Luckily for him she had a good day at work and waited patiently for him with a friend. They walked arm in arm out towards the parking lot, playfully kissing each other every couple of feet.

Valerie had plenty to talk about so Chris listened dutifully, from the time they were in the parking lot, all the way down Richmond Avenue until they reached the Korean War Veterans Parkway. They approached her Annadale exit when Chris interjected for the first time. He wondered this for a while and decided now was a good time as ever to ask.

"Hey, Val, not to interrupt, but can I ask a random question?"

"Sure, pookie." Pookie was her pet name for him, cute in the right setting and downright embarrassing anywhere with people around.

"I'm sure you remember how we met…"

"How could I forget? You almost killed me."

Chris laughed and said, "True true, thankfully I didn't." They exchanged a kiss before he continued. "I guess I'm wondering why you calmed down enough to talk to me?"

"Ohhh I was so angry at you!" she said with a laugh. "Seriously, you ruined my entire day and I really let you have it."

"Yeah you really..." She cut him off without realizing it.

"Honestly, I don't know. Ugh you had that beard. Remember how bad you looked with that thing?" Her question was rhetorical and she continued without waiting for an answer. "You just stood there with this sheepish look on your face and that blue hat of yours pulled down so low that I could barely see your eyes. I suppose I felt a little bad, just not enough to stop yelling. Of course when you came back and didn't freak out when I said I couldn't find my insurance I thought you had to be decent. Plus your hat lifted off your face and I could see those beautiful blue eyes of yours." Valerie leaned over and kissed his cheek before she continued on." The better question is why would you want to be with a girl who screamed at you the way I did?"

"You want the truth?" he asked sincerely.

"Of course, pookie" she said, expecting something sweet to come out of his mouth.

"You were hot," he said with a smile. "Guys can pretty much deal with anything if a girl is hot enough."

"So, if I was ugly?"

"You'd be taking the bus!"

"Hey!" Valerie smacked his arm.

"What? You're hot! Is that a bad thing?"

"I hope I'm more than just eye candy for you."

"Babe, that's just a bonus."

Chris had just given the perfect bailout answer. Valerie squealed, kissed him and laid her head on his shoulder for the rest of the drive.

The summer of 1997 was by far the best summer Chris ever had. By Labor Day his thinking was resolute; this was his first real love.

That night they were at his house, watching her favorite movie, "When Harry Met Sally" for the nine hundredth time. His parents let him have the den whenever Valerie was over and the two kids were sprawled out on their old black leather couch. In his mom's opinion, the den was better than a closed bedroom door. They were up to the part when Harry meets Sally again in the bookstore and Chris had his eyes closed, listening as Valerie recited the lines verbatim while her head was resting on his chest. Suddenly Chris sat up, took a deep breath, gently lifted her head off his chest and said rather abruptly,

"I think I love you."

Valerie stared at him dumbfounded for a moment or two before a smile came across her face. "Do you think you love me or do you love me?"

"I am fairly confident in the fact that I am in love with you."

"Christopher! Do you have to make a joke about everything?" She half jested half complained.

"Okay okay, Valerie Carreon, I love you."

"I love you too" she said in that high-pitched squeal and threw her arms around his neck followed by several thousand little kisses.

Chris never imagined saying I love you meant an assault. After the display of affection commenced, Valerie resumed her spot on Chris' chest and continued watching the movie.

From that day on, Valerie changed in how she acted towards his parents and his younger brother, Eric. It wasn't as if she was shy, just a little reticent. Almost like she didn't know how to act. After Chris proclaimed his love, it was if the dam inside of her had burst. She finally relaxed. A day wouldn't go by without Valerie coming over for dinner, or to drop in and say hi to "Mom." Chris had privately asked his mother if she minded Valerie calling her that and his mom without hesitation said, "of course not." His mom was growing rather fond of Valerie and didn't hide the fact.

A couple of days before Chris' birthday, his dad pulled him aside to talk. The family had just finished the rare family dinner where all four members were in attendance. He had brought his plate to the sink and was about to walk out of the room when his dad spoke up.

"Chris you have a second?"

He stopped and said, "Sure dad what's up?"

"Pull up a chair." Chris walked over to the table and sat in his chair to the right of his father.

Not sure where this was headed, Chris went on his guard. "There a problem?"

"Don't worry, there's nothing wrong, I just have a question. I notice that Valerie spends a lot of time here, not that I'm complaining. You love her and your mom seems to get along great with her. I'm just wondering if her parents mind?"

Chris' entire demeanor relaxed, as he understood what his dad was asking. "Well, her home life is kind of chaotic. She never went into the whole story with me, but from what I gather her dad hasn't been around for a long time. Her mom has been dating over the past couple of years, and according to Val the guy she's with right now is okay."

"Ahhhh okay." His dad took a gulp from the half finished Budweiser sitting in front of him.

"Yeah, I think she likes the whole family thing we have."

"Makes sense." Chris stood up and walked over to the refrigerator. He pulled out a can of Pepsi.

"Are you sort of saying you don't want her here as much?"

"No no no. You know I like her. I was just curious and I figured we have the kind of relationship where I could just ask."

"Okay. Yup. Well that's the deal. I'm heading out. Bye, Dad." Chris took his can and left.

Chris' dad wasn't lying. He did like Val. So did his wife. In fact they would sometimes joke about the over/under on when Chris would come telling them he was going to buy an engagement ring. His dad thought they still had another three years, while his mom would respond by saying when Valerie graduated college in two years. She seemed to be a lot surer of her answer than he was, and one day Mr. Marcum asked why she was so confident.

"Well, you know how girls talk."

"Yeahh."

"One day, I casually asked in a perfect world how old she wants to be on her wedding day? She shocked me when she immediately answered twenty-three-years old. So the way I figure, they'll be engaged when she's twenty-two and married by twenty three."

"So, Chris will be twenty-four; I guess that's a good age. A little young, sure, but at that point they'll know for sure if they're ready or not."

"Chris has a good head on his shoulders; I don't see him rushing into something if he wasn't absolutely sure."

On October 18$^{th}$, Chris' twenty-first birthday was celebrated in style at Leo's with his friends and Valerie of course. At the time Leo's was a young bar—a mixture of college kids and kids claiming to be of legal age. The bar wasn't exactly strict with the IDs. You could slide right up and sit on a stool all night or grab a table and camp out. Monday night was karaoke night, Tuesday was ladies night and Thursday was college night—anyone with a college ID paid half price for drinks. On the weekends a cover band would normally play. When the boys decided on a Leo's night that meant no gel in the hair, sneakers, and leaving with money in your pocket. Ordinarily you would expect a twenty-first birthday to be celebrated in better surroundings, yet Chris was happy enough to keep it local. As long as his lady and his crew of Sammy, Richie and their girlfriends were there Chris could have celebrated his birthday in Bayonne, New Jersey and had a great night.

For the first time, Chris could see a clear path for his life. He was in love with a girl he was sure would be around for the long term. They would have kids down the line, which made his future teaching job convenient for the schedule and the summers off. He would dabble with some writing, maybe one day getting a novel published. From there it would be moving on to a professorship at a university. Chris took a big gulp of his Budweiser and looked over at Valerie, who was talking to Sammy's girlfriend, Stephanie. Maybe this crew would make it long term as well. His best friends Sam and Richie were both dating girls for over a year. They would all get married, live near each other, and their kids would even play together. Suddenly Chris realized what he was doing and laughed to himself. He was worse than Valerie!

# CHAPTER 13

## November 26, 1997

A Wednesday night isn't a typical night to go out to the bar, (even for college kids like Chris) unless the Wednesday night in question happens to precede Thanksgiving. Every bar on Staten Island ran some kind of special to pack the place and Leo's was no exception. This meant Chris was guaranteed a night of battling through kids ranging between the ages of sixteen to twenty-five to grab a drink. Despite knowing they would spend the night shoulder to shoulder, with a drink or two spilled by them or by someone who would be buying them a new one, Chris and his friends Sammy and Richie ventured out to their favorite bar. Naturally, Val was there at his side. The running joke amongst his friends was, whenever you saw Chris, the scent of Curve wasn't far behind.

Chris took things easy that night, holding his Bud more than sipping it. The past week was nothing but going out, between that night, Thanksgiving night and the weekend with Val's friends he needed one night where he wasn't trashed. This made him the de facto driver of the evening and guaranteed there would be drunken friend shenanigans later on in his car. The shenanigans never bothered Chris; in fact if he wasn't driving he was always in the middle of them.

In the four years Chris had been driving he only had one rule. If you had to ralph, either tell him to pull over or at least open the window. You could scream, shout out the windows; do whatever you wanted to do, just don't ruin the inside of his car! Nevertheless before the car insanity commenced, Chris planned on enjoying himself as much as possible while sober.

As the hours ticked away the music had a hard time competing with the drunken babbling that comes from so many in such a tight space. Chris needed a break from the noise and told everyone he was going out to the alley. He made his way out the back door and down the wooden steps into the alley when he felt a vibration come from his left hand pocket. He took out his beeper and saw:

## 11:54 PM – 555-7310

He didn't recognize the number and was going to ignore it, but the powers of curiosity were too strong. It didn't matter what the person wanted, he just wanted to know who it was. Chris made his way past the smokers and kids standing around until he reached the back of the alley where the pay phone was. A couple of rings later…

"Hello?"

"Yeah hi you beeped me, who's this?"

"Are you Eric's older brother?"

"Yeah."

"Okay, hold on, he beeped you. I'll get him." Chris occupied this lull in the action by counting the number of damaged tiles on the side of the bar. He was up to nine when his brother picked up.

"Hey Chris it's me. I need a favor."

"What," he exclaimed with a hint of irritation in his voice.

"Listen a couple of guys want to go out tonight to the bar and I don't have a fake ID. Any chance I could use your old one?"

"And what bar were you planning on going to?"

"Leo's."

"You know where I am tonight?"

"Umm…"

"Leo's."

"So?"

"So that means no shot."

"C'mon! What's the big deal? It's not like I'm going to hang out with you and your *girlfriend*."

Chris wasn't sure if there was a tone when Eric said girlfriend and frankly he didn't care. "Listen, I gotta go. Good luck going wherever tonight, just not here."

"What about the ID?"

"If you can find it sure."

"I'm looking at it right now."

"Then I don't care what you do, just don't come here."

"Fine."

*CLICK*

Chris knew what would have happened if Eric and company came to Leo's. He would suddenly turn into the Mid-Island Cab Company, shuffling everyone back and forth from the bar to their homes. Considering he had a full car already Chris had no desire to make several trips. Besides, he was a good older brother. Eric was going out because of his generosity. The ID was a gift; the least he could do was respect some kind of boundary.

The night went on for another couple of hours before the group decided enough was enough and poured into his car. Chris dropped off Richie and Briana and was now on his way home. Val was sleeping over tonight and he was looking forward to just laying down and passing out, with maybe an occasional kiss in between. She was drunk, but not obnoxiously so—just giggling and touching while he was driving. She put her hand on his leg and felt a vibration, which caused her to go into hysterics. Chris tried to explain to her that it was the beeper but every time he said "bee" she would just laugh harder and louder. It took about five minutes for Chris to actually check who had beeped him because whenever she laughed he couldn't help laugh himself. Finally he saw

## 3:01 AM – 555-0382

That was his house number, which was strange because Chris never had a real curfew before, especially now that he was twenty-one. They were almost home and Chris figured no matter what it was, it could wait ten more minutes.

When he pulled into the driveway, Chris started to get a nervous flutter in his stomach. The living room lights were on and his Aunt Jean was standing in the doorway. Aunt Jean was his mom's sister and by far his favorite aunt, although you can't admit to those things out loud. Chris stepped out of the car at the same time Aunt Jean stepped out of the house. Her presence alone there at this late hour told him this wasn't good, her face confirmed it.

"Chris listen your brother was in an accident tonight." He stopped walking and closed his eyes. There was no way he heard that sentence.

"What?"

"He was in the backseat of his friend's car and they crashed into another car."

"Oh my God!" Valerie clutched his left hand. In a surprisingly level voice he asked, "Is he okay?"

"Your parents went down to the hospital a little while ago." Her response didn't register inside his head and he asked again.

"Is he okay?"

"We know he's alive and that he's hurt. Nothing more." Chris put his hands to his head and let out a deep sigh. Valerie looked like she was about to cry.

"Why didn't they wait for me?"

"Well they beeped you a little while ago and when they didn't hear from you they called me."

"I'm going to the hospital, where's he at?"

"Staten Island North—Chris I'll drive."

"I'm alright Aunt Jean. C'mon lets go."

The twenty minute car ride to the hospital was a quiet one. Val was no longer giggling out of control and Chris didn't have anything to say, although he was doing plenty of thinking. He had such an easy time forbidding Eric from coming to Leo's, why didn't he just say no to him using his ID? A little while ago he was giving himself credit for being a fair older brother and look where his fairness got them. Hell, even if he had given permission to use the ID, did he have to be such a prick about dictating where they went? If he had let them come to Leo's he could have driven them home. Why did he care so much if Eric wanted to come?

When they reached the Emergency Ward parking lot, Chris almost left the car without turning it off. The three of them ran inside and saw his parents standing up, not pacing but not standing still. Chris was the first to reach them and as he drew closer he could tell by her red eyes and puffy cheeks that his mom had been crying. For a couple of seconds the five of them stood in the middle of the room in silence. Their eyes spoke a lifetime of words between them. Finally his dad opened his mouth.

"Chris, your brother is unconscious right now. We know he hit his head and they have him stabilized." For the third time that night he asked,

"Is he okay?"

"The doctors are running tests and hopefully we'll know soon what's going on." Chris noticed his mother take a deep breath and wipe the corner of her eye.

"What happened?" Val said in a quiet voice. His dad began to say something, but his mom cut in.

"Eric went out with his friends tonight and Ronnie was driving. Apparently he was coming down Hylan and went to make the left into the Colinade parking lot when he lost control and hit a car in the left lane. Your brother was sitting behind Ronnie so the force of the impact slammed him against the window and the door."

Valerie spoke up again, "what about everyone else?"

"They're all banged up, but thank God no one died tonight."

Chris stared off into the distance. He heard every word and at the same time still had a hard time processing the information. The conversation was much easier if he allowed Valerie to run it. "What about the driver of the other car?" She asked with some trepidation.

"He's okay too. Shaken up and bruised, but he managed to walk away." Chris felt the gaze of his parent's eyes and looked back at them. His voice cracked a little.

"Can I go and see him?"

"Not yet, the doctor said he'll let us know when we can go in." Chris sat down and stared straight ahead while Val kept talking to his mom and aunt. His dad sat down next to him.

"One detail that your mom left out that I got from one of the EMT guys. Considering the speed of the oncoming car and the fact that Ronnie's truck was in the process of making a left no one can understand how the truck didn't flip over."

Chris said an immediate quick prayer of thanks and resumed staring ahead. It was another hour before the doctor came out to tell the family Eric had suffered a severe concussion, broken his left collarbone, and had scratches and bruises on his face and chest. Considering everything, he was a very lucky nineteen-year-old.

Deep sighs of relief left the lungs of the five people hearing the news. Val came over and gave Chris a hug. His mind would not stop racing and morbid thoughts kept fluttering across his mind's eye.

The next couple of days saw Eric come home and be coddled by everyone in the house, especially Chris. His heart was heavy, although he let no one, not even Valerie know what he was thinking. Instead, he focused his energy on his younger brother. A week later he was in the den watching television with Val. They were sitting on the black leather couch Chris had been watching television on since he could remember, flipping between a college football game and a movie starring Dudley Moore. To be honest he was less interested in what was on the screen and more concerned with trying to get Valerie to rub his feet. His head leaned against the arm of the couch and he was stretched across so his legs draped over Valerie's lap. She let him keep his feet in her general vicinity, but she wasn't going any further.

"Babe just a quick two minute rub. That's all."

"Chris you know I would but I skeeve feet."

"Seriously I would rub your feet."

"Thanks!" Valerie knocked his legs off of her and swung around so her feet were now against his chest. With a sigh Chris started the massage.

"You know what's crazy?"

"What?" he said with severe disinterest.

"A week ago we were out having fun and everything was great. It's amazing how fast life can turn." Chris didn't say anything, just continued to rub and now turned his body so her feet were next to his heart and he could stare at the television.

"I mean to think of what could have happened gives me the chills." Chris continued to not acknowledge the conversation and was now giving a half-hearted rub.

"You know what I mean?" The last word hung in the air for a couple of seconds before Chris shrugged his shoulders and gave a monotone, "yup."

"You okay Pookie?" Val asked as she removed her feet from his grip and sat up. "Fine" he said without any sort of inflection.

"Chris, seriously, what's the matter?"

"Well I wanted a foot massage but clearly that isn't happening!" His voice rose as he said the words.

"No! C'mon you know what I mean."

"Nothing. Nothing." The second "nothing" was said with the same casualness he had earlier in the conversation. "I'm just watching television with you."

"Nothing? You sure?" She waited for him to say something before continuing except Chris wouldn't even look at her. "There is obviously something bothering you. In fact, I noticed it a couple of days ago, but I figured you would talk about it eventually." At this point Valerie was sitting up on her knees and staring at him. Chris remained locked on the television screen.

"Chris?"

"Yeah." More monotone.

"Let's talk."

"About what?" If possible, said even dryer.

"You know. Eric, the accident, everything that happened."

"Yeah everything is good now, thanks." He still hadn't moved his head.

"Why won't you talk to me?" Valerie said with a tone that suggested frustration with a hint of whine. Chris slowly turned his head and finally made eye contact with her, placing his arms behind his head. With a voice that could snap any second Chris replied,

"Please tell me you aren't going to pick a fight with me."

"What's that supposed to mean?" She said with genuine shock.

"It means exactly what it means. You're looking for something that isn't there and you're determined to stir something up."

"What I am is determined to make you talk!" She grabbed his left knee for emphasis.

"About what?" Chris asked with some bass in his voice.

"Eric!" Valerie smacked the couch cushion.

"He's alive everything is fine!"

"Christopher, seriously."

"Enough! No more!" His mother heard the shouting from the kitchen and wanted to check in before his father talked her out of it.

He sat up and stared at her wide-eyed. His face was red and Valerie decided enough was enough.

"Fine, I'm going home."

"Later," Chris said returning to the familiar monotone voice. Val jumped off the couch, grabbed her coat, and came as close as possible to slamming the front door. A couple of seconds later Chris heard the car screeching away. "Finally," he thought, "I can watch TV in peace."

But it was no use—Valerie had stirred everything up and now he couldn't think of anything but last Friday. If Chris were a smoker now would have been a good time to go outside and have one. Instead, he went to his room and pulled out the journal he'd been writing in for a couple of years now.

*12/6/97 11:15pm*

I've been avoiding this for as long as possible but Valerie was determined to make me think about this so fine here I am. The short of it is Eric got into a car accident last Wednesday – not his fault. Severe concussion/broken left collarbone and a scratched up face but he's alive and happy on vicodin! I guess you can say the word of the day is guilt because it's all I ever feel lately.

That night Eric wanted to come to Leo's with his friends, but bc we were all there I stopped him. I let him use my old ID just as long as he didn't come there. Apparently the story I was able to piece together was they went to Nineteenth Hole and all got piss drunk. Ronnie was the most sober out of the five, and since he drove there he decided to drive home. They were going for a bite to eat at the Colinade and as he made the left he lost control of the wheel and wound up getting smacked by an oncoming car. Despite the damage things could have been a lot worse. Dad was told it's a miracle the truck didn't flip. Eric was sitting behind Ronnie and wound up getting smashed by his friends and the car that hit them.

So why I am guilty?

Because the reason why I didn't want him and his friends at Leo's was because I knew they would all get drunk and I knew I'd have to drive my friends home, then them as well. I also assumed that somebody in his group would probably puke and I didn't want to take the chance in my car.

I was selfish and if the truck had tilted an inch more he could be a vegetable or worse....I don't think I'm a completely shitty older brother. When we were younger the year and a half age difference mattered because it meant two full grades of school separated us. But now that we're both getting older we hang out together sometimes, when I'm not hanging out with Val. I'm not sure if Eric likes Val or not because he always makes a joke about us being together constantly. He'll understand when he finally falls in love! I mean me and Eric are close, we might not be best friends but we are a lot closer than what we were.

I wonder if he resents me for not letting him come to Leo's?

Mom said the next morning when he was coming out of the haze he was calling for me which got me choked up for a second. I wonder if I blew it? I mean I graduate college in less than a year, then I'll be working and I'm assuming me and Val will get our own place. All this time we had to hang out and I didn't really take advantage of it.

Ok I'm beating myself up now and I don't want to become miserably depressed. I'm sorry Eric, even if I never actually say it to you.

# CHAPTER 14

## Christmas/New Year's 1997

In the weeks following the accident Chris made every effort to spend more time with Eric, even if he had to blow off Valerie every now and then to do so. Of course that didn't go over as well as Chris would have liked. To go from seeing each other everyday, to telling her "sorry, I'm hanging out with Eric tonight" was not something she was used to hearing.

At that point Chris knew for sure Eric wasn't a big fan of Valerie. He figured it had to do with her constant presence at the house. He knew there were times when she could be annoying, but Eric didn't know the other side of Val, or refused to try and find out. For the time being, Chris' main concern was to balance everything out—Eric, Val, Sammy/Richie, senior year of college, work, and everything else a twenty-one-year-old dealt with.

What added even more stress was this was their first Christmas and New Year's together. Her mom was going to spend Christmas with her boyfriend Don's family; so, Valerie decided to spend it with her boyfriend's family as well. Chris found it somewhat strange that Val and her mom would be apart and asked her about it when he drove her home a couple of days before.

"Not that I mind or anything but can I ask why you're spending both Christmas Eve and Day with me?" Valerie had been staring out the window and didn't hear the first part of his question.

"You don't want to see me?"

"I didn't say that, I'm just wondering why you and your mom aren't going to be spending Christmas together."

"Well she's going to Don's house and his entire family is going to be there."

"So?"

"So I don't want to spend Christmas surrounded by strangers. I'd rather spend it with the person I love, if that's okay with you." Chris could tell he was one wrong word away from a fight.

"You know I want to see you too. I just feel a little, I don't know, bad for your mom."

"She was the one who made plans first!"

"How about you don't stay over Christmas Eve? At the very least that gives you the morning to be with her."

"Why are you so concerned about me seeing my own mother?" Chris opened his mouth to speak but instead furrowed his brow. He didn't have an answer for that. In his head this all made sense, however he couldn't think of a legitimate reason. After a couple of seconds he spoke up.

"I just think it's important in the long term to get along with her." Valerie looked at him and grinned.

"Aw Pook! So when we have kids they'll know both their grandmas?" By this time they had reached her house and Chris pulled up in front.

"Who said anything about kids?" Chris said sarcastically. Valerie smacked his shoulder.

"Fine. If it will make you feel better I'll tell my mom that neither of us should spend Christmas Eve sleeping at a boyfriend's house. Of course I can't guarantee she'll agree to it."

"Now why wouldn't anyone want to spend time with you?" Chris said in an overly genuine tone.

"Sometimes you are so smooth. Give me a kiss."

Valerie's mom agreed with the plan and so the Carreon women would spend Christmas morning together. Then when the Marcums came home from St. Clare's she would come over and they would exchange gifts. In fact, even if she had slept over Christmas Eve Valerie wanted to wait for the day itself to open gifts and Chris simply went along with it. They spent Christmas Eve at his Aunt Jean's house and enjoyed the traditional Italian seafood and pasta spectacular. The conversation was raucous, helped out slightly by the liberal amount of wine flowing. After midnight the party broke up, and Chris and Valerie drove home. They said good night to his parents and went downstairs to his bedroom in the basement. Chris sat on his bed with his back against the wall flipping around the channels while Valerie picked up clothes off his floor and put them in his hamper. After she finished she stood at the foot of his bed.

"Okay Chris I can't wait any longer let me open my gifts now." Chris looked away from the television and smiled.

"Time out" he said along with the hand gesture. "You want to open your gifts when my presents are at your house?"

"I'm a girl so I should be treated extra special!"

"What I'm really hearing is every day in your world is Christmas?"

"Yes," Val said with a laugh. "And since its Christmas Eve I should be treated even more special." She slithered over onto the bed and placed her head in his lap.

"Why can't you wait a couple of hours more?"

"Because" she whined.

"Well I want to wait."

"How about this, let me open up just one gift. I'll open up one gift now and then open the rest tomorrow." Chris could already see he wasn't winning this argument.

"This is unbelievable. And what do I get?"

"A happy and very appreciative girlfriend." Knowing she would carry on for hours if needed, Chris decided to surrender.

"Just one gift and one gift only."

"Yes!" Valerie shot up and clapped her hands excitedly. Chris stood up and went over to his closet. He opened up the doors and went into the back left corner, coming out with a small box that was wrapped somewhat decently.

"I can't wait! Let me have it!"

Chris handed her the gift and Valerie tore it open, discarding the wrapping paper like a piranha onto the floor. She flipped open the box and her face dropped in horrible disappointment.

"Socks? You bought me socks for Christmas!"

"You said one gift." Chris tried to contain his laughter.

"Christopher!" Valerie tossed the package of pink socks with individual green toes at his head and charged at him. Ten seconds later Chris had a black and blue shoulder, which he tried to claim didn't hurt. No matter, the shit-eating grin remained on his face when he dropped her off at her mom's house an hour later and didn't leave until he finally fell asleep.

Christmas day went as expected. The Marcums woke up early and went to nine o'clock Mass at St. Clare's so that his mom had plenty of time to get the house in order. Valerie spent in her words a, "nice" morning with her mom and popped in around noon. The rest of the family was in the kitchen so the two of them went in so Val could say her hellos. After she kissed everyone and wished them a Merry Christmas she turned and threatened bodily harm to Chris if he ever pulled another stunt like he did last night. Chris swore it was a one time only affair and Eric, in mock horror, insisted he did not want to know. Chris told him the socks story anyway, causing the entire family to laugh. Naturally, this aggravated Valerie even more, until she looked around and saw tears pouring out of Chris' eyes. This brought a smile to Valerie's face, which Eric proclaimed to be a "Christmas miracle."

The rest of the day was a typical family affair. You had your eating, your sleeping, and of course exchanging gifts. At Chris' age, the only gifts he received from his family came in the form of clothes or gift cards. Of course his girlfriend made up for the lack of excitement by getting him a couple of books, some clothes, and a beautiful Movado watch with *VC CM* engraved in the back. Valerie was thrilled with her gifts of course, especially the main one, a diamond bracelet that she had casually mentioned a few months back.

By ten o'clock Chris could barely keep his eyes open and Valerie let herself out. Presents, food, laughter, and not having to drive his girlfriend home equated to the perfect Christmas.

With New Year's rapidly approaching, neither Chris, his friends, nor Valerie had given much thought as to what they were doing. Forty-eight hours before the ball dropped, Sammy's girlfriend, Stephanie, told everyone her parents were going out for the night and they didn't care what she did, as long as no one drove home. The fish bowl rule was in effect, where you place your keys in a fish bowl by the door when you walked in, and you took them out the next morning. Chris was elated this came together, as he had no inclination to spend hundreds of dollars at a place where it would be a struggle to move.

The clock began to tick down to midnight and Chris heard Valerie yell out his name. They still had a good three minutes to go but Valerie wanted to make sure her boyfriend was where he needed to be. He navigated away from the bathroom, made his way through the kitchen and dramatically walked into the living room. Everyone was standing, watching Dick Clark count it down. Valerie hurriedly grabbed his hand and pulled him in close. His face came close to hers and he whispered, "We survived our first year."

"Well technically not our first year…"

"I know I know. You know what I meant." He said in mock exasperation.

"We did a lot this year."

"Yeah you could say that" he said with a laugh.

"You know what else?" She said as she stood on her tip toes to get even closer.

"What?"

"This is our first new year's kiss." Her eyes were wide and a large smile crept over her face.

"Correction, the first of many new year kisses" he said with a dramatic flourish.

*5-4-3-2-1*

HAPPY NEW YEAR!

80

# CHAPTER 15

## February 12, 1999

The year 1998 was both busy and successful for Chris. In the spring he walked across a long stage under a large canopy at St. John's University, packed to the brim with dignitaries and received his college diploma. Prior to the big day, Chris decided to further pursue his education and get his Masters in Education at St. John's as well. The original plan was to work somewhere during the day, go to school at night and apply for a job teaching history at the high school level the following spring. His parents were going to pay half his tuition, which combined with living rent free, would allow him not to rush out and get a full time job. At least this was the plan until a friend of a friend informed him of an opening at Tottenville, his old high school a week after he graduated.

Chris didn't mind wearing a suit for an interview on a hot June afternoon and he certainly didn't mind when he shook hands with the Academic Vice Principal and signed a contract. He was hired to teach Global studies to three freshmen and two sophomore classes. When he told Valerie the news, her first thought was how much fun it would be to shop for new dress shirts and pants.

He loved the classroom, even if he didn't like all the students in the classroom. There were tough days, especially in the beginning, but Chris felt like he turned a corner in November and was on his way to becoming a good teacher. He had lucked out with the dean of his department—a guy in his early fifties—who took an immediate liking to Chris. The Mets were a common bond between them and they became friends right away. Steve not only gave helpful advice for inside the classroom, he also gave helpful life advice as well.

If his work life was at an eight, his love life was at a seven. Like his dad once told him, things had gotten back to normal. Val came over almost everyday again, and Chris and Eric weren't hanging out as much as they were right after the accident. Chris rationalized this as the both of them being busy and nothing more. Valerie had begun talking about the future, and Chris estimated he would be ring shopping by the fall. Of course he wouldn't make it to fall if he forgot the rapidly approaching Valentine's Day.

As a teacher, Chris' life was geared towards the calendar. Homework was due tomorrow, tests on Friday, the next paper due in two weeks. Yet somehow, the fact that Valentine's Day was coming up completely slipped his mind. In fact the only reason why he remembered was because of a precocious student of his who inquired what he bought his girlfriend. He paused, realized his forgetfulness and blurted out jewelry. Immediately he knew where he was going as soon as his school day ended, the Staten Island Mall.

There were things Chris knew, and things Chris had no clue about. Jewelry fell somewhere in the middle. He entered one of the mall's finer stores and took notice of the various display cases. He had a vague idea what she liked and had a firm idea of what his price range was. All Chris needed was a salesperson that would legitimately help him and not just try to push him into spending more money.

Chris walked around the different cases when a friendly smile came over to see if he needed any help. The man looked to be in his late forties, hair overly gelled, and a smile that suggested his face might be locked in a permanent position. With some trepidation, Chris explained who he was buying for and gave him a general idea of what he wanted. The man, who exuded an overabundance of confidence, motioned for Chris to come to a case in the corner, saying he had exactly what Chris was looking for "right over here."

While the two men strolled over a random girl followed the same path, leading them to converge at the same spot at the same time. She initially thought the salesman was coming over to help her and started to say, "No thanks" when she realized there was a man standing behind her.

"I'm sorry, am I in your way?" She said in embarrassment.

"No big deal, I'm in no rush."

She smiled and moved over so Chris could slide in. He muttered a low, "thanks" without any eye contact and stepped in her place. To be honest, Chris only saw the back of the girl; he was more focused on the pieces being pulled from the display case. The salesman took out four necklaces, describing their various qualities and laid them on a counter to their left.

"That's beautiful."

Chris intently compared the necklaces and didn't quite hear what was said.

"Excuse me?"

"I said that necklace on your left is beautiful."

Chris finally looked up and his stomach did a backflip. She was beautiful in a natural sense, with blonde hair pulled back, barely a hint of makeup, and deep blue eyes, which contrasted off a tan face. He was even more impressed with the fact she wasn't even dressed up, just a black Guess jacket and a pair of gray sweatpants. Chris smiled as he reminded himself the purpose here was not to flirt, but to buy a Valentine's Day gift for his girlfriend.

"Yeah to be honest I actually forgot about Valentine's Day and now here I am two days before looking for anything. Just don't tell the sales guy." She giggled while the sales guy gave an overly enthusiastic laugh. Apparently he believed forced laughter was a key to any deal.

"It doesn't matter what day you're buying it, she's a lucky girl for you to be buying it at all." Chris liked the tone in her voice and wanted to hear some more.

"Thanks. And if you don't mind me asking why is a girl shopping by herself in a jewelry store?"

"I'm just looking. My boyfriend and I are planning on getting engaged soon so I figured I'd help him out by scouting for rings ahead of time."

"Lucky guy. What do you figure, a thirty- or forty-thousand dollar ring?" He said in jest.

"I don't know, I was thinking one- maybe two-hundred thousand. I don't want to spend all his money."

"Wow, he is a lucky guy!"

"Yeah I tell him that all the time."

"Umm sir, I don't mean to interrupt your conversation, but do you see anything you like?" Salesmen have the worst timing, Chris thought.

"Yes I suppose you have a job to do. You know what? This girl said the necklace on the left is beautiful, let's go with that."

"Wait," she said in surprise. "Don't base what you're buying her on my taste! We could be the exact opposite."

"I already know you are, but that's beside the point." Chris paused as he wasn't sure what he was saying or why he said it. To avoid any further potential awkwardness he said, "Anyway, you seem to have good taste, and I'm sure the man will be flexible on the price tag!

"Yes I'm pretty sure we can work out a fair deal, sir."

"Can you wrap it as well?"

"Of course, let me just put these away and we'll discuss the terms." The salesman put the other three necklaces back in the display case and went to the back to grab a box.

"What about you, see anything you like?" Chris felt his gag reflex kick in from the cheesey double entendre that just left his lips.

"Nope, nothing. Guess I'm not as lucky as you are."

Chris thought he detected a slight blush, although it was up for debate. His mind started to race for something suave to say before she left. Something that would leave a lasting mark. Something that wouldn't make him want to vomit. Then he remembered once again he was buying said jewelry for his girlfriend and quietly said,

"Thanks for the help." The girl paused for a second, and as if picking up on his involuntary cue said,

"You're welcome. I'm going to another store to continue my quest for the perfect ring! Hope she likes the necklace!" The girl turned around and took a step towards the door.

"I'm sorry; I didn't get your name," Chris blurted out suddenly.

"I'm Jen."

"Well Jen, again, thanks for your help."

"Well again, you're welcome," she responded with a smile. She paused as if she was waiting for him to say something else.

"Are you going to make me ask your name?"

"Oh! I'm sorry, I'm Chris." He said as he shook her hand.

"Well Chris, Happy Valentine's Day!"

"You too, Jen. Good luck with the ring shopping."

"Thanks." And with that Jen walked out of the store.

Chris patiently waited while the salesman ran his Discover card and diligently wrapped the necklace. Valerie was going to love the gift, Chris thought assuredly. He was fortunate that girl had been there to help him out; otherwise he would have endlessly debated which one was the right one. When Chris left the store, he wasn't thinking of Val or the necklace, or even the bill in his back pocket. His only thought was those deep blue eyes.

# CHAPTER 16

## May 7, 1999

Chris had adverted a potentially major disaster with the necklace that girl Jen picked out for him. Valerie absolutely loved it and admitted she was a little surprised. She knew Chris had taste but had no idea he had that keen an eye. Chris naturally took the compliment and didn't mention anything at all of having outside help.

The days continued to tumble off the calendar, and when May rolled around Val completed what should have been her senior year at Wagner College. Instead she was still a semester behind, due to not taking college as seriously as she should have her freshmen year. Her arrival into the "real world" wouldn't happen until graduation in January. To be fair, Val had been living in the real world far longer than Chris had. Her folks had split when she was six and to say her mother was flighty would be like saying the sun was bright. Her mother, Brooke had been dating for as long as she could remember, more zeros than heroes in her estimation and Valerie, as an only child, learned early on to be self sufficient. Her current boyfriend, Don had been in the picture for the past four and a half years and he was the first guy who had long term potential. Even though her mother insisted one marriage was more than enough, it wouldn't surprise her if she came home one day to find out they had eloped.

Out of all the many traits Chris loved about her, he valued her independence most of all. While she loved him, she didn't need him. If something ever happened to their relationship she could endure, it was something she was used to. Sure she was a bit domineering at times, he supposed that was part of the trade off.

It was a beautiful Friday afternoon in early May and Chris pulled out of the teacher's parking lot. He had missed his lunch period to talk with a student about why he failed two tests in a row and subsequently was starving. Valerie was finished with classes and only had two finals to go, both on Monday. Thus, she was the perfect candidate to help rectify his current situation. He flipped open his new cell phone and gave her a ring.

"Hey babe."

"Hey," she said in a somewhat somber voice.

"What's the matter?"

"Ugh. I'm not feeling good at all and I have so much to study for my Psych final. I keep reading the same page over and over."

"So take a break and get a bite to eat with me."

"I don't know, even if I could eat I really can't blow this off."

"All right so what time should I get you tonight?"

"I think I'm staying in."

"Really?"

"If you saw how much I have to read you would understand. Of course if you wanted to come over and help me study I wouldn't say no."

"You just said you have a lot to study but you want me to come over and help you?"

"Is that a problem?"

"Well yeah. We both know we would start off studying and end up giggling real fast."

"You mean *we* would start off studying and *you* would get distracted and focus on other things." She said with a playful laugh.

"It's the price you pay for being hot. If you were ugly there would be no threat of any interruption. We could sit for hours and just read." He emphasized the word, "read" with mock enthusiasm to further make his point.

"Chris you know I hate when you talk that way."

"I know. I know. I'm sorry. Seriously, my presence will not help you whatsoever. How about you do what you have to do tonight and we see each other tomorrow."

"Ohhh" she said with a pout, "I wanted to see my Pookie tonight."

"Yeah but it's better for you if you didn't."

"And you know what's best for me because?"

"C'mon Val don't be like that."

"No. I want to hear how you know what's good for me."

"Are we really going to argue about this? Remember I'm the one who wanted to eat with you now and see you tonight. You rebuffed me twice." He remarked with mock indignation.

"Okay, I'll study tonight and I'll see you tomorrow. In the meantime, what are you going to do?"

"I don't know. I figure I'll call Sammy and see what the deal is."

"Don't have too much fun without me."

"I'll be miserable all night."

"I love you too."

"Bye."

"Bye."

When you spend more time with your girl than your friends it can be a tad awkward to call them up and ask what the big plan is for the night. Your friends know the only reason why you're calling is because the girlfriend isn't around, and it's not worth trying to explain to them how it was your decision. He called Sammy and took the good natured kind of joking/kind of serious abuse. The plan was the usual, Leo's, and they were meeting there around ten. What made tonight a little different was the bar was under new ownership. Three months ago the place lost their liquor license due to underage drinking and was now reopened under new ownership. Ordinarily new ownership meant a new name but Leo's carried such cache throughout the Island that it made sense to keep it as is. Of course the fear amongst the regulars was it would become a hip, trendy bar filled to the brink with assholes. The grand opening was last night and supposedly the place was packed with a minimal amount of jerks. The test was how the bar would perform over the weekend.

Chris figured since it was still only Leo's and he wasn't seeing Val, he could leave the stubble on his face for one more night. Besides, he missed having facial hair. He grabbing his black Mets hat jumped in the car and took off.

After he endured a brief line outside, Chris strolled into the new place a quarter after ten and looked around. The bar area had expanded and there were televisions everywhere. Other than that, and some random bullshit up on the walls for atmosphere it was the same bar he had come to know and love. He worked his way through the crowd, and spotted Richie, Sammy, his girlfriend Stephanie, Eddie and some other familiar faces hanging out on the stools lined up in the far corner of the bar.

Immediately, sarcastic cheers went up from his friends, "welcoming him home" and asking him "what prison was really like?" Chris took everything in stride and answered the insincere questions with insincere answers. Richie was on the fence about the new Leo's and asked everyone what they thought. Now it was Chris's turn, except knowing how Chris had a tendency to ramble, Richie limited him to three words or less. Chris went for laughs and said, "paradise it's not," eliciting laughter from the group. Especially since the bartender/owner named Gus had come down and stood right behind him when he said it. Gus was in his mid-thirties, already balding with a short and stocky build. Many a person had commented that he "looked like a Gus," whatever that meant. With a disingenuous smile, Gus asked him what he'd be having and Chris flashed a sheepish grin and told him to just give him a Bud. The night was off to a great start.

While they all caught up on what was going on, Chris noticed a familiar face sitting amongst them on one of the bar stools. Actually, he didn't necessarily remember the face, more like those deep blue eyes staring back at him. If she was wearing any makeup it was probably just lip gloss. A tight black shirt hugged her skin and ran down to the jeans she was wearing. He was certain he knew the girl, he just couldn't remember where from. Chris figured this mystery was going to drive him nuts all night so he danced his way through his friends and settled up next to her against the bar where she was in the middle of a conversation with Stephanie. Ordinarily Chris might have waited for the mystery girl to finish up her conversation. However she was talking to Steph and Chris knew Stephanie wouldn't mind getting interrupted by him.

"Wait," he said as he slid into their view. "This is going to sound crazy and such a cheesy pick up line, but I think I actually do know you." The girl was in mid sentence, stopped and turned to look at Chris.

"You know you really could have thought of something a little more creative than that." She said with a playful hint of annoyance.

"No seriously, I know you from somewhere, what's your name?"

"Hey Chris." Steph attempted to join the conversation.

"Hey Steph." Chris said dryly before he immediately refocused back on her friend.

"You're right, you do know me and I'm insulted you don't know my name." Stephanie surmised her presence wasn't necessary and made a hasty retreat.

"I'm going to go find Sammy, you okay here?"

"Yeah I'm good Steph. He's not, but I'm good." This was now driving him crazy, which drove his enthusiasm up to an eleven.

"Ohhh c'mon! That's nonsense. I'm always good. Now where do I know you?"

"Well, Chris, I just so happened to have saved your life back in the day."

"Okay, so you know my name and you're obviously insane. Give me another hint." She gave a loud laugh, causing Chris to laugh too. After a couple of seconds of staring she asked, "Did she like it?" Chris thought for a moment and a big smile crept across his face.

"Jen! Jen from the jewelry store!"

"Ta-da!" She extended her arms out in a flourish.

"Actually not only did she love it, she was shocked I was able to pick out something like that on my own!"

"You didn't give me any credit? Now I'm shocked!"

"I would have picked it out eventually."

"Regardless I believe you owe me."

"How's a Heineken sound?

"Two Corona's and we got ourselves a deal."

Chris leaned over the bar and caught Gus's attention. "Could you get this beautiful girl a Corona please? And whenever she's done with that give her another."

Gus, still remembering the earlier remark said in his driest voice, "Oh wow two beers. That should impress her." Chris laughed, handed Gus a ten and handed Jen her beer. They clinked bottles and took a drink.

"Question for you, if you're friends with Stephanie how come I've never seen you around?"

"Well, for one, I just turned twenty-one last month."

"Time out! Twenty-one? Seriously? No way let me see your ID!"

"Are you serious?"

"Yes. I cannot believe you are only twenty-one years old!"

"Are you saying I look forty?!" Chris laughed.

"No, I thought maybe twenty-two, twenty-three. But just turned twenty-one? Impossible."

"Okay fine. Here's my ID." Jen reached into her bag and pulled out her wallet and handed him the license.

"Hmm Jennifer Polanski. Born April 14, 1978. Sex: Female. Eyes: Blue. Height: 5'3". Yeah I guess you check out!"

"Gee, I'm glad I have your approval. Thanks," she said with a smile.

"I still don't understand why I never saw you anywhere with Stephanie."

"My ex didn't exactly get along with her or any of my friends for that matter.

"Ex? I thought you were ring shopping."

"Thank God I was only shopping."

"That bad?"

"I'd much rather talk about that beard you're attempting to grow on your face," skillfully changing the subject.

"Why, do you like guys with beards?" Chris playfully stroked his chin.

"Actually I love facial hair."

"I'll keep that in mind."

For the rest of the night they hung out next to the bar and talked. Sometimes others would join in, but for the most part it was just the two of them. It seemed like they had everything in common, from humor to their mutual love of Kevin Smith movies. Jen even surprised the hell out of him when she sang along with the jukebox to "Elderly Woman Behind the Counter in a Small Town."

Around two in the morning Jen and the girls were getting tired, while the guys wanted to get a bite to eat. The group walked out together and everyone gave their goodbyes. When Chris said good night to Jen, they agreed to find each other randomly again, whether it was a jewelry store, a bar, or a Laundromat. Apparently their goodbye took a little longer than everyone else's because they already left in their cars. Chris walked to his with a huge grin, one that didn't leave his face when he walked into Perkins, the diner where they always ended the night. The boys were already in a booth when Chris strolled up, plopped himself down, and grabbed a menu. It was quiet—way too quiet—and he knew something was up. He peered over the menu and saw Sammy, Richie, and Eddie with big dumb grins on their faces. Chris knew what was coming next as they took great pleasure in seizing upon his night with Jen and peppered him with rapid fire questions and comments.

"*You* like Jen!" Richie said in a sing song fashion.

"She's okay."

"Nooooo. you liiiiiiiiike Jen." Eddie said with tremendous glee.

"I get it Eddie. I like Jen."

"Do you looooove her?"

"I'll tell you who I do love, my girlfriend Val."

"We don't care about that, we care about what we just saw and you *definitely* like Jen." Richie was in his glory and Chris was feeling defensive. Without even realizing it removed his hat and ran his fingers threw his hair.

"Well what's not to like? She's hot and we have eight billion things in common."

"So does this mean you're breaking up with Vallllllllllllll?"

"Okay, seriously, don't let Eddie drive home because he's clearly drunk."

"Marcum seriously, break up with Vallllllllllllllll," Eddie was persistent.

"I'm getting the idea you guys don't like her."

"No we like her, but it's not a question of who we like, it's who you like. And you clearly like Jen," Richie said as he grabbed Chris by the shoulders and shook him.

"Okay fine you made your point. Enough." Sammy decided to add his two cents.

"Chris, seriously. Say with a straight face that you love Valerie and you have no interest whatsoever in Jen."

"I love Valerie and I have no interest whatsoever in Jen. Happy?" Chris managed to get through the first part but felt his lips tremble by the time he finished the sentence.

"You started cracking after you said the word interest."

"I can't win!"

"Welcome back buddy, hopefully this isn't a one night stand with us."

The comments kept flying before, during, and after the boys received their food. When the time came to end the night Chris warned them that the next guy to bring up Jen was getting a punch in the face. That didn't stop Richie from calling on his cell phone during the drive home just to ask if he and Jen planned on eloping. Chris faked getting angry but the truth was he didn't care. He figured it was better than getting his balls broken for never being around.

He entered the house, went downstairs to the basement, kicked off his sneakers, and crashed on his bed. Were his friends joking or being serious? He was in love with Val, hell he was probably going to marry Val and those guys would be in the wedding party. Sure, Jen was beautiful and fun to be around, but for all he knew she could be a complete psychopath. Val on the other hand, he knew for sure was a psychopath, just not a complete one. And with that brilliant piece of deductive reasoning assuaging his troubled mind, Chris fell asleep.

# CHAPTER 17

## June 24, 1999

Despite the persistence of his friends, Chris managed to put Jen out of his mind. Like he told them, he was in love with a great girl who made him happy. What more did he need?

With the end of his first year of teaching weeks away, Chris' thoughts turned to the upcoming summer. Some of his friends at work were camp counselors and were trying to sell him on the position, to no avail. The last thing he wanted to see was another child. Ten months with teenage kids had taken two years off his life. He was going to use the two month vacation to decompress. The thing he was looking forward to the most was being able to wake up at 11AM guilt free.

While Chris figured out his summer, Valerie was doing the same. Facing one last summer as a student, her goal was to make as much money as possible. Her mother's boyfriend Don came in handy—getting her a summer job at Merrill Lynch. One thing you could say about Don, he knew people. As long as she didn't drop the ball completely, the company would have a job waiting for her in January. The summer would be hard, but would pay off down the line.

When she told him the plan, Chris was ecstatic for her, and for himself. He was aware that a teacher's salary was a modest one before he took the job, however if Val were able to parlay her summer gig into a full time job after graduation, their combined salary would be more than enough. Chris had been non-committal whenever Valerie brought up getting married. He didn't think at this point in their lives it would be smart move. However, this news put the plans back in play, with October mentally circled in his mind. Throw in perhaps a two year engagement and the wheels were now in motion.

On June 24, Chris turned in his keys and grade book and said his goodbyes for the summer. Some of his colleagues talked about getting together for drinks and Chris gave a couple of insincere nods and smiles. To be honest he wanted a break from everything involving the job as long as possible. Charge up the batteries and be ready for the fall campaign. As he stepped out the back door to the parking lot and walked down the handicap ramp, Chris beamed with excitement. He felt like he was thirteen again. An entire summer at his disposal. The sun was shining; there was not a cloud in the sky, or a worry to be thought of. Simply put, he was content.

He climbed into his new (the car was two years old and used, but it was new to Chris) Mazda he had bought off a co-worker a month ago and thought of his various options. It was only 11:30AM; he could grab a bite to eat or go to the old book store, grab a cup of coffee, and read for the afternoon. Or maybe...

A loud vibration made his left thigh tremble—his eight pound cell phone was ringing and it was a number he didn't recognize.

"Hello?"

"Hey Chris, it's Stephanie."

"Hey Steph, this is random."

"I know. I think this is the first time I've ever heard you on the phone."

"Is it what you imagined?"

"Even better." They both laughed.

"So what's up?"

Nothing much. I was just on the phone with Sammy, telling him how I was going down to Belmar. And he casually mentioned how today was your last day of work and how you might like to lay on a beach with some pretty girls. You interested?"

"Hells yeah. I'm just leaving the parking lot now; figure I'll be home in about fifteen minutes. You want me to drive?"

"Would you mind?"

"Ahh I see. You're just using me for my sweet ride."

"Ohh you got me." They laughed again.

"All right I'll be at your house in a little bit."

"Sounds good. I'll tell the girls to meet up here."

"Girls plural?" This keeps getting better and better he thought to himself. "Who's coming?"

"Eddie's girlfriend Antoinette and that girl Jen you met at Leo's." When Chris heard Jen's name he felt his stomach rumble. He tried his best to be nonchalant and said,

"K. Good stuff. See you soon."

"Yes you will."

"Later."

"Bye."

"God bless Sammy," Chris thought, with a huge smile coming over his face. He loved going to Belmar and could lie out on the sand all afternoon. The fact that Jen would be in attendance had nothing to do at all with his excitement. Nope, nothing at all.

If there was one constant in this world, it's that Christopher Marcum had to take a nap the moment he arrived home from the beach. It didn't matter if he spent all day in the ocean or tanned on the sand the entire time there. It didn't matter if he drove down or slept the entire car ride home. No matter what, Chris slept for at least one hour.

On that particular day, it wound up being three.

When he woke up at 8:45PM, he had two voicemails on his cell phone and two messages waiting for him on his answering machine. Apparently, he was even more popular than he imagined.

Chris stretched his left arm to reach the end table next to his bed and hit the play button on the machine.

```
"You have two new messages."
"First message, Friday, June 24, 12:15PM."
"Hey Poo it's me. Just wanted to see how the last day
went. Call me back. Love you. Bye."
```

Chris hit delete and went to the next message.

```
"Next message, Friday, June 24, 7:30PM."
"Hey it's me. I called your cell phone a couple of
times. Where are you? Call me back!"
```

Chris rubbed his eyes, hit delete again and picked up his cell phone.

```
"You have two new messages."
"First message, Friday, June 24, 2:23PM."
"Hey it's me, just wanted to see what you're doing.
If you're wondering about the echo I'm calling from the
```

96

women's bathroom, and I know what you're thinking pervert! Call me back…love you. Bye."

Chris again hit delete and went to the next message.

"Next message, Friday June 24, 5:14PM."
"Did you get kidnapped or move to China? I want to talk to you! Call me back. Bye!"

Okay maybe he wasn't as popular as he thought, but at least one person in the world loved him enough to think he moved to China. He deleted the fourth and last message and started to dial Val's number when a knock came from his bedroom door.

"Hey Chris just wanted to let you know Valerie called our phone looking for you about twenty minutes ago. I told her you were sleeping."

"Why is she calling your line?" Chris asked in an annoyed tone.

"You're asking *me* about *your* girlfriend?" His mom said in an incredulous tone that made Chris smile.

"Yeah I know. Thanks Mom." The one thing you could say about Val, Chris thought to himself, she was persistent! Chris figured she would be calling again any second so he might as well call her now. The phone didn't get through its first full ring when she answered.

"Ohhhhh good morning, didn't mean to disturb you!"

"Well when you had a hard day like I did you need a nap."

"And by hard day you mean…"

"Tanning at the beach."

"Ahh yes. I can see how that would be a workout—for your eyes."

"There were a lot of good looking girls there Val, mostly *under* the age of seventeen and we both know I like my girls older."

"Yeah thanks. That's reassuring. So you drove down by yourself?"

"Actually Stephanie called me out of the blue and asked if I wanted to go."

"Since when do you two hangout?"

"Since Sammy told her my vacation started today. He gave her my number and I wound up driving her and her friends down."

"Ohhh friends too! Anyone I know?" She asked in mock jealousy.

"Umm, I know you've hung out with Antoinette and her other friend Jen went too."

"Since the love of your life is working this summer are these girls your new crew?" She jokingly questioned with a hint of paranoia underneath.

"I wouldn't call them my crew, but I could see going to the beach every once in a while." Chris instantly knew he had stepped into a bear trap and was praying to God this wouldn't end with him gnawing off his own foot to escape.

"And they know that you're taken by the best girl in the world, right?"

"I mentioned you at least sixty-seven times, so yes they know."

"Good! Well it's Friday and I'm bored out of my mind. Get dressed and let's get a bite to eat."

Bear trap averted. Foot still attached to leg.

"Let me just shower off the sand and the stink. I'll be over in twenty."

"Eww sand and stink, how could those girls possibly resist you?"

"I have no idea Val. I'm normally a smooth talker."

"Yeah I've already experienced the smoothness. Get your butt over here ASAP."

"Love you too."

Chris was normally a straight shooter, preferring to be completely honest, even to his own detriment rather than lying. He figured he had more credibility if he told Val everything, so at least she was aware rather than being surprised by something. Yet for whatever reason Chris casually left out a tiny detail in the course of recapping the events of the day—he traded cell phone numbers with Jen.

# CHAPTER 18

## July 1999

If two summers ago was the best summer of Chris' life, this summer was a very close second. His days began around 11AM with a stretch and roll out of bed, followed by a casual breakfast consisting of either Lucky Charms or a sesame bagel with cream cheese, while reading the Daily News and the Post. With his dad at work at the office, his mom busy with real estate and Eric working full time somewhere (he wasn't sure what exactly Eric did), Chris had the house to himself. After a quick scrub of whatever dish he used he would check the weather outside to see what his day would consist of. If it was a warm and sunny day, he would drive down the Jersey shore to his favorite spot, Belmar. If the day was overcast or rainy, he would spend his time on the couch reading the next book that captured his attention. Valerie was right, he and the girls had become a fun little crew. This was well and good until the Thursday after the July 4th weekend.

Every weather forecaster pegged the day to be a gorgeous one, ninety-five degrees and a clear blue sky. They practically begged beach goers to get to the sand as early as possible. The new beach crew decided Wednesday night on an AOL chat to meet at Jen's real early to beat the traffic and claim the optimum spot, close enough to the water so they wouldn't burn their feet. The plan was whoever woke up first would call the others. Antoinette's eyes opened a little before eight o'clock and Chris was awoken from his restful slumber to hear, "Jen's house at 9 o'clock." He acknowledged Antoinette with a grunt, shook off the sleepies from his eyes and jumped in the shower.

Chris, being the punctual guy that he is, pulled up at Jen's house a little before nine and expected to see the usual cars parked out front. For a second he thought they might have left without him, before remembering there was no way they were going to do the forty five minute drive on their own. He hopped out of the car in his light blue bathing suit, guinea t-shirt, black Mets hat, a pair of blue flip flops Valerie wished he would forget somewhere and strolled up to the front door. This was the first time he was ever at Jen's house and he noticed once again a flutter in the stomach. Laughing at his ridiculousness he rang the doorbell and casually checked himself out in the reflection of the door. He heard a couple of locks being fiddled with and when the door opened Jen was standing there wearing a large pink bath towel around her head, a plain white tee-shirt and a lively shade of green sweatpants.

"Am I early?"

"Nope I'm late and you're the first one to arrive. Come on in." Chris followed her inside, watching her kick aside a pair of shoes. They walked up the three steps into the living room and Jen said,

"I'm going to finish getting ready. You can either sit here in the living room and watch TV or keep walking till you hit the kitchen and knock yourself out."

"I'm good with the television, do what you gotta do."

"I promise I'm not one of those girls, just give me like seven minutes."

"Not ten, not five, seven?"

"What can I say, I'm precise."

"Sounds like it. See you in seven."

The phone rang and Jen ran up the wooden steps to the left of the living room while Chris plopped down on the white leather couch positioned in front of a large fifty inch television set. He was going to put it on before he saw the overly complicated remote control lying snuggly between the opened pages of a People magazine on a glass coffee table. Not wanting to accidentally open the garage door or blow up the house, Chris left the remote alone, stood up and looked at the various pictures around the living room and the dining room. There were pictures of Jen as a little girl, getting pushed on a tire swing by presumably her dad, there were pictures of her graduating high school and college, along with pictures of her mom and what looked to be a younger brother and sister. There was one of Jen at SeaWorld, feeding a dolphin that captivated Chris' attention to the point that he didn't hear her coming down the steps.

"Chris?"

Her voice startled him and when he turned to say something the words jammed up in his throat. Maybe it was the way the light came in from the front window, or how she walked down the steps. Whatever the case, this time something was different. Her hair, lighter from all the beach activity, cascaded down her back and her tan face made those deep blue eyes pop even more. She wore a bright orange tank top and a pair of pink shorts, which stopped just below her ass. Chris did his best not to ogle.

"There's a problem," Jen said.

Of course Chris was ogling and all he heard was "Blah blah blah."

"Chris?"

"What's up?"

"Stephanie called me up just before you got here and said Sammy wasn't working at the firehouse today."

"And?"

"And you know how Sammy is with any body of water." This was true. Sammy hated the pool, the beach, rivers, lakes, lagoons even shallow puddles in a parking lot. Showers were his absolute limit.

"Then I guess it's the three of us."

"More like the two of us. That was Annie on the phone just now. Not to be gross, and don't ever say I told you this, but she just got her period and doesn't feel comfortable going."

"You know you could have given me thirty different reasons why she couldn't come."

"I could have except for one little problem. I can't lie." He smiled. "I'm not sure leaving out a detail is a lie."

"Any omission is an admission of guilt."

"I had no idea I was in the company of a Chinese fortune cookie."

"You have no idea period." She punctuated her remark with a friendly jab on the shoulder.

"Wow that might have been the worst pun…of all time." Chris said as he did his best Chandler Bing impression.

"Ewwww okay how about we continue this philosophical conversation in that car of yours?"

"Oh you still want to go?" This surprised Chris even more.

"Let's see. Underneath this amazing ensemble I'm wearing a bikini and you are in a bathing suit. It's a thousand degrees outside and leaning against the banister over there is a cooler packed with some assorted sandwiches and beverages. What else do I want to do today?"

"I don't know. I didn't want to assume you would still go if it was just the two of us." Suddenly he was nervous and doing his best to hide it.

"Aww! Do you feel awkward? Don't worry Chris I'm not going to attack you in the water," she said in a mocking tone offset with a huge smile.

"Fine. I'll go to the beach with you." He said in a sad voice and playfully stomped his way down her steps and out the front door.

"Way to make a girl feel wanted!" Jen gave him another playful tap on the back and followed him out.

Chris never had a better day at the beach. Between the food, Jen trying to throw pieces of roast beef into his open mouth and hitting everything but his mouth, "accidentally" throwing salt in his eyes, splashing each other in the water, and even an attempt at burying him in the sand—it was a phenomenal day. Chris also discovered his long held theory might not be one hundred percent accurate.

He always believed it was impossible for good looking girls to be funny. They might be unintentionally funny, but they could not get a laugh on purpose. When girls would challenge him by saying guys laugh at their jokes all the time, Chris pointed out these were guys who were trying to go out with them. There was no way God was going to give a girl superior genetics and a sense of humor—it just doesn't happen. Jen wound up getting an asterisk. She made Chris laugh more than Chris made her laugh, and Chris prided himself on being funny. Beautiful, funny, a cook, and very easy to talk to—Jen had everything.

From that day forward, Chris and Jen started hanging out a lot more…as friends. This also spoiled another one of his long held theories—guys and girls cannot be true friends. Of course if Chris truly examined their situation maybe his theory still carried some weight. If the day was beautiful they would hit the beach. If it was raining they might go to the mall together. With Val working the nine to five, five days a week, Chris jokingly referred to Jen as his "During the Week" girlfriend. Of course he only said that to Jen.

This isn't to say that Chris kept Val in the dark about Jen. He wouldn't tell her everything, but she knew they would go to the beach together or occasionally talk online. Chris rationalized it to himself by saying Jen was only a friend, nothing more, who just happened to be a girl. If things went beyond their current situation then it would be wrong.

Their friendship had progressed quickly in a relatively short period of time. They had private jokes and could carry on conversations with simple glances. For the first time, Chris felt like he was with someone who understood him, and as a result he felt his guard coming down.

It was the second to last day of July and the two of them were in Chris' car coming back from the beach. They didn't get two miles before Chris had to slow down. Apparently there was a major accident on the Garden State Parkway and the traffic was backed up for miles. The car crept along another mile or so before everything just stopped. Chris came to the quick realization that they weren't going anywhere so he put the car in park and started to drum his fingers against the steering wheel.

"Well this sucks!" Chris said while staring out the window. Jen was fixing her hair in the side mirror and smiled.

"You're saying it sucks because of the traffic or it sucks because now you're stuck with me for God knows how long?"

"Oh definitely the second one."

"Good, just wanted to make sure we were on the same page." She gave him a playful slap on the shoulder. By this point he was used to the smacks, slaps and the once in awhile punch, although his shoulders still had some remnants of previous encounters. Chris went to change stations but Jen reached over and shut the radio off.

"No radio. I'm confident we can carry an entire conversation from now until we get home."

"You think?"

"I know!" Chris looked over at her.

"I'm waiting."

"No, no, I want to hear all about Christopher Marcum."

"What about me?"

"I don't know, tell me something."

"You are a lousy interviewer."

"Okay fine you need a topic? Tell me about teaching."

"Well what do you want to know?"

"Do you really need a specific teaching question?"

"Again you are the one interviewing me."

"Let me think of a really deep, probing question." Jen looked up at the ceiling for a couple of seconds.

"Umm do you like it?" She barely got the sentence out of her mouth before she laughed all over it.

"It took you four hours to think of that?"

"Just answer the question!"

"I love that I can go to the beach in the summer."

"Come on give me the serious answer. Do you like your current occupation?"

"Seriously? Yes."

"Do you see yourself doing it for the next thirty years?"

"Well, I love my job, but at the same time I can't see myself in a classroom when I'm forty."

"Why not?"

"I don't know. No you know what; honestly I don't see me caring as much as I do now. I could see myself taking advantage of having tenure, taking things for granted and just settling into the routine. I know for sure I wouldn't want to become that."

"You don't think you could keep being the same enthusiastic guy you are now?"

"I think the enthusiasm burns off of everything after a while. Unless it's something you absolutely love."

"Well what do you love?" That's a loaded question, Chris thought to himself. "What are you smirking at?" She asked as she leaned forward to examine his face. Chris playfully helped and arched his left eyebrow.

"Smirking?"

"Yeah. There was definite smirkage."

"I think you're drunk!"

"Whatever" and she sat back down on her seat.

"Enough about me, let's talk about Jennifer Polanski. What about you? Do you think you'll enjoy being in the classroom?"

"I hope so. If things go according to plan I could definitely see myself teaching first grade until I'm fifty. Of course this is all depending on whether or not I get a phone call this week."

"That school still hasn't called?"

"The teacher I would be replacing hasn't told them yet whether or not she's moving. Until she makes that phone call, I'm stuck in limbo."

"Worst case scenario?"

"I sub for a year and hopefully get in the next year after. However our audience is growing weary of my voice and wants to hear more of yours."

"I had no idea this was being filmed."

"Thirty countries, ten different languages and one radio station."

"Just one?"

"Any more would just be ridiculous." They both laughed and Chris swooned quietly to the sound of her giggle.

"As I was saying Mr. Marcum, if you don't see yourself teaching at forty what do you see yourself doing?" Chris leaned to the left so his back was against both the door and the seat.

"Honestly?"

"No I want you to make up a lie. Of course honestly."

"I want to write."

"Really?" Jen dropped the seat back so she could stretch out.

"Yeah if I could spend the rest of my life getting paid to make up stories and characters I would be beyond happy."

"Have you tried?" Chris laughed and replied. "Well if you count keeping a journal then yes, I have tried."

"Aww you keep a journal? Do you write your deepest darkest secrets in there and keep it under lock and key." Chris pretended to be offended.

"That's it. Conversation over."

"No. No stop. I didn't mean it," Jen said laughing. "Tell me all about your girlie diary, I mean manly journal." Chris took a glance at her out of the corner of his eye and took a deep dramatic breath."

"Fine. Just be gentle, this is some serious stuff."

"I promise. Please continue."

"Basically it has everything I can't say."

"What do you mean? You have one of the biggest mouths I know. What could you possibly be holding back?"

"I'll say anything that comes to mind, but for the most part it's either jokes or sarcasm. I'm not real good expressing how I actually feel. In many ways writing is like therapy for me."

"Do you write about meeeeeeeeee?" she inquired while batting her eyelashes. Chris laughed.

"Yeah I think you're mentioned once or twice."

"And what does it say?" Chris straightened up. "I can't tell you. It's personal," he said in mock indignation.

"That sounds juicy! If you refuse to talk about your diary devoted to Jen, tell me something else that's personal."

"Why would I do that?"

"Because you trust me of course."

"Yeah, but me getting personal is just going to bring this conversation down and then we'll be stuck in traffic even more depressed."

"I don't care; we'll just have to be depressed together."

"You're serious."

"I'm waiting." Chris looked out his windshield and saw cars were beginning to move.

"Oh look at that. I can't talk now I have to concentrate on driving again."

"I get the hint. I'll leave it alone." She said in a rather subdued voice.

Chris wasn't sure if she was joking or genuinely disappointed she wasn't going to hear anything. He looked over at her and paused. Whether it was the need to unburden or the way their eyes held for a moment, he wasn't sure. Whatever the reason, Chris decided to talk.

"All right fine. How about this—I think.... I'm.... trapped." Each word hung in the air until the last thudded to the ground and Jen looked at him quizzically.

"Trapped how?"

"I'm just saying this because it's standard when you tell a secret, but don't tell Stephanie or anyone."

"You have my word. Trapped how?" Jen turned her body so that she was staring intently at his eyes.

"This is going to sound horrible but whatever, you wanted truth. Here it goes."

"Just say it already!"

"Okay okay, this is tough give me a second."

"Take a deep breath and just blurt it out." Chris followed her directions, took a deep breath and said,

"I know I love Valerie, but I don't know if I *love* Valerie." Jen pulled the seat back up.

"OHHHHHHH!"

"Yeah." A pregnant pause and then,

"And you still want to marry her?"

"Yeah. Yeah because I love her."

"But you don't *love* her."

"I don't know." Silence lingered for a couple of seconds before Chris spoke again.

"You want to hear something funny? I have the money for the ring all saved up."

"You didn't buy it yet, right?"

"No. Not for another couple of months."

"This is just my opinion and doesn't mean anything, but if I were you I would really think before I went shopping."

"That's all I've been doing lately. Thinking."

"And if, after doing a lot of thinking I still had the slightest doubt I would wait until I didn't." Chris took off the black Mets hat and ran his fingers through his hair.

"But who's to say these doubts ever leave? I don't believe in fate and I don't believe in soul mates. I just think you find someone and you learn to make it work."

Jen gasped and said in her most serious voice, "That is the most horrible description of love and marriage I have ever heard." Chris chuckled.

"Sorry, but I mean, I'm going on twenty-three and I have never experienced complete and total love before. The thing is I do know I love Valerie. But the gooey lovey dovey rest of your life love? The kind where you say to the other person you would be lost without them? That I don't think is real. I think it's just something you see in the movies."

"Well I hope for your sake it works out. I wouldn't want to spend the rest of my life wondering what if."

A loud vibrating sound came from Jen's purse and she reached for her phone. The caller ID showed Stephanie's number and Jen let it go to voice mail.

"You sure you don't want to get that?"

"I said we would be able to talk the entire way home and I'm sticking to…" Before she could finish her thought the phone rang again and once again the caller ID showed Stephanie's number.

"If she's calling back to back it has to be important."

"Nope, she's probably just bored. Where were we?"

"We were talking about whether or not oooey gooey love exists."

"Ahhh yes, you and your depressing views on….oh c'mon Steph!" For the third time in less than a minute Stephanie's number flashed on her phone.

"I think you better take it."

"Yeah so do I. You mind?"

"Go for it."

As soon as Jen said hello Chris could tell by her face something was wrong in Stephanie's world. For the rest of the car ride, Chris listened to Jen and her attempts to calm Stephanie down with whatever she was going through. Even though their conversation had stopped, Jen's words about love echoed in Chris's head.

# CHAPTER 19

## August 17, 1999

Chris woke up and didn't have to peek out a window to know Tuesday would not be a beach day. The weather was miserable, nothing but rain, wind and an overall gloomy attitude. He shuffled out of his queen size bed and made his way to the kitchen and a late breakfast. He had reached his front door and was about to make the trek up the remaining flight of stairs when his cell phone rang. He reached into his sweatpants saw it was Jen and all was right with the world. He had reached the point that whenever the phone rang he was disappointed if it wasn't Jen.

"I'm shocked you're awake."

"Relax it's 11:30, I don't sleep that late."

"Chris I called you last week at 1 and you said you just woke up."

"The exception not the rule."

"Whatever. Get some clothes on and come pick me up."

"Umm have you seen the weather outside? It's brutal. I plan on eating some Eggos, grabbing the newspapers and making a day on the couch. I might not even shower."

"Now you're just being disgusting."

"Par for the course." Chris said in a random French accent.

"Do you mean to tell me you would rather spend your day alone on a couch than with a girl who provides constant adventure?"

"Let me think about it."

"Wow."

"Okay okay. What's on tap for today?"

"How about a matinee and a bite to eat?"

"What are we seeing?"

"A friend of mine saw this movie called "The Sixth Sense." She said I had to see it just for the twist."

"You buying the nachos?"

"Is that a dealbreaker?"

"Yes. Yes it is." Jen let out a mock sigh.

"Fine you win. Nachos it is for Mr. Big Shot."

"And queso. Don't forget the queso."

"Yeah yeah yeah nachos and queso. Get dressed I'll see you in twenty."

"Can't wait."

"Bye."

"Bye."

Two and a half hours later they were sitting in Applebees, waiting for their appetizers to come out. Chris was gushing about how M. Night Shyamalan used the color red throughout the movie when his phone shook. He had placed the phone and his car keys off to the side next to the ketchup and couldn't see the caller ID. Jen's hand was a second faster and she threatened to answer it. Chris asked who it was and she said it was a restricted number. He decided to call her bluff and told her to answer it.

"Hellooooo this is my boyfriend Chris's phone. Who's calling?" She said in a valley-girl accent.

"Excuse me?! Who is this?!" Chris could see something went wrong because Jen's face dropped and threw the phone at him.

"I think it's Valerie," she whispered nervously.

"Shit." Chris took the phone and tried to sound as casual as possible.

"Hey babe, what's up?"

"What the hell was that Christopher? Who are you with?" Valerie's voice came in loud and clear and Chris had to pull the phone away from his ear.

"It was a joke. She thought she could scare me by answering my phone and I called her bluff."

"Stop using pronouns, who are you talking about?"

"Ahh Jen."

"And who else?"

"Umm no one else."

"I'm looking outside my office window right now and it's pouring. I'm going to assume between that and the noise in the background you aren't at the beach."

"Well yeah it's raining so we just went for a bite to eat."

110

"When were you going to tell me?"

"Tell you what?"

"That my boyfriend is a cheating bastard!"

*CLICK*

"Val? Hello?"

Chris removed the phone from his ear and looked to see if she really hung up. As he went to put the phone in his front left jeans pocket Jen spoke up.

"Chris, I'm so sorry for answering the phone. I didn't mean to cause a fight."

"Stop. It's not your fault. I guess it's my fault actually since I sort of haven't been telling Val we've been hanging out by ourselves."

"You what? Why not?"

"Because for one I knew she would react like that and second because I knew she would react like that."

"But we're just friends."

"I know that and you know that but Valerie would never believe that."

"So she thinks I would try and steal you away."

"Yeah I think we have some trust issues to work on."

"No jokes right now Chris."

"Sorry. I'm not sure what to say or do right now."

"I'd say you have a lot of things to work out if you're still planning on popping the question in a couple of months."

"Yeah I know, I know. The problem is I can already hear her saying she doesn't want us hanging out anymore."

"Don't get me wrong I like hanging out, but I mean, is it worth fighting with your girlfriend?"

"Yes," Chris said quietly, but firmly. Jen paused and gave him a look.

"That was more of a rhetorical question."

"Well, for the record you are worth whatever fights I have ahead of me."

"I think it would be better if we just went home now."

"Why? What difference would it make at this point?" His voice was a touch louder.

"Chris I don't want to be the cause of a breakup."

"This isn't your fault at all. I should have just let her know from the beginning except I didn't. I still don't think we did anything wrong, I mean it's not like we're making out or anything." His last sentence seemed to hover in the air above the table. Jen shifted uncomfortably in her seat and leaned forward.

"Chris if I went to kiss you right now would you pull away?"

"What?"

"If I leaned over the table right now and attempted to kiss you would you lean forward or move away?"

"What does that have to do with anything?"

"Everything. Would you move away? Yes or no?"

"Honestly?"

"Always."

"No."

"Now you absolutely have to take me home."

"Why? Because I'm attracted to you? Because I was honest, you have to leave?"

"I just got out of a long-term relationship because I couldn't trust the guy. You are months away from getting engaged. Nothing good can come from us hanging out if you want to kiss me."

"Well you want to kiss me."

"Who said that?"

"You said that with your hypothetical."

"No I was asking if you would, not what I would do."

"Jen are you telling me that if I leaned across the table to kiss you, you would pull back?"

"Honestly, yes. You have a girlfriend."

"Okay. Take Val out of the equation. Would you pull back then?"

"Here are your mozzarella sticks and do you need a refill?" Waiters have the worst timing, Chris thought to himself.

"No thanks," Chris said softly.

"And you, Miss?"

"No. I'm good. Actually could you cancel our order and just bring the check?"

"I'm sorry is there anything wrong?" He said in a stammer.

"Everything. Nothing to do with you, we just have to go." Her body language screamed there was a problem bigger than Applebees and the waiter didn't press the issue any further. He looked at Chris who was staring at Jen.

"Jen, are you serious?" He couldn't believe what was happening. The waiter shuffled his feet uncomfortably, needing to ask one more question.

"Well I'm sorry to hear that. Just give me a second and I'll get the check. Should I wrap up the sticks?"

"Chris do you want to take them home?"

"No I'm not hungry." He mumbled.

"That's okay—just the check then."

"No problem."

"I'll meet you at the car. Here's five bucks." Jen dropped a five dollar bill on the table and walked out of the restaurant.

"What the hell just happened?" Chris said aloud. The day was going great and in the process of five minutes he somehow pissed off the two most important girls in his life.

Chris settled up the bill and walked out. The rain had stopped and Chris sarcastically said "thanks" out loud. Jen was leaning against the passenger side door with her back to him. If she thought his comment was directed at her she didn't acknowledge it. He unlocked the doors and they both climbed in quietly. The car ride was silent, except for the *Dark Side of the Moon* album he had set on random. "*Speak to Me/Breathe*" was starting up, and the heartbeat in the beginning was mocking his own. While that heart had a slow, rhythmic beat, Chris's was on overdrive.

"You didn't answer my question." For the first time since leaving the restaurant Jen looked at Chris.

"You didn't ask anything."

"I meant from before in the restaurant. I asked you if I wasn't with Val would you move away if I kissed you." Jen sighed.

"Chris why do you want to know that?" Her voice was as earnest and as gentle as possible.

"I don't know. Peace of mind?"

"So me telling you that I would kiss you if you were single would make you feel better while you went home to fight with your girlfriend?"

"It wouldn't make me feel better. It wouldn't make this better. I just need to know."

"Your answer is an engagement ring in a couple of months and a wedding in over a year." She said it with such firmness that Chris had no retort. Chris made the left turn and was now in front of her house.

"Chris I don't think we should hang out anymore. I mean in a group yes, but not by ourselves. It isn't right."

"Oh now it's not right, but the entire summer it was?"

"That's completely not fair. You know how I feel about being honest. Your girlfriend thinks I'm conspiring against her!"

Jen removed her seat belt and picked up her purse. Chris didn't want her to leave like this. He didn't want her to leave at all. As his heart searched for the proper words to convey his true thoughts, his mind went on autopilot and he blurted out.

"I guess I should at least thank you for a fun summer. I just wish it didn't have to end like this." He couldn't believe out of everything he could have possibly said, he went with that.

"Me too. Bye."

"See ya."

Jen stepped out of the car, gave him a quick glance, and turned towards her house.

Chris remained until she stepped inside and lingered for a couple more seconds after. Should he step out of the car and ring her bell? What would he say? What good would it do? Why did he feel this way when he was in love with Valerie? That question brought a significant amount of discomfort to his already frazzled mind and Chris decided to not deal with it. His stomach was doing back flips and no matter how hard he tried to ignore that last question, it came circling round back on him. He had no idea that Jen remained on the other side of her front door well beyond the time Chris pulled away.

It had been four days since Chris had spoken to either Valerie or Jen—the day Chris referred to as Armageddon. He knew he couldn't call Jen, figuring that would be the absolute wrong thing to do. Instead he tried calling Val, but coincidentally her voice mail always came up after the first ring or the phone would just cut out as if someone was hanging up on him. Finally, whether he caught her off guard or because she was ready to answer, he got through on Sunday morning.

"Hey," Valerie said with a touch of nervousness in her voice.

"Oh hey. I expected to get your voicemail again." He kept his voice intentionally soft, hoping this would cause Valerie to do the same.

"Chris its nine o'clock on Sunday morning. I assumed someone was dying because you are never up this early."

"I know. I figured that would make you pick up the phone."

"So" she said in a monotone.

"So I want to see you."

"Why?"

"Oh c'mon Val don't do that. I love you, and this is the longest we've gone without seeing or talking to each other."

"Why not just call your friend *Jen*? I'm sure she'll listen to you."

"I haven't called or spoken to Jen since that day."

"Oh I feel so much better."

"Listen I'm wrong and I know I'm wrong. All I want to know is how to make this better."

"Why should I even give you the chance?" Her voice didn't get loud, although there was a distinct possibility it would in the near future.

"Because I don't deserve it or you." Valerie actually laughed in surprise and said,

"That's supposed to convince me?"

"No, I just want an opportunity, a chance. What can I do to get that?"

"For starters don't ever see or talk to that bitch ever again." Even though Jen put a stop to their hanging out, Chris didn't like being told who he could or could not see. Val was his girlfriend, not his mom and he was going to tell her that.

"Val don't you think you're being a little…"

"A little what, Chris? Finish that sentence and we'll see how long it takes you to get me on the phone again." Suddenly, Chris saw himself at the Alamo. He was going to lose and he knew it. The question now was whether to surrender and survive or fight until he was killed.

"You're right, you're right. I'm sorry."

"So you won't see her ever again?"

"Well if we're all in a group and she happens to be there I have no control over that."

"If I were you I'd assert as much control as possible."

"C'mon Val seriously, do you really think I would cheat on you?"

115

"If I did I wouldn't be talking to you right now, would I? But she is a decent looking girl and guys sometimes think with the wrong head."

"She isn't as beautiful as you." Chris put his head down the moment he said those words. Not only was he making himself sick he wasn't exactly sure he meant it.

"Do you think stating the obvious is going to make things better?"

"No, but it's true."

"Chris, don't give me bullshit right now. The last thing I want from you are clichés."

"Well what do you want?"

"The truth Christopher. I want the truth," she said in an exasperated tone. "I always want the truth and I'm afraid either you're holding something back or you are outright lying to me."

"Val how long do you know me? Have I ever hidden something from you before?"

"How would I know if you did?"

"Because you would know. You always know. You know me better than anyone else in the world." Chris ran his hand through his hair as he said those words. He was disgusted with himself. At the same time he heard an audible sigh from her end and knew he was getting somewhere.

"Before I even consider seeing you or continuing to talk to you I need to know something."

"Sure."

"Do you want to be with me?"

"Of course Val. I..." She cut him off before he could say another word.

"No I don't want the automatic answer. I want you to seriously think about this. Do you really want to be with me?"

"Val I don't need to think about this. You are it for me. If I had to think about it then there's a problem. I know from the bottom of my heart that I only want to be with you."

"Are you sure Chris? I don't want to deal with this six months from now." Chris had talked himself into this conversation and there was no turning back.

"I'm as sure of this as I am of anything else. I love you Valerie. End of story."

"Yeah?"

"Yeah."

"Fine you can start making things right by taking me out to dinner tomorrow night." Apparently the war was over and a détente had thankfully been declared.

"Or I could take you out for breakfast in twenty minutes?" said with a hopeful inflection.

"Are you kidding me? Just because we're talking doesn't mean things go instantly back to normal."

"So I'm not seeing you today at all?"

"Nope I have plans."

"What kind of plans?" he said with a trace of jealousy.

"The kind I made before this conversation."

"Is there a guy involved?" said with more than a trace.

"What if there was? You spent the entire summer hanging out with a girl." Chris paused and debated what to say next.

"Okay. Okay. Alright you're right I'm wrong. I'm sorry. Call me tonight if you want or I'll just see you tomorrow."

"Just for the record I'm not hanging out with a guy, unless you count Don as a guy. He's taking my mom and I out to the city for some food and shopping."

"Lucky guy."

"Not as lucky as you are still talking to me." A silence held in the air for a couple of seconds.

"True true. Okay go have fun. I'm going to clean this place up and maybe see what the boys are doing."

"I will and yes I'll call you tonight."

"K."

"Oh Chris one more thing" she said with as light a tone as possible.

"Yeah?"

"If I find out you called Jen, or plan on calling Jen or have any type of conversation with Jen we're done. You understand?"

"Yup" he said with his eyes closed and his head tilted up to the ceiling.

"K love you."

"Love you too. Bye."

"Bye."

Chris hung up the phone and felt worse than he had ten minutes ago. Why? The ice had finally broke with Val and things had a chance to get back to normal. He had made his stand at the Alamo and survived. It had been bloody and near disastrous, but he survived.

A quiet little voice in the back of his mind begged to differ.

# CHAPTER 20

## Labor Day Weekend 1999

Once again, his dad was right. Eventually, everything goes back to normal. The frost had dissipated and he saw Val every night. The Jen comments came fast and furious with Chris dutifully keeping silent. He considered himself lucky the outward hate lasted for only three weeks. Sure there was an occasional comment here or there but it seemed like Val swallowed the anger and the vitriol behind them had frittered away. With another school year soon approaching, Chris was happy to put the drama behind him. However, if he were truly honest with himself he would admit that he wasn't happy. In fact he was miserable. He missed Jen more than he imagined he would. He could talk to Val no big deal, yet he had a hard time being truthful with her.

By truthful he wasn't referring to lies—he was talking about whatever he was feeling inside his heart. There were no conversations of substance with her, through no fault of her own. For some strange reason Chris gave her a dog and pony show. He was more entertainer than honest. The first time he noticed he had a communication problem with her was after Eric's accident, when even though she was right for bringing it up he still couldn't talk about his feelings regarding his brother. Instead he relied on his journal to sort out his feelings and emotions. Talking via the pen. Conversely, with Jen it was different. He felt liberated, compelled to discuss things that previously had no business being spoken aloud. She might know him more in less than two months than Val did in more than two years! He did not feel like a traveling comedy troupe stopping off at her town. Jen came with her own personal sigh of relief. Yet to acknowledge this would only be an effort in frustration, so Chris buried it away.

Labor Day was a couple of days away and the entire group decided to get together and have a jam-packed weekend. Friday would be spent down the shore at Belmar for one last gasp of summer. Saturday Chris was going to the Mets game and Sunday everyone would gather at Sammy's house for a barbeque. Of course Val would be in attendance for everything, including the Mets game. This went without saying.

Friday night was spent at Bar-A and was as always phenomenal. What made the night even better than usual was Val agreed to drive his car home, which allowed Chris to get as drunk as he wanted with Sammy, Richie and Eddie. Eric even came with a couple of his friends and the new girl he was dating, Lisa. She seemed nice and was attractive, but Val said she was kind of a bitch in the bathroom to her. Chris didn't care. All that mattered was everyone was together down the Shore and having a great time.

On Saturday night Chris, Val, Eddie, and Antoinette went to Shea Stadium and saw a thrilling 4-2 New York Mets victory over the Colorado Rockies. Edgardo Alfonzo and Robin Ventura both hit home runs. Al Leiter got his eleventh victory of the year and shocker of shockers, Armando Benitez didn't blow the game. Even though Val said she wanted to sit in the orange field box seats Chris insisted that there was no seat better than in Mezzanine Section 18. Val was resistant at first, believing Chris didn't want to spend the extra cash. By the seventh inning she leaned in and whispered he was right. Very quietly he celebrated the moral victory. Chris was also right when he told Val she shouldn't have another hot dog, pointing out that her stomach is of the sensitive variety. Introducing another mystery dog could only pose problems later on, nevertheless Val insisted she knew her body better than he did.

During the car ride home, Valerie began to feel sick. Apparently Chris knew Val's body better than she thought. They were a couple of minutes from her house when Eddie got off the phone with Sam.

"Sammy said everyone is going down to Leo's to hang out. You guys interested?"

Chris looked at his girlfriend, who had her eyes closed while she clutched her stomach. He knew right away the only place she wanted to be tonight was in her bed or maybe the bathroom.

"I think we're going to pass. Tell everyone I'll meet up with them tomorrow." Val shifted forward and opened her eyes.

"Chris it's Labor Day weekend. Go out and have fun."

"It's okay, I'll stay in and hang out with you."

"Chris, seriously. There is nothing you can do for me. All we're going to do is hang out on the couch and you'll watch me fall asleep."

"No big deal. You would do the same for me."

"You bet I would, but you just saw a great Mets win. Go out and have fun with your friends."

Conveniently for Chris, Eddie had parked his car in front of Valerie's, saving him another trip. He pulled up in front of her house and Chris had no clue how to proceed. He desperately wanted to go out tonight but was fully aware he couldn't do anything without her giving the okay one way or another. At the same time Chris wanted to make sure she wasn't just "saying" to go out. This could be a bear trap and Chris didn't feel like having to spend the night apologizing for gnawing off his foot. While this dance was going on in the front of the car, Eddie whispered to Antoinette to stay inside until he knew what Chris was doing.

"Babe it's no big deal. I can stay in."

"Listen to me. I have no desire to stay in the car right now and go back and forth. I don't feel good and I just want to walk into the house and go to sleep," Valerie said with mild irritation. Chris took a quick glance in the rear view mirror and saw Eddie with a huge grin on his face.

"Are you sure because…"

"That's it I'm leaving. Bye guys, I'll give you a call tomorrow Ant."

"Bye Val," the couple said in stereo.

"Thanks babe. I'll call you when I get home tonight."

"Don't even bother. I'll probably be passed out. Give me a call tomorrow when you wake up."

"Sounds good. Love you babe."

"Love you too Pook."

Chris gave her a quick peck on the lips and Valerie left the car.

"Marrrrrrrrrrrrrcum damn! Any more of that and I was probably going to ralph!" Antoinette punched Eddie's arm.

"I wish you would show that much concern when I wasn't feeling good."

"Oh Marcum wasn't serious, he just wanted to make me look bad."

"Damn right! I'll meet you at Leo's." Chris kissed Antoinette goodbye and bumped fists with Eddie before he drove off. When

Chris came home, he took a quick shower, splashed on the Cool Water and made his way back out to see his friends.

Leo's was surprisingly packed on the Saturday of Labor Day weekend, as Chris figured everyone would be down the Jersey shore. Instead Chris had to battle his way through the mob to the usual corner spot of the bar where his crew congregated. In the course of saying his hellos he felt his stomach flip and noticed a pair of deep blue eyes off to the side. When Sammy told Eddie "everyone," he meant Jen as well.

Feeling like a nervous junior high kid asking a girl to dance, Chris had no clue what to do or say. They made eye contact and he wasn't sure what would be worse—going over to talk to her or her coming to talk to him. Finally he pulled himself together and told himself to just act normal. He went over, flashed a smile, and said "hey." She flashed a smile right back and said "hey yourself." Then Eddie grabbed him by the shoulder because he just *had* to show him something. He looked at Jen and walked away.

For the next hour, Chris drank his Buds and laughed with his friends, while constantly checking out of the corner of his eye to see if Jen was looking at him. He wasn't sure whether it was coincidence or on purpose, but Jen was as far away from Chris as possible while still being able to stay in the conversation. While Chris was sweating Jen was beyond cool and Chris never noticed her glances. However, one of Einstein's unknown laws of physics is that boys and girls plus copious amounts of alcohol equal a lack of inhibitions. The law was in full effect after two hours.

Chris had just finished another Bud and was at the bar looking to grab Gus' attention. Suddenly, he noticed himself right next to Jen, who had her back towards him. One part of Chris just wanted to grab the beer and slide away undetected. The other part hoped that Gus would never see him and he could hangout there for an hour. While Chris debated the pros and cons of each, someone said something funny and Jen roared with laughter, leaning back and falling right into Chris. The moment called for something, anything to be said.

"Are you trying to get my attention?" Her head slowly looked up and her eyes met his. A deep grin formed on her face as she turned around to face him.

"Ha! Said the guy who has been too afraid to talk to me all night."

"I didn't see you strolling over to say hello!" Jen straightened up and was now leaning next to him at the bar.

"That's because you are the guy so you should be the one to come over."

"That is such a cop out, but I'm going to let it go on the account that you are very drunk."

"I'm not very drunk, just slightly buzzed," she said with a slur.

"It's official, you have zero credibility."

"Should you even be talking to me? I wouldn't want to get you in trouble," she hinted sarcastically.

"Oh wow. Hysterical! You're the one who said we couldn't talk anymore!" Jen's face softened.

"Looks like I hit a nerve." Chris immediately tried to steer the conversation back into light heartedness.

"So I'm going to assume you miss me tremendously and cry every night thinking about me." Jen laughed and said,

"Yes Mr. Marcum. You are absolutely correct. I was going to jump out a window, but I didn't want you throwing yourself into my coffin at the funeral."

"Are you kidding me? A girl killing herself over me? That would be a career highlight. Hell I'd even put that on my resume."

"You probably would, sicko!" They both laughed. A couple of beats went by before Jen spoke again.

"So ahhh, I hear you're still with Val."

"You hear?"

"I hear things." She said nodding her head.

"Well you're right. Still going strong." He punctuated the sentence by making a popping sound with his lips. They both took a drink before continuing.

"Are things at least better?"

"Yeah. I had to do some groveling. Some major groveling actually. However like my Dad always says, things eventually go back to normal."

"I'm shocked she isn't with you tonight."

"Well, I told her not to eat a second hot dog at Shea, but she wouldn't listen."

"Doesn't she know that you're always right?"

"Seriously. I should make that into a t-shirt and just point to it whenever she disagrees with me." Jen let out a booming laugh and Chris felt those familiar pangs again.

"Sooo, since I think I know you really well, I think you are miserable without me. Am I right?" She was now semi-leaning on his left shoulder and looking dead in his eyes with a mischievous smile. Chris paused and thought about what he was going to say before quietly saying,

"Honestly, yeah." The smile left Jen's face immediately and she took a step back. An awkward pause hung in the air.

"I don't know why I just blurted that out, but I do. I do miss you, a lot."

"Ok, if we're playing the truth game then I'll admit the same thing." She had spoken the words as soft as possible while still being heard over the din. Consciously or subconsciously they had moved closer. Their eyes were locked on each other, their lips pulling them in and Chris desperately wanted to wrap his arms around her waist.

"What if I said I wanted to be with you?" "I'd say it was the alcohol talking," Jen half giggled.

"Seriously. What if I said I wanted to be with you instead of Val?"

"I'd say this would be a conversation for another day when your head is clear and I'm not spilling my drink." By this point her face was as close to his without touching.

"The thing is I have had this conversation with you about a million times already in my head. I just don't know why I never actually said it to you."

"I know why. You are in love with another girl."

"Named Jen." She took a step back and looked at him, unsure of what to say next.

Despite the shouts of drunkenness around them, the music coming out of the jukebox, and Gus screaming to hear whatever order was being shouted, it was dead silent in the space between Chris and Jen. They were in their own private universe and for that one second things were perfect. She stared at him, not saying anything and Chris took this as an opportunity to swing for the fences. If there was ever going to be a movie moment where he got the girl, this would be it. He stared into her deep blue eyes and in their reflection he saw it all. A kiss followed by another and another followed by a date and a proposal and a wedding and a lifetime of happiness. They would grow old together and the only thing he would need was the knowledge that she would always be there by his side. A huge smile came over his face and he could see one appearing on hers as well. Instinctively his right hand reached out for hers and they stood there, holding hands wearing goofy smiles. Here goes nothing he thought to himself.

"Jen, listen to me."

## "CHRISTOPHER MARCUM!"

Chris turned around to see Valerie standing there, with murder in her eyes. The crowd had spread as if commanded by Moses and everyone stared in rapt attention. In shock he dropped his Bud and the bottle shattered across the floor.

"You piece of shit! How dare you! The first chance you get you go right back to her?"

"Val, listen to me." She cut him off immediately.

"No Chris you listen to me! You are going to decide right now who you want to be with and then no matter what I'm going to kick this whore's ass!" Valerie's face was beet red with anger. Jen didn't want to get involved, however between the drinks and being insulted she was sufficiently pissed off enough to say something.

"Excuse me? Who do you think you're talking to?"

"I thought you were just a slut, but you're obviously a dumb slut as well." The girls stepped forward and things were about to get out of control. Chris jumped between them with his arms extended and said,

"No one is fighting anyone." Valerie, with steam almost visibly rising from her head, knocked his arm away and got right in his face.

"Chris listen to me right now. I am going outside and into my car. If you want a future with me you will get in the car. If you want to be with……*her*…..you will stay here. Either way this fence riding bullshit has gone on long enough. Grow some balls and make a decision."

Val punctuated her statement by screaming "bitch" at the top of her lungs at Jen and stomped out the bar. Somehow it seemed like ten thousand people had crowded into Leo's and were watching their own private reality show come to life. Ignoring the eyes, Chris turned around to face Jen.

"Jen."

He looked right at her and once again saw everything in her eyes. This time the vision was even clearer. He could see the children they would have, the house they were going to live in. He could feel the emotion rising up inside and was never more certain of anything in his entire life. Jen was the girl for him. The out he had been looking for had now appeared like an early birthday present. Now it was time to make it happen. Sure Valerie would be crushed, but he had to do what was right. Jen was everything that was right.

She stared back at him and waited.

He opened up his mouth, but nothing else came out. While his mouth hung open, his heart was screaming do it! Do it now! This was it and yet nothing more came out of his mouth. He wanted to tell Jen how she was the one for him, how he knew since that random day at the jewelers and how his friends even recognized it. And incredibly, he still couldn't say a word. Instead, he stood there like a dumb mute, continuing to linger on in silence. The air was electric and goose bumps rained up and down his arms. Suddenly, he felt like his very essence was drained from his body. His shoulders slumped and his view grew blurry. Christopher Marcum took one more glance at Jennifer Polanski, the girl he knew was the one. He took off his Mets hat and ran his fingers through his hair. Jen's face began to shatter as she realized what was about to happen. Christopher Marcum turned around and silently walked out of Leo's.

# CHAPTER 21

## May 19, 2000

Sometimes Chris felt as if he was outside his body, watching someone else make his decisions. The days immediately after Labor Day weekend were, from the outside, just like any other ones. Wake up, go to work, teach, come home, eat, see Valerie, go to sleep. Rinse, wash, repeat, and continue the cycle the next day. Keep to the script and do not under any circumstance ad lib. In his mind, the last decision he made maybe wasn't the one his heart wanted yet it was the right one. Leaving Leo's and climbing into Valerie's car was the right thing to do. What's done is done and he was fine if he didn't think about it. However there were times at night, maybe a half hour before going to bed that he would randomly think about things and his stomach would churn. Momentary thoughts of Jen would be vanquished as soon as they formed in his mind. He made his choice and now he had to live with it.

A month later, Chris decided to buy the engagement ring, figuring there was no use waiting when he already decided whom he was going to spend the rest of his life with. Chris asked his father to come with him and together they picked out what Chris thought Valerie wanted, a carat and a half with a princess cut. Leaving the store his dad stopped and put his arm around his son.

"I'm proud of you. Your mother and I both love Valerie."

"Thanks Dad. I love her too."

Chris planned on asking her to marry him on Sunday, October 11. The day before though, he was going to a ballgame. And not just any ballgame. Sammy came across three upper deck left field tickets to Game Four of the National League Divisional Series: the New York Mets versus the Arizona Diamondbacks. If the Mets won, they clinched the series and would advance to the National League Championship Series. When Chris told Sammy what he planned on doing, Sammy responded by telling him to consider the ticket a "farewell gift," which got plenty of laughs from Richie, when Chris told him in the car on the way to Shea Stadium. It was a beautiful Saturday afternoon in Queens, and the game was tied going into the bottom of the tenth. Chris had spent most of the game screaming his head off, especially when Armando Benitez allowed the Diamondbacks to score the tying run in the top of the eighth inning. His voice wavered when Mets catcher Todd Pratt stepped up to the plate in the bottom of the tenth, one out and the score tied at 3-3. The count was 1-0 when Todd hit a very high, very deep fly ball to dead center field. Fifty-six thousand people rose to their feet as the center fielder for Arizona, Steve Finley raced back to the wall and jumped. For a couple of seconds, Shea was dead quiet as everyone waited to see if it was a home run or if Finley caught the ball. After what seemed like an eternity Steve put his hands on his hips in either dejection, just plain shock, or probably both. Home run! The Mets had won the series! Chris was out of his mind happy and wound up at the bottom of a crazy dog pile. The bruises and a lost voice were worth it.

The next day, the eleventh of October, was another beautiful Sunday afternoon in New York. Chris picked up Valerie early and took her out for Sunday brunch at one of the finer Staten Island restaurants, the Marina Cafe. He told the owner a couple of days earlier of his plan and everything were arranged perfectly. There was only one slight problem—he had no voice. Over three hours of screaming and yelling had reduced his voice to a whisper and he was concerned that Valerie wouldn't be able to hear the actual proposal.

From the moment he picked her up he was a nervous wreck. When they arrived, he excused himself to go the bathroom and instead went over to check with the owner. The maitre'd told Chris he had everything covered; don't worry about a thing. On the outside Chris did his best to maintain an easy breezy demeanor. On the inside however he couldn't wait until the moment came, when they received their dessert. Time seemed to slow to a crawl, especially when Valerie took forever to decide what she wanted. They enjoyed their waffles, eggs, and bacon and Val talked away without a care in the world. When the waiter came over with a dessert menu he made sure to keep a straight face while Val once again hemmed and hawed. It took a couple of minutes before she chose gelatos for the two of them.

Chris could feel his body temperature rise. The events of the past three months, specifically the last one had all led him to this point in time. He started to believe he had made the correct decision.

Valerie's food came out on a silver serving dish, and was placed gently down in front of her. She went to remove the top when Chris took her hand and with all his might managed to say the following aloud.

"Valerie, we have been through a lot since the moment we met. Our first conversation you hated me, and I managed to dig and dig my way into your heart. You are the most important person in my life and I couldn't imagine living a moment without you by my side. You're everything I could possibly want in a partner and a best friend." Chris slid out of his chair and got down on his right knee.

"Valerie Carreon, will you marry me?" With his left hand he removed the cover off the tray to reveal an engagement ring.

The tears arrived from the first sentence and Valerie tried to compose herself enough to give an answer.

"Oh Chris, oh Chris oh Chris. I love you, you know I love you." Chris smiled.

"I know you love me. I love you too." The smile stayed on his face as he watched Valerie pick up the ring and rotate it around her thin fingers.

"Val you still haven't answered." She looked down at him, leaning on his left leg, anxiously awaiting her next words, words he did not see coming.

"I just don't know." Chris looked up at her dumbfounded. Once again he found himself in a most embarrassing moment in front of a large crowd of people.

"I don't understand."

"Chris a month ago you were trying to decide who to be with…"

"And I made my choice."

"Yes but don't you think I still haven't gotten over that. Did you ever think how hard it was for me? The pain and the humiliation?"

"Val I know and I'm sorry. I'm trying to atone by…"

"By buying an engagement ring? You really think getting married would solve all our problems."

"I do because I know that I made the right choice." Valerie looked around and saw the eyes of the entire restaurant on them. She stood up and said,

"Let's continue this outside. I don't want to give these people a dinner and a show." Chris dutifully obeyed and followed Valerie outside. They walked in silence until they stepped out and felt the sun.

"Val I can't believe you're doing this. Isn't this what you wanted? Aren't I who you want to be with?" He said with tremendous exasperation.

"Yes, yes yes. Of course you are. Again I just don't think now is the time to be getting engaged." The two of them stared at each other, not saying a word. Finally Valerie stepped towards him and wrapped her arms around his waist. Looking up at him she said.

"Trust me, I have dreamt of this moment for a long time. I also know first hand what it's like when a marriage goes bad. I don't want to be my mother Chris. I don't want to be picking up the pieces when I'm forty."

"Why are you so afraid?"

"Do I really have to answer that question?" Her remark scorched him and he instinctively pulled away.

"I know I was wrong. I know I screwed up. I'm sorry."

"Do me a favor. Keep the ring in a safe place and wait. You'll know when the time is right."

"How will I know if I'm already 0 for 1?"

"Because you love me and I love you. I love you enough to tell you to wait. I love you enough to endure your stupidity. All I'm asking now is for you to wait a little bit longer. Can you do that for me?" Chris looked at her. He knew she was right.

"Of course I can babe. I can do anything you want. I love you."

"I love you too."

"Should we go inside and finish our dessert?"

"Umm I'm pretty sure I don't want to go back in to that crowded room again. Would you mind if I stayed in the car while you paid the check?"

"Fair enough."

"Pook?"

"Yeah Val?"

"I love you."

"I love you too."

Chris went inside, embarrassed as hell, walked up to the maitre'd, handed him his Discover card and asked for the check.

In the months that followed Chris knew Valerie was right. He really believed an engagement ring was a problem solver, instead of actually trying to deal with the problem at hand, which was his heart. Everyday he proved to Val that his intentions were true and everyday she began to trust him a little bit more. Whenever the subject of Jen came up, Chris would just say he was dumb and had no rational explanation. If she persisted Chris would always fall back on how, when push came to shove he left Leo's with her, not Jen. Eventually Val let it go, to her later regret.

The following May of 2000 Chris had a bounce in his step as he locked his classroom door. Not only was it Friday, it was a picture perfect Friday and it was quitting time. Chris left work the moment he was legally allowed to, 2:45pm and drove out to Manhattan. Due to Don's initial connections and Valerie's hard work the previous summer, she had been offered a job at Merrill Lynch after graduating college in January. She loved her job, her commute, her clothes and everything else that went along with being in the "real world." Including the paycheck which was immediately larger than his. Once again, things felt right and once again Chris decided to make a scene in front of a bunch of strangers.

He parked the car in a garage and lingered outside her building for a couple of hours, waiting for her to leave. Things would have been easier if he knew exactly when she was leaving, but with her job the time varied. He alternated between leaning against a wall acting casual and slowly walking circles around the front. Finally, at 5:15PM Valerie stepped out of the building with a couple of co-workers. She was saying her goodbyes, oblivious to the fact that her boyfriend was standing eight feet away.

"Valerie Carreon?" Hearing her full name being said out loud stopped her in her tracks and she scanned the area looking for the voice. To her surprise Chris stepped towards her.

"Chris what are you…"

"You were right. You were right when we first met and I wrecked your truck. You were right about Eric. You were right about my stupidity. You were even right about waiting. Bottom line Val is I have come to the realization that you are always right. So I hope and pray that this time the timing is right…" Chris kneeled down and took a box out of his pocket. Valerie put her hand over her mouth and started to cry.

"Valerie Carreon this time I'm not going to give you a speech. I love you. For the second time, will you marry me?"

"Yes, yes, of course I will!" Chris took the familiar ring and slid it onto her left hand. He stood up and they kissed each other repeatedly.

Her co-workers, who had stopped to see what was happening, along with some random New Yorkers clapped and cheered as the newly engaged couple wrapped their arms around each other. Valerie squealed in joy and did a little two step.

"I always had faith in you Christopher."

The newly engaged couple drove over to Valerie's house first so her mom could see the ring and celebrate, and then they went over to the Marcum's. Chris' mom was extremely pleased and they started to discuss the various details of the big day. His dad gave them both a big hug and officially welcomed Valerie to the family. Eric came over and congratulated the both of them, although Chris detected a bit of a smirk when Eric hugged him. Maybe it was just in his head.

Valerie wanted a spring wedding, and they decided rather quickly to attempt to get a May date next year. Despite all the drama, his mom's prediction had only been off by a year.

# CHAPTER 22

## May 7, 2001

The next year progressed rather quickly. Valerie had ultimate authority on the entire wedding, and Chris couldn't care less. The only things Chris wanted a say on were the wedding hall, the menu, and having a Mass instead of a quick wedding ceremony. Valerie at first put up a minor fuss, yet Chris stood firm, insisting the Mass was important to him. Other than that, she would just show him what they were getting or doing and Chris gave his nodding seal of approval.

At the start of 2001, Chris was twenty-four and half way through his third year of teaching. He couldn't believe how fast time was going, and how comfortable he found himself inside the classroom. Through one of his fellow history teachers, Chris developed a contact in the publishing world about an untitled book Chris had been playing with for awhile. Actually what he had was three short stories with no common link, although he was certain eventually he would find one and presto, he'd have his novel. While no promises were made, Allison Wullford, an editor at Starlight Publishing believed Chris' idea was interesting and based on some writing samples thought he had a legitimate shot. Conversely, Val was moving up at Merrill Lynch. Between their combined salaries and his parents' generous wedding gift, which they said they could get before the wedding, they had more than enough to start looking for their first house.

Originally they limited their search to Staten Island, until a friend of Val's who lived in Bergen Beach, Brooklyn told her they should check out her area. It took some convincing before Chris became open to the idea and they started to look around. Two months before the wedding a realtor showed them a listing which looked beautiful on paper. The house was a semi attached, partial brick, and in need of some maintenance. When they arrived Valerie began squeezing his hand, and the more they walked around seeing the different rooms the more they became convinced. The price was a little higher than they wanted to go, regardless; this was the house they were looking for. It had three bedrooms and a semi-finished basement, for their future kids to go crazy in. Sure his commute would now involve crossing a bridge back to Staten Island, and they were also moving further away than his parents would like, but it was still only a half hour away. Valerie was overjoyed when Chris agreed and the wheels were put in motion.

Lawyers, papers, and money all exchanged hands on Wednesday, May 4. Since they were so close to the wedding they agreed while they would move all the furniture in, they themselves would move in after they were married. From his parent's basement to his own house in Brooklyn, not bad for a twenty-four year old soon to be married man.

The night before the wedding, Sammy took Chris out to Leo's for "one last drink." Sammy jokingly said how it was only a couple of years ago when they were trying to see who would throw up first. Now they were the old men at the bar, nursing their drinks and making comments about the "punk kids." The two best friends sat there with their Buds and watched the Mets game. Chris was in need of a refill and signaled Gus over. The man was already running ragged and the night had just begun. He came over and in one breath said,

"Listen Chris your friend told me the big news and I'm all alone here tonight. Tell you what, considering you guys are loyal customers drinks are on the house. The only thing is that if you want a beer you have to go get it yourself." Chris and Sammy let out a whoop and high fived each other.

"Hey hey hey relax. This isn't permanent. One night only. And don't be pigs either!"

The combination of Chris getting married the next day, and not wanting to take advantage of a generous offer kept their visits behind the bar to only a couple. Even still, they both enjoyed the looks from the other patrons whenever they slid over the bar and grabbed what they needed. One kid who might have just turned twenty one thought this applied to everyone and started to hoist himself over before Sammy put his hand on his shoulder and gave him a friendly suggestion to sit down. Smartly, the kid did what he was told.

Chris had known Sammy for what seemed like forever. He probably knew more about Chris than anyone, including Valerie. He was the friend Chris could go to for an honest opinion and Sammy never failed to give it, whether you wanted to hear it or not. After a couple of hours and a very slight buzz Sammy decided to ask a question he had debated bringing up for the last couple of weeks.

"You almost done with your bottle?"

"Yeah Sam, but I think this is it for me. I'm pretty sure Val wouldn't want a hung-over groom waiting for her at the altar."

"I'm pretty sure she wouldn't even realize it. All eyes will be on her right?"

"Have you *met* Valerie?" Chris said with a laugh. "She'll notice if I'm missing a cufflink."

"Yeah, good point."

Sammy twirled his bottle with his thumb and forefinger on the bar. Chris could tell something was on his mind and was pretty sure he was just trying to frame the question correctly.

"This is kind of a messed up question. And I don't mean this in a bad way." Chris cut him off by saying,

"Whenever someone starts off saying that the next words are never good." Sammy chuckled and nodded his head.

"Yeah I guess you're right. And I probably wouldn't ask Richie or Eddie this question, but we've always been direct with each other right?"

"Always." The boys clinked beers.

"So that said... are you sure Val's the one?" Chris did a drunken double take before he laughed.

"Wow! That's a hell of a thing to say to a guy the night before his wedding!"

"Well I don't mean it as an insult, but I've been wondering. And I've been wondering if you've been wondering. So have you been wondering?"

"Say wondering again." Sammy laughed and repeated the word.

"Sam, I'd say you are my best friend correct?"

"You are correct sir." They clinked beers again.

"So, when you say something like this to me, I know you're not saying it to be a dick. You really are serious."

"Of course."

"Can I ask you a question?"

"Are you avoiding answering mine?"

"No, but mine is just as legit."

"Okay I'll answer yours and then you answer mine."

"Deal. Do you like Valerie?" Sam leaned back and almost fell off his stool.

"What kind of question is that?"

"It's just as legit as yours. Do you like Valerie?"

"Do you mean like as in do I want to sleep with her?"

"No. Well, you can answer that one too. I mean do you like being around her?"

"First things first. She's a great looking girl, but I could never. And second, of course I like her, I like her because you love her and I know we're all going to be together for a very long time."

"What if that wasn't the case, would you still like her?" Sammy took a gulp and looked at Chris quizzically.

"I'm not following."

"You're saying you like her sort of because you have to."

"No. Not because I have to. I really do like her."

"Do you think she's the one for me?"

"Ah Ha! I know you better than you know yourself!" Sammy punctuated his statement by smacking the bar.

"What does that mean?"

"I'm going to cut straight to the chase. Jen. You like her. Hell, Stephanie gave me the impression that you could have been in love with her." Chris immediately put the kibosh on furthering that part of the conversation.

"Whatever I was or wasn't is long in the past and that's where it needs to stay."

"Bro seriously if you feel this way you need…"

"No. I don't need to do anything. This is reality; this is how things played out. I made my choice and that's the end of that."

"But if you do…"

"But I don't."

"But if you…"

"I'm going to keep cutting you off. Listen to me. I appreciate the concern but let it go."

"Yeah?"

"Yeah."

"Whatever you want." The two of them clinked beers one more time.

A couple of hours later Sam threw a twenty into the tip jar and the boys said goodbye to their favorite bartender. While they walked over to their cars Chris said,

"Thanks Sam. Thanks for taking me out tonight and even though it's an awkward subject, thanks for bringing up you know who."

"It had to be said. I'm just happy you're happy." The boys hugged, hopped in their respective cars and drove off into the night.

The next day was like a tornado. It seemed like seconds had passed since he woke up and now there he was standing at the altar of Saint Clare's Church, waiting for his bride to come down the aisle. Chris watched as the wedding party, which consisted of Sammy with Stephanie, Eddie with her friend Rose from college, and Richie with Bianca, a girl she had met at Merrill Lynch all came down the aisle. Her cousin, Clarissa, was the maid of honor while Chris stood at the altar with Eric as his best man.

When the organ struck its first note the crowd turned their heads towards the door. Flashes went off everywhere as Valerie took her first steps down the aisle. Valerie, who was being given away by her mother, was radiant. Her dark hair cascaded from her veil down like water to her shoulders, and her face beamed with happiness and tears. Chris was having a difficult time keeping his composure as well and Eric placed his hand on his shoulder and gave a reassuring grip.

When it came time to exchange vows, Chris did his best to hold his composure while tears trickled down Valerie's face. Chris smiled and told her she was going to ruin her makeup and she laughed. They said "I do" and Father Mark told Chris he could now kiss his bride. They kissed, stopped, and kissed again which produced a raucous roar from the packed assembly.

The rest of the day was a whirlwind affair. The reception was out in New Jersey and the newly wed couple was very thankful the event was being video taped because they were sure they missed ninety percent of what happened. They could remember dancing to their wedding song, Faith Hill's "The Way You Love Me" and they laughed when Richie knocked over Eddie to catch the garter. The highlight however, at least in Chris' eyes was the toast his brother gave.

*"For the three percent who don't know who I am, my name is Eric and I am the younger and better looking brother of the groom. I don't want to rattle off some heart felt clichés I found online. I'm sure whoever originally wrote them would probably say them much much better. I'm just going to speak from the heart. Chris, let me start off by saying how much I look up to you. How much I respect the decisions you've made and the life you are carving out for yourself. Growing up I knew you always had my back, and despite the bumpy moments that all brothers go through I know there is nothing you wouldn't do for me and there is nothing I wouldn't do for you.*

*Now Valerie. Valerie, Valerie, Valerie. Thank you for turning my brother into a man. Thank you for cleaning up his act. He was kind of a mess before you stepped into his life, or should I say before he crashed into yours. I'll never forget the gift you gave me, you have no idea how much it meant to me.*

*In closing let me say I look forward to spending the rest of our lives growing even closer and sharing in all the triumphs we are certain to have. Welcome to the family Val and congratulations Chris, you sure picked a great girl. Cheers."*

Before they knew it they were saying goodbye to their guests. Some, such as his parents and her mom and Don were staying overnight at the hotel down the street. The newly wed couple let the merriment continue down at the hotel bar while they decided to head up to their suite. When the elevator reached their floor, Chris scooped up Valerie and carried her to their room. Life was perfect, as perfect as it was ever going to get.

# CHAPTER 23

## Summer/Fall 2001

It wouldn't be fair to say Valerie changed. The Valerie Chris married was the same girl he crashed into four years earlier. The same girl who told him no the first time he proposed. The girl he carried into their honeymoon suite the night of their wedding was the same girl he woke up to the next day. The problem was Chris never changed. He was the same guy who left Leo's without knowing why. He was the same guy who told Valerie what she wanted to hear, instead of dealing with everything swimming inside his head. These problems were significant albeit problems that could be worked out. However there were two events within their first year of marriage that in the end would overwhelm Chris.

The first event happened on July 11th. Because he was on vacation, Chris kept to his usual routine of sleeping till 11AM. Everyday Val would wake him up before going to work and everyday Chris would say goodbye and return back to bed. In his mind it would be a sin to leave a king size bed at 7AM if you didn't have to. One random Tuesday in July, Val woke up for work and Chris heard the usual morning sounds, his wife shuffling down the wood floor in the hallway leading to the bathroom. The shower faucet squeaking awake. He heard those noises everyday and they were simply part of the background, to be incorporated into whatever dream he was having. On this particular morning he rolled onto his stomach and was in the process of falling back asleep when he heard a sound that scared the hell out of him. Valerie had let out a high pitched shriek, which caused Chris to immediately throw back the blankets and sprint towards the bathroom. He opened the door and saw Valerie sitting on the toilet shaking, while she stared at a home pregnancy test. She looked up at Chris and showed him the thin blue line. He stared at the plastic, unable to comprehend what exactly he was looking at. Valerie, seeing his confusion, picked up the cardboard box resting on the sink, turned it over and handed it to him.

They were having a baby!

Chris tried to say something but nothing would come out. Finally he just grabbed Val and they kissed several times before embracing.

"Can you believe this?"

"I-I'm-I" Valerie was so excited she ignored whatever Chris was trying to say and started rambling.

"I missed my period in June and figured it was due to leftover wedding stress. No big deal. Then last week came and went. That got me thinking so two days ago I went out and bought a test but I was nervous so I put it in the medicine cabinet. Then, this morning I had a dream that was so vivid I woke up convinced it was real."

"Yeah?"

"We were at a Mets game with our son. I couldn't see his face but I knew he was ours."

"Wow."

"The rest of the dream is kind of hazy but it was real enough for me to open up the medicine cabinet and see what's what."

"Incredible."

"Christopher are you going to keep on giving me one word answers?" He had sat back down on the toilet and looked up at her.

"I'm sorry Val. I'm just a little shocked."

"Are you at least happy?" She said with a hint of concern that snapped him out of his fog.

"Of course I am! Of course I am. Val I love you. This is phenomenal. I'm going to be a father. I'm going to be a dad. A dad."

"My pookie, the daddy! Awwwwww!" Val grabbed his hands, kissed him hard on the mouth and threw her arms around his neck. Chris couldn't breathe and that was the least of his concerns.

Being the professional that she was, Val still went to work, while for the first time Chris couldn't return back to the king size bed. When he kissed her goodbye he sat in the middle of the living room and prayed simply for a healthy child. Anytime you get the news that you're having a baby it's a great day, nevertheless Chris always assumed this moment would come a year or two down the line, not less than two months after his wedding day.

He meandered into the kitchen in desperate need of caffeine. He grabbed his mug from the cabinet, the milk and the sugar like he was on autopilot. His mind was flooded with too many thoughts and as a result he was unable to maintain a clear head. Chris sat the coffee maker down and leaned against the counter. He drank half the mug in one gulp, allowing his insides to be flooded. He needed a jolt and then he would be able to think. A couple of seconds they all came roaring in at once. How would they afford this? Sure between the two of them they were banking some good coin but did he want Valerie to work after she had their son or daughter? His parents or her mom could help out however it wasn't like they were living five minutes away. On a good day they were a good half hour to forty five minutes away. If he wanted Val to stay home he was going to have to make more money. And if that meant leaving his job then so be it.

Valerie had made an appointment and three days later the two of them were at the doctor's where he confirmed that yes, they were indeed having a baby. It's one thing to learn from a blue strip, quite another to hear it from a professional's lips and Chris had to sit down and collect himself for a second. Now it was real.

They agreed to wait past the first trimester to make sure everything was all right before they told anyone. Of course they couldn't keep this to themselves and had to tell someone. Valerie told her mom, who passed out on the couch. Chris drove out to Staten Island and went for beers with Sammy at Leo's. They settled into their usual spots and Chris ordered the first round. Sammy knew something was on his mind, but never in a million years expected Chris to tell him he was going to be a father. At first, per Sammy's honest nature, he yelled at Chris for spoiling the post wedding glow. But after thirty seconds of that he reversed fields and congratulated Chris for being the first guy in the crew to be a dad. Sammy joked about how his marriage forced him to commit to Steph and now she was going to want a baby right after the wedding. No matter, they toasted, drank a couple more, and drove home in the wee hours of the morning.

The first people they told after Val completed the first trimester were Chris's parents, who they drove over to see one Sunday morning. They gave the expected reaction of shock and happiness. His mom told them whenever they needed someone to watch the baby, or just needed a break they should not hesitate to ask. The girls continued to talk in the kitchen while Chris and his dad plopped down on the couch in the den.

"So do you think you're ready for this?"

"I don't think I have a choice now, do I?" Chris said with a sort of fake laugh.

"Well no, I guess not. Regardless, do you think you're ready?"

"I'm not going to lie, this isn't the best timing."

"If there is one thing I've learned, it's that there is no perfect time to do anything. The key to a good marriage and a happy life is to make the best of whatever life gives you."

"To be honest I'm kind of scared."

"Holy shit Chris, if you weren't at the very least nervous you'd have a bigger problem on your hands. Hell you and Eric at times still give me the shakes." Chris laughed and said,

"Where is Eric? I wanted to tell him in person."

"He's out with what's her face."

"Another girlfriend?"

"I'm not even sure. I have a hard time keeping track these days."

"Should I admit a little jealousy?"

"Nah, you're in a much better place. Wife, house and a baby on the way, who's better than you?"

"Thanks dad."

The first event, while slightly overwhelming due to the suddenness, was a good one. The second event, which took place two months later in September, was the equivalent of a tsunami wave crashing over Chris' psyche.

Sammy was off that Tuesday morning from the firehouse and had plans to go over and help his dad paint the garage. Sammy was a creature of habit and followed his routine of Frosted Flakes and the local news when he saw an airplane crash into the North Tower of the World Trade Center. Sammy called his dad, told him he had to go to work, grabbed his wallet and drove to the station. He tried calling Stephanie on the Verrazano Bridge to let her know what he was doing but one of their lines was down and the call went straight to voice mail. Sammy left a brief message, letting her know what he was doing and that he'd call her when he was coming home.

Chris was in the middle of first period when Mike, the math teacher next door charged in and said he had to talk to him. Chris paused, put his papers down and followed him outside, upon which Mike informed him the country was under attack. When he walked back inside the classroom he tried to stay calm and return back to his lesson. Six minutes later the principal came over the loudspeaker and instructed all teachers to put on their televisions. From that point on, Chris tried to keep his sophomore class (and to be honest himself) from panicking. Valerie worked at the World Financial Building across the street and Chris was scared to death. Fortunately, after the first plane hit she called him on her office phone to let him know that she was leaving right away. When she knew more details she would call, which took forever because cell phones were down for most of the morning and early afternoon.

Chris stayed at school well past 4PM, making sure everyone was getting picked up and talked with whoever needed talking to. Keeping busy meant not worrying about Valerie, who, even though he knew left immediately still hadn't called. Finally around 5:30pm he heard his name over the PA, telling him he had a phone call.

"Chris?"

"Oh my God Val are you okay?"

"Yeah, I mean no I'm not but yeah I'm home and I'm alive." Chris felt a lump in his throat and took a deep breath. Now wasn't the time.

"Oh thank God. Thank God thank God thank God."

"My clothes are ruined and my feet are throbbing but yeah I'm alive."

"Thank God. I've been out of my mind here. How did you know I was here?"

"Called your mom. She told me you guys talked earlier and you said you were staying till the kids left."

"Yeah a bunch of us...."

"Listen Chris has Stephanie called you?

"No. Why?"

"She said Sammy called and told her he was going into work."

"What?"

"I said Steph said Sammy went into work today."

"And?"

"And she hasn't heard from him and she asked me to ask you if you talked to him yet."

"No I haven't."

"Well if he calls tell him to call home."

"I will and Val I love you so much."

"The baby and I love you too."

"Okay I'm leaving work now see you as soon as I can."

"Babe the bridge is closed."

"What?"

"The Verrazano Bridge is closed. You're going to have to sleep at your mom's."

"Okay I'll call her and the moment that bridge opens I'll be home."

"Okay I'm going to go next door and stay with the Clavell's."

"If you need anything call either my phone or my mom's house."

"I will. I love you Chris."

"I love you too Val."

"Call me tonight."

"I will."

"Bye."

"Bye."

When Chris hung up the phone, he grew angry with himself. The entire time Chris has been thinking of Val and their unborn baby but not his best friend? His conscious started doing the good cop/bad cop game. What's wrong with him? What kind of friend are you? No, it's not your fault; you didn't know if he was working. The back and forth continued for awhile until he made a conscious decision to not think dumb thoughts. Sammy was fine and they would go to Leo's on Friday so he could tell him all about today.

Chris arrived at his parents' house twenty minutes later. They ran towards each other and embraced, not saying anything, just squeezing each other tight. On a lark Chris asked if Sammy had called their house and his mom said no he hadn't. Chris grabbed the phone and called Steph.

"Hello?" she answered with underlying panic.

"Stephanie? It's Chris." At once Stephanie's voice broke and he could hear her struggling to get the words out.

"Chris….. Sammy went into…. work today. He was off, but he went to Manhattan," she sobbed.

"Have you heard from him?" Again Chris could hear her voice cracking.

"Not yet."

"Do you want company?"

"I'm at his parent's house. My parents are here too, but if you wanted to, yeah you could come."

"I'll be right over."

Chris looked at his mom and she could tell by his face things weren't good. Without saying a word he climbed into the car and drove over. The six of them spent the entire night together and any time the phone rang they huddled around the receiver. Instead of hearing Sammy's voice it was always a concerned family member or friend looking for an update. This was torture, plain and simple.

For two agonizing days they waited to hear something, anything, regarding Sam. Stephanie was on the verge of a nervous breakdown and to be honest so was everyone else. Finally, a little after four o'clock in the afternoon the phone rang. Sammy's dad reached it first and within seconds his face had contorted into something inhuman. Everyone rushed over to him as he kept repeating the phrase, "uh huh" over and over. Stephanie began shrieking and for the rest of his life Chris was haunted by the sound of Stephanie screaming, "What happened? What happened?"

The wake went by in a blur, and the only thing Chris really remembered were how the uniformed men came over and offered their condolences and admiration for how great a guy Sammy was. Stephanie sat in the front of the room, in a zombie-like trance. Every once in a while she would cry and someone would take her hand and bring her out of the room. Sam's parents seemed to age twenty years overnight and Chris spent most of his time attending to the three of them. He found the best way to cope was to concentrate on someone else's pain and ignore your own.

Chris managed to keep the straight face throughout the wake and the funeral, although he almost lost it when he gave Sam's eulogy. He knew if he looked up and saw the grief inside the pews he wouldn't be able to continue.

*"Sammy wasn't just a friend. He wasn't just a best friend. He was my brother. Whenever something had to be said, Sammy would be the one to say it. If there was a problem Sam fixed it. If someone was hurting, Sammy hurt along side of them. And if there was someone in danger, Sam was the first person to jump in. He died*

*doing the one thing he's always dreamt of doing and I couldn't be prouder. I love you Sam, we all love you and we will all never forget you."*

Chris stepped off the altar and was greeted by Sam's parents and Stephanie who threw their arms around him. Despite the tears all around him Chris kept his composure. In fact he kept everything inside until the cemetery, when they started laying roses on the coffin. When it came time for Chris to step forward and drop his rose the dam broke. He couldn't take it anymore and a tidal wave of pain and emotion washed over him. Thank God Valerie was there. There was no way he could function on his own. Strangely enough, this was the first time Valerie ever saw Chris cry. She had seen tears before but she had never truly seen him weep. His best friend, his confessor, the guy who could truly say he knew Chris inside and out was gone, and there was nothing he could do to fill the void.

That night they decided to just go to sleep early. The room was quiet and Valerie knew Chris' mind was on overload. She also knew he didn't like to talk about what was inside his head. She stroked his hair while Chris rested his head on her chest. After awhile Val felt it was a good time to talk.

"Can I ask you a question?"

"Okay."

"It's a religious question actually."

"Shoot."

"Why did God allow this to happen?"

Chris remained quiet for a minute. He was going to talk about how God gave everyone free will, and how they were casualties of men who had abused it. He was going to talk about her decision to leave work immediately and how God kept both her and their baby safe. Instead he just lifted his head up so their eyes met.

"I don't know."

She knew not to push it any further and gently brought his head back down. The silence hung like a curtain and Valerie was afraid to peek behind it. He was angry, and for the first time in a long time, Chris went to sleep that night without a simple prayer of thanks.

# CHAPTER 24

## March 5, 2002

The last seven months of the newly married Marcum's life had been stressful. Chris had decided a week after finding out Val was pregnant to sign up for night business courses at the College of Staten Island, starting in the fall. The sooner he started the faster he would be making more money to support the family. There were times Valerie would get upset at Chris for "abandoning" his pregnant wife and Chris would have to calmly re-explain why he was breaking his back. Teaching five days a week combined with going to school at night meant either constantly grading papers or writing his own.

Thankfully for them, both mothers were hands on in helping Valerie when Chris couldn't. Chris didn't know exactly when it happened, but his mother had started to look older. His dad had been on the slippery slope of middle-age for years now, up until point his mom had somehow evaded the march of time.

She was a graceful five foot six and had always kept her body fit. About ten years ago she cut her brunette locks short and it went perfectly with her face. Her green eyes often told everything you needed to know about whatever she was thinking and Chris learned that fast growing up. With her high cheek bones and pouty lips, Chris's dad had married a looker. Today, though, there were hints of gray scattered throughout her brunette forest, and there were hints of wrinkles around her eyes. Then again, for a forty-eight year old woman, she still looked good.

As of right now this would be his last year teaching. If he loaded up on courses the following summer he would have a minor degree in business and a foot in the door, except Chris knew nothing in this life was certain.

They had decided to find out the sex of the baby beforehand, so that way they could get a room ready, and so people would know what to buy. Even though Chris told anyone who asked that he didn't care what was coming out (as long as it was a healthy and happy baby) he really wanted a boy. They could have two or three daughters and that would be great, as long as he had a son as well. When the doctor informed them of what they were looking at on the ultra sound Chris pumped his fist and screamed. He received his wish—they were having a son.

The question now was what to name him. The baby had gone from "baby" to "him" and Chris wanted to now go from "him" to an actual name. Valerie suggested naming him Christopher Junior, but he didn't like the idea of people calling his son junior. She suggested Mark, but Chris pointed out Mark Marcum didn't exactly slide off the tongue. He liked Greg or Matt, but Valerie immediately vetoed those ideas. One night they were flipping through the channels and heard James Earl Jones' voice in one of the commercials. Val commented how she always loved hearing his voice and when Chris, who wasn't paying attention asked who, she said James Earl Jones. Two seconds later Valerie smacked Chris's arm and before he could even ask what he did wrong, she said that's the name!

"Earl? Really?"

"No fool! James!"

Chris fiddled with it in his mind and the name sounded right. James Marcum. He wanted him to have a middle name but for now James was perfect.

The due date was March 9. The closer they came to the date, the more Chris would wake up in the middle of the night, having dreamt that it was time to go. He insisted on packing her bags and kept them by the door for weeks prior. It was a good thing he did.

They had spent Monday night, March 4, in bed watching "The Sixth Sense" on HBO. Val had a hard time getting comfortable, due to the oversized basketball hanging off of her. Chris tried whatever he could to help to no avail. Eventually they fell asleep with the television on and a half eaten bowl of popcorn on Chris' nightstand. At 3:23 in the morning it started.

"Wake up!" Chris shot up like a bolt of lightning.

"I'm awake I'm awake."

"Chris I think this is it!"

"Honey we've had these false starts before. You sure it's time?"

"Yes! This baby is coming and we have to go now!"

Chris knew it would be ridiculous to argue the point with the person who was actually having the baby and hustled Val into the car. The hospital was about fifteen minutes away and most of the ride was a straight away shot. Chris wanted nothing more than to blow through red lights. He always imagined himself racing through intersections before a cop appeared out of nowhere and flashed the sirens. He would then calmly explain the situation and receive an escort for the rest of the way. Chris could vividly see this scenario play out while he showered or daydreamed at work and when he saw the first red light ahead Chris was ready to start honking the horn.

Except the light turned green. As did the next one.

Whether it was fortuitous timing or bad luck (for him), Chris had timed the lights perfectly and was now riding the green wave directly to the hospital. Valerie noticed he was strangely agitated and knew it had nothing to do with the approaching birth.

"Chris what's the matter?"

"Nothing" he said as he leaned forward to check his side mirror.

"C'mon Pook tell me."

"It's dumb."

"Chris!" She said emphatically.

"All right all right remember I already said it was dumb. All the lights are green."

Valerie stared at him in confusion.

"Isn't that a good thing?"

"Yeah normally, but I really wanted to go through some red lights."

"Christopher please tell me you are not reverting back to ten years old the night you're about to become a father."

"Damn it another green light." He smacked his steering wheel in disgust.

"Christopher please don't get us killed on the way there!"

"I won't if all these lights keep turning green."

They arrived at the hospital at ten to four. Valerie managed to call both sets of parents on the way over to let them know the moment was here.

In the delivery room, Chris casually mentioned he brought a video camera with them, just in case she wanted to document the momentous occasion.

"Chris if you think you're going to video tape me screaming and yelling and looking like a mess you're drunk. And if you think you're going to video tape the actual birth..."

"Okay okay I figured I'd give you the option."

"No. The only option I want right now is to be knocked out. Being on camera looking like this is not an option!" The nurse gave Chris a look as if to say "what were you thinking" and Chris gave a sheepish grin.

Six hours later Chris came out to announce the arrival of James Samuel Marcum into the world, weighing a whopping eight pounds and four ounces! Both mother and child were doing well, and Chris was proud of his wife for doing the childbirth naturally. He was quietly even prouder of himself for not passing out when he witnessed a couple of delicate sights. Plenty of cheering and cigar smoking followed.

He was a father! The thought of it made him weak in the knees. In less than a year he went from being single to married to a father. If the party wasn't over before, it was certainly over now.

Over the weeks and months to follow Chris would wake up in the middle of the night just to stare at his newborn son. He couldn't comprehend how he had a part in creating a brand new life and was beyond thankful that James was healthy. Several times Chris vowed to do whatever it took to ensure his happiness and when Val would ask what he was saying in there Chris would say he was just having a man to man talk with his son.

# CHAPTER 25

## 2002

The rest of the school year was one big blur. The days of long, restful sleep were a vague, distant memory. Valerie had three months of maternity leave, which took them up to the beginning of June. They learned as they went, as all first time parents do. Whatever they didn't know was answered with a phone call to either his mom or hers. Thankfully James was a good and healthy baby. There was one slight fever back in late April, nothing major besides the anxiety Valerie had.

Ordinarily, with two weeks to go in the school year, Chris would be looking forward to a long, peaceful summer. Not this time. This summer, instead of 11AM mornings and casual pajama days, Chris would have four college classes and a ton of work to do. It would be killer, but in doing so he could bang out a minor in business by the end of August. There was just one small piece of business he hadn't addressed yet—his teaching contract.

It had been awaiting his signature for the past month and Chris had put off going near it. The form sat on his desk at home and everyday Chris would sit down to grade a test or homework and see it out of the corner of his eye. Honestly he wasn't sure what to do. Should he sign it and if he received a job offer in the business world give his notice in January? Or should he not sign it and hopefully find something by September? His parents said they would help them out if needed, but Chris didn't want to go down that road. He was not only a married man, but a father as well, and he wanted to handle things himself.

And by handling things, he meant avoid making a decision for as long as humanly possible. Things came to a head the first day of finals when his principal cornered him in the library.

"Mr. Marcum do you have a second?"

"Sure Mrs. Mancini. What's up?" although Chris had an idea.

"On my desk right now is the schedule for the rest of finals, paper work I have been avoiding, and my computer which has been giving me a hard time for the past three days. Do you know what's not on my desk?"

"No I don't," although Chris now knew exactly where she was going.

"Your teacher's contract."

"I've been meaning..."

"There is no need to dance around this. I know you have a lot on your plate and I have tried to give you as much time as possible, but I can't wait any longer. If you are coming back fantastic, I'll be happy to have you for another year. If you aren't coming back then I need to go out and find someone else. Do you understand where I'm coming from?"

"Yes I know and I appreciate your patience, especially at this time of the year when everything else is chaotic."

"I'm happy you appreciate it because I'm going to put you on the spot. Are you coming back next year?" Chris looked Mrs. Mancini in the eye. He realized there was no more room for dancing and took a deep breath.

"No."

"If you don't mind me asking, is it because you have another teaching job lined up?"

"Oh no, not at all. It's not like that at all. I came to the hard decision to leave teaching and see what's out there in the business world."

"I see."

"I love this place and you and your staff have been very good to me. I would never teach anywhere else, but I have my wife and son to think about first."

"I totally understand Chris. Good luck with whatever you wind up doing."

"Thank you Mrs. Mancini." They shook hands and Mrs. Mancini walked out of the library. Despite the emptiness he felt, Chris knew he had made the right decision.

Chris finished his courses at the end of the summer, thanks to his mom and his mother-in-law. If they weren't in the picture Chris didn't know what he would have done. Valerie was dealing with post-partum depression, not helped in her mind by Chris either not being home or not being accessible when he was home. His contact in the publishing world, Allison Wullford had emailed him in mid-July asking Chris about his book idea. Embarrassed, Chris told her things were starting to come together, when in reality Chris had not typed a word in almost a year. That night, Chris sat down and vowed to his wife to type at least five pages every day. Valerie wasn't too pleased with this until Chris said he would only work when she wasn't home. That seemed to placate her.

Chris felt himself being pulled in four different directions, taking care of his son, getting his course work done for school, trying to develop his novel and keeping his marriage strong. Occasionally, the tension building up underneath would rise to the surface and they would have what Chris wouldn't call fights, more like passionate arguing. When the summer finally ended with Chris obtaining his minor, he promised Val from now on things would be better. There would be no more distractions to keep him away from his wife and son. Now it was simply a matter of finding a job.

Valerie had been back at work for three months, each day coming home more and more miserable. She missed James and didn't like leaving him in the morning; even with Chris home. At first the hints were subtle, a casual mention of a friend of hers who was a stay at home mom. Things came to a head one Tuesday night in the beginning of September. Valerie had to work late and came home in a bear of a mood. Chris had dinner waiting for her except she didn't feel like eating. The only thing she wanted to do was lay down. Sensing a storm coming, Chris stayed away for a bit, letting her get changed and relax. After a half hour he gently made his way into the bedroom.

"Babe? Can I come in?" Valerie was lying on the bed and barely turned around.

"Just leave me be."

"Is everything all right? Can I do anything?"

"Unless you found a job today I don't suppose you can." Her comment annoyed him and he did his best to keep his cool and not volley back.

"Still waiting on an interview and a headhunter contacted me today."

"Fantastic."

"C'mon Val. It's not like I'm sitting on the couch all day goofing off."

"Oh yes I'd much rather deal with staying after work for an hour and dealing with constant bullshit than staying home looking for a job. You should be jealous." Again, Chris bit his tongue.

"What would you like me to do?" Valerie perked up at his question, sitting up against the headboard.

"What would I like? What would I like Chris? What I would like is to quit this job, stay home and raise our son." Chris sat down on the bed next to her.

"Babe even when I get a job it's not like I'm going to start off making six figures. We don't have millions stashed away we have thousands and not enough to get by on one income."

"Why not? We're doing it right now."

"Yeah on your income. You were making more than me as a teacher and odds are your salary will still be better than whatever I wind up getting."

"We don't need to be rich. We could survive."

"You say that, until we need to get James something and I'm forced to call my parents."

"What would be the problem? They wouldn't say no."

"Val I'm twenty six years old, the days of hand outs are long gone." Val went to say something, held back and started to tear up. Frustrated, she stood up.

"What's more important, your pride or your wife's happiness?" He realized right there it would be impossible to have a rational discussion. She had made up her mind what she wanted to do, and until that day came their lives were going to become increasingly miserable.

"Fine."

"Fine? Fine what?"

"What if when I get a job, we wait a month, see what's what and then you can quit."

"A month after? What's the difference between your first check and your second?" Chris thought for a moment and figured since he had already given ground it didn't matter how much more he bent.

"Fine. After the first check. After the first check you can quit your job and we'll somehow get by. I don't know how but I suppose we'll have no choice." Valerie crawled over next to him and gave him a big kiss.

"Thank you Chris. You have no idea how happy I am."

"If it prevents us from tearing each other's throats out it'll be worth it."

"Now please please pretty please with sugar on top find a job!"

Obtaining a job proved to be more elusive than getting eight hours of sleep at night. James had become a colicky baby and between the depression and Valerie coming home everyday asking how the search went, the tension Chris thought would leave the house only intensified. Everyday that passed without employment was in Chris' mind another failure on his part to do right by his family. Depending on her mood, Val was either supportive or aloof.

September came and went with a couple of interviews and nothing further. Even worse, Chris was battling his own case of severe depression over the death of Sammy and thousands of other Americans the previous September. He desperately needed someone to talk to except that he didn't feel comfortable talking to Valerie about his emotions. She now hated her job and, in his mind was in no mood to lend a shoulder to cry on. His depression deepened to the point where he didn't have writer's block, he had writer's paralysis. The common thread he thought for sure would be easily transparent between his short stories was nowhere to be found. A couple of times he sat down at the computer and just stared at the blinking cursor. Once he even had the idea of writing something about Sammy, just to try and shake something inside of him. Instead he grew angry at himself, angry at his life, even angry at Sammy who had put him in this funk. Frustrated he had taken a brief break, in the hope that time would bring forth a solution. To combat all these problems, Chris began pouring himself a casual drink at night, just to help with the dreams.

October saw an increase in interviews, and even a couple of call backs but again, all for naught. He tried to keep a calm exterior but inside Chris was frantic. What was he doing wrong? He bought books on the proper way to interview and even went through a couple of mock ones with Val and it sounded like he had everything right, yet no one shook his hand in congratulations. Valerie, however, did not hide her frustrations and there were several nights where Chris enjoyed the company of his couch cushions while Valerie enjoyed the comfort of their king size bed.

By mid-November they were starting to eat into a significant portion of their savings and Chris thought about taking several part time jobs and making that work. Finally, Don, his maybe future father-in-law, heard about an opening at one of his competitor's companies and told Chris to go for it. It was everything Chris was afraid of growing up—mindless numbers and cubicles—but it didn't matter; his family came first.

The first two interviews took place within a week of each other and he felt good about his prospects. The third interview however seemed to be going down the same road as all the other failed interviews had. He felt the pressure build and in his mind gave some muddled replies to fairly easy questions. He was blowing it and there was nothing he could do when the man behind the desk threw out a random question.

"So you know Don?"

"Umm yes. He is the long time boyfriend of my mother-in-law."

"I was talking to him last night and he put the good word in for you. I'm assuming today that you're just nervous?"

"Ahh yes sir that would be correct."

"I'm also assuming if you were to get this job you would work even harder to keep Don's reputation pristine."

"Absolutely."

"Then I guess the last question is, when can you start with us?" Chris wanted to say now but didn't want to come across as too desperate.

"Next Monday would work for me."

"Next Monday it is. Congratulations and welcome to the team!"

Chris wanted to jump out of his chair, pump his fist, and scream; but instead, like an adult, he calmly rose from his seat and shook his hand. He came home that night like a tornado and Valerie knew immediately things had finally broken right for him. He tried to scoop her up however Valerie insisted on being put down. For a second Chris was tempted to say something and instigate another fight but thought better of it. This was a day for celebrating not arguing. They sat down at the table and Chris promised her that from now on there would be no more worrying and no more struggling. That night he called Don up and profusely thanked him. He waved off the credit

156

saying he knew the type of man Chris was and had no doubt he would be a success. The door had finally opened. Things were going their way.

Christmas was Chris' favorite time of the year, and this year would be extra special. This would be their son's first Christmas. Following the example of how the French and German forces had an un-official ceasefire on one Christmas during World War I, a cease-fire was declared during this time. Chris once again enjoyed coming home to a house filled with smiles and laughter, instead of interpreting body language. Chris and Val were invited to Don's house for Christmas Eve, while Chris and Valerie would drive out to his parent's house for Christmas Day. Everything went smoothly, with nary a snide remark to be found. As they watched the ball drop from their television on New Year's Eve, Chris believed they had turned a corner. The first year of marriage was tough, but they had survived and produced a beautiful baby boy to boot. As the clock struck midnight Chris and Val kissed, while Chris prayed in the back of his mind for a quiet and drama-free 2003.

# CHAPTER 26

## 2003

The way 2002 ended gave Chris much hope for 2003. Chris hoped that the détente that had been declared during the Christmas season could last well into 2003. Surprisingly, it did. They enjoyed the first two months of the year in tranquility before potholes appeared all over their road.

Chris had done a remarkable job of leaving the past in the past when he made his choice that fateful night at Leo's and had not allowed himself to look back. It was understood by all their friends not to bring up the name Jen Polanski, or even the word "Jen" in a general sense. This was tough on everyone because Stephanie had grown even closer to Jen since losing Sammy. At the same time, in the months and years since his passing Chris had slowly drifted away from his friends. Whenever he felt guilt about not seeing the guys anymore he thought of his wife, his son, his job, his college courses. There simply wasn't enough room for anyone else in his life right now. Of course, in cutting everyone off he made certain that he would never have to see Jen ever again as well.

In fact, since the incident in Leo's, the only time Chris saw her again was at Sammy's wake. She had shown up on the first night and Chris, who was standing off to the side talking with Richie, had happened to look at the entrance when Jen walked in. They locked eyes for a second before she turned and signed the guestbook. The rest of the night Chris felt anxious and nervous. If Val noticed her she didn't say anything and when it was time to leave Chris debated whether or not to say goodbye. The decision was made for him when Jen walked out first.

It was a windy night in early March when Chris waited for the bus to come and take him home. Another commuter attempted to catch up on his reading and had the previous Saturday edition of the

Staten Island Advance. The problem was the gusting wind, which roared unrepentantly and the stranger came out on the losing end. With a huff, he folded and refolded until he could control his newspaper. Chris could plainly see the wedding announcements on the back of his paper and didn't give it a second thought until he saw the following:

## Chamberlain – Polanski

Henry Chamberlain and Jennifer Polanski
were married at Holy Child Church,
Saturday February 22, 2003

Despite seeing those words Chris still wasn't sure if it was Jen or just a coincidence. His doubts were laid to rest when the man folded the paper again and Chris could plainly see the picture of Jen and her husband. It was as if a giant vacuum had sucked all the air out of his immediate area. With billions of thoughts muddling his mind, Chris sat down on the curb. If some woman hadn't knocked her purse into the back of his head he wouldn't have even seen the bus pulling in.

When Chris came home that night, despite his best efforts, he was irritable and curt towards Valerie. She was sitting in the kitchen with James, feeding him his dinner and having a hard time with it. His face would squish up and his body would squirm whenever Valerie tried bringing the spoon to his mouth. Christopher merely watched his wife struggle and didn't say a word. She had recently cut her hair so that it was barely above her neck and there wasn't an ounce of makeup to be found on her face. Chris realized she had turned into a mom and hadn't even noticed. The svelte figure of her youth had been chipped away by the extra pounds courtesy of a baby. He wondered, rather shallowly, if he was even attracted to her anymore.

When she had finished with James and asked him why he was so quiet, Chris copped out and blamed it on a bad day of work. The entire time Chris knew it wasn't fair to act this way, especially when things had gone so well; but no matter how hard he tried, he couldn't get the wedding announcement out of his head. The more he thought about the newspaper, the more he thought about the conversation he had with Sammy the night before the wedding, which made him even more depressed. He asked Chris point blank about Jen and Chris had dismissed the thought immediately. If Sammy was alive he could call him right now and talk on the phone, or go grab a drink at Leo's. He would talk and Sammy would understand, commiserate and eventually goof on him and by the end of the night his mind would be free and clear. Instead, he was miserable and in his mind, horribly, horribly alone.

That night he stared at the ceiling wide awake from the moment he climbed into bed. Valerie passed out right away, her prone body less than six inches away, facing the opposite direction. At one point he wanted to wake her up and talk. The problem was how could he talk about this with his wife? What would he say, "Babe are you awake? Good because I wanted to talk to you about how I'm depressed. Why? Because the girl you hate, the girl who almost broke us up just got married and I'm regretting my choices." Oh yeah, a conversation like that would go over splendidly. Val would give him a big hug and kiss and just like that all their problems would be solved.

He finally gave up trying to get any semblance of sleep and got up around 3AM. He made his way to the kitchen in the dark, opened up the fridge and grabbed a Bud. He went to go sit down and stumbled over the leg of a chair, dropping the glass bottle all over the kitchen floor. He waited a couple of seconds to see if he woke up his blushing bride and when his silence was met with more silence he went about cleaning up his mess. Cursing himself, he grabbed some paper towels and went over the floor, soaking up the lost beer. While he swept the glass shards into a dust pan, he started to think of the last time he dropped a Bud, that night at Leo's. He was standing so close to Jen that he could feel her pulse racing. Or maybe it was his. Either way the air was electric and if he had been given one more second they would have kissed. Perhaps one kiss would have been all he needed to stay. No, that's a cop out. He didn't need to kiss Jen to know he should have stayed. He knew from the moment he met her at the jewelry store. That night should have been the culmination of a friendship blossoming into love. Instead it ended with broken glass and two broken hearts.

"I guess she's over me." He thought to himself before immediately taking the thought back. It wasn't a fair statement to make. He had left her. In her mind she probably thought he had long since forgotten her. If only she knew.

After that night, it was as if a match had been thrown into a forest that hadn't seen rain in months. Over the next ten months, simple conversations or looks would be misconstrued and both parties were guilty of doing so. Chris wasn't sure if maybe he was the cause by bringing his overall dissatisfaction into every conversation, or if Val was going stir crazy inside the house all day with the baby. Either way the Marcum's communicated like North and South Korea.

They reached their breaking point on a Thursday night, exactly one week before Christmas 2003, when Chris came home after another long day of work. He was in the bedroom getting changed when Val came in and started to talk about the day she had with James. He was half listening, half nodding at the appropriate moments. All he wanted was a moment of silence, couldn't she see that? Right before she turned to leave she casually gave him a note. It was a phone message from two days ago:

*Allison called – where are you on the book?*

Ahhh yes the book. The book Chris had talked about doing for a number of years now. Due to his work hours and having a baby there was no time to actually work on said book. Everyday that passed pushed the idea further and further from his mind. In all honesty he had nothing to say to Allison. Staring at this two-day-old message caused the dam that held all of Chris's frustrations to burst. The anger Chris had for his own choices and actions, or lack there of, had been pent up for so long. He now had a reason for letting them out and his belief that his dreams of writing were dead was the excuse he needed to unleash with a fury towards his unsuspecting wife. He held the note up.

"Let me get this straight. Allison called two days ago, wondering about my possible book and you give me the message now?!" Valerie had already gone downstairs into the kitchen and took a second to realize the tone in Chris's voice was directed towards her.

"Chris, I'm sorry. I just forgot! Between James and everything else it just slipped my mind." Chris realized they were on the precipice of a major fight, and it would be his fault for starting it. Sure he was irritated at not getting the message sooner however there was nothing to say to him. If anything the fault was on him for not writing. He couldn't understand why this was suddenly so important to him.

He was on the verge of letting it go when a little voice inside his head spoke up, livid that she was blaming his son for her forgetfulness. He had to hold her accountable! With a flimsy line of reasoning Chris charged ahead with both barrels blazing. He charged down the steps and met her in the kitchen.

"That's bullshit! Don't blame James for you forgetting. Do you know how important writing is to me?"

"I guess not when you never really talk to me." His eyes went wide.

"How the hell am I the bad guy in this? You forgot to give me the message. I didn't do anything wrong."

"That's right Chris, you didn't do anything," Val said sarcastically.

"What's that supposed to mean?" James started crying and Valerie went into the living room and picked James up from the Pack and Play to soothe him.

"You don't do anything Chris. How long has it been since you typed a word?" For a second he stood there dumb founded but quickly recovered.

"How the hell can I do that when I don't have time to do anything when I get home?"

"Well if you were still teachin..."

"Time out! I left teaching to take a job that I'm not in love with to make more money so you could stay home and I'm the bad guy? Do you not remember the fights we used to have?"

His voice was now the equivalent of a megaphone and anyone in a three block radius could hear his screaming.

"No one told you to quit teaching!" Valerie tried keeping up in terms of volume but couldn't match him.

"No one had to tell me! It was the right thing to do!"

"So then don't blame me for your life!" Christopher's voice switched to a barely audible whisper.

"Blame?

"What do you want Chris? What's going on with you?" Valerie was trying to diffuse the situation. She wanted to have a conversation. They needed to have a conversation. All Chris wanted was blood.

"What do I want? I'll tell you what I want. When I get a phone call from someone who can save me from my shitty life all I want you to do is give me the fucking message!"

162

The fury of his words, the hate dripping from each syllable brought tears to her eyes. Sure they had fought before and some of those were real doozies. The difference between them and now was the notable absence of love behind his words. She wanted to fire back, wanted to get as cruel and as vicious as he was and found all she could do was stand there with an open mouth and tears running down her cheeks. Placing James, who was also crying, into his high chair Valerie whispered,

"I gotta get out of the house. I'll be back." Valerie walked over to the closet next to the front door, grabbed her jacket, and reached for the car keys on the hook. Chris was right on her heels.

"You have to leave? What the hell is this? How did you get to be the martyr?"

"How did you get to be an asshole?"

"Someone made me the man I am today."

She was full-on crying now as she made her way out the door. For a second Chris felt guilty. Actually guilty isn't the word. Chris felt like a monster. He wanted to calm things down and apologize. Things had gotten out of control. Hell, he had gotten out of control. He had said things she would never forget and possibly never forgive either. He had to apologize right now. He started to form the words when James' crying intensified. Would she really abandon her son in his time of need? What kind of mother would do that he thought to himself. A selfish one, a selfish bitch that was constantly putting her needs above everyone else in this house. The bitterness had returned and he loved the feeling.

"That's right leave the house. Don't deal in reality. Go escape somewhere else. I'll stay here, dealing with your mess. This is reality!" Chris slammed his fist into the front door. James, who was crying before, shrieked even louder in fright. He stood there, screaming like a lunatic while he watched his wife peel out of their parking spot and off into the night. His heart was racing, his eyes were bulging out of their sockets and now his right hand throbbed from fighting his front door.

"What the hell am I doing," Chris thought to himself as he went to calm his son down. "Seriously, what the hell am I doing," this time he uttered the words out loud. "Did I really just chase my wife out of my house? What's wrong with me?"

Chris had plenty of time to ponder those questions because he didn't see his wife until the following Monday. No phone calls, no letters, no contact whatsoever. Due to the shame of his actions Chris didn't reach out to anyone to see if they had heard from Valerie. He assumed she had gone to her mother's. The last thing he wanted was the rest of the world knowing how big a jerk he was. The first day without Valerie was a Friday, so he arranged for his neighbors, the Clavell's to watch James. He hoped that by the time he came home from work Valerie would be sitting in the living room waiting to talk. Friday came and went, as did the weekend. Chris used a personal day and took off Monday, this time hoping Valerie would come home to get some clothes and he could surprise her. Instead he was the one surprised as the hands on the clock continued to spin and Valerie remained a mystery. Finally, around 10PM he heard the front lock wiggle. Not wanting to play any more games, Chris decided to greet her at the door.

"Hey." Valerie looked at him briefly and walked past him up the steps and to the bedroom.

"Val?"

"Don't even Chris. You said enough."

"I know and I want to talk about that."

"What for? You meant everything you said, I'm surprised it took that long for you to say the words."

"No Val I didn't mean it. I was angry, unbelievably angry and I took it out on you. I'm sorry."

"Wonderful. I appreciate your apology. Now do me a favor and grab the suitcase out of the closet."

"No way. I'm not going to let you leave. We need to settle this." Valerie laughed which caught Chris by surprise.

"You're not going to let me leave? That's great, I'm glad you won't. The only thing is I'm not leaving. You are."

"What?"

"For the past four days I have thought out all my options and finally realized this is my house just as much as it is yours. I'm going to stay and take care of James, you're going to leave and find whatever it is that will make you happy."

"You and James make me happy."

"Ha, that's twice you've made me laugh so far. Congratulations I thought this would be sad and emotional. You're making this much easier than I thought."

"What do I have to do Val? Tell me right now what I have to do and I'll do it."

"Pack your clothes in the suitcase and whatever toiletries you need as well."

"No. What do I have to do to stay in this house?"

"Stay? Oh, you want to stay? Sorry that ship has sailed."

"I refuse to believe that. We have way too much history to throw it all away on a stupid fight."

"Stupid fight? Do you really not remember what you said or how you said it? Do you not remember punching the front door or screaming at me like a psychopath for the entire neighborhood to hear? Do you not remember humiliating me?" Chris stared at his wife, unsure what to say. His silence encouraged her to continue.

"You know my history, you know the dysfunctional house I grew up in. I will not become my mother. I will not let history repeat itself. You screwed up Christopher and you have to accept the consequences."

"I'm sorry Val. I am so sorry. Please, one more chance. Anything you want, I'll do it. Whatever it is, whatever you want me to do I'll do it. I can't lose you and James. You two are my world." His voice started to crack with emotion, something that legitimately surprised his wife.

"Why should I bother? Six months, a year from now, five years from now, whenever it is we both know at some point that anger is going to rise up again and I refuse to be your emotional punching bag."

"Please Val. Please give me one more chance. Please give this family one more chance. I want James to grow up in a loving home with two parents."

"You have some balls you know that? Bringing up our son like that. How dare you? You didn't seem to mind screaming in front of him did you? Now you're mister remorseful and things are different huh?"

"I promise things will be different because I know there are no more chances with you."

"How many chances have you had with me already since we started dating? Ten? Forty?"

"C'mon, that's not fair."

"That's not fair? Really? That's what you're going to say back to me? That's not fair? Ohhhhh I could kill you sometimes Christopher. You make me so damn angry I could kill you."

"The day I can't make you angry at me is the day I know I've lost you forever. I love you and I know you love me. C'mon Val, Christmas is in four days. At the very least can we just make it through the holiday and then if you still feel the same way I'll temporarily leave and give you your space?" Valerie stared at her husband considering his proposal. Despite the rational part of her brain screaming at her that her jerk of a husband has had enough chances and it was time for him to go, the emotional part of her brain considered his offer a fair one. After all, Christmas was only a couple of days away. Did she really want to spend Christmas answering questions about her failed marriage? Once Christmas passed, then she could revisit her options.

In Chris' eyes, every second Valerie didn't answer was evidence that their marriage still had a heartbeat. They stood there staring at each other, each holding their own inner monologue while waiting for the other to say something. Finally, after what seemed like forever and in all actuality was less than forty-five seconds worth of silence Valerie spoke up.

"This is it Chris. Our marriage depends on these next four days. Any more screw-ups, any more fights, any more unhappiness and we're going to get divorced."

"I promise, no I guarantee that I will do everything in my power to make you as happy as you were when we first met."

Christmas came and went that year, as nondescript a Christmas one can possibly have. Chris made sure he was on point with his wife, attending to her every need, making sure he was doting and attentive without being obnoxious. Valerie recognized the effort her husband was putting in and decided to not even bring up the conversation again. She didn't want to fight anymore. All she wanted was a happy marriage, a healthy son and a normal, boring life. At the very least she wanted a drama-free 2004. As long as Chris met her needs, their marriage would survive. If he faltered then so would they.

# CHAPTER 27

## May 5, 2006

As Chris struggled with the day to day life of marriage, his brother Eric was busy living his own life. Over the past two years, Eric bounced around as a freelance graphic designer, doing well for himself and padding his resume. His last project had gone so well, and the manager had been so impressed, that they offered him a job within the company. The only catch was he would have to relocate down to Austin, Texas.

For him, the timing could not have been better. Eric had just broken up with Coleen, his girlfriend of over three years and decided the time was right for a fresh start. With some help from his parents, and a generous package from his company, Eric relocated down to Texas in the spring of 2004. Chris was sad to see him go, but it wasn't like they were hanging out on a regular basis. With the bridge separating them, there simply wasn't enough time. Truth be told, even if there wasn't a bridge, married life kept a man busy; a struggling marriage kept that same man exhausted. If he was lucky he saw Eric maybe twice a month at his parents for a weekend dinner. Other than that it was the random email or the rare phone call. If you asked him, Chris would say he felt bad, but they were both busy guys. There would be plenty of time down the road to sit down and talk.

It had been a stressful Thursday in July at work and Chris was eager to just get home and put his feet up. He hoped Val would be in a good mood and he could sit down, grab a Bud, watch the Mets game, and decompress. This sounded like a good plan on the bus, and an even better one walking to the house, except now, as Chris jiggled the key inside the lock to let everyone know daddy was home, he was having second thoughts. There was no way Val was going to let him sit around and do nothing. Chris braced for impact as he opened the door to find a beaming wife jumping up and down on the phone.

"Chris! Chris! Guess what?" Not used to such a happy reaction it took a second for Chris to think of an appropriate response.

"We hit the lotto?"

"Better!" He did a double take.

"What's better than hitting the lotto?"

"There are plenty of better things now guess!"

"Seriously I don't think so. If we hit the lotto that means no more bullshit job, no more back breaking commute, and…"

"Christopher it is not the lotto, would you stop about the lotto!"

"You told me to guess!"

"I'm not going to fight with you on such a happy day; your brother is getting married!"

"Eric?"

"Yes!" A big smile, a surprised smile, but a big smile just the same came over his face.

"To who?"

"Hold on I'll find out." Valerie went back to the phone talking a mile a minute.

"Mom what's the girl's name?" Based on how long Valerie was listening Chris assumed he would be getting much more than just a name.

"Her name is Danielle Montegrago and according to Eric she's fantastic."

"Are you talking to my mom?"

"Yeah."

"Let me have the phone." Valerie passed the phone to her husband and excitedly scooped up James and danced with him.

"Mom what's going on?"

"Your brother met a girl down in Texas and they're getting married!"

"Wait a second; if Eric is getting married why isn't Eric calling me?"

"Well it was supposed to be a surprise, but Valerie called me up right after I found out and I couldn't help myself! I told Eric what time you normally get home so when he calls you act surprised."

"Mom!"

"Don't make me feel guilty Chris." His mother hated feeling guilty.

168

*BEEP*

"Mom I think this is him. I'll call you back."
"Okay Chr…"

*CLICK*

"Eric?"
"What's up Chris?" Those were the only words he could make out because Valerie was talking in the background.
"James we're going to have to buy you a suit. Aww you're going to look so handsome."
"Eric hold on I can't hear you." Chris lifted the phone from his ear.
"Valerie I can't hear what Eric is saying would you please stop shrieking!"
"Everything all right over there?"
"Yeah my wife goes crazy every now and then but you get used to it."
"Well I hope mine doesn't because I'm getting married."
"Hey! Wow, congratulations!"
"Thank you thank you."
"This came out of nowhere."
"Well not really. I met Danielle when I first moved down here and we've been going out ever since." Chris lowered his voice to a loud whisper.
"Eric listen I should be the last guy offering marriage advice, actually maybe I'm the best guy to do so— do you know what you're doing?"
"Chris trust me. She's the one."
"I'm assuming we're flying down."
"Yup. Cinco de Mayo 2006."
"That's less than ten months from now."
"It's also two days before our anniversary" Valerie said with a smile.
"Val please, I'm having a hard enough time hearing him."
"What did she say?"
"She said you're getting married two days before our anniversary."

"Oh wow I totally forgot about that. It's not a problem is it?"

"Are you kidding me? I'm pretty sure we can share the same month."

"Just making sure, don't want to start any family wars." The brothers laughed.

"Still, you giving yourselves enough time?"

"I know we're doing it fast. She has everything basically planned out already and we found a hall."

"No shot of a New York wedding?"

"Christopher!" Valerie said in a harsh tone.

"What? He's my brother I can ask."

"I would have had the wedding up north but she has a busload of family down here and I mean, they say it's 'her' day anyway."

"Totally understand. Don't even worry about that. Just get everything straight and enjoy it because the time goes fast."

"Okay bro I have a million other people to call so I gotta run. Oh and thanks for acting surprised. I know mom told you guys already."

"Noooo she didn't."

"Yeah, and on that note, see you in ten months."

Like Chris had said, the time did go fast and in what seemed like a blink of an eye the Marcums were on a plane down to Texas. The wedding itself was a simple one, none of the pomp and circumstance Chris was used to. Chris was a little surprised yet completely honored when Eric asked him to be the best man. Just seeing his younger brother all grown up really touched him. They had gone from sharing toys to sharing an ID (or not) and all the drama that followed to now a wedding in Texas. Eric asked if James could be his ring bearer and Valerie beamed as she watched their four-year-old son walk nervously down the aisle. He was dressed in a little tuxedo, blue eyes glowing and a nervous grin peering out from the corners of his mouth. Anyone who saw him said he had his father's blue eyes and smile. The blonde hair he inherited from Valerie's mother, although Chris always assumed she had it dyed (his mother in law, not his son). The blonde hair was always a topic of frustration, as Valerie adored the golden locks and hated to let a scissor get anywhere near them. Chris believed they should at least clean it up a little. For the wedding they compromised and went with a gelled version of a messy mop top. Hearing all the "awwws" and "he's so cute" coming from the crowd made Chris even prouder. This was his son! At one point Chris thought James was going to hook a right and run out the church, but he walked tall and his father's chest swelled with pride.

From the moment Danielle took her first step down the aisle a gasp rose forth from the assembly. She looked positively stunning! Her pale white face and brown eyes made a beautiful contrast off the shimmering white wedding dress. Chris couldn't believe his younger brother was somehow going to marry this gorgeous twenty-three-year-old girl!

When it came to the rest of the wedding, Chris was kind of hazy on the details. They all started drinking in the limo after the ceremony and by the time he gave his best man's toast he was pretty toasted himself. Fortunately for his well-being he was coherent enough to deliver the speech, mainly because Valerie would have murdered him if he hadn't.

*"Ahh hello everyone. For those who don't know me, and there are plenty of people here that have probably never even seen me, I'm Eric's older brother Chris. I'm six foot one, enjoy long walks – wait wrong speech. Today I am lucky to stand up here and say how proud I am of the man Eric has become. He was always independent, and he did something I could have never done, which was move down to Texas by himself. Of course no matter how great a guy can be, he is nothing without an even better woman standing beside him and I think Eric has hit the jackpot with Danielle. Danielle, let me officially welcome into the Marcum clan. May your happiness outweigh your tears, may your joy far exceed your pain and may everyday bring more love than the last. Cheers."*

As for the post wedding plans, Eric and Danielle had a beautiful house on the outskirts of the city. Between the money Eric was bringing in and the money Danielle made as an accountant the newlyweds were doing very well for themselves. The only bit of advice Chris offered his brother before they departed for their honeymoon was. "Don't rush into having a baby."

# CHAPTER 28

## January 16, 2008

At this point, Chris and Valerie were married for over six years now. Six long, tough, borderline apocalyptic years. Since "The Fight" right before Christmas 2003 he had tried to control his temper and anger with Val. He tried his best to be an attentive and loving husband, one who gave willingly and freely of himself. To her credit Valerie also tried to be a better partner. She tried to listen more and better understand Chris' moods. Their marriage was slowly healing itself and Eric's wedding even brought out the lovey dovey side in both of them for a bit. Unfortunately for the both of them, the advice his father gave him years ago once again proved prophetic, eventually everything goes back to normal. Normal for the Marcums meant distance and resentment.

At thirty-one, Chris was starting to face facts. He was in a loveless marriage, and things weren't getting better any time soon. They had briefly talked about having another baby before they realized that would only make a bad situation worse. Chris also thought to himself that in order to have a baby they would have to have sex, which in their marriage was like finding Bigfoot. There was only one reason to stay together and that was James. Because they both fiercely loved their son they started to see a marriage counselor at the start of 2007. The goal wasn't to light the flame of passion, the goal was to find a way to co-exist.

Every Thursday night for a little over a year the Marcums dropped off James at the Clavell's and went to deal with whatever was going on inside their marriage. Dr. Caitlin Haggerty had come highly referred by one of Valerie's friends due to her easy going nature. She was probably in her mid-fifties and based on all the diplomas and licenses on her wall she had to have some credibility. The doctor insisted on two things when they first started. One, they call her Kate. Two, don't hold back. The only way they would get to the root of their problems was unmitigated honesty.

Chris learned right away he didn't stand a chance.

"He's emotionally distant Kate. I try to talk to him and he just gives me one word replies or a shrug of the shoulders."

"Oh c'mon Val you are just as guilty as…"

"Now Chris, when we're here we have respect for the opinions of others. Especially your wife. Let her continue."

"See Kate? He's constantly doing that."

"MmmHmm okay, and how does that make you feel Valerie."

"Like I'm a secondary character in his own personal novel." She started to cry and Kate passed her a tissue, while keeping her focus on Chris.

"Do you think you put as much into this marriage as you do other facets of your life Christopher?"

"Well Kate, yes I do. I…"

"Do you like your job?"

"I…"

"He hates his job Kate. And he blames me for it."

"I thought you said…"

"Hold on Chris, let your wife finish." Chris leaned back with an exasperated look on his face.

"He was a teacher but he quit to make more money to support us, even though I was making more money than he was, and would still be making more money than he does right now if I was working."

"Chris do you feel threatened by Valerie and her potential earnings?"

"Come again?"

"Does her potential salary emasculate you to the point you subconsciously take it out on her."

"Doctor…"

"Please, Kate."

"Doctor," Chris said firmly. "First off I don't know where to begin with that statement. It was her idea! Not only was it her idea but she hammered me on it every single night!"

"Perhaps from your perspective it was her idea. However did you ever stop to think that you could have projected your feelings on to her? Maybe these brooding thoughts of yours came out subconsciously."

"That's some dynamite doctoring you just did Kate. Bravo."

"More sarcasm Kate. It's all I ever hear. I just want you to know I genuinely do believe you're doing a great job."

"Why thank you Valerie."

Chris endured the criticism under the belief that if this is what it took to save the marriage than so be it. He didn't believe in the idea of divorce growing up and wouldn't jump on that bandwagon now when times were tough. Chris decided that no matter what he wouldn't be the one to end things. He had made his choice nine years ago and, for better or for worse, he had lived with that choice. If she wanted out she would have to be the one who lived with the guilt.

The stress of a failing marriage was taking its toll on the both of them. Around Halloween Chris started sleeping in the guest bedroom. It wasn't something they openly discussed. One night Chris stayed up late watching "The Sixth Sense" for the thousandth time and when he went up the steps to the bedroom saw the door was closed. He figured if he opened the door Val would wake up so he crashed in the other room for the night. The next night Chris was really tired from staying up late the night before and Valerie was watching television in their bedroom so once again he crashed in the guest bedroom. Every night after he found another reason until that just became his room.

Christmas came and went, New Year's passed without an acknowledgement either; they were both asleep before 11pm. They had reached the point where the only time they truly had a conversation together was at Kate's office and that was more each of them talking to Kate than talking to each other. If their marriage was a person then they were wasting away somewhere in a hospital bed, just waiting for death to come.

January 16 was your typical Wednesday. Chris came home from work at 6:45PM and expected to find his dinner waiting for him in the oven. Gone were the days of Val sitting with him while he ate and listening as he talked about his day. Chris didn't care about that, as long as his boy came charging towards the door when he walked in he was happy. Today would be different. Chris jostled the key in the lock, but he didn't hear any noises inside. When he opened the door there was no insanely happy boy ready to jump into his arms and hug him tight. In fact, there was no noise coming from the house at all. Just a note:

*I took James to my moms. We both know this isn't going anywhere and there is no point wasting any more time. I loved you when I married you and I hope everything works out with you. I'll call you when I'm ready.*

*Valerie*

I guess a Dear John letter is apropos, Chris thought to himself. At that moment he wasn't angry or hysterical. A form of melancholy crept in and took hold of him. He had fought and fought and still it was no use. It was finally over. The important thing no matter what was James. He would do whatever it took to keep the peace with Val so that his relationship with James wouldn't be affected.

Three days later Valerie called.

"Hey."

"Hey."

"Listen I know this is uncomfortable but we have to discuss how we're going to handle things."

"What's to discuss Val? The bottom line is James and I'm willing to do whatever it takes to make sure he doesn't suffer."

"Well I appreciate that, I really do however there are still details to talk…"

"You get the house."

"What?"

"You and James take the house, I'll move in with my parents till I find something else."

"You sure?"

"Yeah it'll be easier for everyone."

"I'm not going to lie Chris, I thought this would get ugly."

"I'm done fighting and arguing Val. I'm tired of it and I know you are too. It didn't work out with us so why should we continue to make things miserable? All I ask is from this point on you remember James is my son and grant me the respect that goes along with it."

"Of course. I still can't believe it's going to be this easy but I'm more than happy to be wrong. I guess my lawyer will be in contact with yours."

"I guess so. You're welcome. Bye."

"Bye."

When they hung up Chris felt like a thousand pound weight had lifted off his chest. Although he was slightly confused—his wife had officially left him and he didn't feel that upset. To him, it was further proof that love and all semblance of love had left a long time ago.

In the following months Valerie was good about sharing James. They worked out a schedule and they were actually getting along better now than at any time since their first married Christmas in 2002. Whenever Chris thought about this he would always think about how his marriage only had five Christmases. Five. A deep shame would then follow and Chris would think back to their wedding day and how "I do" meant forever and not for five years and change. Once he shook off that line of thought he would think about how it took breaking up to be happy again. Though was he really happy? Or was it rather just the case of him enjoying the absence of hostility and resentment? Did he really know what happiness was? Of course he did—he was happy whenever he picked up James. But what happened when the day came where he couldn't pick James up anymore? Will he still be happy or will he be content to not be happy?

Still, whatever this was, it was working for now. They were communicating and it was all because both of them put the interests of James ahead of their own. Their love for James was their common ground.

For seven months they kept things civil. Better than civil, they had even rounded past tolerance and moved towards friendliness. Of course that couldn't stay permanent. Happiness was always temporary when they were married, why should divorce be any different?

Even though it made no sense at all, Chris had moved back to Staten Island at the start of the summer. If he stayed in Brooklyn he would remain close to his son and his commute to and from Manhattan would be shorter. Instead he packed up his things and returned home. He said the reason was because he found a great deal on a condo near the Ferry. Valerie suspected he just wanted to be as far away from her as possible.

Mid-August of 2008, Valerie dropped off James at his condo and seemed a little withdrawn. He was going to say something before a realization came over him: It's not my problem anymore. Instead he said goodbye and closed the front door. Later on Chris took James to the park. He pushed him on the swings while they discussed his son's favorite topic—dinosaurs—until he mentioned something curious.

"Brad thinks dinosaurs are cool too."

"Who's Brad? Is he a school friend?"

"No Daddy, he's Mommy's friend." Alarms immediately went off in his mind, nevertheless he kept his cool for his son.

"So Mommy has a new friend, huh? Do you see him a lot?" The words were coming out through his gritted teeth.

"Yeah."

"Do you like him?"

"Yeah he plays with me and stuff."

"How long has *Brad* been playing with you? A long time?"

"No Daddy it's been soon."

Chris decided to not go any further. If he wanted to know anything else, he could just ask Valerie. He didn't want to put his son in the middle of a spy game. When he dropped James off at the house, he asked Val if she had a second.

"Yeah but make it quick I have to get ready." She had already put in one earring and was now putting in the other.

"Seeing *Brad* tonight?" Valerie never had a good poker face and Chris knew right away he had scored a direct hit.

"How do you know about Brad?"

"Well when you let him hang out with our son it's only natural for James to tell his daddy."

"You used James to get information about me?"

"No. James brought him up; I thought maybe he was a school friend. Instead our son tells me he's a mommy friend."

"Well it's none of your business who he is."

"Oh it's absolutely my business when a strange guy is hanging around my son."

"What are you suggesting, Chris?"

"I'm not suggesting anything. I'm saying I don't know the guy and I don't like another guy playing daddy during the week."

"If he's only playing I would love to see him do it for real because he's doing a fantastic job." Chris was momentarily stunned by the remark and could only muster up,

"Oh really?"

"Yeah and maybe if you did a better job you wouldn't feel so threatened." Their guns were drawn and firing indiscriminately towards each other.

"Drop dead Val. Maybe if I had a real wife my marriage would have lasted."

"Oh so that's how we're going to play Chris? Fine! We'll see what happens now!"

"Time out. You're going to try and threaten me now? Go ahead! I already endured five years of marriage how much worse can it get?"

"Believe me Chris, things can get much much worse. Now if you'll excuse me I'm going out."

A week later Chris was using every profanity in English, Spanish, and Italian to describe his ex-wife and her new guy, *Brad*. After months of his six-year-old son asking and begging, Chris felt it was time to take James to his first Mets game. Besides, this was the last year the Mets would ever play at Shea before moving next door to Citi Field. James had to see the place once before they tore it down. They were playing the Astros that Friday, August 23$^{rd}$ and Chris bought seats in his favorite section, Mezzanine Section 18. He felt like a little kid himself all week and work seemed to take forever. The night before he was watching the Mets finish up a 3-0 victory over Houston when his phone rang. As soon as he saw Valerie come up on the caller ID his heart filled with dread. She never called him, especially this late.

"Hi Chris sorry to bother you this late…"

"Is everything alright? Something the matter with James?"

"No James is okay but he is the reason why I'm calling."

"Yeah?"

"Sorry to do this to you on such short notice but James has something to do tomorrow."

"What?"

"Yeah like I said sorry to do this on short notice but he has something and you'll have to see him next weekend."

"That's bullshit Val. I got tickets to take him to his first Mets game. He's been begging me for months."

"There's still a month left in the season, plenty of time to take him."

"I can't believe you're doing this Val. I can't believe you're using our son to get back at me."

178

"Using our son? How dare you." In the background he heard a male voice. He couldn't make out what he was saying except he was sure the comments were directed at him.

"Who was that?"

"Who was what?"

"The guy talking in the background, is that *Brad*?"

"Yes it is."

"Tell *Brad* to mind his own damn business."

"Babe you don't have to defend me to your dead beat husband." A voice said loud enough to be heard in the background.

"Did he just call me a dead beat? Did that asshole just call me a dead beat husband?!"

"I'm sorry Chris but you can't have James tomorrow."

"Bullshit he's my son too! Valerie I swear to God do not do this!"

"Chris listen I'm sorry but I have to go."

"Don't you hang up..."

*CLICK*

He was long accustomed to frustration and anger, except this was a whole new level of fury he had no idea existed. He paced his condo muttering to himself incoherently outside of the word bullshit, which he repeated at least twenty-five times. Needing something to do, if only to distract him he went into his bedroom and looked at the couple of boxes he still had left to unpack. After sorting through the first two he opened up the third box marked, "MISC" and saw it immediately.

The watch.

The watch Valerie had given him for their very first Christmas eleven years ago. He turned it over, and read the engraving one last time: *VC CM*. Shaking with anger Chris brought it into the kitchen and gently placed it onto the table. Then he opened up his toolbox and took out a hammer. Thirty seconds later Chris had destroyed the watch and left marks on the table. Calmly, he collected the pieces that had scattered onto the floor and threw them, along with what remained of the watch into the garbage. Feeling satisfied with himself, he reached into the refrigerator and took out a Bud. Five minutes later he reached in and grabbed another one. Forty-five minutes later he was passed out on the couch surrounded by eleven glass witnesses.

# CHAPTER 29

## March 26, 2010

For the past forty-five minutes Chris had sat on his barstool with his head in his hands. His musical selection of Pink Floyd's *"Time"* had ended many turns ago. Apparently someone had chosen Alice in Chains because Layne Stanley's voice screamed from the speakers. Everyone had left him alone except for Gus, who eventually came over to make sure he was still breathing.

Chris was breathing all right, and remembering. Gus could hear him murmuring to himself but couldn't quite make out what he was saying. With a gentle nudge of the shoulder Gus said, "Chris….Chris…are you singing or talking in your sleep?" His head slowly lifted from his hands and Chris's half opened eyes met Gus'.

"Sorry Gus. I'm just in one of those moods tonight."

"Yeah that's obvious for all to see. There is no way you're driving; I'll call you a cab when you're ready. Just let me know."

"All I want right now is another Bud. The cab can wait a little bit longer."

"No the cab isn't out front, I'll call the cab….whatever, listen, just tell me when you want to go home."

Chris laughed to himself. Home? And where was home exactly? The condo down by the ferry here on Staten Island? Is that what he was calling home these days? A big empty bed to go along with his other empty rooms? Was Leo's home? For good or for bad he had plenty of memories sitting right here in this very spot.

This spot.

This bar.

This life.

Jen.

Maybe he should call Jen just to say hello. You know the friendly eleven-years later phone call where you exchange small talk and chit chat before asking "hey are you satisfied in your marriage?"

Because that would work.

Nope, that boat had sailed. Sailed away in this very spot, at this very stool actually. She was standing six inches away and if Chris closed his eyes he could remember exactly what she looked like.

Pony tail.

Tight black shirt.

Jeans.

A little bit of makeup.

Tan skin.

A smile that never left her lips.

And those deep blue eyes…

Don't walk out the bar with her Chris. Stay here with me. Stay here and talk to me some more. Stay here and hold my hand. Stay here and fall in love and get married and have children. There is nothing outside for you Chris. Nothing outside but eleven hard years followed by God knows how many more lonely years. I'm sitting right here. Happiness is staring you right in the face and she's telling you to stay.

A stranger walked past and accidentally bumped Chris's shoulder, temporarily jostling him from this fantasy world. Chris looked around and for a second had an intense desire to make whoever had jostled him apologize. A bar room brawl, the cherry on top of a shit sundae. The thought had some appeal, before he realized he probably couldn't hit anyone if he wanted to. He would probably swing and if he was lucky fall on the floor and remain there. Or worse, get the shit kicked out of him by some guy and his friends. He was better off putting his head down and falling asleep.

He closed his eyes and returned to his haunted memories. He could see with perfect clarity the fury in Valerie's eyes and the hope in Jen's. He didn't stay. He left. He didn't stay here at Leo's to live happily ever after. No, he left Leo's and walked into a world of misery. He chose his fate and like the last living knight at the end of the Indiana Jones movie had said, "He had chosen poorly."

Well no more choosing poorly. No more bad choices. And definitely no more regrets. At thirty-three-years old he had enough regrets to drown a man in a dark and lonely river. He needed someone to throw him a life preserver. With no one around to do it, it might as well be himself. The doubts and fears he had would no longer control him. He would not let their weights sink him to the bottom of a bottle or something worse.

Things had to change.

Did he want to be "that guy" sitting here when he was fifty-four? The old, washed up drunk that everyone openly pitied and privately mocked? Chris felt that on his current course he was well within reach of that shoreline, and it scared him to death.

"You know what Gus" he slurred, "I think I'm going to settle up and hop in that cab."

"Don't worry about the tab tonight Chris. Just go home and get some sleep."

"Thanks Gus. I think I will."

Chris got up off his stool and put a fifty dollar bill under his glass. For good and for bad Leo's had been his home, and Gus was a friend. If this was the last time he would be in Leo's he had to leave a thank you note.

# CHAPTER 30

## 2010 - 2013

He tried. He really, really tried to stay away. The problem was alcohol is an enticing mistress. When Chris left Leo's that night he had every intention of never coming back. However, every man has needs, and when those needs aren't being met, others take their place. For Chris the answer was simple, he was lonely.

The solution wasn't as simple.

The bottom line was Chris didn't trust his own judgment. He didn't believe he had the necessary tools to choose the right person. As a result, he was in no rush to get involved in another serious relationship. If you pressed him, he wouldn't say he was scared. Scared had such a negative connotation and it made him feel like he was a little kid. No, the phrase Chris would use to describe his current outlook towards members of the opposite sex was "gun-shy." That expression was vague enough to work.

The problem then was a circular one. Chris was lonely, but Chris didn't want to meet anyone. Therefore, to overcome the loneliness, Chris drank. Chris didn't want to drink anymore, but he felt helpless to do anything else to cope with being lonely.

Over the next three years Chris continued this never ending circle, which felt more and more like water in a sink, running down the drain. Eventually he was going to hit bottom, and he was scared after everything that had happened to him already, what could bottom possibly be? Anytime the thought of bottom came into his mind, another voice would pipe up to defend his actions. His drinking hadn't affected his work, which numbed his mind on its own. Nor had he ever made a public spectacle of himself. And it wasn't like he carried a flask around. Chris just went down to Leo's, the closest place he could call home and toasted himself and if he was in the mood anyone else there. Better yet, the people down there loved him

184

too. Last time he looked he was legally allowed to sip a beverage or two, so why not?

The problem was, Valerie and *Brad*—who was now the love of Valerie's life—knew about his drinking. And their knowledge meant they didn't trust Christopher with James. Things came to a head during the summer of 2013. Chris was supposed to pick up James at *their* house at 7PM Friday. Work had been beyond stressful that day and Chris decided he needed to get a sip or two to calm down. A sip or two turned into a beer or two, which turned into a shot or two, which then turned into Valerie calling his cell phone at 8:30PM.

"Hellooo."

"Chris where the hell are you?"

"Oh hey Val, I'm on my way. I just had to make a quick stop."

"Well James has been waiting for you for an hour and a half."

"I'm sorry things got hectic at work."

"Really? Doesn't sound like you're at work."

"Well I…"

"I nothing. Clean yourself up and start acting like his father."

"What are you talking about? I'm clean…"

"Chris I hear the music and the noise, I know you're at a bar, and if I had to bet my life on it I'd say it was Leo's. Can you even drive?"

"Of course I can…"

"You know what? The very fact that I have to even ask that question tells me I'm not comfortable with you taking James tonight."

"First of all stop cutting me off. Second I am perfectly capable of…"

"Downing shots. Yeah Chris I know. You're capable of going out and drinking instead of picking up your son."

"Stop cutting me off! I'm leaving now."

"Don't bother coming. You can't drive, and you are certainly not driving with my son in your car. Call tomorrow when you sober up and you can see him then."

"This is ridic.."

She cut him off one more time with the sound of a click.

Chris was furious and decided if he was going down he might as well do it as fast as possible. He called for the bartender, some new kid named Billy, who had no idea who he was and ordered another beer and two shots of Jack Daniels. If his wife thought he was drunk

185

now, she'd have to invent a new word come morning. Five hours later Billy took his keys and called him a cab.

The next morning the phone rang, which was like a trumpet announcing his hangover. He looked at his clock and saw 10:00AM. With a groan, Chris stretched out his left arm and picked up the phone. It was Valerie. Great, just the person he wanted to start his day talking to. She informed him that they needed to talk right now, but not on the phone. This would have to be done in person. Chris told her to give him an hour; he had some "things" to do around the house first. And by "things" he meant getting a ride down to Leo's and picking up his car.

Chris arrived at Valerie and *Brad's* a little after 11AM. When he rang the doorbell he expected James to come running and answer, but instead a rather curt Valerie opened up and let him in.

"Where's James?"

"At his grandmother's."

"Hey! I see him on weekends."

"Chris you were too drunk to see him last night, so I dropped him off at my mom's. She has him till tomorrow."

"Val that's ridiculous. He's my son."

"No what's ridiculous was your behavior last night."

"Cut the dramatic crap Val I was fine."

"Regardless, we have to talk. Would you come in please?"

Chris stepped inside, closed the door and followed Val into the kitchen. She had moved in with *Brad* a year ago and from the looks of things was living the high life. The house looked good from the outside and was even more beautiful inside. They had spared no expense furnishing the place and Chris wondered if this was Valerie's attempt to throw it in his face.

"And where's *Brad?*"

"Out doing some shopping. It's just me and you. I figured you would be more open this way."

"Open to what?"

"Chris, Brad asked me to marry him."

"This is what you had to tell me in person? Valerie no offense, but I don't spend my nights thinking of ways to win you back."

"No, that's not what I had to tell you. And for the record I am much happier with Brad now than I ever was with you." The years had not quelled the hostility.

"Yeah great. I'll be going now." He turned and headed for the door until Val called after him.

"No wait. Wait, I don't want to turn this into a stupid fight. Listen, I called you over to tell you that yes I'm marrying Brad. More importantly, his job is transferring out to California and I'm going with him."

"That's great, congratulations." He said with a surprising amount of sincerity. "What about James?"

"That's why you're sitting here in my kitchen. Chris if you are honest with yourself you will admit that you aren't the best of dads. You drink way too much for your own good and.."

"And nothing! There is no way I'm letting you take my son!" Chris' eyes radiated with defiance and anger. Valerie paused for a second, to collect her thoughts.

"Chris please. I understand your position, but look at it from your son's. Brad is already doing well for himself, as you can plainly see. With this promotion, James and I are going to be set, and James won't want for anything."

"Oh. So because *Brad* can buy him stuff I'm supposed to say yeah sure, take my son away from me?"

"No it's not just that. It's opportunities. It's about being able to afford private schools, and putting him on a good path for his future. We both want the best for him. Well now he can get that."

"I make a good salary myself. Remember? Remember how I quit teaching and got this miserable job for the paycheck? For you? For James?" Valerie let out an audible sigh.

"Please don't play the martyr game again. Yes you do make a decent salary and you have never let me forget that it's my fault. Besides, I know your paycheck. Yours is nowhere near what Brad's will be." That last comment almost set Chris off, but he kept his composure and a level voice.

"I don't care. You will not take my son away from me."

"Chris you let me do this and you won't have to pay another dime in child support. We won't need it and I'll make sure it's changed."

"Are you shitting me right now? You can't buy me off Valerie."

"Damn it Chris stop being greedy and think of your son."

"What the hell do you think I'm doing? I'm his father!"

"Act like it then!"

"Let me get this straight. By letting you take my son across the country I'm being a good father?"

"When you put it that way, obviously no. It's when you think of the endless benefits and possibilities James will be exposed to. All new doors will open up for him."

"Doors that don't exist in New York?"

"I didn't want it to come to this. I really didn't. My other option is we can go to a judge and say your drinking has gotten so out of control that you are a danger to James."

"Bullshit! That's bullshit Val. Not only that I would fight you every inch. We'd be in court for the rest of your life."

"Sure you could and I'm pretty sure Brad's wallet could absorb the bills that would flood in. Could you?"

"You are not taking my son away from me, threats or no threats." Valerie lowered her voice and began to plead.

"Chris look at me. I am not trying to be spiteful or vindictive. All I want is for James to have a life that is better than yours or mine. I know you hate Brad but he can make sure our son has every single opportunity to succeed. Besides you could come out whenever you wanted to and I'd even be willing to let you have summers if that's what it takes."

Despite himself Chris paused and Valerie knew immediately he was starting to consider the proposition.

"You can't drop this on me and expect an answer immediately. When do you need to know by?"

"I'm getting remarried on August 17."

"That's two weeks away."

"Well Brad just received the offer."

"Let me think about it."

Chris walked down the driveway towards his car. For the second time in his life, Chris was leaving a place and agreeing to something he wanted nothing to do with. Coincidentally both times involved Valerie. Did he really just tell his ex-wife he would think about letting her, *Brad*, and his son move three thousand miles away? What was wrong with him? When he stepped inside his car Chris let loose with a couple of punches to the steering wheel. Of course the only result from slamming his fist wasn't his son staying here with him, only a bruised right hand.

# CHAPTER 31

## August 11, 2013

Chris already knew his answer when he left Valerie's house. He was stuck. If he fought her on this, his drinking would come into play and he could quite possibly lose his visitation rights. If he voluntarily let his son go he would still retain his rights and Valerie would owe him a favor at some point. When he added it all up he kept coming up with the same conclusion, he had to let James go. If his life could be an easier one, filled with advantages he wouldn't get here, how could Chris say no? Sure it would be *Brad* playing the role of dad, except was there room here for ego? On top of all this, Chris would save a tremendous amount of money by not paying child support.

Wow that was selfish, Chris thought. Get that out of your head immediately. He is your son and you shouldn't have a price tag on him. If his reasoning for letting James leave was solely for his son's benefit that was one thing, it was another to do so for monetary gain.

The question was when he would tell Valerie. Tuesday night seemed like the right time. When he came home from work he would eat dinner, relax for a little while, and pick up the phone.

When Tuesday arrived, Chris didn't get an ounce accomplished at work. All he kept thinking about was the phone call and whether or not he was doing the right thing. The hours seemed to drag. After he arrived home at the usual 6:45PM, he didn't want to eat or relax. All he wanted to do was get it over with.

"Hello?"

"Val? It's Chris."

"Oh hey."

"I made up my mind, and if it's the best thing for James then I won't say no."

"Are you serious? Thank you Chris!"

In the background Chris could hear Brad asking what's going on. Valerie informed him of the decision and he heard Brad say, "Get the hell out of here." He wanted to tell Brad to drop dead but before he could Valerie resumed speaking.

"Listen Chris I know that must have been very hard for you to decide and I'm very proud of you. You're doing the right thing."

"I don't care what you think. All I care about is my son and his future."

"I understand."

"Okay I'm going to go. Bye."

"Bye."

Chris hung up the phone, somewhat in shock. He walked over to the fridge, pulled out a Bud, and sat down at his kitchen table.

Friday night Chris raced over to Valerie's house to pick up James. With the wedding next weekend this would be the last time he would have James for an extended period of time without either of them traveling. Fortunately, he didn't have to get out of the car and ring the bell as James was waiting by the window. He saw Valerie come to the door and kiss him goodbye and pretended to fiddle with the radio. He wasn't going to acknowledge her, even with a head nod. When James climbed into the car he gave his dad a hug and they were off.

James was excited about the wedding, and throughout the drive told Chris all about how he was in the wedding party and how *Brad* and mom said he was a real important part of the wedding. Chris listened and faked enthusiasm, considering it was hard to show genuine happiness for anything involving his ex-wife. Was it really that long ago when James was a ring bearer at Eric's wedding?

He took his son out to Applebees at the mall and let him do the talking. With a passing thought Chris remembered how a long time ago he was here with someone else, and how bad that went. He hoped this time they would finish their meal. Chris was content to sit back and listen to his son do most of the talking. Sometimes Chris wouldn't hear what James was saying because he was too busy looking at him and remembering how he looked when he was a baby. James still had a young face but there were hints that puberty was right around the corner. His blue Mets hat hid the bushel of blonde hair that crept out the back. Valerie had resigned herself to the fact that her son would need haircuts now and again a couple of years ago. Nevertheless she still tried to stretch out the intervals.

Chris began to show signs of his age as well. He still had the youthful face and he had grown a nice looking beard but at thirty-six-years-old Chris was beginning to find a gray hair or two.

Several times James paused and asked if he was listening, to which Chris would always lean forward and say with a French accent, "Hanging on your every word." For whatever reason that always made his son laugh.

Saturday Chris took James to Citi Field to see the Mets play the San Diego Padres. James wanted everything in sight, from hot dogs to those big foam fingers and Chris gladly ponied up the loot. Chris loved going to ballgames with his son. In fact, pangs of regret sprouted up when he realized this would no longer be a regular occurrence. Chris shoved the horrible thought out of his mind and tried to concentrate on the clear and present moment.

All weekend long Chris debated when to have the conversation with his son, and decided to do so on Sunday. They woke up early, went out for breakfast and then they drove down to Belmar. James took after his father's love of the beach and once again during the drive down Chris had pangs of regret.

The day was perfect—not a cloud in the sky and a dry ninety degrees. The sand was crowded with towels, blankets, and umbrellas so it took a little while before they found a good spot to claim. In the past Chris had been a "lie down and enjoy the rays of the sun" kind of beach guy. With James that wasn't an option. Reminding him of another beach experience from so long ago, they hung out in the water for most of the day, throwing the football around or catapulting James high into the air so he could cannonball into the water. They came out a couple of times to get some pizza or some ice cream but for the most part the day was spent laughing and enjoying the water.

Again, Chris debated exactly when it would be appropriate to have the conversation with James, and finally decided to have it on the way home. They had just pulled onto the parkway.

"So I heard that you, mommy and *Brad* are going to be moving." James gave his dad a strange look and said,

"You always say Brad's name in a funny voice."

"Do I? I never noticed," he said with mock surprise.

"Do you like him?"

"Sure he's an okay guy. More importantly, do you like him?"

"He treats me good and doesn't tell me to do stuff."

"That's good." Despite his personal feelings for the man, Chris was happy his son liked him.

"Yeah he makes mom happy so I guess I like him." Silence hung in the air for a minute until Chris resumed the conversation.

"Are you excited about the move?"

"Yeah out to California, but I'm not sure if I want to go."

"Why not?"

"All my friends are here."

"Well all Marcum boys are both popular and good looking, so you'll make friends no matter where you go in life." Chris looked over and grinned at James and James smiled back.

"Yeah, but what about the Mets? I don't want to be a Dodgers fan!"

"How about if you can't get Mets games out there I buy you the ticket on the computer that lets you watch all the games."

"But what about you?"

"What about me Jimmy?"

"Aren't you going to miss me?" Chris didn't see that coming and a knot rose into his throat.

"Well of course I'm going to miss you! I'm going to miss you every day and every night. We can still talk on the phone or skype or email and fly back and forth to see each other!"

"It won't be the same dad and you know it!"

"Jimmy you know I never lie to you, and I'm not going to start now. You're right it won't be the same, and it's going to be very hard for me to get used to it. I probably never will. The important thing though is you. Your life is going to get so much better."

"Not if you don't live there with me." Chris was doing everything to keep his composure, made even harder when James began welling up with tears.

"I know, I know. It's tough to understand it now, but in ten years you're going to look back and be grateful." There was another pause in the conversation and the Marcums sat in silence. James fidgeted and out of nowhere blurted out,

"Dad are you doing this because you're tired of me?" The fifty pound knot just increased to one hundred.

"Absolutely not! Who do I love going to Mets games or the beach with more than you? You are my son and I would do anything in the world to make sure you're happy. The same goes for mom and *Brad*. They only want to see you happy as well. Trust me California is going to make you happy. Beyond happy. So even though it's really tough for me, it's the best thing for you."

"Yeah but no one asked me," James insisted soft, but firmly. Chris was once again caught off guard. He was right, this was something his mother could have at least pretended to include him on. Make him feel like he was part of the process. Truth to be told, Chris couldn't even remember asking his ex if she had.

"You're right and that wasn't fair. One day, when you have a son or a daughter there are going to be moments when you have to make the tough decision and you don't ask them what they think. The thing is, you decide because you know what's best for them."

"Do you promise to come visit?"

"I promise that you will see your obnoxious dad in a Mets hat yelling at Dodger fans any time I see them. As long as you promise to stay a Mets fan!"

"Of course!"

Chris reached out with his right arm and squeezed his son's left shoulder. For a couple of minutes the only sound to be heard was from the cars on the road. James' eyes grew heavy and Chris knew he was about to pass out.

"And Jimmy, any time you need me all you have to do is ask and I'll be on the next plane. Because no matter what you're mine. Okay?"

"Okay Dad."

"I love you and I hope you know that. Just like I know you with absolute certainty you are going to be asleep in less than a minute." His son yawned and replied,

"I love you too. How do you know?"

"A father knows everything. I'll wake you when we get home." Thirty seconds later, his son's head leaned back against the seat. For the rest of the ride, Chris kept his left eye on the road and his right eye on his son.

# CHAPTER 32

## December 29, 2015

Everything happened way too fast to process. One second Chris was at the airport picking up James, who came home for Christmas. The next second he was in his car pulled over to the side of the road, only a couple of blocks from Leo's. No matter how hard he tried, he couldn't stop shaking, his fingers wrapped in a death grip on the steering wheel. Chris looked at his hands, saw his knuckles were white, and slowly began to loosen his grip. He wasn't breathing, more like panting as he felt the cold sweat roll down his back.

Nine days ago, Chris stood anxiously outside the terminal, waiting to see a glimpse of his almost fourteen-year-old son. This was the first time James had come back east, as Chris had always been the one to go out and visit him. Chris' parents were excited as well, they hadn't seen James since he left, over two years ago. As for Chris, the last time he saw Jimmy was nine months ago for his thirteenth birthday, and he missed him ever since.

He almost didn't recognize James as he walked out of the terminal gate. Teenage James had grown at least three inches and his blonde hair was now down a little past his shoulders. Either he was trying to grow some facial hair or didn't shave the random hairs sprouting above his lip and on his chin. Excitedly, Chris yelled out his name and went to give him a hug and kiss. James had other ideas and Chris had to settle for a lukewarm hug. He figured his son didn't want to be seen kissing his dad in public so Chris shrugged it off, took his bags, and led him to the car.

The week seemed to go too fast and was at times a battle of wills. James was now a teenager and seemingly accustomed to getting his way. The slightest thing would churn up an undercurrent of bitterness. First off, James no longer wanted to be called James anymore. He only answered to Jimmy. Chris would suggest they get some pizza and

James would snap that he doesn't eat pizza anymore. When Chris asked why, James gave him a semi-blow off answer, "I just don't." This happened all week—little battles that chipped away at Chris. The last thing Chris wanted to do was fight with the boy. At the same time, he was his father and he wasn't going to get walked all over.

Chris and James slept over his parent's house on Christmas Eve and then spent all of Christmas Day there as well. For most of Christmas Day, James was on his phone either going on twitter, playing some game or texting his girlfriend, if you could call anyone that young a girlfriend. Chris wasn't even aware James liked girls, and when he asked who he was talking to James exclaimed, "The person I should be spending today with."

The day had been a slow, steady stream of snide remarks and Chris had just about had enough. He let James be and decided they were going to have a conversation during the car ride back home later that night.

They had just turned off his parent's block and the timing seemed right.

"All week it seemed as if you didn't want to be here. Is there something wrong?"

"No Dad. There's nothing wrong. I'm here and that's the way it is." Despite receiving answers from James like that the entire week, his suddenness and abruptness took Chris by surprise.

"You don't seem happy to be here. I thought we had a good relationship so what's the matter?"

"Honestly? I miss Tara and I wanted to spend Christmas with her and her family. But instead…"

"Tara?"

"My girlfriend," James said as if he was talking to a five year old.

"Ahhh okay. Instead you had to fly out to see me."

"Yeah you didn't even ask if I wanted to come. You just talked to Mom and the two of you decided. Just like you decided two years ago to move me to California."

"I figured you wanted to come back home and…"

"My home is in California now Dad, not here." The curtness in his son's voice momentarily threw Chris.

"I understand that. I just figured you wanted to see me and your grandparents."

"Yeah I know. I really wanted to see Tara. Her family goes out to some fancy restaurant every year and they get waited on hand and foot and eat whatever they want."

"Doesn't grandma wait on you hand and foot?" Chris's attempt at levity went over like a ton of bricks and James just gave him a look.

"James listen—"

"Jimmy."

"James, Jimmy whatever. You're here for two more days, I want to enjoy them."

"So you don't have any more guilt?"

"Guilt?" He was both surprised and relieved at hearing the word. The circling was over, he was going to get some answers.

"Yeah for ditching me!"

"James I—"

"Jimmy!"

"Fine Jimmy! I didn't ditch you, I…"

"No Dad, when you send someone away you are ditching them. And that's exactly what you did to me."

"Your mother married *Brad* and they were moving. In all honesty I had as much a decision on this as you did."

"The guy who preaches responsibility is the one who passes the buck. Way to set a good example." He wanted to be patient and understanding. He wanted to have an open and honest conversation. However the digs and the remarks and the disgust registering in every syllable was too much to bear. Chris did the only thing he knew how to do at this point, anger, some yelling and a pair of furious eyes.

"I've had enough! I don't know what you can or can't do with Mom. I don't know what they let you get away with out there, but here I am your father and damn it you're going to show me a little bit of respect!"

"Whatever."

"Don't whatever me!"

"Or what? You'll only see me once a year instead of twice?"

Chris didn't know what was worse; his son's sharp commentary or the defiant look on his face. They had reached his condo and Chris pulled up in front. Immediately, James shot out of the car and ran to the front door. Chris took his time getting out and strolled over. The moment he opened the door James stormed past and the last form of communication done between the two was the slamming of his son's bedroom door.

The next two days were agonizing. There was nothing Chris could do to get back on common ground. James spent most of his time awake connected to his phone and despite some earnest attempts by Chris to engage that's where James remained. Conversations were either muted or simple one word replies and Chris was tired of fighting. If his son wanted to talk to Tara more than his father then fine, so be it.

During the car ride to the airport Chris once again tried at least to build something for the next time he saw his son, but James was having none of it. Chris was with him as he checked his bags and wanted to wait around until it was time for his departure, however James told him he was old enough to do this on his own. With a deep sigh, Chris resigned himself that this was the way it was going to be. He went to give him a kiss but James turned his head. Instead, Chris shook his hand, gave him a hug, and let him go.

Chris was off until January 2, and decided he was going to spend his remaining vacation days blotting out all memory of this visit. The first two nights he went to Leo's he walked in and preemptively placed his car keys inside the fish bowl that Gus had designated as the official home for Chris' car keys. If he were good at the end of the night he would get them back. Otherwise they would be there come morning. Both nights ended with his keys remaining in the fish bowl.

On Sunday, Chris walked into Leo's at noon, automatically dropping the keys off, watched football and poured the beers back. After the Sunday night game ended around 11:30pm, he was out of his mind drunk. Billy the bartender told him he would call him a cab and Chris replied by saying he was just going to hit the bathroom before he left. He stood up and for whatever reason locked eyes with his car keys. Billy was distracted by a cute blonde in a halter top and didn't notice Chris sliding his hand into the bowl and taking back his keys. He walked into the bathroom, did his thing and walked out without anyone noticing. A harsh January night awaited him and he was greeted with a bitter wind. Chris wanted nothing to do with battling a wind like that and thought about going inside and getting that cab. Instead, he spotted his car down the block, and at the same time felt the car keys in his coat pocket. He stood there, debating what he should do until another gust of that horrible wind compelled him to do his thinking inside that warm car. From there things just snowballed. His home was a short, easy breezy, fifteen minute drive away and he already started to sober up. This was an easy decision. The key was to just go slow, if he drove cautiously nothing bad could happen.

From the moment he stepped on the gas and peeled out of the spot, everything became a blur. What Chris did remember is how the young couple darted out of nowhere into the street while Chris came charging down. He still didn't know what made him see them, because the street light was out and they were in dark clothing. Everything was aligned for Chris to at the very least hit them with his car, at worst kill them both.

Yet nothing like that happened.

Instead his eyes widened at the last second, he swerved and jammed on the brake. The car screeched and skidded to the left, careening into a couple of garbage cans.

Somehow his car had narrowly missed them. Chris sat there shaking in his car, half on the sidewalk, half on the street, covered in garbage. His knuckles were white with tension and Chris became increasingly aware of how such a stupid decision could have permanently wrecked three lives. All because of that stupid wind.

No, that's not right. There was no wind inside Leo's when he grabbed his keys and snuck out like a thief in the night. In fact there was no wind inside Leo's at all this weekend, as he spent each night getting completely obliterated. The truth of the matter was this all had to do with James, or should he say Jimmy and how he had turned into a shitty father. Of course to deal with any sort of pain or emotion was out of the question. Why would he force himself to deal with cold hard truths and realities when he could just as easily drink eight or nine Budweisers and polish them off with three or four or maybe even eight shots of a little Southern Comfort? He was upset so he had to drink. This had been the rule for at least six years now and if Chris was honest with himself the signs were there long before that.

Well not any more. Chris made the sign of the cross and began to pray. God had spared him and at least two innocent people from a horrific moment and Chris had to acknowledge what was going on. He swore he would never touch another drop of alcohol ever again. All these years he thought he was at rock bottom. Now, months before his fortieth birthday, Chris believed he finally smacked the cold concrete.

# CHAPTER 33

## August 8, 2021

Unlike the first time he swore off alcohol, this time Chris kept his promise. As hard as it was, he never went back to Leo's or had a drink on the couch. There were times he was tempted, until he remembered the fear, panic and the "what might have been" thoughts and they were enough to overcome any sort of craving.

Since that fateful night, (he referred to it as RB—rock bottom) life was almost the same. He had risen up in his job to middle management. With the increased paycheck came increased problems and stress, but Chris didn't care. Those added problems kept him distracted from his personal life—one that no longer included his son. Over the past six years Chris called and emailed and received little more than a terse response. At first it bothered Chris immensely, except as time passed he grew defiant. What had he done to deserve this treatment? It was probably Valerie and *Brad* poisoning the well. Chris assumed his son simply had no interest in talking to his father.

Chris approached his forty-fifth birthday, the definition of middle-aged, and refused to play any more games. Instead he found happiness with the bulldog named Chonky he brought home six years earlier. Chonky was more of a pig than a dog, fat and stinky and Chris loved him even more because of it. He was all white except for a hint of black fur around his eyes and ears. Chris spent hours on the floor wrestling around with him, or taking him to the park to run around. Any amateur psychologist could tell you Chris bought Chonky to fill the hole in his life where his son used to be and they would probably be right.

Outside of a failed relationship with his son, Chris had no complaints. He had begun to date again with some success. Cynthia was in the picture for almost two years; the only problem being she wanted marriage and Chris was still gun-shy about going down that road again.

On August 8, Chris was walking in the mall, taking his time on a hot Saturday. He had some things to buy and was in no hurry to do so. After doing some fine dining in the food court at Arthur Treachers, Chris went down the escalator and walked into what used to be Walden Books, where he worked eons ago. There was a new name and new signs, yet the books remained the same. He figured there was nothing to look forward to on the docket that day, so he would sit and read for a bit. Chris walked up and down the fiction aisle, looking for something to catch his eye. Except it wasn't a book that caught his eye; it was the woman on the end of the aisle.

Casually, Chris gave her a look over. He guessed she was in her late thirties, at most her early forties. She had blonde hair, a beautiful face, and a tight figure that meant either excellent genes or a gym membership. Apparently Chris wasn't as casual as he thought he was, because the woman detected his stare.

"You don't work here do you?"

"Me?"

"Yes you" she said with a smile. "I'm looking for something to read during my breaks."

"Well first, no I don't work here and second where do you work?"

"I teach fourth grade at PS 42."

"Ohh yeah? I used to teach too."

"Really. Where?"

"This was a long time ago. God, what, twenty years? I worked at Tottenville High School."

"I think I had a friend who worked there around that time."

"Oh yeah what's their name?"

"Joe Noti." Chris thought for a second before responding,

"No, don't think I know him."

"If you don't mind me asking, why did you leave?"

"Oh it's a long story."

"Oh," and she made a face. Chris imagined what she was thinking and found it amusing. He laughed again.

"No. No, don't get the wrong idea. Nothing to do with students or the police. More to do with family circumstances."

"Ahh the mysterious family circumstances. Well if you won't tell me why, can you at least recommend a good book?"

"That depends. What do you like?"

"Anything with a good story and a believable plot."

"I'm partial to Stephen King myself."

"Eh, he's too graphic for me. Too much gratuitous violence."

"That's not always the case. You know he wrote *Shawshank* and the *The Green Mile* too."

"I love the *Shawshank Redemption*, it's my favorite movie."

"Originally it was a short story. You should check it out."

"Lead the way," she said with a grin.

"Will do" and Chris navigated his way to Fiction.

"I'm Susan by the way. Susan Donovan."

"I'm Chris Marcum and here's your book." He took "Different Seasons" off the shelf and placed the book into her hands. As he did they brushed against each other. Chris noticed a lack of a ring on her finger and was pretty sure she checked his hand out as well.

"You know even though I don't work here tips are appreciated." Susan laughed.

"What did you have in mind?"

"Nothing too extravagant, maybe a twenty, or a really crisp ten dollar bill."

"What about dinner?"

"A date?" Chris inquired with a nervous laugh.

"You can call it whatever you like." Chris appreciated her forward nature.

"Where do you want to eat?"

"If you like, we can go to the steakhouse across the street."

"Sounds good to me."

"Let me just pay for this," pointing to the book, "and we'll be on our way." They walked to the counter and Susan paid for the book. As they walked out she said,

"Do you mind strolling around the Mall a little bit more? I have to return a blouse."

"I believe that's doable. Lead the way."

Chris followed Susan as they walked to the clothing store. The conversation throughout was light with laughter mixed in and there was a feeling of easiness between them. No forced conversation, no awkward pauses, it was as if they had known each other for years.

With her business finished, they walked into the parking lot, climbed into the respective cars and made the long trek across the street to the steak house.

At the restaurant Chris told Susan all about his teaching experiences and the various stories he had no idea he remembered. It was if all these memories were in storage, waiting for the day they would be pulled out, dusted off, used for the entertainment of others. Susan had her own stories as well, considering she had been teaching for almost twenty years now. She told him how when she was younger she loved teaching kindergarten, until she eventually decided she needed to have a real conversation, no matter if it was coming out of the lips of a nine-year old or not. To Susan, fourth grade was the perfect age to teach. They were kids, but with experience and they weren't corrupted by hormones.

Susan asked Chris why he left teaching and once again he tried giving her the "family circumstances" story except Susan remained persistent. Her curiosity had peaked and said if he didn't mind she would love to hear the details. She had already grown fond of his story telling abilities.

Chris couldn't say no, so he took a deep breath and gave her one more warning, telling her how long and dramatic it was. She smiled and said she had nowhere to go, leaned forward, and placed her hands under her chin. Her look was warm to the touch and Chris felt an odd sense of reassurance. He stretched out his hands and began to talk. He talked about getting married to Valerie, finding out he was a father soon after, and his desire to provide for his family overtook any desire for job satisfaction. Susan found it both noble and sad that Chris did what he did and asked him if he missed being in the classroom.

"I think about it every now and then. The autonomy of being in control, the ability to impact a life, but most of all I miss all the vacations."

Susan laughed and Chris decided he wanted to hear that laugh again. When they finished eating Susan said she would love to see him again. Chris, not used to a woman being this forward, commented on how she doesn't play games.

"Chris, I'm forty. Games ended a long time ago. Can you handle that?"

"Music to my ears," he replied.

They traded numbers and said goodbye, he debated whether or not to lean in for a kiss before ultimately deciding against. No matter the age, his stance remained the same; he was not a fan of the PDA—public displays of affection, especially in a parking lot near the Staten Island Mall.

Their next encounter was for another bite to eat and the days and meals kept on coming. For the first time in years, Chris believed he was actually falling in love. Sure there had been chaos, trials, and tribulations over the course of his life, however Chris believed through Susan he had found redemption, a way to make things right.

She was perfect for him—challenging, but at the same time submissive. Adoring, but not over the top. He knew if they had met twenty years ago it wouldn't have worked out. Immaturity and youthful inexperience would have soured the relationship. However at this stage of their lives, it was as if the stars had aligned perfectly. No jealousy, no pettiness; just two people who enjoyed each other's company. Of course being immensely attracted to each other helped, as they could carry on like a couple of teenagers at times, although there was more to them than just the physical. With Susan he could let his hair down and be honest in ways he hadn't been since Jen. Long story short, he was happy.

# CHAPTER 34

## 2021 - 2026

Over the course of Chris' forty-five years on earth, he had never been happier. Susan proved to be the companion he was looking for. She was still beautiful at forty and was financially independent due to the death of her husband, Tim, to lung cancer six years earlier. She had a great sense of humor, and best of all a kind heart. She could read Chris's moods and instantly know how to diffuse any situation—a talent Valerie never possessed or acquired. Chris told her several thousand times that she should have introduced herself thirty years ago and saved him a lifetime of aggravation.

Because she was a widow, Susan had no desire to get remarried, something Chris was very much in agreement with. They didn't need a piece of paper to affirm their love, just a house, which they bought two years into the relationship. How they happened upon their dream home was a complete fluke.

While driving around Staten Island one Sunday afternoon in early June of 2023, they saw a beautiful center hall colonial with a "For Sale" sign out front. A real estate agent had just exited the house with a young couple and Chris suggested they pull over and take a look. At first Susan didn't see any reason, but Chris was persistent and she agreed to just take a look. They had no interest in buying; a fact the real estate agent didn't need to know. In the meantime, it was a fun way to kill a lazy Sunday. They pulled over and parked behind the agent's car. Chris stopped the agent before she opened her car door and asked if it was possible to see the house. She responded with a quick yes and ten minutes later they were getting the tour.

The house was even more gorgeous on the inside—four large bedrooms, a modern kitchen with all the amenities, even a Florida room with cathedral skylights. The more they saw the more this became an actual possibility. By the time they saw the jacuzzi, Chris was ready to buy the place. They took the agent's card and told her they would be in contact.

The drive home wasn't a conversation about the house itself; they both agreed it was perfect. The question was did they want to take that next major step? Dating and enjoying each other's company was one thing, but living together was a completely different animal. Chris' vantage point was slightly colored by the fact he was still living in his condo. It had never bothered him before, but after seeing that house he was painfully aware of what he didn't have. On the other hand Susan had a high ranch and had been living there for the past fourteen years. It was the house she had bought with her husband and it held a lot of sentimentality. Not wanting to pressure her, Chris said he understood where she was coming from and if she wasn't ready to move in with him he would of course understand. She was conflicted in the fact that she loved her house and loved the independence of separate residences. Yet at the same time Susan missed waking up next to someone and she loved Chris, there was no doubt in her mind about that. The conversation ended with the two of them agreeing this was too big a decision to make on the spur of the moment. They would take their time and if and when the relationship was ready they would both know for sure. The next morning Chris was at work when Susan called.

"Hey babe what's up?"

"I was doing a lot of thinking last night and I want to do it."

"Do what?"

"I think we should make an offer on the house." Chris laughed.

"What happened to taking our time?"

"I thought about it all last night!"

"And?"

"Honestly I knew by the time you dropped me off. I just wanted to make sure."

"Really?"

"Yeah."

"Are you sure? Like I said I would completely understand if…"

"Chris listen to me. It's perfect, you're perfect, let's do this."

Two months later, on August 29 thanks to the insurance money she had left over from her late husband Tim, they closed on their dream house. For the first time in fifteen years Chris owned a real home. Back then he was thirty-two and married with a son. Now he was forty-seven, divorced, with an estranged son. His new family, Susan and Chonky moved into their new house on September 1, 2023. She referred to Chonky as her "adopted son" and Chonky had fallen in love with her from the moment he met her two years ago. Chris was thankful they didn't have to wait until they sold their respective places first, which surprisingly happened in less than four months. Things were good, they had all settled in and Chris, for the first time in a long time was able to kick back and relax.

Three years passed with nothing of note except Chris was about to turn fifty. Of course the big 5 – 0 also meant a trip to the doctor's. He felt fine but at this age it would be irresponsible not to get checked out. On a fine Friday morning in September he ran the gamut, from throat to prostate. Upon completion of the examination, Chris zipped up his pants and his doctor told him barring anything unforeseen he'd see him next year.

The weekend came and went as all weekends do—fast. With the weather still summer-esque, they decided to have a picnic at Wolf Pond's Park on Sunday afternoon. They found the perfect spot underneath a big sprawling tree and lay their blanket down. After he finished his potato salad Chris pushed his plate aside and proceeded to place his head in Susan's lap, while she leaned against the great big tree. As she scratched his head Chris closed his eyes and said thank you.

"For what?"

"For everything."

"Oh stop."

"No, seriously. You know my story. I never thought I would be at this point ever again in my life. Hell, I'm not even sure I was ever at this point. Thank you."

"Well you know you saved me too. I had my own personal nightmare that you helped me recover from. I'd say we're even."

"My entire life I've had problems telling people how I really feel, and even though I've told you before I felt you should hear it again. Thank you and I love you."

"I love you too." The two of them kissed as if they were teenagers. Things were absolutely perfect.

Monday morning at the office had been busy and only grew worse as the day went on. Chris was swamped with a pile of things he had to do and a pile of things he had to do last Friday. He looked at the wall and saw 2:13PM. This might be a late night. He had to call Susan and let her know to eat without him. He was in the middle of prioritizing his to do list when his iPhone rang and his doctor's face appeared on the screen.

"Hello Dr. Bennett."

"Hello Chris."

"How do I look?"

"That's what I'm calling about. I was wondering if you could come in later today."

"Why?"

"Your test results came back and I want to go over them with you."

"How do they look?" Chris felt his stomach rise up in his throat.

"Chris if you could come in today that would be best." On screen Dr. Bennett had the face of a professional poker player. It was the lack of emotion in his voice that worried Chris.

"But is everything okay?"

"Chris..." Frustrated with his doctor's evasiveness he snapped,

"Doctor yes or no, am I okay?" Dr. Bennett started to say something, thought better of it and stopped. Chris was about to scream at him when his doctor blurted out,

"We found something in your prostate and we want to do more tests."

"Oh."

Chris leaned back against the chair. It was as if someone had sucker punched him. After a couple of seconds, the doctor asked, "So what time do you think you'll be able to come in?"

"I'm leaving now."

"Listen, this doesn't mean anything, it just means more tests." Quietly, almost inaudibly Chris replied,

"I know. I'll be there in an hour."

The car ride over to his doctor's was agonizing. Normally at that time a Manhattan to Staten Island drive would take at most forty five minutes. That day however the BQE was slow moving and the Staten Island Expressway was backed up before the toll booths. Chris sat in his car and despite his best intentions could not stop horrible thoughts from taking hold of his mind. He was tempted to call Susan and have her meet him down there until he thought better of it. If this was something serious he wanted to hear it alone. He could tell Susan later, at home if needed.

Chris sat on the cold recliner in the middle of sanitized waiting room #2 and this time was successful in keeping out the negative thoughts. Actually he kept out all thoughts altogether. He had just run through another battery of tests and was mentally exhausted. If he let his mind wander he would start thinking about the tests. If he started to think about the tests he would begin to worry, if he began to worry…

The door opened and Doctor Bennett came inside.

"Sorry for the wait. I'll have the new tests results in by 9AM tomorrow. As for right now, like I said when you walked in, your last prostate test came back inconclusive, so this is just standard procedure."

"Okay."

"This new test should tell us all we need to know. We'll have the results by the latest 9AM tomorrow."

"Okay. Thanks doc."

"I know it's impossible, but try not to think about this. Go home, get some sleep, and carry on like you were never here."

"Yeah that's going to be impossible but thanks again."

From the moment Chris walked in the house he was distant and quiet. Normally Chonky greeted Chris at the door and they wrestled for a bit. Instead he walked over and gave a halfhearted scratch to his excited dog. Susan noticed the change in his demeanor immediately and when she called him on it he blamed it on the avalanche of work at the office. Until his desk was cleared, he would probably remain in this fog. In fact, the day was so consuming, he should probably go to sleep early. God knows tomorrow would probably be worse.

That night Chris lay wide awake, either staring at the ceiling fan, Susan's back, or the alarm clock. Chonky's snoring was worse than normal yet he didn't hear him at all. All he wanted was to see Susan's face. Even though everyone looked peaceful when they're sleeping Susan had a different look. It was as if she had a secret she kept to herself. She wasn't just peaceful she was almost blissful. Blissfully unaware of her surroundings, locked in whatever happy dream her mind had concocted. Her hair would scatter in such a way to suggest sunbeams. Whenever Chris thought this way he would laugh to himself. Comparing the love of your life's hair to sunbeams was a true blue sign of not just plain love, but fanatical, gooey love. The kind you see in the movies. The kind he once told someone a long time ago didn't exist. Somehow he had stumbled onto it here in the real world. The one thing that comforted him was Susan.

"This is ridiculous," he thought. "Why am I waxing poetic right now? I don't have cancer, I have an inconclusive test. I also have a very long day at the office tomorrow, so if I don't pass out now I'm going to be dead tomorrow." That last sentence made him chuckle aloud.

Chris briefly debated when he woke up whether or not he should call out of work, but after a little bit of thought, realized it would do no good to sit at home. His reasoning was confirmed when the obvious thought of Susan at work popped in his head, which meant would be home by himself. Why be by yourself when you could have the company of an impatient boss and wide-eyed people underneath waiting on your every decision?

He arrived early at the office and just threw himself into his work. He didn't even notice the time and was jostled when Dr. Bennett appeared on his phone minutes after nine o' clock.

"Hello Chris,"

"Hey doc" he said warily.

"I just received your test results."

"And?"

"And I'm sorry to say it came back positive."

Chris' mouth twitched and his voice locked. After a minute he thought he hit the ultimate mute button because the phone, the office, his world had gone dark.

"Chris?"

"I'm here. Now what do we do," he asked quietly.

"Well you'll come back in today and we'll discuss your options. I suggest we go on the offensive with strong, aggressive treatment. The fact that you're almost fifty increases your odds of not only beating this but living a long, productive life."

"Thanks Doc. I'll be there in a little while. Just have to finish up some things here."

"This isn't a death sentence, just a bump in the road."

"Yeah I'm familiar with bumps. Bye."

When Chris came home that night Susan knew right away something was wrong. She was in the kitchen making dinner and heard him walk in. Chonky jumped up and placed his paws on his belt and Chris once again gave a half-hearted scratch to his ears. He somberly walked into the kitchen and she could see it in his face.

"Chris honey what's wrong?"

"I found out some bad news today."

"What happened? Your job?" Chris took a deep breath and couldn't even look her in the eyes.

"No I got my test results back from the doctor."

"Test results?"

"From my physical."

"And?"

Chris took another breath.

"They came back positive for prostate cancer."

"Oh my God Chris." Susan started to cry, which caused Chris to well up as well. Chonky heard the commotion and whimpered into the kitchen.

"Don't worry. The doctor said I'm young enough to beat this and I'm going to."

Susan didn't say anything back; instead she threw her arms around his neck and hugged him tight. They walked into the living room, sat down on the couch, and Susan laid her head on Chris's chest. After a couple of minutes she remained quiet and Chris needed to hear her voice. She always knew how to calm him down and right now Susan was exactly what Chris needed.

"Talk to me."

"What do you want me to say?"

"I don't know. Something. Anything."

Instead of talking Susan began to sob. Suddenly Chris realized the roles were reversed, she needed him. She needed him to be strong, and so he was.

"Babe I promise you, no I guarantee you I'll beat this." Upon saying that, tears began to pour down her face like a hurricane. She was sobbing uncontrollably and he had never seen her lose control like this. Chris did his best to try and soothe her to no avail. Finally after a couple of minutes she calmed down. She started to say something before she cut herself off abruptly.

"I'm sorry babe what?" Susan lifted her head from his chest and looked at him.

"Nothing, sorry."

"What did you say?"

"No, nothing it doesn't matter."

"Please don't do that to me. What did you say?" Susan stood up, went into the bathroom and blew her nose. After taking a second to compose herself she came back into the living room.

"I'm sorry it's just that it felt like I was having a flashback."

"Why?"

"I remember having the exact same conversation with Tim." Her voice began to choke up. "I remember trying to reassure him and having my throat seize up on me. When you told me to say something I remembered hearing those exact words from him."

"Oh babe I'm sorry, I'm sorry." Chris stood up and pulled her in close.

"This is so surreal, like a dream."

"I wish it was babe, I really wish it was."

A couple hours later they were getting ready for bed. Susan was inside washing up and Chris was shutting off the living room lights. For whatever reason he thought of the conversation they had earlier. There was something about Susan's reaction that led him to believe there was more than what she told him. He was going to let it go before he decided it was something he had to know. He walked into the bathroom as Susan was drying off her face.

"Babe, I don't want to pick at this, but it seemed like there was something more before."

"What do you mean?"

"You started to cry and then you really started to cry."

"Are you kidding me? The man I love just told me he has prostate cancer. How else would you expect me to react?"

"No I know. I know. I just feel like..."

"Chris let it go."

"What?"

"Just let it go." Susan walked out of the bathroom and into the bedroom. Chris followed right behind.

"Please Susan this is not what I need right now."

"Why do you do this? We both had a real shitty day. Why press this?"

"I don't know."

"So then drop it."

"The more adamant you become the more obsessive I get."

"Glad to see you haven't changed."

"Please Susan. Please. I'll try to stop this obsessiveness from this point on if you just give in this one time." Susan let out a long sigh and sat down on the bed.

"You're not going to drop this are you?"

"No."

"Fine. I didn't want to say this because I didn't want to put any negative thoughts in your head."

"What are you talking about?"

"Tim said the same thing."

"What?"

"Tim made the same promise to me thirteen years ago. He swore that he would beat cancer. He swore that he would never leave me. He…" Once again Susan started to cry and Chris felt like the world's biggest asshole.

"I'm sorry. I should have listened." For a minute they sat there in silence until Susan composed herself.

"No, don't. This isn't about me, it's about you." Chris sat down next to her and wrapped his arms around her.

"Susan I am not Tim. I'm not…" Susan wiped her eyes and put her hand over his mouth.

"No more promises."

The rest of the night was subdued. They watched television in bed and Chris massaged her head while she laid on him. Eventually he knew she was asleep. Before he went to sleep that night he didn't ask God to cure him, or for him not to die, he simply thanked Him for bringing Susan into his life.

# CHAPTER 35

## January 8, 2027

Dr. Bennett told Chris his best shot at beating the cancer would be to undergo seed therapy. It would be a one time visit and the treatment would be enough to knock it out. Despite her emotional baggage, Susan was the rock Chris imagined she would be and was at his side the entire time. He knew if she wasn't his attitude and total mind set would have been much much worse.

Chris was lucky that they had caught it early on, and that seed therapy was available to him as an option. He felt sluggish for about a week afterwards although thankfully he didn't have the side effects he had read about on his iTV. Once again, Susan was with him every step of the way, his own personal live at home nurse, with fringe benefits of course.

A little more than a month later, on October 18, 2026, Chris celebrated his fiftieth birthday with a cake, the love of his life, and the hope that he would never have to deal with cancer ever again. Two weeks after that the two of them sat down with Dr. Mike Bennett and Chris had his wish granted. The treatment worked! He still wanted to see Chris every six months just as a precaution, other than that congratulations, he was cancer free! When he heard the word, "clear" Chris squeezed Susan's hand. They looked at each other with glassy eyes and smiles that were more relief than celebration. It was now almost December and Christmas was weeks away. Happily, Chris already received his present.

Their Christmas was a quiet one. Eric had called him a week prior to his doctor's visit and told him he was inviting the entire family to Texas for Christmas. Their parents were going and he would love to finally meet Susan. Since he didn't tell his parents or his brother about his battle with cancer, and not being sure if he would be physically up to it Chris declined, blaming work. His brother warned him that at his age he better be careful or else he'd work himself to death.

If only…

Susan had lost both her parents years ago and as an only child had no other family to speak of. There was a cousin or two but no one she kept up with. Ever since Tim died this was a rough time of year for her. Because of that, since their very first Christmas back in 2021, Chris always took Susan out to eat both Christmas Eve and Christmas Day. He knew she didn't want to cook or go nuts. By going to a restaurant, it was less about the day and more about them. This year would reflect that even more so. Christmas wasn't about presents; it was about savoring each other and understanding how precious life is. New Year's was the same, a quiet night home, just the two of them. They stayed up to see the ball drop, toasted each other with some cranberry juice (on account of Chris' sobriety) and crawled into bed a little before 12:30AM. After the drama of the past year, Chris hoped 2027 meant the return of a mundane life.

Chris came home early from work on Friday, January 8, to find Susan's car out in the driveway. Strange, he thought to himself. She always parked in the garage. He brushed off the oddity and unlocked the front door. "Susan you home?" he shouted and the only response was from Chonky who seemed agitated. Chris bent down and scratched the bulldog's head and ears. No big deal, he thought. She was probably out for a jog. Chris climbed up the steps and walked into the bedroom to change. Instead, he stood at the doorway and watched as Susan stuffed clothes into a suitcase. He was confused; she hadn't mentioned any overnight trip that weekend.

"Susan what are you doing?" She was in the middle of folding a shirt and the expression on her face said it all.

"Chris! I didn't expect you home this early."

"Why are you packing your clothes?"

"Chris I swear to God I didn't want to do this. I love you and I always will love you. But I can't go through it again." Chris went to sit down on the bed until her words straightened him right up.

"What do you mean?"

"I lost Tim to cancer twelve years ago this April. I can't do that again. I can't go through that again."

"You won't. I beat it. I'm cancer free remember?"

"For now, but what if it comes back?"

214

"I'll beat it again! I'm not going anywhere!" Her eyes were beginning to well with tears.

"You can't promise me that! Tim made me that promise and I buried him two years later!"

Susan closed her suitcase and walked past Chris out the bedroom and down the steps. Chris reached for her arm and she pulled herself free. Chris followed right behind her in a panic.

"I'm not Tim! I know you lost him and I can't imagine what that must feel like! But I'm not Tim, damn it! I beat this because of you, you can't leave me now!" Susan reached the bottom of the stairs and turned around.

"Chris if God forbid you left me too I couldn't deal with it. It's going to be bad enough growing old without children. It took a long time but I've grown to accept it. However, to be childless and have to lose the two most important men of my entire life would be too much. I couldn't deal with it."

Chris was right behind and stopped three steps above her, his eyes more desperate than angry and his voice reflected this.

"So you're just going to run away? You're afraid of losing me but you're going to leave me. You're afraid of growing old without me except that's exactly what you're going to do!" His eyes were wide and he felt his heart surge with adrenaline. Susan said nothing and continued to stare blankly at him. Her silence fueled his anger and now his voice boomed.

"Damn it I'm not going to die! I'm going to live and I'm going to live for a long time and you will be with me for a long time! I love you and I need you more than anything in my life!"

"I know," she said in her soft voice. Chris gripped his head with his hands, as if to prevent it from rolling off.

"If you know that, then why are you doing this? Where will you go?"

"I called Kristin; she said I can stay with her until we sort this out."

"Sort this out? I don't understand this at all. You're walking out of my life what's left to sort out!"

"I didn't expect you to understand and that's why I planned on leaving before you came home."

"Oh so you could sneak out just like Valerie did? Would I get another shitty Dear John letter where you tell me it's not my fault?"

215

"It isn't your fault. It's my fault and I know that." For a couple of seconds neither knew what else to say. Chris ran his fingers through his thinning hair, searching for the magic words.

"So you leave. What then? What about the house?"

"Well you can stay here until we figure out what to do." Her tone and her quick response infuriated him. This wasn't some spur of the moment plan based on emotion. She had thought this out.

"This is bullshit!" Chris slammed his fist into his hand. "This is bullshit!" He slammed it again. "Do you hear me? Bullshit!"

"I know, I know."

They stood facing each other in the front hall of the house. Chris looked around. This was their house. This was their home, and now the roof was caving in.

"I really don't believe this. I get cancer, I beat cancer, we celebrate, we have Thanksgiving, Christmas, and New Years, and now you leave?"

"I know." Susan couldn't bear to look at him anymore, keeping her glance down towards the floor. Tears cascaded down her face like a waterfall and she felt helpless to stop both her sobs and the situation. Chonky danced around her legs whimpering.

"Stop saying I know! I know I know I know. You don't know shit!"

Susan looked at him with eyes that pleaded for the forgiveness she knew she didn't deserve. He tried to stay angry to no avail. He loved her. Chris sat down on the steps and took a deep breath. He had to keep his cool if he had any chance of changing her mind.

"What do you know Susan? Tell….Me….What….Do…..You…. Know?!"

"I know this is wrong." Chris thought he sensed a breach in her defense. He walked down the last couple of steps and was standing right in front of her. Calming his voice the way he would when James was younger and needed reassurance, he said,

"So."

"But I know I have to do this."

Chris couldn't fathom this. He couldn't wrap his head around her actions or logic. Exploding with a mixture of hurt and anger he exclaimed for the block to hear,

"No! No, you don't have to do anything! We don't have to do anything! We have choices in this life, and sometimes you make the right one and sometimes you make the wrong ones, but damn it we have choices! You don't have to leave; I don't want you to leave! I need you Susan, for the first time in my life I have love and I'm not letting it leave me! Do you know why? Because I am not and will not DIE!"

Chris was breathing heavily and felt the sweat drip down his face. He felt himself choke up and swallowed hard. If there was one thing he would not do right now, it was cry.

"I hope you're right. And I love you and need you just as much. I just can't take the chance Chris. I am not strong enough to take that chance. I'm sorry and I love you but I'm not as strong as you are."

Chris stopped and heard her words rattle around his head. He couldn't believe this was happening and once again searched for the magic words that could convince her not to walk out the door. His voice was reduced to almost a whisper; it was if he was begging for his life. In many respects he felt like he was.

"Susan you are infinitely stronger than I am. I am nothing without you. I was nothing before and if you walk out the door you might as well sign my death certificate because I'll have no reason to wake up tomorrow morning. That's not me being dramatic, that's not me trying to guilt you into staying, that's a fact. You have given me the best six years of my life. You resuscitated a walking corpse when you met me in the bookstore. Please, for me, for us, don't leave. Please don't leave me." Susan didn't say anything; she couldn't even look at him. She fumbled with her keys for a couple of seconds and whispered,

"I love you Chris and that will never change. And I hope what I'm doing is wrong, because that means you lived a long life. I really hope I regret this for the rest of my life, because that means you still have plenty of years to live. I'm sorry. I'm so sorry. I love you." Not knowing what else to say Chris looked at her.

"Can I have one more kiss?"

They walked towards each other and kissed, then hugged before they kissed again. Susan continued to cry and Chris felt like his head would explode from the emotional pressure building up. He didn't want to let go, he couldn't let go of the woman who gave him a second chance on life. Eventually Susan slowly pulled away from his grasp. She picked up her bag, walked toward the front door and opened it. Chris stood there, desperate and as helpless as he had ever felt. Chonky, who spent the entire conversation whimpering, lumbered up to the door and howled. If Susan heard him she didn't acknowledge it. He wanted to scream out her name. He wanted to say everything he had written on his heart. Instead he watched her walk out the door and kept watching as her car backed out of their driveway and out of his life.

# CHAPTER 36

## January 9, 2027

The light had turned green for almost thirty seconds and Chris had yet to make a move. Car horns screamed at him and a brave driver decided to jump into the other lane and go around him. The man made sure to slow down long enough to give him a curse/gesture combination. Chris couldn't care less and instead focused his attention on the clock radio, which had moved a minute ahead to 7:42pm. He had been on the road for an hour now, driving aimlessly up and down Hylan Boulevard. The longer he drove, the louder that voice in the back of his head grew. At first he couldn't make out what it was saying, now he understood perfectly.

Beer.

Leo's.

A reunion.

One big happy family. His only real family.

Temptation was too much to bear; he had made his promise and kept it for what, over eleven years now? Was it a coincidence it had been over eleven years since he last saw James? No, he thought; push that out of your head. Nothing good could come of going down that road. The bottom line was he had lived up to his word so where was God's word? Where was God in all of this? Oh, he knew where God was all right. God was the one who gave him cancer. God was the one who made Susan leave. God was the reason why a fifty-year old Christopher Marcum was driving up and down Hylan Boulevard, alone with no prospects in sight. Well no more playing the fool. No more blind faith. It was time to play Doubting Thomas. More importantly, it was time to hit up Leo's and see how much the old girl had changed.

Chris made a right up Nelson Avenue and felt a cheer rise up from his chest. He started whistling some old Pink Floyd song, whose name he could not remember. Something with clocks. No matter, he could definitely find it on the jukebox. That jukebox had every possible song you could think of. He approached a stop sign and Chris eased his way to a halt. He gazed off into the distance while he thought about the first drink he would buy. Definitely a Budweiser, probably with a side of Jack Daniels. In his humble opinion that was the best way to reintroduce himself to the wonderful world of alcohol.

He felt the burn at the back of his throat at the same time he noticed the large cross on the roof of Saint Clare's Church. Oh! The place where it all began! The very place he married Valerie and began his descent into hell. Because this was hell, right here, right now. His life was hell and he was its prisoner. No escape, no chance of redemption. Any hope given would be snatched away without fail. Well if he was stuck in prison he wanted to go meet with the warden. Give him a piece of his mind. Let him know the conditions here sucked and the food was worse. He would hit up Leo's afterwards. First he wanted to pull into the parking lot up ahead and have a conversation, however one-sided it may be.

As if his body was on automatic, Chris drove up to the entrance of the lot and pulled in. He stepped out of the car with a purpose. He wanted answers and somehow, someway he would get them. Chris walked toward the front door and noticed the sign out front

## SATURDAY NIGHT CONFESSION 7PM – 8PM

The situation just went from ridiculous to preposterous he thought. Confession? What did he have to confess? That his life was a pile of shit? That he was utterly and truly alone? Absolution? Ha! That was a joke. If anything God should be seeking out his pardon.

An elderly couple came out outside and held the door open for Chris. He gave a half-hearted thanks and stepped inside. The church was empty, which Chris thought was as good an analogy as any he could think of. He walked up the main aisle and saw a green light above the confessional to his left. With a grin that could best be described as maniacal, Chris walked over opened the door and kneeled down. His heart beat rapidly and he tried to find the words to express the bile within.

"You may begin whenever you like." Chris chuckled to himself, the man with the calm voice had no idea what he was in for. Another fifteen seconds passed before Chris decided to go the direct route.

"Father I'm angry."

"Say again?"

"I am so angry right now my hands are shaking." Despite the dark confessional he could see them tremble.

"Why are you angry?"

"Why am I angry? Wow. Why am I angry?" He saw the silhouette lean forward towards the confessional window.

"Is everything alright?"

"I can honestly say no. Everything is not all right. In fact we are as far away from all right as humanely possible."

"How can I help?" That was a great question he thought. How could this anonymous man help him? How could anyone help him? What's the point? He was hopeless and it was a mistake coming…

"Actually would you rather just step outside and talk?" Chris didn't expect that either.

"What?"

"Clearly you are hurting right now. If you wanted to, we could step outside and just have a regular conversation. If I can do anything to help you I promise I will." Chris was knocked off balance and paused. This priest was full of surprises.

"Okay. Yeah let's talk outside."

Both men stood up and left the confessional. The moment they locked eyes there seemed to be something familiar about him. The priest looked to be in his early fifties, with a receding hairline. His thin-framed glasses hung off the ridge of his stub nose. The priest was a couple of inches taller than Chris and had a slight paunch.

"Do you want to sit in a pew or somewhere private?"

"Sure right here is fine." He was flippant bordering on sarcastic and the two men sat down facing each other in a pew. They stared at each other for what seemed like an eternity before the priest spoke up.

"I want to help you any way I can."

"That's the problem, there is nothing you can do for me."

"Well you can't feel that way completely otherwise you wouldn't be here."

"I'm not here for a solution, I'm here for answers." Without realizing it Chris' voice rose and the word "answers" echoed throughout the church.

"Okay you're looking for answers. What kind of answers?"

"For starters where the hell is He?" The priest picked up on the allusion immediately and answered,

"He's here right now and He's listening."

"Well when does He start answering for all the crap in my life?" At that the priest laughed, a loud booming laugh that filled every crevice and corner of St. Clare's.

"You want answers? Son step to the back of the line, there's a world full of people who were here first." Chris leaned forward and remained quiet.

"My name is Father Bob but you can just call me Bob if you prefer."

"I'm Chris."

"Well Chris I think we'd be better off if I heard your story." Chris moved back against the pew and let out a deep sigh. He felt less anger and more vulnerable and didn't like it. Anger was easy. Lashing out was easy. To actually talk, to feel, was hard.

"Okay, alright, fine. Wow, okay let's see. What I should lead off with? For one, I met the woman of my dreams. For five and a half years we laughed and cried together. For five and a half years I found happiness—the type of happiness I never knew existed." Chris paused and looked up at the ceiling.

"Only instead of getting the happy ending, I only got a taste, and on top of that I get prostate cancer. And this woman, this beautiful woman is my rock, my strength, my inspiration to be strong and brave and beat it and I did! I beat cancer, Father! But then she tells me how she lost her first husband to cancer and she can't go through it again and she leaves me. She leaves me for a 'what if'. She leaves me for a hypothetical. Her entire basis for walking out the door is on a possibility."

"I'm sorry."

"Oh it gets worse. I've had horrible luck when it comes to relationships. How about years ago I married the wrong woman in this very church."

"Excuse me?"

222

"I actually had the choice between two women laid out in front of me, like a movie, and I chose the wrong girl, Father. We had a son together and things were all right for a time before it all fell apart. And because I made the wrong choice not only am I divorced, not only is my ex-wife remarried and living on the opposite coast, but my son thinks of me more as Chris than dad."

"I see." Father Bob took off his glasses and rubbed them on his shirt.

"So here I am—in my fifties, divorced, dumped, a cancer survivor, and as a bonus I have a non-existent relationship with my son! And after all that, after all the punches to the face, do you know what the worst part of this is Father? Do you know what haunts me at night?"

"What?"

"In the end, my life will mean nothing. When it's my time to go I will be put into the ground and if I'm lucky someone might come out to acknowledge my death. I will leave nothing behind. Nothing that says Christopher Marcum walked this earth." Chris leaned back against the pew, ran his hands through his just as much salt as pepper hair, and took a deep breath. Father Bob was experienced enough to know there was still more to be said and sat there patiently. Chris looked to the Church ceiling and felt the tremors of emotions bubbling. He brushed them off and continued.

"A long time ago I wanted to be a writer. I dreamt of one day getting published. That was my dream, Father—to one day walk into a bookstore and see my book on the shelf. I didn't even hope for a *New York Times* bestseller. I wasn't looking for a book tour or working the lecture circuit. No, all I wanted was one book, one book that had my name on it. My words inside a cover that someone would see in a bookstore or a library and think 'hey, I want to read that.' All I ever wanted was to be on someone's nightstand or maybe a shelf in a den somewhere. Evidence of a life lived. Instead, I work the nine to five, I wear my tie, and I'll be retired in a couple more years. Off to live God knows where on a modest pension and social security." Chris leaned back and exhaled deeply. He had said everything that was on his mind. Actually, there was still something that bothered him. Father Bob leaned forward and said,

"Now..."

"Wait, I'm not finished yet. Father, As crazy as it sounds I believe. Despite the hate I have in my heart I obviously believe because I'm here talking to you. He has a plan for everybody, isn't that what the kids are taught growing up? Do your best and live a good life and you'll receive your just rewards. Well where are my rewards, Father? Where are my rewards?" His eyes watered and he contorted his face to control his emotions. The priest straightened up and then leaned towards Chris. He took a deep breath.

"I heard everything you said, Chris, and I empathize with you. I truly do. However, I think right now you're looking for a scapegoat when, if you're honest with yourself, you should really look in the mirror." Chris did a double take, not sure if he heard him correctly.

"What? Wait, you're saying it's my fault? Father you're about to lose another Catholic."

"Chris, please listen to me. I'm just going by what you said, your own words. You said you made the wrong decision involving a girl. Your choice. You said you don't have a relationship with your son. Again I would say that's partially your choice. You are bitter about the other woman walking out of your life; the one you said gave you the inner strength to beat cancer. So you are angry at God for letting her walk out of your life, but not grateful for bringing her into your life to help you beat the disease?"

"Father, I'd rather die than live without her."

"I know you feel that way now, but let me continue."

"Sorry."

"That's okay. And lastly, you said that you regret never getting published. Am I accurate so far?"

"Yeah."

"Chris, it sounds like you want a God who comes down from the heavens and tells you, 'no Chris don't do that,' or who pushes you in the right direction. It sounds like you want a God who will take you by the hand and bring you to happiness. The problem is, Chris, that's not the way things work. We believe in a God who loved us so much He became one of us to feel our pain, our concerns, our anxiety, and He was killed for His troubles. Our God is love, but what He isn't is an overprotective daddy who won't let his child run. Chris, He gave us free will for a reason, and it wasn't to hurt us, it was to let us go out and live—to make mistakes, to make choices, to let us stumble and fall, scrape our knee, and cry; but, the most important thing: to make us get back on our own two feet and keep on running. You want a God who snaps His fingers and gives us instant happiness, but what kind of happiness would we have if that were the case? We would be fools living like sheep."

"Father, I hear what you're saying, but c'mon, a guy can only take so much. How many more times can I keep getting knocked down before I stay down?"

"Each person has their own private threshold of pain. For some people the first time they get knocked down is one time too many and they give up. Other people get knocked down their entire life and keep dusting themselves off and getting back on their feet. What you think is an excessive amount is someone else's dream life. The bottom line is that we are all responsible for our choices, all accountable for our actions. This is your life Chris and while it sounds like you've had more valleys than peaks, the bottom line is you are still here. You are still standing and breathing and you have a chance to see the sun rise tomorrow. God gives us the day; it's up to us to make it."

Chris looked at him, and for a second, didn't know what to say. He was stunned. All the hate and vitriol he walked in with was gone.

"Father I—" but no words came forth. Instead a tear appeared and fell down his face. Father Bob stood up without a word and embraced him. The two men stood there until Chris was able to gather himself.

"Wow, thank you Father, I really needed this."

"What you needed was to be listened to. The worst thing in the world isn't suffering, it's suffering in silence. You have plenty of years left to live, go out and live them."

"Thank you Father Bob. I hope God gives you extra credit for this."

"Believe me; I need all the help I can get. Even though I have this collar on, I have sat where you sit now and I have talked the way you talked tonight. The problems might be different but the feeling of despair is universal. Just remember, you are not alone."

"I am not alone."

"And you are loved."

"I am. Thank you Father. I can't say that enough."

# CHAPTER 37

## January 16, 2027

The conversation Chris had with the priest had stirred something deep inside, and ironically it wasn't what the priest said that moved him the most, although he needed to hear every single word. It was what he had said himself:

*"So here I am—in my fifties, divorced, dumped, a cancer survivor, and as a bonus I have a non-existent relationship with my son! And after all that, after all the punches to the face, do you know what the worst part of this is Father? Do you know what haunts me at night?"*

*"In the end, my life will mean nothing. When it's my time to go I will be put into the ground and if I'm lucky someone might come out to acknowledge my death. I will leave nothing behind. Nothing that says Christopher Marcum walked this earth."*

*"A long time ago I wanted to be a writer. I dreamt of one day getting published. That was my dream, Father—to one day walk into a bookstore and see my book on the shelf. I didn't even hope for a New York Times bestseller. I wasn't looking for a book tour or working the lecture circuit. No, all I wanted was one book, one book that had my name on it. My words inside a cover that someone would see in a bookstore or a library and think 'hey, I want to read that.' All I ever wanted was to be on someone's nightstand or maybe a shelf in a den somewhere. Evidence of a life lived. Instead, I work the nine to five, I wear my tie, and I'll be retired in a couple more years. Off to live God knows where on a modest pension and social security."*

Chris had a hard time sleeping that night. He kept hearing his words reverberate inside his head. He didn't know why out of an entire conversation filled with truth that he would focus on that part of the conversation, but there he was, unable to sleep with his words being played on a loop. The answer came to him on the other side of 3AM. He was an asshole. Not just a regular asshole, but a greedy, self-absorbed asshole. In his entire diatribe he mentioned his almost twenty-six-year old son once and actually said that not being a writer was worse than not having a relationship with his flesh and blood. Deep shame came over him as his eyes finally opened. Sure he had blamed Valerie and her new husband Brad for his absence in his son's life, but wasn't that a cop out? Isn't that what the priest had said: to take personal responsibility for his actions? Chris was dancing around and blaming everyone else instead of just looking in the mirror. He was the father; he should have been more determined, more insistent. To do that would have been too much work wouldn't it? Instead, he chose the easier route of blaming someone else. Well, no more.

For the past twelve years, Chris was in "birthday card with a check inside" mode. Phone calls had stopped years ago due to what he felt was wasted breath. There was always a battle to fight, an attitude to deal with. Cards were inherently simpler because there was no frustration on the other end. All he had to do was just sign his name, write out a check, and mail it. Chris resolved to change that first thing tomorrow.

At 10AM the next day Chris dialed his son on the iTV. Maybe if things went well they could talk regularly. Baby steps. As soon as the call connected a sick feeling came over him. What if this went bad? What if James didn't want to talk to him? He shook his head at the thought. It didn't matter, at least he would know.

"Hello?" There, on his bedroom wall was his son. His grown son, live and in the flesh.

"Hey James."

"Dad?" James said in complete shock.

"Yeah it's me."

"Is everything okay? Are you sick?" A wave of shame washed over him. James wasn't aware of his bout with cancer.

"Yeah I'm fine son, I'm good. More importantly how are you?"

"Actually Dad I'm real busy right now. Can I call you back?"

"Yeah, sure, sorry about that. I just wanted to say one thing and then I'll let you go."

"All right. What is it?"

"I realized I was a shitty dad and didn't want to just say that over an email. I figured you deserved to actually hear the words coming from my mouth."

"Oh." Here comes the awkward pause and the silence; Chris fervently wracked his mind to think of something to fill the gap.

"I know this is coming out of the blue, and I know you're an adult with your own responsibilities, but I was wondering if I could fly you here. Or if I flew out to you to, you know, we could hang out for a couple of days."

"Wow Dad, I mean, yeah except that my life is really busy right now. Kristina and I are looking at rings and my job is really busy and..."

"James, listen, I know and I understand. I just really want to see you. I can't make up for what didn't happen but I can do my best to make sure things get better. So for now on how about I just keep calling you maybe like once a week, and then maybe at some point you'll find a weekend or something in your schedule that could work for us. Is that fair?" Chris realized he was rambling so he paused, both to breathe and let his son respond.

"Dad listen I really respect what you're doing right now. I really do and I appreciate it. It's just that after all this time you want to come in, give an apology, and expect we're back to normal?" He paused a second, deliberately weighing his words.

"No, James, I know it's going to take a lot of work. I'm willing to do whatever, and wait however long to make things right with us."

"Did you know I was engaged?"

"No."

"Do you know I'm getting married in eight months?"

"Chris I had no idea, your mother..."

"No, don't blame mom. I'm tired of you blaming her for all your problems! If you wanted to know you would have found out. I suppose birthday cards are more your specialty. Don't get me wrong, I appreciated the checks inside but the gesture came off empty to me. I held a lot of resentment towards you for a lot of years. Thankfully my doctor and Kristina helped me to stop blaming myself and come to grips with it. I've done fine on my own and at this point, when I'm

228

just about to start the next chapter of my life I'm not sure I want you to come strolling in. You want a relationship with your son? Buy a time machine." Every single word was like a little dagger and his last sentence was a machete. Chris had a hard time dealing with it so naturally anger crept into his voice.

"James I'm your father damn it..."

"No. Brad was really my father. He was the one who took me to ball games and helped me with my homework, and was there when I needed him." More daggers; Chris was bleeding out and in desperation he deflected.

"You moved away! What was I supposed to do?!"

"I don't know, visit? Call? Keep in contact?!"

"I did and the last time I saw you your girlfriend was more important than I was!"

"That was twelve years ago! Twelve years! Where the hell have you been?" James screamed at him.

"I'm sorry. Okay? I'm sorry." His voice was reduced to a whisper. "And I know that doesn't fix things or change things but I can't tell you how sincere I am right now." The phone remained silent as both men deliberated over their next words. James spoke first.

"You don't know how long I've waited to hear you say I'm sorry. And now, when I finally have I realize I don't care. I honestly don't care." Chris had no words; there were no words.

"I think we're done. Thanks for calling."

"James I—"

*CLICK*

Chris stared vacantly at his bedroom wall. He saw his son. He heard his voice. And his son told him in so many words to drop dead.

He went downstairs and sat in the Florida room for an hour, staring up at the gray sky above. Chris obsessed over every word in their conversation. He was beating himself up and decided to get a drink from the fridge and since alcohol was a no go, ice tea would have to do. When Chris put the container back and closed the door he happened to notice the Mets calendar he had up. When he saw the date he paused. There was something significant about this day. After a couple of seconds the answer dawned on him and the realization caused him to stumble back into his kitchen chair and for the third time in his life drop a beverage.

Twenty years ago today Valerie left him, closing the door on their marriage. Twenty years later to the day, his son hung up on him, closing the door on any chance of a relationship. That would be enough to drive a man to drink. Instead he silently wiped up the mess on the floor.

# CHAPTER 38

## May 28, 2030

When you reach your sixties, you have the right to reclaim your life. If you are married with kids, the majority of your life has been devoted to their needs and their happiness. Your own needs, wants, desires are second or third depending on how much you love your spouse. Christopher's parents had lived for their children their entire lives. They lived their lives based on the needs of their children, and as their children grew to adulthood, on the needs of their potential grandchildren. That plan hit a bump in the road when Eric moved to Texas and Chris lost his marriage. For years they debated the pros and cons of leaving New York and retiring some place warm. Despite the guilt his mother had for leaving Chris, they decided to enjoy their remaining years in the sun and warmth of Arizona. Both Chris and Eric were happy for them and encouraged them to go have fun, for however long that would be.

And so they did.

The Marcum's moved to Arizona in 2019 and never looked back. At least once a year the boys would fly west and visit them for a week or ten days, depending on vacation time. Chris and Eric exchanged emails regarding the change in their parent's demeanor. It was like they were teenagers; they had their clique of friends, parties, and were constantly on the move. Chris figured at this rate they had at least another twenty years to go. They would just be too busy to die.

Meanwhile Chris and Susan sold their house five months after she walked out. Chris never saw her again, as she would only come to pack up her things when she knew he was at work. A couple of times Chris tried to take her out to dinner but she refused. This was how things were, and the sooner he realized it the better off the two of them would be.

With his share of the money Chris bought a small semi-attached house about twenty minutes away. He was back to living by himself, made even harder when Chonky was put down a month later. He was now truly alone.

The call came a little after six in the morning on May 28, 2030. The iTV must have rang at least three times before Chris heard it. Finally he clicked the remote on his nightstand and saw his father's face staring back at him. There were tears pouring down his cheeks and he looked like he aged fifty years.

"Dad? Dad you okay?"

"Chris..." His father's mouth hung open and in his eyes was a panic he had never seen before.

"Dad what is it? Is mom okay?"

"Your Mother..."

He put his head down and started to violently shake in anguish. "Dad! What happened? What happened to Mom?"

His dad looked back up at the screen and seemed to shake his head free of the grief. He pulled himself together and cleared his voice.

"She fell. She fell Chris right over there." His Dad pointed towards the bathroom. "She's gone." Chris couldn't believe what he was hearing and didn't want to waste anymore time.

"Okay Dad okay I'm coming out there. I'm going to get a flight and get out there as soon as possible." His dad went to say something in reply and found that he couldn't. He couldn't even look up at the screen.

"I'll call Eric and we'll be out there first thing." Once again his dad tried to talk and couldn't get the words out.

"I love you." He saw his father nod his head in reply and they were disconnected.

Chris immediately called his brother and told him. Eric seemed to be in shock because he took the news rather calmly. They cut the conversation short so they could both book flights out there and said goodbye.

He searched on the iTV the moment the conversation ended and looked for the next available flight out of Newark Aiport. He found one for an affordable price departing in two hours and put it on his American Express. With that out of the way he gathered his clothes and some necessities, threw them into a bag and ran out the door. At first he was going to call for a cab before he decided to take his car and pay the long-term parking. He wanted to be on the road five minutes ago, not fifteen minutes from now.

Eric and Danielle touched down a little after 8AM Pacific Time and Chris arrived fifteen minutes later. He was in contact with Eric for the duration of the flight and when they realized they would be arriving at the same time it made sense for them to wait for each other, share a cab and see dad together. Later on, Eric thanked Chris for making him wait. They were all shocked to see how much their father had aged. His white hair was a mess and his eyes had sunken in. Chris thought on video he gained fifty years. When he saw him in person he thought the actual number was seventy-five. Their father blamed himself for his wife's death and wore the guilt all over his elderly face.

His seventy-seven-year old mother had been complaining about indigestion for most of the evening. Even though his father wanted to bring her to a doctor, she just blamed it on the Mexican food they had for dinner. By 11PM she claimed things had settled, they kissed each other good night, and went to sleep.

Three and a half hours later his dad woke up to go to the bathroom and found his wife face down in the doorway of the bathroom. By the way she was facing he could tell she was on her way back to bed. His father called 911 immediately, unlocked the front door, and sat on the floor next to his wife of fifty-seven years holding her hand and stroking her head. Twenty minutes later she was declared dead in the ambulance, cause of death was a massive heart attack.

If only he had insisted they go to the doctor's. If only he heard her get up. If only he heard her fall. What if she cried out for him? Chris and Eric told him he couldn't think that way but that's all he could think about. It was his fault his wife was dead and no one could say anything different.

Danielle put a pot of coffee on as the three of them sat in the kitchen, alternating between silence and tears. What could they possibly say to their dad to assuage his pain? At the same time they were grieving the loss of their mother. Their dad refused to eat and said he was going back to bed. Except instead of going into the master bedroom he shuffled into the guest bedroom next door and closed the door. Danielle rinsed off some silverware left in the sink and said,

"Do you think one of you guys should go in and keep him company?" Chris and Eric looked at each other and immediately came to the same conclusion.

"Hon right now it's best to let Dad be. He hates showing emotion, even now, and I think if Chris or I went in there he would just get embarrassed."

"He's your father and he just lost his wife."

"Eric's right. It's too raw for him right now. He'll let us know when he wants company."

"Well in that case after your coffee why don't you guys find out what time the funeral home opens and start making the arrangements. Maybe hit the supermarket too considering we'll be here for a little while. I'll stay here with Dad in case he does want that company."

"Sounds good babe" and Eric turned to his brother.

"Here comes the fun part."

Chris couldn't have been more impressed with the wake. It seemed like the entire state of Arizona came out for his mother and he was shocked at how many friends they had made in eleven years. The boys made sure to be point men on everything so that their father didn't have to deal with any of the details. Later on Chris wondered if that made it worse on him. Maybe if their dad was involved it would have kept his mind distracted, or as distracted as one can possibly be after losing a spouse.

Chris stayed strong all throughout until it was time to place a rose on his mother's coffin. The emotions of losing his mother, combined with remembering the pain of Sammy's death, on top of not having Susan was too much to bear.

Growing up the running gag in the family was that Dad would be lost without Mom. The boys had no idea how much truth there was in that statement until they saw it first hand in the weeks following their mother's death. Dad was despondent and openly talked about his desire to meet up with his wife. He shunned the friends they had made and mostly kept to himself in the house. He would no longer sleep in the bedroom and instead slept in the guest room. Eric and Danielle told him to come back and live with them for a little while but he refused. Chris told him if he came back to Staten Island he could see all the neighbors and friends that he hadn't seen in years. His father said that would be worse, because then it would be nothing but "I'm sorry" and "Do you need anything" and he didn't want anyone's pity. To be honest, Chris wouldn't have minded the company, but his father was insistent. Bottom line was, this was their house and he wanted to stay. Chris felt that he wanted to stay out of guilt, not wanting to "abandon" his wife again.

A couple of nights after burying his mother, Chris couldn't sleep and made his way downstairs to sit out on the screened porch. He was startled to see his father sitting there, staring out into the darkness.

"Hey."

"Hey Son."

"Mind if I joined you?"

"Pull up a chair." Chris grabbed one of the chairs and pulled it closer to his dad. They sat there in silence for a couple of minutes, the sounds of the night filled in the gaps.

"Your mother loved this right here. Every so often I'd wake up and realize she wasn't in bed and find her outside just like we are right now."

"Hmm."

"She loved this place. Loved the weather, loved the scenery, everything about it. If she could have convinced you and your brother to move out here as well things would have been perfect. Even without the two of you, it was pretty damn close." Chris was going to say something but his dad resumed talking.

"She was a great wife. I'm not sure if I told her enough how lucky I was to have her." Chris and his father sat back and once again listened to the sounds, which emanated from the darkness. Minutes passed before his dad spoke again.

"Do me a favor Chris. When it's my time I don't want any of that flower nonsense at the cemetery. Say whatever prayers necessary, grieve if you must, and lower me into the ground. I didn't like roses when I was alive so why would I want them if I was dead?"

"Okay Dad."

"Why do they do that nonsense? I always thought it made things harder."

"Same here."

"When your Great Uncle Tommy passed we had to do that."

"Yup."

"I hated it. I absolutely hated that."

"I know Dad."

"You know your mother loved this spot right here. Absolutely loved it. I'd wake up in the middle of the night and find her sitting right where we are. I'd ask her what she was doing and she'd say thinking or praying."

"I know Dad."

"Your mother was probably first on Saint Peter's list. No waiting for her. She was a good woman."

"I'm sure God let her in through the VIP entrance." His dad paused and looked over at Chris.

"CID? What's that?"

"Nothing Dad. Just saying Mom's in heaven."

"That's for damn sure Chris." Another couple of minutes passed.

"I wish I went first. I don't know how I'm going to live without her."

"Well you have Eric and I, and the community here..."

"Yeah that's great during the day, but where are they at night? You know if I close my eyes I can still feel her next to me, and I don't know if that's worse." Chris looked at his father and even in the dark could see his eyes beginning to well up.

"Go back to bed Son. I'll be okay."

"It's okay Dad I'm fine sitting out here…"

"No, go back to sleep. I'll be up soon enough."

"Ok. Night Dad." Chris stood up and kissed his dad and returned the chair to where he found it.

Before they went back home a couple of the neighbors pulled the boys aside and told them they would keep an eye on their dad. Whether it was bringing food over or taking him out to watch a game, they would do their best to keep him active. The boys appreciated it, but they also knew their father. The sole reason why he did anything was because his wife wanted to. He gained enjoyment out of her enjoyment. If she wasn't around anymore, what was the point of going out?

Less than four months later, Chris settled into his office chair, getting back from a nice lunch. He just started to check his email to see if he missed anything when his iPhone rang. The moment he saw Eric's number his stomach sank, and the feeling was confirmed the moment he touched the screen and saw his face.

"Chris."

"Hey Eric."

"They found Dad in the house."

"Wait, what? Who found Dad?"

"Nick and Amanda had a key to the house. They called him up to see if he wanted to get breakfast and he didn't answer. Knowing how Dad never sleeps late they went over and knocked on the door. A couple of minutes later they found him."

"Found him how?"

"He was in bed. He went to sleep last night and never woke up."

"Shit....shit shit shit."

"Yup. Listen there's no need to rush out there. I'm heading out now. Take your time."

"No that's okay; I'll see what flights are leaving from Newark."

"See you soon."

"Yup, bye."

Whether it was because they were still numb from losing their mother, or because they felt relief for their father, this time things felt different. There were no tears, just quiet acknowledgements. Their father had a pronounced influence on the both of them and had given them plenty of great memories growing up. Regardless of the pain they were once again dealing with, they knew their dad was miserable without his wife and no man deserved to live out his remaining years miserable and broken. Chris thanked God for alleviating his pain and allowing him to meet up with their mom in heaven. Once again seemingly the entire state of Arizona turned out at the wake, which Chris and Eric greatly appreciated and on September 4 the Marcums buried their father. He was less than two months away from his eightieth birthday.

At the cemetery Chris gave a private thank you to his father because he didn't want "that flower nonsense." The boys shed a couple of tears when they saw that the tombstone had already been engraved.

# MARCUM

**Maureen Marcum**

**Born: November 11, 1953**
**Died: May 28, 2030**

They assumed in a couple of months Brian Christopher Marcum would be engraved on the right side.

Losing your parents is never an easy thing. Losing both in less than six months is even tougher. Chris and Eric went down and spent a week cleaning out the house, tidying up loose ends and settling whatever problems there were with the estate. Chris was thankful that he and his brother were on the same page. No one contested anything and there was no fighting over money or possessions. An hour before Chris was set to leave for the airport he told Eric that he loved him and that they would have to get together more often. The emails were nice but it would be better to see each other in person. Eric agreed, and when Chris boarded the plane he was happy to have a brother like Eric.

# CHAPTER 39

## October 16, 2040

The solitary energy saving florescent light bulb, while excellent for lowering his energy bill was not kind to Chris for when he wanted to look in the bathroom mirror. Every single blemish and flaw was exposed for the entire bathroom to see. His hair was predominantly white. He could also count those brave surviving black hairs, fighting to the bitter end in his neatly trimmed goatee. There were wrinkles in the corner of his eyes and his laugh lines were much more pronounced than he remembered. So this is what sixty-four looked like, he thought to himself. It seemed like the last ten years happened in a flash and he tried to remember the steps that brought him to this moment.

Three years after the death of his parents, Chris found himself involuntarily retired. His company went through three rounds of layoffs and Chris faced the firing squad on round number two. At least the buyout was generous, a year's pay as well as a bonus paid to his 401K. The plan had been to work till sixty and then reevaluate, except now there he was fifty-seven-years old with nothing but time. There was time now to do all the things he always wanted to do. He could travel anywhere in the world; he could move wherever he wanted to. Hell, he could even take up writing again. The only benefit to living a lonely life was the opportunities it presented. And an opportunity presented itself to him one Saturday night at 5pm Mass at St. Clare's.

Chris casually perused through the parish bulletin when he noticed there was a need for CCD teachers. Specifically, they needed someone to teach the sixth grade class on Mondays at 7PM. Chris reasoned to himself that not only was his social calendar free during that time, it would also allow him to return to the classroom. He couldn't believe that thirty years had really passed since he was teaching those freshmen and sophomores all about global history. It was unbelievable to think that back then he had the tools necessary to teach kids of that age, and to last four years. Thank God for Steve.

Chris called the rectory Sunday afternoon and was told to come over to meet with the Director in charge of Religious Education the next day. When he arrived Monday morning he happened to bump into Father Bob, the same Father Bob who talked him off the ledge a couple of years earlier. He was carrying a couple of boxes and the priest informed Chris he was being transferred to a parish up in Paramus. When he asked Chris why he was there and Chris told him Father Bob put his boxes down and together they walked into the Director's office. The meeting was short and brief as Mr. Ridgwell listened to Father Bob vouch for his character. His response was, "If he's good enough for Bob he's good enough for me," and hired Chris on the spot. The next chapter of his life started two weeks later. He loved every second of it.

After he finished his first year of teaching CCD Mr. Ridgwell asked if he was going to return next year. Two years turned into four, then six, and now at the present moment he was in his seventh year at the program. Except he wasn't just a CCD teacher; he had also taken on the task of leading the youth group, which met on Friday nights. Chris found contentment and peace working with kids and finally felt like he was doing something worthwhile with his life. Sometimes he thought it was sad that it took sixty-four years to find peace before thanking God for finding it, no matter how long it took.

Chris would have continued down this stroll of memory lane if his iPhone didn't loudly announce his doctor's visit was in ten minutes. He checked himself one last time for anything rogue on his face or head, gave the mirror a silly grin and shut the lights. Time to go.

Chris walked into the doctor's office as if he was a conquering hero. He had been coming there for so long that he knew everyone, both worker and patient. Paige, the twenty something year old receptionist, told him Dr. Bennett was running a little late yet Chris didn't mind. Where was he rushing off to? With a smile he sat down and struck up a conversation with Mrs. Saccenti, who he had seen coming in and out of the office for the past nine years. If there was one thing Chris Marcum had an abundance of, it was time. Twenty minutes later Paige stuck her head out and said,

"Chris, Dr. Bennett will see you now."

"Thanks honey." Chris was in the middle of talking about the Mets chances in the World Series with some random stranger and excused himself.

"Chris, do you know everybody on this island or just pretend to?"

"What can I say Paige? I have a friendly face." They walked into the room and Chris sat on the table.

"You know the drill by now, the doctor will be here in a couple."

"Thanks darling, see you outside." Paige waved and closed the door behind her.

Chris knew the room inside and out. He could recite the words on the health posters with his eyes closed. He knew where the supplies were; he could even read back verbatim the toxic chemical warning on the white chest where they disposed of needles. A couple of minutes later Dr. Bennett walked in. He didn't look a day over sixty, even though he was actually three years older than Chris. Either the man kept in shape or had phenomenal genes. One day Chris would ask him. Dr. Bennett came in with a smile, walked over and shook Chris's hand. The ominous feeling returned immediately and Chris knew the next sentence would not be a pleasant one.

"With most people I would look to soften the blow, but after knowing you for the past thirteen years I know you don't want it sugar coated."

"I appreciate that doc. Let her rip."

"Chris your cancer has returned and it's much more aggressive than what I initially feared."

Amazing, Chris thought to himself. Absolutely amazing that at his age he still had to deal with life's nonsense. Although, to be fair at his age this stuff should be expected. A queer smile came over his face and he took a deep breath.

"Okay so now what."

"Well it's your prostate again, but to be honest I'm concerned about the possibility of it spreading. I think you should undergo radical prostatectomy. It's a surgery to remove the whole prostate gland and the nearby lymph nodes."

"All right."

"I'll want you to donate two pints of blood just in case we have to do a transfusion. It's unlikely, but I'd rather be safe than sorry."

"Fine... when are we doing this?"

"A week from now. You can donate the blood tomorrow. Chris, ordinarily I'd comfort the patient, however I'm confident you don't need my words and I'm even more confident that a week from now things will be fine."

"Thanks doc I appreciate it. See you in a week."

Dr. Bennett put on the brave face, gave the good speech, and Chris had gone along with it like an actor on the stage. His role was to assure the doctor that he believed what he was saying and that he wasn't apprehensive whatsoever. In fact Chris put on such a good performance that he even believed it during the drive home. It's no big deal he thought, I beat cancer once I'll beat it again. This is just another bump, and just like the thousands he encountered already, he'll drive over it and keep going. He pulled into the driveway, parked the car, walked into the dark house and out of nowhere a lump formed in the back of his throat.

"No way," he said out loud. "Ain't happening. There is no way in hell one single solitary tear will fall from my eyes. This will not be a pity party. I will not rant and rave. I will beat this like I have, like I always have. After all the nonsense I'm still alive and that's not going to change." He finished his speech with a shout and walked into his kitchen.

All Chris wanted right now, besides a clean bill of health was a nice juicy steak, washed down with a tall glass of ice tea. Then he realized he was giving blood tomorrow and couldn't eat or drink. One last bonus punch to round out an already happy day. Maybe for his birthday on Thursday someone could come over and light him on fire. Or maybe he could get mugged and left for dead. Why not? Apparently life was in a generous mood this year!

When Chris prayed that night he prayed for an all or nothing scenario. Either let the doctors get everything, or let them open him up, see that the cancer had spread and close him back up. In his mind there were only two options, life or death. No in-between.

# CHAPTER 40

## October 25, 2040

For the first time in his life, Chris truly felt alone. No matter the circumstance, he always had his parents, a brother or a woman. Not anymore. His parents had passed, his brother had moved away, the women in his life were non-existent. All he had left was prayer and pray he did.

At that very moment he did feel something, the presence of tubes, probes, and an uncomfortable hospital bed making his back bark. He had been laid up at Staten Island University for six days, recuperating from the surgery. Barring something unforeseen, this would be his last night there. Although he was increasingly susceptible to nostalgia in his old age, there would be nothing in this hospital Chris would miss. Not the 3AM blood taking, not the sterile white walls or the drab view of the building next door. Chris had already committed to memory the pattern the floor tiles made in white and green and he was not eager to memorize the ceiling grid.

He was also inundated with cards, flowers, balloons, and visitors, none of which were for him. His roommate on the other side of the room was a man in his early eighties who suffered a heart attack. All day long guests flocked in and out and so did the gifts. It's one thing to feel alone, it's quite another to have the fact slammed over your head with a sledgehammer. He would occasionally detect a pity stare from one of the guests or a whispered question from someone asking his roommate about him. Chris would imagine the questions. "Who's that lonely old man over there?" "Does anyone come and visit him?" The combination of self-pity and paranoia had created a wall of silence that Chris put up to shield from unwanted conversation. Ask me no questions and I shall tell you no lies, he thought to himself.

There was only twenty minutes left for evening visiting hours and Chris had immersed himself in a book he had brought with him, *Empty Faces*. The author, Joe Brady was one of his favorites and he made sure to always grab the latest story. The writing style had a sense of familiarity about it, as if he was hearing the story from an old friend. This one however took forever to get going. After the first one hundred and forty five pages things finally picked up when he heard a familiar voice come into the room.

"Uncle Charlie!"

"Hey there's my favorite niece! Oh and she brought the hubby! How ya doin Henry?" The man named Henry walked over to the side of the bed and gave a hug.

Meanwhile, Chris lost interest in the book and tried in vain to see whose face belonged to the voice. As of right now all he could see was the back of her head.

"Come over here darling and give your favorite uncle a hug!"

The woman walked over and gave him a gigantic kiss and hug. When she turned around Chris' stomach did eight backflips, his jaw dropped and the heart monitor he was connected to went off like July 4th. If he didn't calm himself right this second the end result would either be a heart attack or a stroke. To be honest, those two options were probably easier to deal with than this one.

He couldn't believe it; just could not believe this. Here he was, alone, dealing with his second and even scarier bout of cancer, and who should walk into the room to shatter the last remnants of his will, but Jen. The Jen. "Remember Jen?" He sarcastically asked himself. "The love of your life, the perfect girl, the one you left inside a bar? That Jen. And not just Jen, she's with her loving husband!"

Chris did not want her to see him, not like this. Nor did he want to have any sort of catching up conversation. More importantly, he could not bear to see an ounce of pity in her eyes. Chris turned over onto his right side and faced the door. If he didn't make eye contact and pretended to be asleep, this would be over soon enough.

The minutes moved as if they were hours and every single word he heard her say was like getting punched in the stomach. He had forgotten how much he loved the sound of her voice. How her laughter made his stomach flip and produced goose bumps on his arms. Chris heard all about Henry's new restaurant opening up and how their daughter Allison was pregnant with her first child and their son Teddy was married seven years and living in Boston. This was torture, outright torture, and Chris felt the heat radiate off his body. His back was soaked in sweat and his joints ached from how tense his body had become. The only hope he had was to hear the chimes, which signaled the guests that it was time to leave. Instead another ten minutes of idle chitchat went on until those melodic bells finally appeared. Chris tried to block out all the kisses, goodbyes, and "I love yous" and breathed a sigh of relief when he heard footsteps marching towards the door. In a couple of seconds, if his body permitted it, he would sit back up and resume his book. Suddenly one pair of heels stopped making noise. In fact it sounded like they stopped around the foot of his bed.

"Chris?" He wasn't sure if he actually heard the word Chris or whether he had just fallen asleep and this was a dream.

"Chris Marcum?"

"Huh?" He said as he slowly rolled over in dread.

"Chris! Oh my God Chris! It's me Jen!" She was almost screaming in surprise and he wanted to scream as well. Instead, he pretended to be drowsy and began rubbing his eyes for the full effect.

"Oh wow Jen. Wow. Hi."

"I was walking out of the room when I just happened to see your chart and saw your name. When I saw your face I knew it was you. Oh my God is everything okay?"

"Yeah everything is fine. Just came in for some minor surgery."

"Honey who's this?" Of course her husband had to come over.

"Henry I used to be really good friends with this man a long time ago."

"Over forty years ago if I'm right." Chris tried to sound nonchalant, as if he didn't know exactly how long it had been.

"Wow forty years. Well I'm Henry." Henry flashed his perfect teeth inside an even more perfect smile.

They shook hands and even at sixty-four-years old Chris sized up the guy. He had the perfect haircut, jet black hair (had to be a dye job he thought), bronzed skin, and dressed immaculately in a three-piece suit. In short, he projected authority. Someone of importance. In comparison, Chris projected old and feeble, what with his hospital gown and tubes running out of him. He estimated maybe a two year age difference give or take, with a two hundred mile wide ravine separating their lives. The haves and the have nots.

"Honey if it's all right I'm going to wait outside."

"Yeah sure, okay," she said without diverting her gaze from Chris' face.

Jen waited a couple of seconds until Henry left the room before she resumed the conversation. In those seconds a lifetime of words took place in their eyes. She had aged yet she was still Jen underneath the wrinkles and her still blonde hair. Her deep blue eyes still pierced right through him and her smile was powerful enough to put a grin on his dour face.

"Oh my God I can't believe this. Is it really forty years? I guess it is."

"Yeah goes fast. So how are you?" Chris was doing his best to prove that a man in his condition could in fact be blasé towards the girl who got away.

"Well, I'm going to be a grandma for the first time in a couple of months. Can you imagine? I'm a grandma!"

"Honestly?" Jen laughed immediately and said,

"Always."

"Actually, no, I can't to be honest," Chris said with a laugh.

"I know it's crazy! So how are things with you, I mean besides the whole hospital thing? How's Valerie?"

"Oh we've been divorced for a number of years now." Jen looked like she swallowed a lemon and quickly tried to get the conversation back on course.

"Oh. Oh, I'm sorry." Chris wanted to keep things light and immediately asked,

"Do you still talk to Stephanie?"

"Every once in a while on the iTV. She moved to California about ten years ago with her husband."

"Oh yeah? Good for her."

"Yeah she managed to carve out a life for herself. Although to be honest I'm not sure she ever got over Sam."

"To be honest neither did I." There was a pause and Jen said,

Besides that, is everything else okay?"

"Yeah. Everything is great, well as great as great can be considering."

"If you had to be in the hospital, at least it's for minor surgery." Chris smiled a little uncomfortably and nodded his head.

"Good, well when I come back tomorrow to visit my uncle I'll be sure to include some cookies for you."

"Ahhh shit. I'm checking out tomorrow morning. Thanks though. That would have been nice."

"Excuse me, visiting hours are now over." Nurses have the worst timing.

"I guess that's my cue. I'm sorry we had to see each other like this but I'm happy that at least we did. If that makes any sense."

"No it does and I am too." Jen leaned forward and looked at him. With a smile she came around to the left side of his bed.

"If I hugged you, would I be knocking out any important wires?"

"I'm pretty sure if you did there is a nurse somewhere that could plug them back in."

With a laugh they hugged and his senses were immediately overwhelmed. She still smelled the same. Not her perfume, or her shampoo, but her actual scent. Forty years later and she still smelled like Jen.

"Hopefully next time we'll talk in better circumstances."

"Yeah same here. Bye."

"Bye."

Chris watched as Jen walked out the door and took hold of her husband's hand. One last punch. Chris' eyes lingered on the empty doorway and he let out a deep sigh.

"So you know my niece?" Because he was still somewhere far away in his mind, Chris didn't hear Uncle Charlie.

"I said, so you know my niece?"

"Oh I'm sorry. I didn't hear you."

"Were you friends with Jen?" Chris paused.

"Yup. A long time ago," he said with some not so hidden anguish.

"You're going to think this is strange, but when she said your name out loud it clicked inside my head. This entire time we've been in this room and I never gave your name a second thought. Then just now it came to me. She used to talk about you."

"Excuse me?"

"Jenny is my niece and my goddaughter. As you know she was a beautiful girl growing up, still is as a matter of fact. She was one of those girls who never had a problem with a boy. For one, it wasn't in her to get upset over one and secondly, who would be dumb enough to drop her you know?" Uncle Charlie started to laugh.

"However there was one time; I think she was in her early twenties when some guy actually made her cry. I mean like depressed, can't eat, leave me alone cry! Well I couldn't stand to see my little Jenny upset, and with some careful prodding and gentle nudging I got her to start talking. I don't remember the story now; I'm an old man. All I know is this guy really hurt her. I remember telling her that this guy was an asshole and that her prince, the one who was meant to be would come and make her forget all about this jerk. She said she felt better but I knew she didn't believe me. When you're young you can't see the forest from the trees, but we wound up joking about that story at her wedding." Chris laid in his bed, dumbfounded at what he was hearing.

"I can't believe this. I'm sharing a hospital room with that guy! It's you! *You* are that asshole! Wow, what a small world!" Chris managed to squeak out a fake laugh.

"You're right it is a small world. I guess we just weren't meant to be."

"Yup I guess not. Henry is a great guy so at least everything worked out."

"I guess it did." Chris gave an exaggerated yawn.

"I'm exhausted and think I'm going to take a little nap."

"At 8:07?"

"Yeah I think this asshole needs it."

Chris pretended to be asleep for at least an hour before he finally fell asleep. His mind raced and his dreams made no sense whatsoever. They were a blend of distorted images and faces. The most vivid dream of all was the one of his wedding day.

Everything was the same but the details were off. They were at St. Clare's but it wasn't the same. While everyone was there on his side, he didn't recognize anyone on Valerie's side. The dream then went from Chris talking with Eric on the altar to the organ playing and Valerie walking down the aisle. Except the dress wasn't hers and a man was walking her down instead of her mother. When Valerie reached the altar Chris took her by the hand and realized it wasn't Valerie, it was Jen! He looked deep into those deep blue eyes and felt happy. The perfection of the actual feeling. She smiled and said I love you and then…

248

Chris woke up with a jolt, short of breath and disoriented. His face was flushed, his back was drenched in sweat and he couldn't get his bearings. Looking over at the clock Chris saw 2:18AM and realized he was in the hospital. It was so real! Chris desperately tried to remember every single detail but the majority was drifting away. The only thing that stuck with him was Jen at the altar in her wedding dress saying I love you.

"It's not fair!" He murmured under his breath as he sat back and closed his eyes. "It's not fair!" he repeated, this time out loud while his mind continued to replay Jen saying I love you over and over. In the darkness, Uncle Charlie stirred while Chris' mind did 140mph down the Expressway.

Thirteen years ago he charged into St. Clare's loaded for bear and Father Bob talked him off the ledge. Talked about personal responsibility and owning up to your choices. Fine, he had. He dealt with the imperfections in his life and tried to atone for his sins and what did he get? Cancer Part Two and you know sequels are always worse than the originals. And then as an added bonus he got Jen rubbed in his face? Out of all the hospital rooms her uncle had to be placed in his? He had to meet the perfect husband and hear about her happy family? He had to be called an asshole, and not just an asshole but an asshole who was mocked at her wedding?!

*"I can't believe this. I'm sharing a hospital room with that guy! It's you! You are that asshole! Wow, what a small world!"*

Enough!

Faith was a one way street. Chris gave and he gave and he gave till he bled, and then he gave some more. He was alone in a hospital room, with no one to come and visit except cruel memories. Belief? Faith? They were merely buzzwords for the desperate and the weak. And if God did exist, he certainly wasn't love, like everyone says He was. If He was love then apparently Chris was His red headed stepchild, unwanted and abandoned. No, if there was a God He was cold and removed from the scene. He didn't care what happened to you, whether you lived, died, loved, cried, laughed whatever. It was all simply a random series of events, and for anyone to claim they made sense of them or to have any insight whatsoever into the grand plan was delusional at best and crazy at worst. Well, it was time for

Chris to cast off his shackles, the chains that had burdened him his entire life. At sixty-four-years old he was declaring himself a free man. Free from belief, free from the premise of God. Chris wasn't a masochist! If he was going to suffer he wasn't going to get down on his knees and thank his tormentor at the same time.

Chris turned over and closed his eyes. Tomorrow he would be leaving the hospital not only cancer free, but free from the burden of belief, no longer handcuffed to the myth of an all mighty, all loving creator.

# CHAPTER 41

## April 2, 2043

Even though it was almost three and a half years since his last bout with cancer, Chris still went for check ups every six months. At almost sixty-seven years old he was diligent about his health. He wanted to live as long as possible in the best possible shape. There were signs of a belly underneath his shirt although you couldn't confirm simply by looking at him. When his eyesight started to become an issue a year and a half ago, Chris went in and had the laser corrective procedure. He still had most of his hair and he let it grow long. He also grew out a thick goatee with a permanent five o'clock shadow, homage to Frank Lapidus, the pilot from his favorite television show, LOST.

From the outside, his demeanor seemed the same as before the last cancer scare. The only thing that had changed was his involvement in CCD. A part of him thought he could continue on volunteering, simply because he loved being around the kids so much. The problem was after a lifetime of faith he was bone dry and more importantly he didn't want to lie to the children. No more lies. He didn't want to be held responsible for indoctrinating another generation of children into the cult of religion. To help pass the time he tried taking up different hobbies. At first he wanted to get back into writing but it was no use. He would sit in front of the iTV for an hour, with only a paragraph to show for his efforts. Worse, a type of anxiety would flood his system. The only way he could describe the feeling was a painful version of deja vu. His thoughts would swirl around Jen and the various imagined scenarios they would have experienced together. In fact there was one time when he typed the phrase, "for the guy on the train and not for the professor in Maine." over and over like he was Jack Torrance from "The Shining." This went on for a month before he finally decided to quit writing for good.

The real problem was the need to keep his mind and hands busy. A potential cure was art, so he decided to try and teach himself how to paint. He would never become a Picasso although he did have his own deep blue period. As a result, Chris spent his days in a black smock staring intently at a canvas, trying to decide what his next stroke would be. Even though he wasn't ecstatic, Chris had found some sort of peace, and at this point of his life that was good enough.

The latest doctor appointment was for 2PM, and Chris arrived a half hour early so he could socialize. Debra the receptionist with the Boston accent told him he had plenty of time to kill and Chris laughed. He loved Deb's morbid sense of humor. He strolled into the same waiting room he had been coming to for sixteen years now; a waiting room he knew like the back of his hand. With no one else around, he sat at the iTV terminal for waiting patients and browsed the grid. Twenty minutes later, Chris was in the middle of conversation with a man in his early forties when a girl came out of one of the rooms. She was walking toward the door when she turned around and locked eyes with him.

"Are you waiting for someone or are you sick too?"

The girl couldn't have been more than fourteen-years old. She had long blonde hair and pink cheeks that contrasted off her creamy white skin. Her green eyes were almost cat-like in shape. The girl was also rail thin and couldn't have been more than five feet tall.

"Neither at the moment, I'm here for another checkup."

"Yeah so was I. Hope everything goes well."

The girl smiled and told her mother, or the person Chris presumed to be her mother, that she would be waiting outside. Chris looked over at the woman and saw puffy cheeks and what appeared to be the remnants of mascara down the left side of her face. She had been crying. He waited until the two left the office before he walked over to the counter.

"Deb you know I'm a nosey guy. Is everything okay?"

"Oh that was Gloria Avery and her mother. They just found out Gloria's Hodgkin's disease returned and they have to start treatment again."

"That's terrible. Again?"

"Yeah this is the third time."

"How old is she?"

"Thirteen."

"That's horrible."

"I know. She's a great girl with a strong will."

"Why haven't I ever seen them around here?"

"I don't know, especially since you seem to know everyone. Guess it's just a simple case of different schedules." Chris leaned on her counter and drummed his fingers.

"I guess so. So she's thirteen and this is her third go around?"

"Yeah it's so sad, and she's a great girl too! Extremely positive, you never see her without her smile. Her mother on the other hand is having a hard time coping."

"When does she come back?" Debra leaned back in her chair.

"You are full of questions today!"

"I'm an old man with plenty of time on his hands. If you don't mind me asking, when does she come back?"

"Chris you're lucky I like you, otherwise I'd politely tell you to sit down and mind your own business. She begins treatment in four days. Would you like to know the time?"

"If you wouldn't mind."

"They must be brass because you have a set! She comes in at nine. Happy?"

"Thanks, Deb."

Four days later Chris just happened to go to the doctor's office at nine in the morning and just happened to bump into Gloria and her mother while they waited to get called in. Mrs. Avery was using the iTV and Gloria was looking around for something to do. Chris took off his jacket and draped it over the back of his chair, which was three down from Gloria and her mother. As he sat down their glances met.

"Hey didn't I see you the last time I was here?" Chris gave her a coy smile.

"Yes ma'am. I believe you did."

"Oh my God did you get bad news?"

"No I just have a crush on Debbie so I'm going to wait right here until she'll marry me. Right Debbie?" Deb yelled back.

"Yeah Chris, hope you brought a sandwich because it's going to be a while!" Chris, Gloria, and her mom shared a laugh. After a couple of seconds Gloria looked at Chris and said,

"Well, while you're waiting for Debbie I'll be going in to get treatment."

"Yeah I've been there. So far I'm 2-0 against cancer."

"Well in a week or so I'm going to be 3-0. Looks like I'm winning."

"And I'll be very happy to let you beat me."

"What's your name?"

"I'm Chris Marcum. What's yours?"

"Gloria Avery. This is my mom—Maggie"

"Nice to meet you Mr. Marcum," Maggie said with a wave.

"Hey Chris, I hope you don't fall in love with them too." Debbie had come out front, holding a medical tablet in her left hand.

"Do I detect a hint of jealousy, Deb? C'mon, you know I only have eyes for you."

"Well I'm sorry to break up the party Gloria but Dr. Bennett is ready for you."

Gloria slid off her chair and bounced to her feet.

"All right. Chris do you think you'll be here when I get out?"

"Yeah I'll probably be bugging Deb for a little bit longer. Why?"

"Gives me something to look forward to," she said with a cute little smile.

"That sounds like a plan. See you in a few." Chris turned around and took a seat at the iTV. An hour later he heard them coming down the hallway.

"Mr. Marcum, you still here?" Gloria asked in a somewhat weak voice.

"Yup I'm right here. How are you feeling?"

"Like crap. How do I look?"

"Beautiful, of course!" Gloria turned around to see if her mom was behind her.

"Mom I like this guy. Do you think you'll be here next week?"

"If you want me to."

"Good. Now when I think of coming back here I have something to look forward to."

"So do I. I guess I'll see you in a week." Taking her daughter's hand, Maggie helped her put on her black leather jacket and they walked out the door together.

"So that little girl just did a chemo session and she had the ability to not only smile at me, but have a conversation? Unbelievable!" Chris was back at Debbie's desk.

"I told you Chris, that girl is unreal. Where she gets her strength I have no idea."

Over the next two months Chris made sure to be in the waiting room before and after Gloria's treatment. Even though he drove her crazy, Debbie didn't mind Chris' presence, if only because Gloria seemed to enjoy it. When Gloria's final treatment was completed she asked him to be there when she got the results and of course Chris said yes.

Three days later, Chris paced the waiting room, awaiting the verdict. In all the visits here, he didn't think he was ever this nervous. Fortunately his wait wasn't long and when he saw Gloria come down the hallway with a glow he let out a sigh of relief. Even better, Gloria greeted him with a backbreaking hug. She was now 3-0 against cancer and Chris felt that hug in his knees and his legs for weeks after. It was worth it. The three of them were getting ready to leave when Gloria said,

"Mom can Mr. Marcum come out to eat with us?" Maggie Avery looked at her daughter and smiled.

"I don't know. He might have somewhere else to be."

"Can we ask him?"

"Gloria, we're talking right in front of him. I think you already did." Chris laughed.

"I would love to eat with two beautiful ladies. Where will we go?"

"All I want right now is a cheeseburger, I don't care where."

"Well Mr. Marcum why don't you leave your car here and come with us."

"You sure?"

"If we invited you out to lunch I'm pretty sure it's okay to come in our car as well."

"Well then I'm going to have to insist you ladies start calling me Chris. Mr. Marcum makes me feel like I'm ninety!" The three of them laughed and hopped inside Maggie's car.

The next hour was the first time Chris really talked to Gloria and Maggie. The past two months had been jokes, smiles, and pleasant conversations, nothing of substance. Gloria dominated the conversation, as teenage girls often do. She rambled on about school, her friends, her parents and her previous battles with Hodgkin's. He couldn't believe a thirteen-year-old girl who had been through so much was this happy and positive a person. When Chris mentioned how brave she was, Gloria smiled and said she just had a lot of faith.

"Just like I'm sure you had a lot when you went through your battles, right Chris?" Chris gave an awkward smile and before he could say anything Maggie interjected.

"Gloria you can't assume just because you believe in God so does Chris."

"Mom he beat cancer twice! I beat it three times! How else do you explain that?" Chris was now in an uncomfortable spot and was trying to calculate his words when Gloria spoke up again.

"Chris seriously, don't tell me you don't have any faith in God. That makes no sense whatsoever."

"Let's just say I have had an interesting relationship with Him over the years."

"What does that mean?"

Maggie gave her daughter a look and Gloria let it go. The conversation quickly went back to Gloria talking about her parents and other exciting things and events in her life. When it was time to leave Chris insisted on paying the bill. After a couple of minutes of protest Maggie relented, but not before she informed him they would have to invite him over to eat to make it up to him. Chris agreed and they climbed back into the car. After a short drive, they reached the doctor's office and Maggie pulled up to let him out. He was about to leave the car when Gloria spoke up.

"I'm sorry I made you feel uncomfortable when I asked about God."

"Oh don't worry; you didn't make me feel uncomfortable. Besides we're friends now, you can't be uncomfortable around your friends."

"Well if that's the case then you won't mind if I keep talking about Him, right? He's important to me and I don't want you to feel weird." Chris paused.

"Sure why not. Thanks for the company ladies. You made an old man very happy."

"And you made my daughter very happy, it's the least we could do." Chris blushed at the sentiment and was surprised even further when Gloria leaned over and gave him a big wet kiss on the cheek and hug.

"I love you Chris." Chris looked at Maggie who had a big smile on her face.

"Love you too kiddo."

"Talk to you soon."

"Bye."

"Bye."

# CHAPTER 42

## June 28, 2045

Despite Chris feeling a little out of place Gloria insisted on his attendance. And when Gloria insisted, there was no question whether or not Christopher Marcum would be there. This was a big day and Gloria wanted all her family and friends to celebrate her Sweet 16 in style. After two years, Chris had become the grandpa that Gloria never had. Both of her grandfathers had died before she was born, and her paternal grandmother had died when she was five. All she had was a Mee-Mah (her affectionate term for grandma) and her Chris.

At first Chris was hesitant to get so involved in the Avery family. He didn't want to impose and certainly didn't want to become one of those people who overstay their welcome. Yet the dinner invites kept coming, as did the invitations to spend Thanksgiving and Christmas together. The Averys had done the old man a tremendous favor; they had given him the family life he longed for. The only time Chris would refuse an invitation from Gloria was when she asked him to come to church. He told her she could talk about God as much as she wanted to, and Chris would always listen, but in return she had to respect his decision not to go. Gloria adhered to the first condition, talking about God whenever she had something to say, and ignored the second. Even though she ignored the second condition, she tried to be tactful about it. Instead of asking every week, her invitations to join them at church were sprinkled liberally throughout. Chris couldn't even get mad at her persistence, how could he get angry at someone whom he considered a granddaughter?

Gloria told him in the weeks leading up to her Sweet 16 that a certain boy might be coming, and she might like this certain boy. Chris joked around and called the mystery boy George Glass, after that Brady Bunch episode about Jan's mysterious boyfriend, a fact that went over her head. Chris had to remind himself that he almost fifty-three years older than she was, therefore he would have to update his jokes and references.

Before Chris left his house, he took a look at himself in the mirror. He was wearing a black pinstripe suit with a navy blue shirt and a light blue tie. He threw some wax into his long thinning hair, gave his goatee a neat trim and thought all things considered he was still a damn handsome man.

When he pulled into the parking lot and saw the teenagers and other faces he didn't recognize his stomach began to churn. Sure he was comfortable around Gloria, Maggie, and her dad Ben, but this was different. All her family and friends were going to be here. Did Chris belong? He stepped out of the car and took a look at himself in the reflection.

"Nonsense," he thought to himself. She wanted him here; he was here and no matter what, he would have a good time. Chris walked into the hall and stopped in front of the seating chart. He spotted his name and breathed out a sigh of relief. Maggie had put him at the family table, along with Gloria's parents, mee-mah, and a couple of aunts and uncles that Chris had met. Not only did save him a night of awkward, forced conversation, it really drove home how much the Averys thought of him.

As he began to walk to the door he heard a young voice scream out.

"Chris!"

He turned around just in time to get walloped by a charging Gloria who threw her arms around him in a big hug. His knees felt the jolt but Chris shrugged off the pain. People stopped to see what the commotion was all about, and Chris was slightly embarrassed by all the attention.

Gloria looked radiant in her bright yellow dress and projected a feeling of class. She had grown beautifully into early adulthood and was no longer the rail thin girl he met two years ago. He still had her in height, although they were almost even with her in heels.

"Chris I'm not going to lie, I was afraid you weren't going to show up."

"Now how could I miss the social event of the season," Chris said with a wink.

"Are you going to dance?"

"Probably not."

"Oh c'mon! It's a party, how are you not going to dance?"

"I wouldn't want to embarrass all these young guys. How could they compete if I started spinning on my head?"

"You could do that?" she asked sarcastically.

"When I was younger."

Gloria grabbed him by the hand. Her mysterious boy was walking over and trying to stay cool about it. Her face turned beet red as the boy smiled and kissed her hello. Chris made a face as if to say, aren't you going to introduce me and Gloria obliged.

"Derek this is the guy I consider to be my grandpa—Chris."

"Nice to meet you, Chris."

"Very nice to meet you, Derek," and they shook hands. Chris knew the kids wanted to talk and excused himself.

"I'm clearly due for a nap. Gloria I'm going to go find my table. Derek it was nice meeting you."

The night was spectacular and Chris couldn't believe the extravagance. The food was delicious, in fact, there seemed to be a waiter delivering another course every ten minutes. If one felt so inclined and were of legal age you could spend the night getting soaked at either of the two wet bars located on opposite sides of the room.

Gloria loved to dance and spent most of the night on the dance floor with her friends (and Derek). Several times she waved over to the table for Chris to get up and join in, but Chris would laugh and shake his head. Twenty years ago Chris would be up on the dance floor, sometimes in rhythm, sometimes not so much. These days he was content to drink his coffee and enjoy the festivities all around him.

All events need to be recorded for posterity and Gloria's Sweet 16 was no different. She had placed mini 3D recorders on every table so her guests could record a personal message and make a little movie of the evening. When it came time for Chris to record his message he kept it short and sweet.

"Happy birthday sweetie. You look beautiful and that smile hasn't left your face all night! I hope this is the first of many best nights of your life. Lots of love."

They reached the point in the evening when Gloria had her candle ceremony and Chris sat back and watched as her parents, aunts, uncles, and Mee-Mah all went up after a touching speech and lit their candle. Then the friends went up in different groups and Derek as well. Finally Gloria announced her seventeenth and final candle.

"As everyone knows, the final candle to be lit is the person who inspires you. I gave this careful thought and consideration before realizing the obvious. Christopher Marcum, even though you aren't really my grandpa I consider you to be one. We met two years ago at the clinic and from the moment we met you have tried to look out for me. You were there waiting for me at the beginning and end of every session and you have no idea how much that meant to me. I thank God every night that he brought you into my life and I hope you never leave me! So Chris would you come up and help me light my seventeenth candle?"

Chris rose from his seat, slightly embarrassed by all the attention, and began to walk to the middle of the dance floor. Keeping a stiff upper lip and grinning, Chris walked up and helped light the final candle. Then Gloria looked at him and said I love you, followed by a big hug. His eyes welled up with tears and he told her to keep hugging him so no one could see him crying. Gloria laughed. Chris dried his eyes and walked back to the table, beaming. How ironic, he thought, it only took getting cancer to finally gain a granddaughter.

# CHAPTER 43

## March 22, 2048

March 22, 2048 was supposed to be an easy day, a quick visit to the doctor's and a small series of tests. Afterward, the results would come back negative and they could go get a cheeseburger. Instead, what was discovered was the worst possible news—and Chris heard it over the iTV. He was watching a movie when the call came through. Ordinarily he wouldn't have been alarmed by a Gloria video call. However, when he saw a picture of her at her Sweet 16 instead of a live image of her face he knew something was wrong.

"Chris you have to come over right now." Gloria's voice fluttered and he suspected she might be crying.

"Why what's the matter Gloria?"

"My Hodgkin's returned. They said it's very aggressive."

"Oh my God." He sat down on his couch and arched his head back.

"Chris I'm scared. Would you come over?"

"I'll be right there."

Chris spent most of the afternoon at the Avery house alternating between the living room and the kitchen. They talked, they laughed, they cried. After the initial shock had worn off, Gloria was resolute in the fact that she would be beating cancer again for the fourth time. Three times already it had tried to beat her and failed. This would not be different. Eventually, Gloria excused herself to call Derek and tell him the news. A silence hung in the air for a moment before her father Ben filled it.

"You have no idea how thankful we are that you are so involved in Gloria's life. You truly are a Godsend."

"Thanks, but I think she's even luckier to have two parents who aren't divorced, especially in this day and age." Her mother took his hand and said,

"Chris, we think you should know this. Gloria is in trouble. This isn't like the last time."

"What are you saying?"

"All we're asking is for you to just keep being you. That's all." Ben stood up, wrapped his arms around his wife and tried to stifle any display of emotion.

Almost a year later, February 12, 2049, things had grown progressively worse. Chris pulled into the hospital parking lot with a knot in his stomach and a brick in his throat. Gloria was in trouble. Her body had started to break down and they had to withhold treatment until she was better able to handle it. Chris made sure to visit every day and would sit with her until he felt it was time to go. At first that would be when she fell asleep; but she woke up one time, saw him leaving, and grew really upset. She wanted him to stay, just like the first time they met, so that way when she woke up she had something to look forward to. Chris would sit there and watch her sleep while his heart silently broke. Her eyes were gray and drawn into her face. Her lips were dry and chapped. The glow she always emitted was now a dull hint. Chris estimated she lost at least twenty pounds. In these quiet times Chris would rail against the God Gloria believed in, the God he had once wasted his time with. What good is it? How can you possibly explain this one? A sweet innocent girl a couple of weeks from her twentieth birthday trapped inside a dying body? Where was the justice in that?

When Chris returned to the hospital that night, Gloria was asleep and her mom sat next to the bed, doing her best not to cry. He walked over and Maggie fell into his chest, violently sobbing. After a couple of minutes she calmed down and Chris told her to go get a bite. He'll sit here and keep her company. Maggie thanked him and asked if he wanted anything from the cafeteria downstairs. He didn't.

Chris sat and looked around. How long ago was it that he was in a bed like this, except he had no one to visit him? And now here he was, the healthy old man visiting a young sick girl. He was about to go off on another rant when her eyes began to flutter open. Chris leaned in close and said,

"Hey, hey Gloria. I'm right here."

"Hey Chris," she said with as much energy as she could muster.

"Your mom just went for a bite. She'll be right back."

"Chris, I want to talk to you." Chris took hold of her somewhat lifeless left hand. Tenderly he began to stroke it.

"About what?"

"Chris I know you don't like hearing it, but I've been doing a lot of praying lately."

"No. No, stop!" He said in a soothing voice. "That doesn't bother me. You can talk about praying as much as you want."

"I haven't been praying for me, I've been praying for you." Chris was taken off guard and replied,

"Me? Why?"

"Chris I made my peace already." Chris began to protest but she waved him off. "I know…you know, and my parents know what the deal is. And I'm okay with it. When I was four they told my mom if I was lucky I'd see six but here I am, still going."

"Gloria stop."

"No I need to say this. I'm right with God and I know you are not. I've avoided talking directly about this with you because I didn't want to make you upset, but now I figure I have you trapped. It's not like you're going to leave my side now, right?"

"Oh great, take advantage of the old man. Good job!" His eyes began to glisten.

"I don't know what happened that made you stop believing. And I know it's none of my business why. But I don't want to spend eternity in Heaven and not have you there with me."

"At my age you might see me sooner than you think."

"See you're joking to avoid talking about it. Chris, do me this favor and just talk to me. After today I'll never bring this up ever again. You have my word." Chris paused and took a breath. He ran his right hand through his thinning hair.

"What do you want to talk about?"

"Why you lost your faith."

Chris let out a deep sigh and crossed his arms. Then he ran his fingers once again through the remaining hairs on his scalp.

"It wasn't one thing, Gloria. I mean I had rough patches but I always came through. It was just too many things. Too many moments, too many people, too much time."

"That still doesn't sound like a good enough reason."

"Well I think I told you I was married once, right? Well I also have a son, who I haven't seen in over," he paused for a second as he

264

thought just how long it was. "Thirty years. Thirty…years." He took a breath and Gloria waited for him to continue. "As a result I was alone for a long time. A very long time. It's my fault and I've tried to rectify the situation but he doesn't want anything to do with me. Regardless, at least I have a chance to fix that relationship. What kills me, what still causes me to lose sleep at night is something I can't go back and fix. And what makes it worse is I know, once again, it's my fault. Back when I was younger I had the choice of two pretty ladies and I chose the wrong one. And I knew immediately I made the wrong choice but what could I do? Life moved forward and I just went along for the ride. The entire time I wanted to stop and go back. Back to the girl I should have been with. When my cancer came back for the second time I was laid up in a hospital bed, depressed, lonely, and to be honest a little bit scared. I had a roommate, an elderly man who I really tried to avoid talking to. Turned out he was the uncle of the girl I should have married!

"Wow." Despite her weakened condition Gloria managed to put some passion behind the single word.

"Do you know how I found that out?"

"No."

"Because Jen and her husband came in to visit him."

"Oh Chris."

"And I saw the two of them together and I heard about her kids and her life and how happy she was and it was just too much. Her uncle had balloons and gifts and cards and people streaming in and out and I had no one. And the one person I wanted more than anything else in this world walked into my room, except she was there for someone else."

"I see."

"The whole reality just became too much to bear. There are other things, little drops that by themselves aren't big, but put them together and suddenly I'm drowning in the Pacific Ocean! So finally, in that hospital bed, alone and miserable after seeing Jen walk out the door and grab her husband's hand, I declared that I had enough with the whole God scene. I believed my entire life and I received nothing but pain, heartbreak, and cancer."

"Chris I'm sorry, I really am but the God you think is unjust is the same God I thank every night for bringing you to me. He gave me a grandpa to help me beat cancer. How lucky am I?"

"Yeah and look at you now. I'm old and healthy; you are young and sitting in a hospital bed. How is that fair?"

"I don't know, Chris, and I've thought about that sometimes myself. It is what it is. I can't change anything and there's no use complaining about it. I just have to deal with it. I know it's hard to be on the other side of the bed, but you have to accept it. The one thing I'm grateful for is that this isn't the end for me. When I die I *know* it's not the end of me; I get to go on to another place where there isn't cancer or suffering. That's our reward for the struggles of this life—a promise that nothing will be hard ever again."

"See I refuse to accept that. I refuse to believe that I should be fine with my personal pain because better days are ahead. I still don't see how a God can justify pain with the promise of another better life."

"It's not up to us to understand, it's up to us to live our lives and just trust that He knows more than we do. It would be like me telling you about life when you clearly know more than I do."

"Right now I'm questioning that."

"Stop. You're older and wiser than me. You have experienced much more than I ever will. So I trust that when you tell me something it's the truth. Well God is older than both of us; I trust that He's telling me the truth as well."

"Well what if you're wrong? What if there is no God?"

"I already know there is. Before you tell me I was dreaming, or it was the drugs just listen. Promise?" Chris could tell by her face this was important and gave her his word to listen.

"Last night an angel came into my room and I actually talked to it! I had never seen anything more beautiful in my entire life. At first all I could see is this blinding bright light, until somehow I was able to look directly at it without squinting. Then it started talking to me and I really thought I was hallucinating. I'm telling you it was as real as the conversation we're having right now. The angel asked if I truly believed in God and tested me by asking if I wanted to prove my faith by living my entire life all over again."

Chris just stared while she told him the tale and felt vaguely uncomfortable. As if he already knew the story. He chalked it up to déjà vu and continued to listen.

"I told him God doesn't need proof of my love. He already knows what's in my heart. The angel seemed to get annoyed at that answer and asked me again, even saying that in this alternate life I wouldn't have cancer, but I refused. This is the life God gave me and I'm happy living it. I actually said that to an angel! I don't remember the rest of the conversation, the one thing I know for certain is he left unhappy."

"I'll tell you what. If anyone else told me that I'd say they were crazy, but I actually believe you."

"So if you believe me then believe in Him. I can't guarantee the rest of your life will be happy; however I can guarantee that you'll be able to see me again, and that's something right?" Chris became choked up and tried to say something. Gloria leaned forward and squeezed his hand.

"Listen to me; He brought us together for a reason. You helped me beat cancer and now it's my turn to help you." For the first time in a long time, Chris thought long and hard about what he was hearing. Then he looked down and saw Gloria's ravaged body and a deep-seated anger took hold of him.

"No! It's not fair that I will be visiting your grave instead of you visiting mine. I don't want to believe in a God who does that!"

"Chris, it sounds like you want a God who comes down from the heavens and tells you, no Chris don't do that, or who pushes you in the right direction. It sounds like you want a God who will take you by the hand and bring you to happiness. The problem is, Chris, that's not the way things work. We believe in a God who loved us so much He became one of us to feel our pain, our concerns, our anxiety and He was killed for His troubles. Our God is love, but what He isn't is an overprotective daddy who won't let his child run. Chris, He gave us free will for a reason, and it wasn't to hurt us, it was to let us run. To make mistakes, to make choices. To let us stumble and fall, scrape our knee and cry, but the most important thing, to make us get back on our own two feet and keep on running. You want a God who snaps His fingers and gives us instant happiness, but what kind of happiness would we have if that were the case? We would be fools living like sheep." Chris paused and this time knew he heard those words before.

"All right let's say everything you just said is right. What now? Do you think I should fall to my knees and beg for forgiveness?" Gloria managed a feeble laugh and replied,

"It doesn't have to be as dramatic as that. We could just say an Act of Contrition together. I'm not a priest but I'm pretty sure saying a prayer where you are asking for forgiveness would work."

He took a deep breath. He still felt angry yet at the same time felt something deep inside. For the first time since God only knew Chris began to pray. He was surprised at how easily the words came back to him.

*"Oh my God I am heartily sorry for having offended you. I confess all my sins because of your just punishment. But most of all because they offend you my God, who is all good and deserving of all my love. I firmly resolve with the help of your grace to sin no more and avoid the near occasion of sin ever again. Amen."* Gloria began to cry and Chris panicked, thinking there was something wrong.

"Why are you crying?"

"Because now I know I'll definitely see you again." Gloria put her arms out and Chris met them in long embrace. It would be their last conversation.

The morning of Valentine's Day, around 4AM, Chris was awoken by the sound of his iTV chirping. It was Maggie, calling to inform him of the bad news. Gloria had passed peacefully an hour ago and Maggie and Ben were with her during her final moments. They were on their way home now and she had to call him. She also thanked Chris for practically living at the hospital with them and tried to say more but was too overcome with emotion to continue. Chris said he would be right over and hopped in his car. He was thankful he owned one of those new cars with the automatic driver option, at that moment there was no way he could drive.

Almost four years ago, Chris sat nervously in his car outside a hall, wondering if he belonged at a gathering of Gloria's loved ones. That occasion was a happy one and Chris left that night ecstatic and at peace with his life. Four years later, Chris sat nervously in his car, up a couple of blocks from Scalia's Funeral Home. Unfortunately, there would be no laughter or smiling faces, except this time he didn't need Gloria's insistence to know he belonged. He just dreaded walking in and facing reality. Of seeing Maggie and Ben and looking at their devastated faces. And absolutely scared to death to see Gloria in her coffin. Chris took a deep breath and said a quick prayer asking God for the strength he clearly lacked. Another deep breath and he left the car and walked to the funeral home.

The place was packed with family, friends, and practically every single person she ever went to school with. The line encompassed the entire room, through the hallway, and out the door. Fortunately one of her aunts who Chris had sat with at the Sweet 16 saw him walking in the parking lot and brought him inside with the family. He couldn't bear to go up to the coffin, instead he spent his time talking with people he had nothing in common with except their love for Gloria.

Chris made sure to keep his composure in front of everyone. They had a two-day wake to ensure anyone who wanted to come could, and there were pictures of Gloria everywhere, along with enough flowers to fill three houses! Ben was strong, and made sure to stand up front and thank everyone for coming, while Maggie had her moments when she would just walk up to the casket and silently cry.

It was at the cemetery when it truly hit him. They were placing roses on top of the coffin when Chris was overwhelmed with grief and memories past and could no longer hold back the tears. He walked away from the scene and just let everything out. Out of all the losses he had experienced, out of all the moments he had taken away from him this was the worst. Ordinarily he would take all the pain and anger in his heart and direct it at the idea of a loving God. Only this time was different. Instead, he silently thanked God for bringing Gloria into his life.

# CHAPTER 44

## Thanksgiving/Christmas 2049

The days and weeks following Gloria's death all seemed to run together for Chris. Most days he just wanted to stay in bed and shut the world out, before an odd sense of guilt would force him to get up. It wasn't like he had to go to work, or see anyone. Rather, he knew he couldn't spend the rest of his life in his bed. He developed a consistent routine of waking up, eating breakfast, watching something on the iTV (most often a movie from the twentieth century), having lunch, going for a walk, tinkering around the house, dinner, paint for a little while, and sleep. Just going through the motions of a life lived. He was seventy-three years old and felt every minute of it.

The first year following her death Chris remained in contact with the Averys. They still invited him over to eat although after three or four times Chris felt worse afterwards and he was pretty sure they felt the same. When Maggie called up to ask Chris if he wanted to spend Thanksgiving with them Chris politely declined, making up a story about going out to see Eric. He wasn't sure if it was paranoia or genuine, but Chris could have sworn he detected a hint of relief in her voice when he said he couldn't make it. It wasn't that they didn't like him; just his presence reminded them of what they had lost.

The Monday before Thanksgiving Chris sat around the house, with the conversation he had with Maggie still reverberating in his ears. Even though he lied about seeing Eric why not give him a call and see what he was doing? The guy was his brother, no matter the distance. Chris pulled up Eric's number and waited for the iTV to connect them.

"Hello?" On Chris' screen was a default picture of Eric and Danielle, perhaps from a recent party. He gathered she wasn't presentable for the live screen.

"Danielle?"

"Chris?"

"The one and only."

"Chris, oh my God how are you?"

"I'm good. I'm good. How about you guys?"

"Hold on one second. I want to make sure I look good before turning off the default."

"Oh stop. You're beautiful no matter what."

"And you're a sweet liar. Okay here we go." Danielle came into view and it was like the hands of time hadn't moved in years. Danielle still looked like Danielle, beautiful as always. Even now in her sixties she was a striking woman who could turn some heads. She had cut her long hair and gained a couple of wrinkles but it made no difference. She possessed the confidence of someone assured of who they were and he could hear it in her voice.

"So how goes life in Texas?"

"Oh we are so happy! Seriously life couldn't be any better. Eric putters around the house getting in my way, but after ten years of retirement I'm finally starting to get used to it."

"I can imagine. Wow he's retired ten years? It goes fast."

"Sure does. Seems like yesterday we were planning a wedding and now here we are, a couple of old farts."

"Hey what does that make me then?"

"*Much* older!" Danielle waited for the laughter to die down before speaking again.

"So what makes me so lucky to see your face?"

"Well I was thinking that we haven't seen each other in God knows how long and that's not right. So I was wondering if you guys are going to be around over the holidays would you mind a visitor?"

"Oh we would love that! All we were going to do was have some friends over for Thanksgiving. The two of us would love for you to come. Get on a plane and get out here." The great thing, (or depending on the circumstance, not so great thing) about the iTV is you could see if the person's words matched up with their body language. In this case it was plain to see Danielle was legitimately excited.

"Really?"

"Absolutely."

271

"Sounds good. I'll go and check out what flights are available and I'll email you to let you know when I'm coming in."

"Great and listen, I'm not going to tell Eric, let's make it a surprise."

"Sounds like a plan—talk to you soon."

Chris was able to book a flight leaving in two days time, Wednesday morning. Barring any unforeseen setbacks, he would touchdown in Austin at 11AM. He emailed Danielle the flight info and packed his things. It had been a long time since he used a suitcase. Forty-eight hours later Chris was stepping out of the terminal, looking for a familiar face. Danielle saw him first and ran as fast as a woman in her late sixties can run.

"Chris!" He turned around and they kissed and hugged.

"This is so wonderful! I'm so happy you came! Eric is going to be so surprised."

"He still doesn't know?"

"Oh my husband can be oblivious at times, I'm sure you know that!" Danielle said with a laugh. "I can't tell you how great it is that you are actually here!"

"I know, I can't wait to see my brother."

Eric was in the garage messing around with his tools when he looked up and saw the car pulling in. He was about to ask Danielle where she snuck off to when he saw who was getting out of the front seat.

"Chris!"

The two men ran towards each other and embraced. Chris could still see the Eric he grew up with despite the bald ring on top of his head. Chris joked he had put on some weight since the last time they saw each other, which Eric attributed to Danielle's cooking. Outside of the belly, Eric was in great shape. When Eric asked Chris how this came about, he immediately turned to his wife, who had a sheepish grin on her face.

"I figured you would enjoy the surprise."

"I did but you almost gave me a heart attack from the shock."

Thanksgiving was spectacular, as Danielle went all out with the food, cold antipasto, salad, lasagna, turkey with all the rest, and pies galore for dessert. Chris joked that there should be a doctor on call just in case after the meal. Eric introduced his brother to his friends, two couples around their age. Jon and Kara were originally from

Chicago before moving out to Austin twenty years ago. Rich and Melissa were Texas natives. They were all neighbors for eighteen years now, after Eric moved to the neighborhood. Chris told them all stories about the two of them growing up. Of course Chris had to throw in some embarrassing stories as well.

Afterwards they retired into the den and now it was Chris' turn to listen to the stories about Eric since he moved out there. The conversation went long through the night and through various bottles as well, although Chris stuck with ice tea. It was well past two in the morning when everyone decided to go home. Chris was in the living room helping Eric clean up, while Danielle washed the glasses in the sink. Eric paused and looked at his brother.

"Thank you. I had forgotten how much fun we had together and I just wish we didn't wait this long to do this."

"Listen Eric, the blame lies just as much with me as it does with you. We both should have called but for whatever reason we didn't. All we can do now is make sure that never happens again."

"When do you plan on leaving?"

"I think my flight is sometime in the early afternoon on Monday."

"No no no. That is way too soon. We don't see each other for years and now we only get five days together? You're going to have to come back for Christmas and New Year's." Chris smiled.

"Would I be staying at a five star hotel?"

"Well we might not be five stars but we do have a maid."

"Hey I heard that!" Danielle chimed in from the kitchen.

"No, I was umm, talking about someone else." The two men laughed while Danielle gave a loud, sarcastic chuckle in response.

"Seriously, Chris, come back out and spend more time with us. And don't worry; I'm not going to make you keep flying on your dime. We'll pay for your plane tickets as your Christmas gift."

"Wow that's much better than the usual Christmas card I get."

On December 21, Danielle once again picked up Chris, this time with Eric driving. He was stiff as a board getting off the plane and attributed the pain in his legs to them not flying him out first class. He would be staying until the second of January. This way they would have plenty of time to enjoy each other without feeling the rush of the calendar.

Chris woke up a little disoriented on Christmas morning; he wasn't used to this kind of weather after spending a lifetime in the cold of the northeast. It was a beautiful day outside and the three of them decided to have breakfast out on the patio. After they were finished, Chris went inside and brought out his gifts, as did Danielle. At first Chris thought they were all for her husband, until he noticed a couple of boxes addressed to him as well. He quickly protested that their agreement was the airfare, but Eric told him to be quiet and open up his gifts. Chris protested mildly for a couple of seconds before he tore into the various boxes. The first gift was a couple of shirts and dress pants. The second box had a heavy blanket that Danielle had made herself, and underneath was a picture of Chris and Eric when they were kids playing out in the backyard. Eric was covered in dirt and Chris had the biggest grin on his face.

"Where did you find this?"

"I was cleaning out my dresser awhile ago and found it in a white envelope. I love this picture so much it's sitting on my nightstand. Danielle suggested we make a copy and give it to you."

"Well I can't thank you guys enough for…"

"Chris stop. It's fine. We're together and happy, that's all I care about."

Christmas day was spent at Rich and Melissa's, who treated Chris like they knew him for years. The relative ease at which they all became friends surprised Chris and later on he commented to his brother how lucky he was to have such great neighbors.

Two nights later the boys decided to just stay up late and talk. There was so much that hadn't been said and questions needed to be resolved. They went out on Eric's back porch and enjoyed the night almost as much as they enjoyed each other's company. They sat next to each other on the rocking chairs and took everything in.

"Eric can I ask you something?"

"Sure."

"It's something that used to bother me but now I couldn't care less. Still I'm curious."

"Oh boy this could get interesting," he said with a laugh. "Okay, go ahead and ask."

"Did you ever like Valerie?" The question caused Eric to start laughing even harder.

"Sorry, I didn't mean to laugh; it's just that it came out of nowhere."

"Well did you ever? I mean did you think I was making the right choice when I asked her to marry me?"

"You want the honest answer?"

"Eric, I'm divorced how many years now? I'm pretty sure this isn't sensitive anymore."

"Okay then. Don't get me wrong, she was a nice girl."

"But."

"But she always rubbed me the wrong way. It was like she was trying too hard to fit in. The way she would hang out with Mom, I mean who does that? And she was kind of patronizing at times."

"Did you think that was reason enough to not marry her?"

"Wait. Before I answer that I'll give you a story. It'll help give a good idea of where I'm coming from. Remember that girl Lisa I was dating?"

"Yeah; that didn't last that long right?"

"Yeah only a couple of months. Anyway did you know her and Valerie almost got into a huge fight in the bathroom at Bar-A?"

"Wait, what?" Chris asked with a half laugh.

"Yeah, apparently Lisa had too much to drink and thought Val was flirting with me. She followed Valerie to the bathroom and waited for her to come back out. When Valerie opened the door Lisa was in her face." With a surprised look on his face Chris waited for more details.

"Of course Valerie thought she was joking around and said yes it was true, we were having a secret affair behind everyone's backs. Like I said Lisa was drunk and more than a touch possessive and went red with anger. She started to yell but before she could get out her first threat Valerie shoved her, causing Lisa to stumble and fall on the floor. When she got back up Val got right in her face and told her she would be on the floor again if Lisa didn't apologize and walk away."

"What?" Chris said in shock.

"Yeah and Lisa had at least five inches on her, so it was more like Valerie's nose to Lisa's neck."

"This is crazy. How didn't I ever hear about this?"

"Hold on. Stephanie hears the commotion and goes over to see both girls nearly ready to beat the hell out of each other. Fortunately, she broke it up and that was the end of that."

Chris started laughing again.

"Tell me again what the point of that story was?"

"Well even though Valerie didn't do anything wrong she just couldn't let things go. Lisa was a nut job, which is why we didn't last long. Instead of Valerie just ignoring her and walking away, she was ready to fight her." Chris couldn't get over the story and the boys kept laughing.

"So to answer your question again, honestly yeah. I thought you were making a mistake, but what did I know? I was your younger brother and you were madly in love with the girl."

"Well you could have said something to me."

"Chris seriously, let's think about this. If I pulled you aside forty years ago and said you shouldn't marry her how would you have taken that?"

"Now it's my turn to be honest. I might have listened. I mean I was actually on the fence between her and this girl Jen. Do you remember Jen?"

"Remember her?" Eric's chair jerked back in surprise. "Holy shit Chris I had a huge crush on her! I was so jealous of you that you were going to the beach with her and seeing her in a bikini!" A big smile came over Chris's face as he remembered what she looked like in a bikini.

"Really? When did you ever see her?"

"One night at Leo's I was hanging out with my crew and I saw Stephanie with her friends across the bar. I went over to say hello and couldn't take my eyes off of Jen. Steph told her I was your younger brother and her eyes lit up! Remember those eyes?" Chris smiled and nodded his head.

"Later on my friends couldn't believe that not only did I know that girl, but my older brother wasn't going after her.

"And did you tell them the reason why was because I was with someone else?"

"Yeah but they didn't care. They thought you were stupid for turning it down!" Both men laughed.

"Well it wasn't exactly offered to me." Eric gave his brother a look that suggested otherwise.

"Yeah so getting back to what I was saying, anytime after I saw her at Leo's I would always make sure to go over and say hi. Between that and talking to her online…"

"You talked to her online?" Chris was laughing at his own ignorance.

"I told you I had a huge crush on her!"

"Well did you..."

"C'mon! Stop that!" Eric was hysterical.

"What? Is it that crazy?"

"Damn right it's crazy! I was too young for her. Besides even if I was older she had a thing for you."

"She said that?" Fifty years later and it still mattered to him.

"She didn't come out and say it but it was no big secret."

"Damn." Chris couldn't believe any of this.

"To say the least! We all thought for sure she was the one for you. Hell, Mom and Dad were convinced you were going in that direction. Instead it seemed like out of nowhere things changed and the next thing we knew you were engaged." Chris laughed again.

"Time out! How did Mom and Dad know about her? I never brought Jen to the house."

"You know our mother. She knew you were hanging out with a girl who wasn't your girlfriend and wanted to know who she was. Next thing I know I have her and Dad peering over my shoulder as I show them pictures of Jen online."

"This is unbelievable!"

"Hey you wanted to know!"

"Did you ever hear about our little incident at Leo's?" Eric stopped rocking and leaned forward on his chair.

"Oh everyone knew about that! Word spread pretty fast. Did the girls really fight on top of the bar?" Chris let loose with a loud booming laugh.

"Fight? Nooo. There wasn't a punch thrown. Although Valerie went ballistic and talked a good game. Jen didn't seem to back down either."

"Ohh you were so lucky. Two hot girls fighting over you!"

"Yeah and looked what happened."

"Yeah." The boys paused, smiled, and started to laugh again. After the laughter subsided Chris spoke up.

"There was something else I always wondered. Remember the speech you gave at our wedding? You mentioned something about a gift she gave you that meant a lot to you. I never found out what the hell you were talking about."

"Ohh yeah I remember that. Hell of a speech if I do say so myself. You mean to tell me she never told you?"

"Nope."

"Well it starts off a couple of weeks after that car accident I was in. Remember?"

"How could I forget?"

"Well you were in the shower and I was in the den watching television when she walked in. I gave her the casual hey and went back to watching whatever it was, probably a Mets game. She waited a couple of seconds before walking over and dropping a book on my stomach. She said to look for December 6, 1997, and read what was on the page. I looked at her and she smiled and left the room."

"Are you telling me…"

"Yeah apparently you did a horrible job of hiding that journal of yours because she read it pretty regularly, or at least back then she did. However this time she shared the wealth and everything made sense. A couple of days later I thanked her for doing that for me. I referred to it at the wedding because I wanted her to know how grateful I was."

"I had a hard time actually telling you how I felt, which is why I guess I was your servant for those first couple of weeks."

"Yeah I didn't understand why you were being so helpful and friendly until I read that. Don't worry Chris, I never blamed you or held any sort of resentment towards you. It wasn't your fault at all and I hope that thought left your mind a long time ago." Chris ran his hand through his remaining hair and looked away.

"Well it has always been one of those nagging thoughts that rose up every now and then. I'm glad to hear this coming from you. Thanks Eric."

"No, thank you. No matter what you were good to me, and I'm glad we're spending the time together now."

"Same here."

A moment went by as the boys stared off into the darkness, with the sounds of the night filling in the silence. Eric spoke up again.

"I don't mean to be forward, but have you ever considered you know, moving out here. To be closer to us I mean." Chris looked over at his brother and smiled.

"The thought crossed my mind once or twice, but my home is up East. I haven't had the most stable of lives but it's where I'm comfortable."

"I understand, I'm just saying that though, if you ever wanted to, we would love to have you as a neighbor. I'm sure Rich and Jon wouldn't mind having you here either!"

"I don't want to say never, but at my age I think I'm done moving."

"I feel the same."

Once again the conversation quieted down and Eric asked if Chris wanted a drink. Chris said he would take an ice tea, chilled, which got a laugh. Two minutes later he was back with two glasses.

"Is the glass chilled enough for your liking sir?"

"Yes I believe it is thank you."

They sat back, Chris sipping on his drink, Eric on his wine enjoying the comfortable silence. Chris couldn't get over all the stars in the sky! A slight breeze would blow through every now and again and Chris smiled. This is the way God intended the night to look. After a couple of minutes, Chris turned to his brother with another item.

"It's my turn again. But this isn't a question, more like a confession."

"Oh man this doesn't sound good at all."

"Well it wasn't, but at least it's in the past."

"All right let me have it."

"I've been diagnosed with cancer twice in my life." Eric choked on his beverage. He wore a look of hurt and confusion on his face.

"You mean to tell me you had cancer twice and you never told me?"

"Not to downplay it, but it was prostate cancer, and they detected it early enough before I was in any real danger."

"What the hell does that even mean? How did you know how much real danger you were in? I'm your brother! I know we didn't talk that often but I mean c'mon! Why didn't you tell me?" Chris knew immediately he had messed up.

"Honestly, I don't know. I guess I figured I could handle whatever was thrown at me."

"Was this before or after Mom and Dad died?" Chris paused a second to remember.

"Actually once before and once after."

"Damn it Chris!"

"If I was going to tell anyone it would have been you, not them."

"Wow. Cancer." Eric didn't know what to say and stared off into the distance.

"Eric you have my word. At this point in my life I'm done playing the silent hero. If I need help I'm going to ask. You have my word."

"You better. I don't want to hear you kept something like that from me ever again."

"I promise."

For the next half hour or so the boys brought up various memories from their childhood. When they heard the clock chime one o'clock they agreed to turn in for the night. The brothers stood up, embraced, and said they loved each other before they retired to their respective rooms. Chris slid under the covers and already felt himself drifting off. Relief poured all over him and he felt free of whatever guilt had lived secretly in his subconscious. That night was the best night of sleep Chris ever had.

Come New Year's the three of them went down to the local banquet hall and the neighborhood celebrated together. Chris watched Jon repeatedly toast the table and laughed when Kara kept interrupting. As the ball began to fall and the countdown began Chris looked at his brother and marveled. They were about to see the year 2050 together. Chris would be turning seventy-four; his brother would be turning seventy-two. Chris regretted all those wasted years not spent together, but at the same time was happy for the here and now. No matter what happened from this point on he had his brother.

# CHAPTER 45

## September 6, 2052

When the doctor asked him about the first time he felt "the pain" in his legs Chris remembered the flight out to Eric's for Christmas. His legs and lower back were killing him, although he chalked up the discomfort to an uncomfortable plane ride. After that the pain would come and go, mostly arriving at night when he was in bed. It felt like he was twelve years old again and he was experiencing growing pains. At the same time, he didn't have anyone around to talk to about this and he didn't want to concern his brother with what he associated as the aches and pains of growing old. Therefore, Chris kept his mouth shut. This had all culminated when he was doing his routine cleaning around the house and banged his right knee on the coffee table. Immediately the knee began to swell and Chris couldn't walk on it. The pain was ridiculous, more so than he felt was normal for a bruise. An hour went by and he still couldn't stand, so Chris decided enough was enough and called 911.

At the hospital the diagnosis was a fractured right knee cap and the doctors wanted to do some more tests. When he heard "more tests" his alarm went off. They already knew it was fractured, what else was there to find out? The next step was sound waves, and he knew its purpose was to find anything sinister lurking within. Within an hour the tests came back. Chris was busy counting the tiles on the ceiling when the doctor walked in. He looked to be much younger than Dr. Bennett, to the point Chris wondered how long ago did he graduate medical school.

"Chris Marcum?" Chris straightened up on the bed.

"Yes, doctor?"

"My name is Dr. D'Angelo. I took a look at your scans."

"Yes." The man paused and his silence drove Chris nuts. He looked down at the tablet and said,

"I'm not sure how to say this."

"Then just go ahead and say it."

"I'm sorry to say your tests came back positive for bone cancer."

"Again?" Chris blurted out in annoyance. Of course he was a veteran of two cancer wars previously so it wasn't like he was surprised. The doctor however was and stumbled over his words. While Dr. D'Angelo tried to compose himself Chris looked him dead in the eyes and with utmost confidence said,

"I've been through the ringer before, when do we go on the attack?"

"Here's the problem. If this had happened six months ago, we could have formulated a plan for treatment. If this was a year ago, absolutely we could beat this. The problem is at this hour the cancer is ravaging your body from the inside out. It's all over your legs and your lower back as well. I'm sorry to say that at your age we don't think treatment is a viable option."

Chris stared at him dumbfounded. He had slacked on going to the doctor's ever since Gloria died. Whenever he received a reminder to see his physician he would throw it out with a hint of guilt. Now he would pay the price for his willful ignorance.

"Are you telling me what I think you're telling me?"

"Well…"

"Doctor at this point there is no need to hold back. I'd rather you be blunt."

"Okay then. I'm sorry to say this is terminal. I'll say three months, six if things go right. In the meantime, you'll be staying here in the hospital with your knee in the shape it's in."

Chris didn't say anything while his right hand balled up into a fist. The doctor's words wouldn't quite register in his mind. This wasn't possible.

"So I'm going to die?"

"I'm sorry."

"You just told me I'm going to die and you want me to spend my remaining days in a hospital bed waiting to die?" His voice rose in anger.

"Well, Chris, I mean you're not forced here against your will. If you know someone who could take care of you that's a different story."

"If I said I do?"

"Then I have no problem releasing you. Although if you are alone, then you have to stay here until your knee heals. There is simply no way you could manage on your own."

"Then this is an easy decision. Let me call my brother," he said sharply.

"Take your time. I'll be walking around seeing other patients. If you need anything or have any other questions do not hesitate to ask." Chris realized it wasn't the doctor's fault and grew embarrassed.

"I'm sorry. I'm taking this out on you and..."

"No need to apologize. Anything I can do let me know."

"Thanks doc."

Before Chris called his brother he wanted to figure out what he was going to say. His mind raced, as the doctor's words began to sink in. It was the way he said terminal that really smacked Chris upside the head. The entire time Chris thought how this wasn't that big a deal, that he had plenty more years to live, but the word terminal was like a missile launched right at him, exploding with an impact. He thought of all the things that had to be done. His finances would have to be in order—the house. Of course he would have to call Eric and Danielle. Who else? His mind suddenly hooked a sharp right into morbid. Is there anyone else who would show up at his funeral? The idea of only Eric and Danielle at his grave caused a large lump in the back of his throat. The absolute worst part was that he would spend the last remaining days of his life on crutches. He couldn't go for a walk in the park or couldn't do his own driving down the expressway. Christopher Marcum was officially being held hostage by his own body. He shook his head and tried to get a grip on things. First things first, he had to call Eric. He had plenty of time to be morbid.

Chris pulled out his iPhone and facetimed his brother. He put the privacy option on and chose the picture Eric had given him when they were kids. He didn't want his brother seeing how worried he was, which was ridiculous considering the circumstances. Within two rings Danielle answered.

"Hey Chris what can I do for you?"

"Hey Danny. Listen. Can you do me a favor? Can you get Eric?" Between the privacy screen and the tone of his voice Danielle knew something was wrong.

"Sure, Chris. Is everything okay?"

"Yeah everything is fine. I just need to speak with my brother."

"Okay hold on one second."

Danielle stepped away from the screen and went to get her husband, while Chris sat on the examining table and waited. After a minute Chris saw Eric appear.

"Do me a favor, take off the privacy, and let me see your face."

"Hold on one second." Chris flipped it off and now the brothers were staring at each other.

"Chris, what's wrong?"

"Remember how I promised no more secrets?"

"Oh no."

"It's bone cancer."

"Oh no."

"They found it when I came in today after I fractured my knee."

"Oh my God Chris! We're going to get the first flight out there and take care of you every step of the way. Don't worry about anything!"

"Listen I don't want you guys coming out on my behalf." That statement might have been the most disingenuous thing Chris had ever said.

"Are you kidding me? That's not even up for discussion. You are my brother and you would do the same for me."

"Well if you are coming up you should have an idea of how long you're staying."

"What does that mean?"

"The doctor is giving me somewhere between three and six months." They stared at each other through the screens, and Eric desperately tried to think of something to say.

"You know doctors can be wrong right?"

"Yup."

"Danielle is already getting the travel info. We should be there by tonight. Can you wait?"

"Well I'm not dying tomorrow!" Eric winced at the comment and didn't reply.

"Sorry, you know me. That's not a problem. I'm at Staten Island North and they said you can sign me out when you get here."

"We'll get there as soon as we can. Chris, I love you."

"I love you too, Eric. See you soon."

Due to a delay at the airport, Eric and Danielle's flight didn't arrive in New York until 2AM, which meant Chris had to spend the night at the hospital. Before Chris went to sleep that night he prayed to God. Not for a cure. And he didn't pray for God to alleviate the pain. All he asked for that night was courage. He could now see death off in the horizon and he didn't want to spend his final months on Earth afraid. Let him face whatever was coming his way with dignity and strength. Help him not to fear death, but find peace in the idea. Finally, he prayed that he would get one more conversation with James.

# CHAPTER 46

## September 24, 2052

Chris hadn't been waited on like this since the days of Susan. Nor had his house been this alive in God knows how many years. Eric and Danielle told him they would be there for as long as possible and do whatever was necessary. A part of Chris felt guilty for interrupting their lives like this, at the same time Chris realized he was weeks away from his seventy-sixth birthday and God knew what else. He had to face facts. Independence was a luxury he could no longer afford.

The first thing Eric insisted upon when they brought him home was to convert his living room into a bedroom. Chris wasn't having anything to do with it. There they sat, on separate couches in the midst of a spirited debate. In fact, this was probably the closest thing they had to an argument since they were teenagers.

"Eric I'm not an invalid! I can navigate up and down the steps."

"It doesn't make sense for you to battle twelve steps a day. If you sleep upstairs you're going to be a prisoner up there."

"I hear what you're saying, but that's my bedroom and my bed and I don't feel like changing up the routine."

"Look at it from our vantage point. This staircase isn't wide enough to support Danielle and I on either side of you."

"Like I said, I can navigate the steps without any help."

"Chris I know this is a tough time for you, but try to be reasonable."

"I *am* being reasonable, you're just not listening!" Danielle remained quiet the entire time, but saw the exasperated look on her husband's face and decided to speak up.

"Chris we are only here to help you and so far you aren't letting us do that. Eric is right, but I understand why you're hesitant. All I'm asking is that you think about it." Chris stared at his sister-in-law. She was right. Why was he fighting them? They were there five minutes and Chris was already making life difficult for them. He turned red with embarrassment.

"You're right. I'm wrong. The living room idea makes sense. Let's do it." Eric looked at his brother, shocked at the complete one hundred eighty degree turn he just did.

"It's not a question about right or wrong. It's about making you comfortable."

"I know Eric, thanks."

Danielle kept herself busy during the day, and none of her duties, for the most part, involved Chris. She learned first hand that he abhorred the very idea of dusting and went to work immediately dusting every single item in the house. When she pressed him on his laziness, Chris answered that it was a war he couldn't win. No matter how often he would dust, it would return post haste. Why would he want to bang his head against the wall repeatedly? It made much more sense to just ignore it.

After a couple of weeks passed, the three of them had fallen into a series of routines. Chris found it funny that he was living on borrowed time but nothing really seemed to change. Sure he had to be extremely careful due to his brittle bones, and he had to rely on his brother to help him with certain things; yet, for the most part, he didn't feel any different. There was only one unresolved issue and Chris wasn't ready to face it just yet. The subject of his son came up on one of the daily strolls the three of them took through the neighborhood. If it was just a quick walk around the house Chris could manage on crutches. However for these types of walks Chris climbed into the wheelchair and let Eric or Danielle push him along.

"You cold, Chris?"

"Nope. I'm okay Dan. It's a beautiful September day isn't it?" Danielle had her hands in her pockets and had a slight shiver.

"When you spend almost your entire life in the warm climate of Texas this is killer."

"What about you? You ready to move back down to Texas?" Eric walked along side of the wheelchair, listening but mostly lost in thought.

"Eric?"

"Yeah?"

"I said are you ready to move back down to Texas?"

"Not yet. But this weather is brutal." Chris turned his head around and shared a knowing smile with Danielle. They passed the Redine place and Angie was on the porch with her bulldog Primo. She waved hello and Primo lifted his head up in greeting.

"Is this the famous brother I've heard so much about?" She said with a smile.

"Eric, Danielle I'd like you to meet the Mayor of Eltingvile, Angela Rendine." They both waved and said hi.

"How long you think you'll be off your feet?"

"Oh I'm sure just another month or so. I don't want to miss your famous Halloween party."

"Chris has told us all about it. Apparently your haunted house is known throughout the tri-state area," said Danielle.

"I wouldn't go that far but yeah we do all right."

"All right? Last year you probably had over a hundred people inside and about another million hanging around outside waiting their chance."

"Okay Chris you're right it's the biggest party of the year. You better do double time on the rehab!" The four of them laughed.

"Alright we're going to continue the walk before my brother freezes to death standing here. I'll talk to you soon." Eric rubbed his arms together and playfully hopped up and down to keep warm.

"I don't know how you survive this tundra."

"It's sixty degrees out!" Angela said incredulously.

"I know, like the Artic!"

"Go take care of your brother. I'll talk to you Chris. Feel better."

"Thanks Ang."

"Nice meeting you two."

"Bye," they all said in unison. The three of them continued down the block as Eric jokingly blew into his hands to keep warm.

"Yeah yeah I get it Eric" Chris said mockingly.

"You have such nice neighbors," Danielle observed.

"Yeah I really got lucky when I moved onto the block. They always made me feel included."

"You didn't tell her…"

"Nah I don't want the attention. Maybe if you guys weren't here I would have reached out. You know how I am about asking people for help." Eric put his hand on his brother's shoulder and let out a knowing laugh.

They walked past three more houses and reached the corner. The path was always the same—walk down the block, at the corner cross over to the other side of the street, go back down the block and cross when they were across from his house. Nothing crazy, just long enough to feel like they did some exercise. As they crossed the street Danielle made a face at Eric and Eric shrugged his shoulders in reply. She made another face and Eric spoke up.

"Chris I've wanted to bring this up, I'm just not sure if it's my place to."

"We're not kids anymore, Eric. You can say whatever you want." Eric took a pause and looked at his wife, who gave him a nod of encouragement.

"Well Dan and I were thinking about James and whether maybe you should try calling him and letting him know about...this." Chris looked up at his brother.

"I'm not going to lie; I've thought about it. I just don't want him talking or seeing me because he feels bad for me. I want him to want to talk to me! The last thing I want from anyone is pity and I'm afraid that's exactly what I'd get from him."

"Shouldn't you at least let him know?"

"Eric, I know what you're saying and I appreciate it. I'm still holding out hope he'll call me first out of the desire to speak to me."

Eric knew Chris wasn't changing his mind and it was pointless to continue the conversation. He had listened and that was all he was willing to do.

# CHAPTER 47

## October 20, 2052

Chris was sitting in his wheelchair on the porch, staring off into his backyard. He just attempted to eat the breakfast Danielle had prepared, but his appetite wasn't as strong as it once was. Leaving a copious amount of eggs, half of his bacon, and most of the sesame bagel on his plate, Chris asked to be wheeled outside. Eric and Danielle exchanged a glance before Eric got up. He asked if Chris wanted any company, but Chris wanted to be left alone.

Outside he could hear the clattering of dishes as Danielle loaded them into the dishwasher. The noise, along with the beautiful fall foliage was barely within the limits of his scope of perception. His mind registered the senses, processed them, and let them be. There were other, more important matters to attend to.

His recently turned seventy-six-year-old body was growing more susceptible to tiredness, and naps were now a regular part of his schedule. The pain was, for the most part manageable and when it wasn't Danielle gave him a pill. Every once in awhile Chris' frustration level exploded at the thought of his limitations. Here he was, a man with a finite amount of time remaining, and he couldn't do the simple things. He had been on his own for at least half of his life and used to picking up and going whenever he wanted to. Not anymore. Despite the automatic feature, he could no longer drive. Gone were the days of a casual afternoon drive up and down Hylan Boulevard. They now had to be planned and organized within the timeframe of whatever Eric or Danielle was doing. It wasn't a question of them saying no, more of Chris not wanting to inconvenience them. After all, they put their lives in Texas on hold while they met his every need. Chris didn't want to be an overbearing patient. He needed them, but he didn't want to be a burden.

A couple of days after Chris' birthday, his frustration level was amped up to a whole new degree. No matter his complaints, he could at least navigate around his own house using the crutches. Now, Chris had discovered that using crutches was putting a tremendous amount of stress on his upper body and the discomfort was too much to deal with. The wheelchair became both his best friend and his archenemy. He hated the essence of the thing but at the same time depended on it. Because crutches were now out, he needed to ask his brother for help going to the bathroom and other simple activities. He could deal with dying, it had been accepted and in a strange way welcomed, but he couldn't deal with the way his body was quitting on him.

In any event these were the usual thoughts and were as regular as eating or sleeping in Chris's life. Routine thoughts however don't make you stare off into the distance on your back porch by yourself. What was consuming Chris was the conversation from two nights ago where he tried once again to bridge the gap between father and son.

In the month since Eric had casually mentioned getting a hold of James, Chris had alternated between calling him right then and there and putting it off for another day. Eric and Danielle hadn't brought his name up since, although Danielle had to talk Eric out of doing so several times. They knew when the time was right he would be in front of the iTV.

The moment came on October 18, the night of Chris' seventy-sixth birthday. Eric and Danielle had gone above and beyond celebrating the day. The three of them watched a movie of Chris' choosing on the iTV, which of course was horrible. His taste in movies was in a word, interesting, as he would gamble on the potential when everyone else could see it was garbage. No matter, the three of them plowed through an hour and forty-five minute movie that caused him to immediately apologize as soon as the credits appeared. Next came a lunch of tomato soup and a Caesar salad, followed by spending the rest of the afternoon and early part of the evening in the local bookstore. To Chris, this was the perfect day. It was topped off by a delicious bowl of pasta a la Danielle for dinner and a big chocolate cake with one candle awaiting his breath. Of course Chris' appetite was no longer what it once was and he nibbled and sampled both the dinner and the dessert. He made sure to tell Danielle it wasn't her cooking, something she already knew.

Following the cake, the three of them retired to the living room and was going to spend the rest of the night watching the iTV and joking. Chris had other ideas. All day his stomach had been churning at the thought and if ever a moment would be appropriate, it would be his birthday.

"Eric would you mind if I called James?" Eric did a double take at the casualness of the question and held in a laugh.

"No I don't think I would. Danielle you want to join me on the porch and give the man some privacy?"

"Sounds good. Good luck," and she patted him on the shoulder as they walked out of the room. Chris waited until they left before he turned on the privacy feature. He didn't want James seeing him as an invalid, instead he would see him at a happier time. Chris scrolled through his pictures before settling on one taken by Gloria's mom at her Sweet 16. By the end of the night his entire table had gotten up to dance, leaving him all alone. Some of her aunts felt bad and wanted him to come join them on the dance floor but Chris shrugged them off and told them he was happier watching, which he certainly was. The actual picture was a side profile of Chris sitting down with his right arm resting on the empty chair next to him. There he sat, facing the dance floor, watching everyone with a grin on his face. Gloria loved that picture, said it made him look classy. With the privacy setting taken care of Chris pulled up James and waited. Three rings later his only son James was on his living room wall.

"Hello?" His son was distracted with something else and wasn't looking at the screen.

"Hello James." Upon hearing the words James did a slow turn towards the screen.

"Dad?"

"Yup."

"Oh... hi." Chris watched James settle into a leather chair.

"Hi."

"How are you?"

Chris had decided beforehand that he would not mention the cancer unless the conversation progressed to the point where they might talk again.

"I'd say I'm doing well for a seventy-six–year-old guy."

"Why do you have the private screen up? Is everything okay?" Chris was quick on his feet (how ironic) and said,

"Yeah the screen broke a couple of months ago and I'm too old to care." James gave a laugh that sounded forced, Chris couldn't be sure.

"So how are you doing James?"

"I'd say I'm doing well for a fifty-year-old guy."

"Wow, I can't even fathom that you are fifty-years-old."

"Yeah I had a hard time with it too for awhile. Kristina and Autumn have been real supportive."

Chris didn't want to jinx it but the conversation was going surprisingly well so far.

"Autumn?"

"Yeah, my daughter."

And just like that a chill went up and down his spine. His son had a daughter! He had a granddaughter! He tried to keep a level voice.

"How old is she?"

"She turned seventeen a couple of months ago. I can't even believe this but she's going into her senior year of high school already."

"Yup time goes fast."

"Sure does." Both men let out a sigh as the conversation waited to be resumed. "Is everything okay on your end? I mean work wise?"

"Yeah I'm a cop and actually approaching retirement real soon."

"A cop?"

"Not a cop, a captain!" Chris heard the voice in the background and said,

"Was that your wife?"

"Yeah that was Kristina. Honey you want to come over and say hello?" James could see his son make a face and eventually Kristina walked into the picture.

"Hi," she said without masking her discomfort. Chris didn't care, he just wanted to meet his daughter-in-law.

"Nice to meet you."

"Listen babe I have stuff to do—"

"Hey listen I understand." Kristina made a face as if to say I don't care that you understand, in fact I hope you do understand the animosity I have towards you but instead she smiled and said,

"Goodbye."

"Listen James I don't mean to bother you but I was just wondering. I mean it's been so long and I would love to maybe see and talk to you face to face? Perhaps maybe…eventually meeting Autumn?" James paused as he deliberated on an appropriate response.

"Sure Dad…things are really busy right now, but maybe after New Year's we'll see what we could do."

Chris debated telling his son he might not live to see 2053, but didn't want to influence James' thinking.

"That would be great James. Listen, I'm going to let you go. If you ever want to sit and talk for a bit feel free."

"Sure thing Dad, thanks for calling."

"You too."

"Bye."

"Bye."

Chris sat in his chair and continued to stare at the now black screen. He wasn't surprised that James didn't wish him a Happy Birthday, but a part of him was hoping for it. His son hadn't yelled or screamed or hung up the phone although his wife certainly wanted to, that much was clear. Yet despite her wishes James didn't, so that was a victory and he agreed to see him next year. Baby steps.

So there he was sitting on his back porch while he debated whether or not he should have told his son that he was dying. Did it matter at this point whether or not it was out of pity? His time was short and if James really wanted to see him he would have to do it soon.

Chris had made his peace with everything else in his long life, thanks to Gloria. He had come to terms with his failures and regrets. He no longer flinched at the thought of lost opportunities or what might have been. Things had happened, for good and for bad, and there was nothing he could do to change that. The only exception to this line of thinking was James. He had been a failure at fatherhood and in subsequent events to make things right he had been rebuked. And now, as his calendar counted down the days, he still could not breach the gap. He wanted love, not pity, and that could only happen if James didn't know. The more time that passed, the more certain he was that he would never see his son ever again.

# CHAPTER 48

## December 27, 2052

A couple of days after Christmas, Chris' body declared open war on him. The past three months had been filled with sabotage, which he handled with an equal balance of acceptance and rage. Some days he would get depressed and moody, despite the fact he could still function normally day to day. That was no longer the case. At first it was a simple cold and Danielle had been diligent in keeping on top of it. After two days the cold progressed into a fever and chills and Danielle knew this was becoming a serious problem. She pulled Eric aside and told him that if things didn't get better by tomorrow morning they were going to have to get an ambulance.

Chris didn't sleep at all that night. He didn't have to be told what the deal was. He was fully aware, and he planned on telling his brother to bring him to the hospital when he woke up. There was a part of Chris that wanted to die peacefully in his own bed, surrounded by his loved ones and all his worldly possessions, however few there were. However that part, that needy, selfish part he had listened to for most of his life was finally overruled by the other part, the rational, practical side that didn't want to emotionally bankrupt his brother and sister-in-law. They had done enough; it was time to let the professionals take over.

As he sat in his bed he started to look around. This would be the last time he ever slept in his own house, in his own bed ever again. In all likelihood he would not be coming back. He had been living there for twenty-five years now, yet it never truly felt like a home. Chris liked to say he did a good job despite not having a woman's touch. Seemed like yesterday he was saying goodbye to Susan and moving into this place. Whatever happened to Susan, he wondered. Realizing those thoughts were nothing but an effort in futility he shook them loose and returned his attention to the house.

He tried to focus on every single detail in the living room and think of what his bathroom looked like. His kitchen. The old bedroom upstairs. How the outside of his house looked in the summer when the grass was green and lush. How it appeared with snow on the ground in the middle of winter. The way his house creaked when the wind came roaring through, or the sounds that came from the boiler. All the details that Chris didn't want to forget, because all these details made up his life. There was a cruel passing thought of no one being there to comfort him before he remembered that his brother and his wife were there. Chris suddenly became very frightened when he realized he had forgotten they had been here for the past three months. All he had left was his faculties and he would rather die tonight than linger on without them.

The only thought that caused him to get emotional was when he realized that Eric couldn't take him to the hospital by himself. Chris was too much to carry out to the car, especially for two people who were also in their seventies. They were going to have to call 911 and get an ambulance sent to the house. Angela and the rest of the neighbors would be watching as they took him out, and he did not want to be put on display. Chris remembered as a kid watching Mr. Dorney get carried out of his house on a stretcher by two EMTs. Seemingly the whole block came out to watch as his wife walked along side of him holding his hand. Even at an early age, Chris knew he wasn't coming back. He didn't want people to think that way about him.

As he sat waiting for the sun to rise, his thoughts traveled over to Gloria. He tried to imagine being in this position at her age, knowing she was going to check into a hospital and not check out. Chris was happy that at the very least he spent almost every available second at her side. She never had the opportunity to feel alone because I was always right next to her, he thought.

Gloria had brought him back to God, and he knew that some day soon he would be meeting up with Gloria once again. Chris wondered if she would try and come to him in a dream, or appear in a vision before dismissing the thoughts as nonsense. This wasn't Hollywood—she wasn't going to show up and start talking to him. Then again he knew if he closed his eyes and listened, he could feel her presence. And that alone was what made waiting for the day to arrive somewhat tolerable.

Eric was surprised the following morning to see Chris sitting up in his bed waiting for him. Eric had thought convincing his brother it was time to go to the hospital would have been a battle, and he was prepared to be as patient and loving as he could. To his shock, Chris spoke first and put to rest any of his concerns.

"Eric, listen to me. I'm sick and I'm not getting any better. We all know this and I appreciate everything you and Danielle have done for me over the past three months. I think it's time I went to the hospital." Eric stood there for a second not saying anything before a smile came across his lips and he nodded his head.

"Why are you smiling?"

"Because I can't believe how after everything you are still in control."

"Well I am your older brother!" The boys shared a melancholic chuckle.

"Seriously, thank you. And when Danielle walks in here I'll thank her too. You guys have done more for me than I deserved and I could never pay you back." Eric's eyes welled up.

"No need to get sentimental now. We'll have plenty of time for that. Just know that we were happy to do so and will continue doing so for however long it takes."

A lump formed in Chris's throat, and instead of saying anything else he opened up his arms and beckoned Eric over for a hug.

# CHAPTER 49

## January 11, 2053

Chris celebrated New Year's in style, propped up by pillows in his hospital bed while Eric, Danielle, and his elderly roommate named Vinny watched the iTV. They didn't stay awake long enough to see the ball drop, but the intention was there.

In the days that followed Chris would ask about his house—if the grass needed cutting or if the bathroom faucet was still dripping—and Eric humored him by answering him no matter how many times the question was repeated. Eric and Danielle both noticed Chris' habit of repeating himself, or forgetting they just had the same conversation twenty minutes ago. His naps were also growing in both frequency and time.

Every day they came to see him, there was less conversation than the day before. One night Chris found himself nodding off ten minutes after nighttime visiting hours had started and apologized to the two of them for being a bad host. "Nonsense," Danielle said, "get your sleep. We'll be here when you wake up." Remembering how he said that to Gloria put a smile on his face, and he went to sleep.

Over the next few days Chris woke up less and less. The doctors told them to brace themselves because it was just a matter of time now.

"Is that my..."

"Yeah Autumn, that's your Grandpa."

"Remind me again when was the last time you saw each other?"

"God I can't even remember. Too many years."

"Do you hate him?"

"No," he said with a pause. "Honestly no. I don't understand him, but I don't hate him."

"Do you think he's going to wake up?"

298

"I hope so kiddo."

They stood at the edge of the doorway, quietly looking at Chris. James put his hand on his daughter's shoulder and they began to walk away. Autumn stopped and said loud enough so Chris could hear,

"You can't die without meeting me first."

At the same time, although he appeared to be sleeping, Christopher's mind was racing.

"What the hell is going on? I'm asleep, but I'm awake. I can't talk, but I can hear everything! Is that James? Is that my granddaughter? Damn it! Why can't I wake up?"

Six hours later, Christopher was wide awake and staring up at the ceiling. Bored out of his mind he blurted out how he wished someone were around to talk to. His roommate Vinny was being prepped for surgery and the room was empty. As he counted the ceiling tiles for the twelfth time Christopher felt a rustle and the unmistakable feeling of being watched.

"You can always talk to me."

Christopher stopped counting and looked around the room. Believing that he imagined the noise, he closed his eyes and tried to fall asleep.

"Christopher Marcum."

The words were as clear as a bell and goose bumps ran up and down his fragile body. Christopher's mouth went dry and he looked around in fright. After a couple of seconds passed without hearing anything else he said out loud,

"I'm sick. I'm sick and the drugs are making me hear things."

"I am not a hallucination, nor the byproduct of any drug."

Christopher began to tremble. He had accepted the demise of his body on the condition that his mind stayed sharp. If he was hearing voices that meant his mind was breaking down as well. The thought sent panic up and down his body.

"I can't go crazy now. Please God, take me before that happens," he managed to get out in a rough voice.

"You aren't going crazy Christopher. I am right over here. Would you prefer to actually see me or continue to just hear my voice?" Christopher nodded yes.

"This has to be the morphine talking," he thought.

Suddenly, a faint gray outline appeared to be growing out from the corner of the room. In a matter of seconds it became a tangible form, if you could call light a form. Whatever it was, it was beautiful. He couldn't tell if it was a man or woman or how old or young it was. Yet he couldn't take his eyes off the figure. Before he could even annunciate a syllable of questionable thought the light provided an answer.

"Christopher I am a type of angel sent to those who are about to come over to our side. Don't worry, you aren't going to die right now, but the moment is rapidly approaching. I'm here to make sure your final hours are comfortable. Do you need anything?"

Inside Christopher was shocked and became flooded with words. This is why he considered it somewhat of a personal triumph when he managed to get out a faint "no."

"I understand this is a shock to the system," the voice went on. "You obviously have plenty of questions to ask. We'll get to them when you feel a little more at ease. For now let's talk about you. Are you satisfied with the way your life turned out?"

"I don't know," he stammered.

The angel softened its tone and leaned in closer.

"Christopher, listen to me. Take a deep breath. I am here and you are not dreaming. We can have a conversation, but not if you can't talk. Is there any particular reason why you don't know if you're satisfied or not?"

Chris took that deep breath and a small smile came over his face. He still didn't believe this was happening but he wasn't going to fight it.

"I lived my life afraid and because of that I missed out on a lot. At the same time I had some good times too."

"Do you hold God responsible for any of it?"

"No. Sure there was anger at times. And resentment. But I made my peace with Him a long time ago."

"Good to hear. How about regrets? Do you have any regrets?"

Chris quietly chuckled to himself.

"I don't think I could list them all in the short time I have left."

"How about you give me the biggest regret then." Chris didn't need to think about this, the answer rolled right off his tongue.

"I had the choice between Jen and Valerie and I chose the wrong girl. In fact, there hasn't been a night since where I didn't think or dream about Jen."

"See now that's very interesting. It sounds like you actually feel pain at the mere thought of her."

"In a way, yes I do."

"And there's nothing in this world that could heal you?"

"I suppose the only possible cure would be Jen herself." Even though he couldn't make out a face on the angel, he could tell there was a smile on its face.

"Here's a question I often ask people who have such deep rooted pain. Do you wonder why God didn't prevent you from making the wrong choice?"

"What do you mean?"

"Well I think it's fair to say you have been a faithful servant for most of your life correct? Yet things didn't go the way you wanted. Why would God punish someone like you when people with little or no faith get to have everything they have ever dreamed of?"

"The thought has crossed my mind, but I understand that He gave us free will and we are responsible for the lives we live."

"Do you truly believe that?"

"A seventy-six-year-old man who is about to die has no reason to say otherwise." Upon hearing those words the figure seemed to grow in height.

"I don't believe you truly mean it. I think you believe that God owes you a better life. I bet you if you lived a privileged life your tune would be different right now."

"I'm confused. I thought you were here to help me."

"I am Chris. That's the point. Do you want to die with any sort of resentment in your heart towards your God? What if I told you I had the power to make certain changes to your life?"

"How would you do that?"

"Let's just say I have the ability to rewind the clock and let you live your entire life over again. You wouldn't have the knowledge you have right now and you wouldn't be given the same burdens you were given in this life. You would live an entire lifetime again and we would be right back here all in the blink of an eye."

"You're telling me that I could live my entire life all over again all in a couple of seconds?"

"Basically, yes. Seventy-six years would pass and we would be right back here before you knew it. Once you came back, you would know for sure how much love God has for you. After all, you don't want to face the Lord Himself with any hesitation in your heart, correct?" Chris' voice picked up with excitement.

"So you're saying I wouldn't make the same mistakes again? That I would wind up with Jen and not Valerie?"

"I can't guarantee that. You will live your life and, what's that old cliché? The chips will fall as they may. However I will say that you will be blessed with an extraordinary amount of good luck. Things will work out in your favor and people will comment on how things always seem to go your way. Does that sound fair?" Chris shifted in his bed and pondered it over for a moment.

"I don't know if it does." The angel didn't expect to hear that answer and said,

"What did you say?"

"If things were given to me then I'd just be a fool, living like a sheep."

"No you would be happy! Since you already mentioned her four times in this conversation alone, what if I guaranteed that this time you wouldn't pick Valerie over Jen?" Chris thought for a moment. There it was, the one thing he would have given anything for. At the same time…

"It still wouldn't be the same. If we were meant to be then we would find each other naturally, not forced upon each other."

"Christopher I have been watching you all your life. You haven't been truly happy for over fifty years. Fifty long, lonely, miserable years. Why are you being so stubborn now? Let me give you the opportunity to correct the one mistake which you have admitted still haunts your dreams." This time he didn't have to think about it, his response was instant and certain.

"No. This is the life God gave me and I've accepted the choices I made. If I'm going to die tonight I want to go happy, not bitter and filled with resentment." The being grew frustrated and had grown so large out of anger that the mere sight of it overwhelmed Chris' senses.

"It's funny that you say the life God gave me."

"Huh?"

"Chris I hate to be the bearer of bad news but you just failed your test." Chris stared at the being in confusion.

"What?" Chris turned his head both ways as if he was looking for hidden cameras.

"None of this is real. Your life, the life you just led was nothing but an illusion."

"I still don't understand," but in the back of his mind something about this seemed familiar and he could feel the panic rising up in his chest.

"In your real life you were dying of cancer. You were alone and afraid and calling out for someone to save you. Naturally I heard the request and appeared in your hospital room. Oh you were so pathetic, prattling on about how you weren't ready to die and how unfair your God was. I calmed you down by bringing up your favorite conversation, your wife Jen."

"My wife?"

"Yes, in your real life you and Jen were married. Although to be perfectly honest, it was more a marriage of convenience than love."

"Jen and I?"

"Yes you and Jen. In the course of that conversation you insisted that you and Jen were soul mates and could find each other no matter the incident or obstacle. I, a being who has always been and will always be naturally disagreed and we set up a bet." Chris sat in horror as the memory of his encounter came back to him. He couldn't remember what they had talked about but he knew there was some truth in what the creature was saying.

"The deal was I would let you relive this life, naturally with some changes to make things harder. If you married Jen and lived happily ever after you won. However, if you and Jen did not enjoy a fairy tale ending you would give me your soul."

"No! That's not true!" Everything had come back to him now. He remembered this being visiting him and he knew they had reached an agreement but he was positive this was a lie.

"I'm sorry to say it is. You tried your best and you failed. Twelve hours from now you will die and your soul will belong to me."

"No!" His eyes went wide in a mixture of fury and fear.

"I'm sorry Chris, a deal's a deal."

"No!"

"Of course we could make another deal," the being whispered with a smile on its face.

"STOP!"

Chris looked to his right and screamed in shock and delight. It was as if the gates of Heaven opened up and let loose a torrent of white light. Coming in through the ethereal was Gloria! Her face shone in glory and her brown hair seemed to flow like waves in the ocean. She looked older, and if he didn't know her, intimidating. He had no idea what was going on right now but he immediately felt a calming sense of peace. Gloria walked to the foot of his bed.

*"Christopher Marcum do not listen to the words spewing from the mouth of the beast. You made no such deal for he is the father of lies. Cast off your illusion and present yourself for what you truly are!"*

A deep rumbling came from the distance and Chris had no idea what was going on or what to do. All he knew was that the angel whom he had been talking to, this angel that tried to take his soul now screamed in agony and changed form right in front of his eyes. Gone were the beauty, splendor, and illuminating light that should have blinded him, and in its place could best be described as the absence of light. There was a void standing in front of them yet he his mind somehow saw an image, the image of a beast. A beast with malice and hate emanating from its very core. He would have been scared to death right now if Gloria wasn't next to him.

*"Christopher do not fear this thing. And fear not them which kill the body, but are not able to kill the soul: but rather fear him which is able to destroy both soul and body in hell. This creature holds no power over you except for what you yourself grant it. Remove thee from my sight satan, or shall I call down Michael and the armies of Heaven to do so for thee?"*

The beast screamed out in agony and said something in a language Chris could not make out yet still understood. Gloria wasted no time and immediately responded.

*"In the name of Jesus leave this place!"*

What sounded like a sonic boom erupted and the beast disappeared from the hospital room. Chris was overwhelmed and didn't know what to say or feel. All he knew was that Gloria had saved him from whatever the beast had planned.

*"Christopher when I was dying I told you if you believed in God we would meet again. God our Father sent me to you so that on this day you would be protected. The beast was correct in one respect;*

*this life wasn't your real life. It was a trap designed to capture your soul.*"

"What? What are you saying?"

"*I'm going to remove the blinders from your eyes, so you can understand.*"

In what could best be described as reality shifting, Chris now stood with Gloria outside a hospital room. Chris looked in and saw himself in a bed, with Jen asleep in the chair next to him. She had changed her mind and came back to stay with Chris. Tears came to his eyes and cascaded down his face as he looked back at Gloria.

"Is that Jen?"

"*Yes.*"

"So none of that was real. My doubts, the anger I had, all of it..." More tears came to his eyes, this time from embarrassment and shame over his lack of faith.

"*We are back to where you should be and you will never see the beast ever again.*" Gloria put her arm around him and continued. "*Do not be ashamed Christopher. With enough tragedy and heartache, the most fervent believer could eventually lose his way. Everyone has their own breaking point, and it was determined to reach yours. Its goal was to get you to deny your faith forever, and for a time the beast almost succeeded.*"

"Wait he said this was about Jen..."

"*He knew of the deep love you have for your wife and believed that was where your faith resided. He thought if you didn't have her, you would stray from your devotion to God.*"

Once again shame rose up from his depths and he said,

"Well I suppose for a time he was right. I was so sad and lonely for all those years."

"*If you had come to this point with anger and hatred towards your God you would have been easier to obtain. Because you regained your faith it tried using another tact, tricking you with Jen.*"

"You should get the credit for that as well. It was because of you that I went back to God."

"*I was just a helping hand. I couldn't force you to do anything for all human beings have free will. The only thing I could do was to present you with the choice.*"

"And what if you didn't arrive just now? What would have happened to me then?"

*"The creature would have coerced you into another deal which would have trapped you inside another illusion. Your life would have been even worse than the last one."*

"Didn't it say I wouldn't have picked Valerie over Jen?"

*"Of course the beast said that because in the next cycle you wouldn't have met Valerie. You would meet someone else and pick her over Jen and the cycle would have continued until he eventually wore you down and you stopped believing all together."*

Chris leaned against the wall in shock. His brain was on overload, and he was having a hard time processing everything he had just seen and experienced.

"It felt so real."

*"It was a world of the devil's own creation. Think of it as the highest form of temptation."*

"So Valerie?"

*"Was there to keep you from Jen."*

"Is she real?"

*"Oh yes. In the real world she was married to her soul mate Brad for over fifty years before he passed a couple of months ago."*

This made him happy. Regardless of what was or was not real he wanted Valerie to be happy.

"Besides yourself were there any other angels?"

*"Not angels per se, just people sent by God to help you in times of need."*

"There is one thing I'm still confused about. What about you? Didn't you tell me that it came to you before you died?"

*"I am your guardian angel. My job is to help you in whatever way possible. I told you that story so you were aware of outside forces working against you."* Chris sat down on the floor and put his arms on his knees. This was too much and he felt exhausted.

"I know I said it before but I can't say it enough. Thank you for saving me."

*"I did nothing of the sort. You made the choice to believe in God. It was your free will that brought you back here."*

"So now what happens? Am I going to die?"

*"Everyone has to die and you are no different. Today is your last day on Earth. Enjoy it with the ones you love."*

"Will I remember any of this when I wake up?"

*"It will be a dream that will quickly leave your mind. You might remember a detail or two, but it will fade as the minutes pass. Enjoy your final day in peace."*

"Can I ask you one more question?"

*"Of course."*

"Is your name really Gloria?"

*"Yes."*

"Thank you Gloria. Thank you for everything."

Gloria knelt down and they embraced. A feeling of peace came over him and he visibly relaxed. Chris closed his eyes and for a brief moment felt like he was falling before he went to sleep.

# CHAPTER 50

## January 12, 2053

It was a little after ten on a beautiful Sunday morning when Chris' eyes began to flutter. Jen sat in her chair reading one of Chris' books when she noticed he was waking up. A huge smile came across his face as he stared at his wife of fifty years. An even bigger smile came across her face and she said,

"Good morning handsome."

Chris continued to stare at his wife. He felt like he hadn't seen her in a long time and started to get emotional. He tried to talk but nothing was coming out of his struggling mouth. Jen gently took his limp right hand and leaned forward.

"Don't struggle love. Relax. Take a deep breath and be patient. The words will come when you're calm."

Chris looked deeply into his wife's deep blue eyes and could feel his body start to relax. After a couple of breaths, he gathered himself.

"I love you so much." Jen immediately began to well up.

"And I love you even more than that."

"I know. I was dreaming last night and all I can remember is that I was chasing after you but I couldn't reach you. When I finally caught up to where you were I was too late and you were gone."

"Honey, I've been right here all night. I've always been right by your side and I always will."

"I want you to know that I would give up everything, my books, the money, the success—everything and anything if it meant losing you."

"Well I'm happy to say you'll never have to make that decision." A giggle escaped from her mouth at the same time a tear slid down her cheek.

A couple of hours later Eric and Danielle came in. Chris' eyes lit up as Eric came over and wrapped his arms around him. The four of them sat down and reminisced about past stories and funny moments that only the four of them knew of. Chris was more alert than he was over the past few days and Danielle commented on that later on while she returned from the restroom with Jen.

"It's as if someone flipped a switch."

"I know Dannie."

"When did it start?"

"This morning. It was amazing, he just opened his eyes."

"Unbelievable."

"Do the kids know?"

"Yeah I called Peter and told him to tell Brittany and James for me. They're coming here in the afternoon." The women were now standing outside his room.

"Let's stay outside a little longer and let Eric have a moment with his brother." They heard a loud obnoxious laugh coming from inside the room.

"I don't know how you lived with that laugh all these years," Danielle said with a giggle.

"You know the first time I heard his bellow I was horrified," she said with a smirk. "But now years later I can't imagine life without it."

"He even looks better. Have you spoken with his doctor?"

"He was encouraged although he said not to get my hopes up. The main thing he stressed was to enjoy this window of opportunity."

After an hour or so Chris grew tired and they let him rest. The three went down to the cafeteria, as much to eat as to give Jen a break. Over a poor excuse for macaroni they talked.

"I went over your house today to get the mail and water your plants."

"Thanks, Danielle. I really appreciate it."

"Whatever we can do for you we will," Eric echoed.

"I know. Chris and I are thankful that you two decided to fly up and be here for the past week. You don't know how helpful you two have been," Jen said as she moved her pasta around her plate.

"Oh stop it. My brother would be there for me if we needed it."

"Whatever we can do Jen, you know that" and Danielle took hold of Jen's hand.

309

"All I hope is that my brother doesn't suffer. If he has to go at least let it be quick and peaceful."

"I don't know what to make of this. Yesterday concerned me. He slept most of the day and even when he was awake he wasn't responsive. Now today he's awake and he's joking and laughing. I don't know what to think.

"C'mon, let's go back up to the room." Eric grabbed the women's trays to throw out the garbage. Danielle stood up but Jen remained sitting there, staring off.

"Jen?"

Since the diagnosis, Jen had handled everything deftly and without hesitation. She was on top of every problem or concern, mainly as a way to distract her from the situation at hand. She hadn't shed a tear because she hadn't allowed herself the time to shed a tear. Except now, sitting in the sterile environment of the hospital cafeteria, reality was setting in. Seeing Chris return to his old self had made her realize what she had been missing and even worse, what would be taken from her.

"I can't do this. I can't lose that man."

Jen's lip began to tremble and slowly but surely the tears fell from her eyes. Quickly she was overcome and openly sobbed into her hands. Danielle came over and put her arms around her. Eric turned away, wiping his eyes. Jen kept repeating, "I love him" over and over with her face buried in Danielle's left shoulder. Danielle tried to keep her composure, but was also having a hard time doing so.

"I'm not ready, Dan. I'm not ready to say goodbye."

"Neither are we."

The kids arrived a little after 1PM. Chris was in and out of sleep and hadn't had a conversation since Jen, Eric, and Danielle came back from lunch. Peter walked in first, followed by Brittany and James. His kids all gathered around his bedside and Chris began to stir. As he opened his eyes a smile came over his face, however when he locked eyes with James, Chris started to cry.

"What's the matter honey? What happened?" Jen asked with some urgency.

"I'm sorry James. I am so sorry!" Chris kept crying.

The kids looked around at each other and grew upset as well. James leaned in and asked what exactly was he sorry for?

"Was I a bad dad to you? I think I was a bad dad."

"You were the best dad! You took me to Mets games and the beach and were always there for me."

"I left you. I left you." He started to shake and James looked at his mother who was at a loss. He placed his hands on his father's face and said,

"Shhh. Dad it's okay. It's okay. You never left. You never left." Chris continued to sob, although his body had stopped shaking. Brittany and Peter took their mother by the hand and the three of them stepped out of the room. James deserved a private moment with his father. He continued to speak softly and reassure his dad. Eventually Chris settled down and fell asleep.

Their spouses and the grandkids came in later that night. Jen warned them that Chris had been asleep for awhile now and to prepare themselves for what might happen. Instead, as day turned into night he awoke from a deep sleep and rather shockingly, seemed to grow in strength. Chris was awake, alert, and acting the way he was when he woke up that morning. Nurses would come in every now and then to remind them this wasn't a bar—it was a hospital, so please keep it down. Chris would then smirk and remind them his voice didn't come with a whisper.

The hospital staff allowed the family, as long as they kept reasonably quiet, to stay past normal visiting hours so they could watch one more baseball game as a family. Peter selected the clinching game from the last time the New York Mets won the World Series in 2049 on the iTV and the family watched the by now memorized classic.

Three years ago they had all gathered at Chris and Jen's house as a family to watch the game live, and Chris frequently sited that as one of the greatest moments of his life. Not only because the Mets won, that was obvious. What made it special was being able to share it with his entire family. It would be something Chris would never forget and he told Jen he had an idea for a book based on the events of that night.

The best moment of all took place after the game was over, and they were all celebrating in front of the house. Chris had a tradition of keeping champagne on hand, to be broken out only when the Mets won the World Series. After the last out, the Marcum men ran to the refrigerator and grabbed the bottles of champagne (for the adults) sitting on the bottom shelf patiently waiting for this very night and some oversized bottles of water (for the grandchildren). Meanwhile the women and the children ran outside to celebrate on the front lawn.

As per tradition, Chris was the first one to uncork his bottle and poured champagne all over Jen's head. This was something that started years ago, one that at first Jen tolerated, then accepted and now, years later loved. Peter and James were running around like kids on the front lawn and Brittany snuck up and doused her father. The grandchildren were spraying water all over each other as well, shrieking and laughing. Chris saw his youngest grandchild John, who was four at the time, running around, screaming and yelling like everyone else. Finding a bottle on the lawn which had a little bit of water left inside, Chris picked up Johnny and poured a little on his head and face causing him to shriek in happiness. Brittany had her 3D recorder out and managed to capture the moment. Chris held John in his left arm while he poured water with his right. He had the biggest smile staring at John, who had his eyes closed, mouth wide open and his hands up in the air. It was one of Chris' favorite pictures. So much so that when they brought Chris to the hospital Jen made sure to grab it off his desk and bring it with him.

By eleven o'clock Chris' eyes were starting to get heavy, so John climbed up on the bed and snuggled in next to his Pop-Pop to tell him what was going on. When the final out came down in the glove of second baseman Ryan Brookaley, a jubilant Mets team celebrated in the middle of Citi Field while Chris celebrated one more time with his family. Each one of his kids, grandkids, his brother and sister-in-law came over to kiss, hug and tell him how much they loved him. Jen waited for everyone to be finished before she came over and kissed him. Chris looked at his wife and smiled. He had everything a man could ever want, the career, a close loving family and most of all his faith. He whispered I love you, and with one final burst of energy held Jen's hand. The last image he saw before he closed his eyes was of Jen, who managed to smile between the tears. When he opened his eyes, Jen's hand became Gloria's and Chris went home.

## October
The Capture by Erika Wilde

## November
Elusive Hero by Joey W. Hill
Falling or Flying by R.G. Alexander
Master of Pleasure by Lauren Hawkeye
Her Desert Heart by Delilah Devlin

## December
Delicious and Deadly by C.C. MacKenzie
Pleasure Games by Jessica Clare
How to Tempt a Tycoon by Daire St. Denis

## Want to Know More about the Invitation to Eden series?

Like what you just read? Sign up for our mailing list to receive new release alerts! For more information about the island of Eden, check out our website.

Make sure to check out the rest of Invitation to Eden series, as follows at your favorite e-book retailer or book seller!)

**March**
Master of the Island by Lauren Hawkeye (**FREE Prequel)**

**April**
Random Acts of Fantasy by Julia Kent
Yours Truly, Taddy by Avery Aster
Escape From Reality by Adriana Hunter

**May**
Hydrotherapy by Suzanne Rock
Fight for Me by Sharon Page

**June**
Breaking Free by Cathryn Fox
Hold Me Close by Eliza Gayle
Queen's Knight by Sara Fawkes

**July**
Dare to Surrender by Carly Phillips
Ivy in Bloom by Vivi Anna writing as Tawny Stokes
Second Glances by Elena Aitken

**August**
Rough Draft by Mari Carr
Blurring the Lines by Roni Loren
Return to Sender by Steena Holmes

**September**
Pleasure Point by Eden Bradley
Wild Ride by Opal Carew

life changed forever, subtle changes occurring each time she dreams, but which never change the painful outcome. At her darkest hour, she's gifted with a decadent island getaway she hopes will help her shed her sorrow. Instead, she meets a man so like Marc, he makes her ache for what she once had. With her waking hours consumed by him and her nights spent roaming her dreams in search of Marc, she begins to lose herself, to dream of another reality where dreams do come true.

# Have you read Invitation to Eden's other November releases?

**Falling or Flying by R.G. Alexander**
Joely knows the island well. A pilot for its most exclusive clientele and one of the few employees who has ever spoken to Eden's Master face to face, she has finally found a place to bury her troubled past and her personal fantasies where no one will ever find them…but the island still has a few secrets left to share.

Austin Wright is a regular visitor, and though his first invitation was meant to mend his spirit after the accident that changed his life forever, each time he's returned his desires have remained stubbornly unfulfilled. He wants Joely. She's resisted him for years, but when a moment of weakness turns into a week of wicked debauchery, there may be no going back. She'll have to take a leap of faith, and hope the landing doesn't break her heart.

**Master of Pleasure by Lauren Hawkeye (The Island)**
Billionaire Theodosius Vardalos has lived on the island of Eden for over ten years. Though his horrific scars have made him a recluse, he has turned Eden into a resort where the lines between fantasy and reality blur… A place where he sees no one face to face, not even his staff, who have dubbed him "Master of the Island". Even as Theo helps fulfill the fantasies of his guests, he waits… Waits for the mysterious woman who was shown to him when he first arrived on Eden. He recognizes Noelle Davis the second the nosy reporter steps foot in his castle… But the dream woman is nothing like he anticipated. He yearns for her submission. But he wonders… can a woman as beautiful as Noelle truly be happy with a beast?

**Her Desert Heart by Delilah Devlin**
Aislinn Dupree always prided herself on living in the present, free of her family's dark predilections for magic. However, after losing her partner and lover in a shootout, Aislin is tormented by her memories of the past and the day she lost Marc LeBrun. Her nights are haunted by vividly erotic dreams of them together, and of that painful day her